PENGUIN BOOKS

THIS SWEET SICKNESS

Patricia Highsmith was born in Fort Worth, Texas, in 1921. Her parents moved to New York when she was six, and she attended Julia Richmond High School and Barnard College. In her senior year she edited the college magazine, having decided at the age of sixteen to become a writer. Her first novel, *Strangers on a Train*, was filmed by Alfred Hitchcock, and her third, *The Talented Mr Ripley*, was awarded the Edgar Allan Poe Scroll by the Mystery Writers of America. She has commented that she is 'interested in the effect of guilt' on her heroes. Miss Highsmith enjoys gardening and carpentry, painting and sculpture; some of her works have been exhibited. She now lives in Switzerland.

Patricia Highsmith's books include *Deep Water*, *A Dog's Ransom*, *The Cry of the Owl*, *The Glass Cell*, *Ripley Underground*, *A Suspension of Mercy*, *Ripley's Game*, *The Boy Who Followed Ripley*, *Found in the Street* and several collections of short stories, *Eleven*, *The Animal Lover's Book of Beastly Murder*, *Little Tales of Misogyny*, *Slowly, Slowly in the Wind*, *The Black House* and *Mermaids on the Golf Course*.

Patricia Highsmith

This Sweet Sickness

Penguin Books

Penguin Books Ltd, 27 Wrights Lane, London w8 5TZ (Publishing and Editorial)
and Harmondsworth, Middlesex, England (Distribution and Warehouse)
Viking Penguin Inc., 40 West 23rd Street, New York, New York 10010, USA
Penguin Books Australia Ltd, Ringwood, Victoria, Australia
Penguin Books Canada Ltd, 2801 John Street, Markham, Ontario, Canada L3R 1B4
Penguin Books (NZ) Ltd, 182–190 Wairau Road, Auckland 10, New Zealand

First published in the United States of America by
Harper & Row, Publishers, Inc., 1960
First published in Great Britain by
William Heinemann Ltd 1961
Published in Penguin Books 1972
Reprinted 1978, 1980, 1981, 1982, 1986, 1987

Printed and bound in Great Britain by
Cox & Wyman Ltd, Reading
Set in Linotype Granjon

To my Mother

I

It was jealousy that kept David from sleeping, drove him from a tousled bed out of the dark and silent boardinghouse to walk the streets.

He had so long lived with his jealousy, however, that the usual images and words, with their direct and obvious impact on the heart, no longer came to the surface of his mind. It was now just the Situation. The Situation was the way it was and had been for nearly two years. No use bothering with the details. The Situation was like a rock, say a five-pound rock, that he carried around in his chest day and night. The evenings and the nights, when he wasn't working, were a little bit worse than the daytime, that was all.

The streets in the neighborhood, residential in a shabby, run-down way, were now black and deserted. It was just after midnight. David turned a corner into a street that sloped down toward the Hudson River. Behind him, he heard a faint sound of car motors starting: the movie on Main Street was letting out. He stepped onto a curb and dodged the trunk of a tree that grew inward, sloping over the sidewalk. In the upstairs corner room of a two-story frame house a yellowish light was on. Was somebody reading late or just going to the bathroom, David wondered. A man passed him, weaving lazily, drunk. David came to a DEAD END sign, stepped over a low white fence onto pebbly ground, folded his arms and stood staring at the blackness in front of him that was the river. He could not really see the river, but he could smell it. He knew it was there, gray-green, deep and rolling, and more or less dirty. He had left the house without his jacket, and the autumn wind blew sharp. He stood it for five minutes or so, then turned and recrossed the little fence.

His way back to the boardinghouse took him past Andy's

Diner, an aluminum boxcar set cater-cornered in a vacant lot. Without desire for food or even warmth, he walked toward it. There were only two customers, men, a long way apart in the row of stools, and David sat down midway between them. The place smelled of frying hamburger meat and, faintly, of its weak coffee that David disliked. A muscular, slow-moving man named Sam ran the diner with his wife. Someone had told David that Andy had died a couple of years ago.

'How you tonight?' Sam said tiredly, not even looking at David, and gave the counter a perfunctory swipe with a rag.

'Fine. I'll have a cup of coffee, please,' David said.

'Regular?'

'Yes, please.' With milk and sugar the coffee tasted rather like tea, and certainly would not keep anybody awake. David put his elbows on the counter, made a fist of his cold right hand, and squeezed it hard with his left. He stared unseeing at a brightly colored photograph of a plate of food. Somebody came in and sat down beside him, a girl. David did not glance her way.

'Good evening, Sam,' the girl said, and Sam's face came alive.

'Hi-i! How's my sweetheart tonight? What'll it be? The usual?'

'Uh-huh. And plenty of whip cream.'

'Make y'fat.'

'Not me. I don't have to worry.' She turned her head to David. 'Good evening, Mr Kelsey.'

David started and looked at her. He didn't know her. 'Good evening,' he replied, automatically smiling a little, then looked in front of him again.

After a moment the girl said, 'Are you always so quiet?'

He looked at her again. She wasn't a cheap girl, he thought, just an ordinary girl. 'I suppose so,' he said shyly, and dragged the mug of coffee toward him.

'You don't remember me, do you?' she said with a laugh.

'No, I don't.'

'I'm staying at Mrs McCartney's too,' she said through a wide smile. 'She introduced us Monday night. I've seen you every night in the dining room, but I have breakfast earlier than you do. My name's Effie Brennan. Glad to meet you for the second time.' She gave a nod that made her light brown hair bounce.

'Glad to meet you,' David said. 'Sorry my memory's so bad.'

'Maybe for people. Mrs McCartney says you're a whiz of a scientist. Thanks, Sam.'

She bent over her chocolate, smelling its vapor, and though David did not glance at her, he was aware that she wiped her spoon surreptitiously with her paper napkin before she put it into the cup, and that she played with the dollop of whipped cream, turning it over and over with the spoon in the chocolate.

'You weren't by any chance at the movie tonight, were you, Mr Kelsey?'

'No, I wasn't.'

'You didn't miss much. But I like practically any kind of movies, I guess. Maybe it's not having a TV set any more. The girls I was living with before had one, but it belonged to the girl who moved out. I had one at home, but I haven't been home in six months. To live, I mean. I'm from Ellenville. You're not from here, are you?'

'No. California.'

'Oh, California!' she said with awe. 'Well, Froudsburg isn't much, I guess, but it's bigger than what I'm used to. Which isn't saying much, of course.' She smiled her big smile again. She had large, square front teeth and a rather thin face. 'I've got a nice job here. I'm a secretary in a lumber yard. Depew's. You probably know it. I had a nice apartment, but one of my roommates got married, so we had to give the place up. Right now I'm looking for another apartment I can afford. I can't say I'd like Mrs McCartney's on a permanent basis.' She laughed.

David didn't know what to say.

'Would you?' she asked.

'Oh, it's all right'

She sipped again, bending low. 'Well, maybe for a man. I don't like this business of sharing bathrooms. Have you been there long?'

'A little over a year,' David said, feeling the girl's eyes on him, though he did not look at her.

'Gosh. Then I guess you must like it.'

Other people had said the same thing to him. Everyone, even this girl who had just come to Mrs McCartney's, knew he made a good salary. Sooner or later someone at the house would tell her what he did with his money.

'But Mrs McCartney told me you had an invalid mother to support.'

She knew already. 'That's right,' David said.

'Mrs McCartney thinks that's wonderful of you. So do I. I don't suppose you have a match, Mr Kelsey.'

'I'm sorry. I don't smoke.' He raised his hand. 'Sam, could you let her have a match?'

'Sure thing.' Sam handed David a book of matches with his free hand as he walked by.

The girl held her cigarette in her mouth between two fingers with painted nails, expecting him to light it for her, but he presented the book of matches to her with a smile. Then he laid a dime down on the counter and slid off the stool. 'Well, good night.'

'Just a sec and I'll walk with you. That is, if you're going home.'

David said nothing, trapped. He found himself opening the sliding door for her. She was talking again, something about coming to the diner for her coffee breaks, because the lumber yard wasn't far away. She chattered on, and David pretended to listen. She asked him what kind of consulting work he did at Cheswick Fabrics, and he replied that that meant various competitors came to snoop around the factory and find out, for instance, the formula of the rinse they used for the plastics.

'Aw, I bet you're kidding! Mrs McCartney said you were the head of Cheswick, and people have to come to you instead of you going to them, because your company can't spare you for a day,' the girl ran on, her voice loud and clear in the sleeping street.

'I don't know where she got that. A man named Lewissohn is the head of it. I'm just the chief engineer. Just a chemist.'

'Speaking of chemistry, I bet you've got a brand new kind of element in Mrs McCartney's upstairs bathroom,' she said through a laugh. 'Did you see that orangey stuff in the tub underneath the tap? Good grief!'

David, who knew the orange deposits well, laughed too, and glanced at the girl as they walked under a street lamp. She was about five feet five and perhaps twenty-four, not pretty and not unattractive either. Her light brown eyes looked up at him frankly and with a naïve mischief.

'We're here. Isn't that it?' she asked, pointing at the dark house in a row of houses.

'Yes,' said David, who could have found the house blind-folded, guided by the irregularities of the sidewalk under his feet.

The girl stopped on the short front walk, and an instant later David saw what she had seen. It was Wes. He had been sitting on the front steps.

'Well, well,' Wes said softly, looking at the girl.

'You didn't wake Mrs Mac, did you, Wes?' David asked.

'No, just one of the old guys downstairs.' Wes bowed to the girl.

'I'd better say good night,' David said to her in a quiet voice.

'You're not going to introduce us?' asked Wes.

'I'm sorry. This is Wes Carmichael. Miss –'

'Brennan,' the girl said. 'Effie.'

'Effie,' Wes repeated, smiling. 'How do you do?'

'How do you do, Mr Carmichael? Well, I'll be going in. Good night, Mr Kelsey.'

'Good night.'

Before she had unlocked the front door, Wes said in an urgent, flat tone, 'Dave, I want you to come home with me. Don't argue. I'm in no mood for arguing. I had enough.'

'It's late, Wes, it's late.' David extricated his arm gently from Wes's hold.

'No, you're going to come. You can do more good by just putting your nose in that house than I can do with a million words. Words! What good're words with Laura!'

'Another bad night?'

Wes stood swaying with his face in his hands. 'People over for drinks. *My* friends, and they didn't leave soon enough. She started blowing her top even before they left. Come with me, Dave, please. I'll drive you.'

'I'm not going.'

'You've gotta. You've never even met her, and boy, tonight's the night.'

'I don't want to meet her, ever. I'm sorry, Wes, but I don't. Now we both have to be at work at nine.'

'Oh, it's not that late. What is it, about eleven?' He tried to see his wristwatch dial and gave it up.

'I'll drive you home and walk back. How's that?'

'You'll drive me there and come in. *Come in*. Jesus, she's probably broken every dish in the house by now.'

'Sh-h-h. Come on.' He pulled Wes toward his car, a green Oldsmobile blocking half of Mrs McCartney's driveway. He pushed Wes into it and got into the driver's seat.

During the ten-block drive David heard more details of the evening, which was no different from many other evenings he had heard about, though Wes was always convinced a new evening was different from all the others, and that things were getting worse between him and Laura.

'And then she expects me to make love to her!' Wes was saying with indignation. 'How can I? How could anybody? Maybe some guys could, but I can't.'

Wes's voice was like a distant violence that did not concern David. He scanned the Carmichael house warily as he approached it, not wanting to encounter an enraged Laura on the sidewalk or the lawn. A light was on at a side window in the back of the house, probably the kitchen where all the breakage had taken place, and there was also a light in an upstairs room. It was absolutely quiet. David said that Laura had probably gone to bed and that there wasn't any use in his coming in at this hour, and after a few feeble protestations, Wes shut up. It was depressing to David that the mere proximity to Laura could so demolish Wes's courage and his intension.

'Dave, take the car and pick me up in it tomorrow morning. Don't walk back.'

'No, no, Wes. Now turn loose. I'm fine.'

Wes stood up suddenly tall and clapped David on the shoulder, but there was a scared look on his face and tears of drunken melancholy in his eyes 'You're the best pal a guy ever had, Dave. You're the greatest guy I ever knew.'

'Take some aspirin and drink a lot of water before you go to sleep,' David whispered.

'Sleep. Hah.'

David waved to him and walked off into the night. He felt strong and free, free of all the tragic mess that Wes was in. He even smiled at it, and shook his head pityingly. David had met Wesley Carmichael just after his honeymoon, and he remembered envying Wes his happiness. Bitterly envying it. He had almost been jealous. He had heard at the factory about Wes's easy, whirlwind courtship, about the beauty of Laura, et cetera, et cetera, and maybe there had been three months or so when Wes still wore that aura of happiness – a little mortal, touched for a while by the gods – but that time had been so brief, David really hardly remembered it. There had been a swift descent to hell, and that was the level on which Wes lived now. Often Wes visited David in the evenings to escape from Laura's tongue and from her neurotic housecleaning. David pitied Wes on weekends, when (though Laura didn't have a job) the housecleaning was on full blast, because Laura, according to Wes, accused him of messing a room if he merely entered it. David shook his head again. To let as precious a thing as marriage rot like an apple before your eyes! It would never happen to him and Annabelle, David swore to himself, as he had sworn before. With the thought of her, a warm, tender pulse struck once throughout his whole body, like a mighty heartbeat. He was on the front walk of Mrs McCartney's.

He heard the telephone start to ring before he reached the front steps. David unlocked the door and went quietly down the hall and grabbed the telephone accurately in the dark. 'Hello,' he whispered.

'Dave, it's Wes. She was asleep, thank God. What do you think of that?'

'Good.'

'Listen, I'd like to see you tomorrow night. I'll invite you out to dinner. Let's just sit somewhere and have a couple of beers and maybe –'

'Tomorrow's Friday, Wes.'

'Oh, Christ. You're right.'

'I'm sorry, fellow, otherwise, I—'

'I know, I know,' Wes interrupted him in a tone of misery. 'Okay, pal. I'll see you tomorrow.' And he hung up as if he were breaking down in tears at the thought of the long weekend ahead.

David silently replaced the telephone and tiptoed up to his room, which was on the west side of the second floor. There was a slit of light under another door at the rear, next to the bathroom, and he supposed that was where the girl's room was. He unlocked his door with a long key. 'Effie — isn't that an awful name?' she had asked apologetically. 'My father named me after one of his old flames.' David wondered if her father were still in love with his old flame, Effie, and had got himself married to a shrew?

Life was very, very strange, but David Kelsey had an invincible conviction that life was going to work out all right for him.

2

Every Friday afternoon at approximately five-thirty, David went to Mrs McCartney's to pick up the blue duffel kit in which he presumably carried a fresh shirt and pajamas, toothbrush and razor. Actually, he would not have dreamed of taking any personal possessions that he used at Mrs McCartney's on his weekends. The little bag might contain books, a bottle of gin or wine, or a small thing for the house, but none of his possessions that he used from Monday to Friday. And really, he did not drop by on Friday afternoons for the duffel bag, which he might easily have taken with him to work on Friday mornings. He came back to the house to see if a letter had come from Annabelle in the 10 a.m. mail. It was a compulsion for him to see, though in the two years he had been living in the town, Annabelle had written him only twice. And he had written her only four times: it would be a serious mistake, he thought, to inundate her with letters.

His room, like David himself, was orderly and curiously evocative of some forgotten past that one might have experienced, if one was old enough, or that one might only have read about or seen pictures of. People like Mr Harris, the potbellied piano tuner who lived in the downstairs middle, or Mr Muldaven, the widower, downstairs front, or Mrs McCartney herself, when they happened to stand on David's threshold for one reason or another, always stared at the room for a moment with dazed expressions before they opened their mouths to announce their business. (David discouraged visitors, kept his own broom and dust rags, and cleaned his room so well there was no need of Sarah the clean-up girl ever to enter his room, though he knew she sometimes did.) The room was of a general faded yellow color and its furniture was like the furniture of all the other rooms, a tasteless mixture of the old and new, providing the minimum necessities – bed, straight chair, armchair, chest of drawers, table. In David's room the chest of drawers was absent but in lieu of it stood a tall, dark wardrobe with two drawers in its bottom. The carpet was large and worn out, brushed threadbare by brooms and carpet sweepers, its two holes more or less concealed by the hideous brown double bed with its too short counterpane of machine-made crochet and by the plain writing table on which stood a row of David's books. The maroon easy chair was the newest piece in the room and probably twenty years old. It was both the absence of clutter – David had no pictures at all on the walls – and its invariable order that might first have made people stare at the room, but then came a sense of *déjà vu*, an awareness of a peculiar antiquity which was even stronger when David's tall, quiet figure was there. Mrs McCartney spent little time savoring all this. She merely considered David Kelsey her ideal roomer, a fine young man, 'a young man in a million'. He neither smoked nor drank, never had a girl visit him even before ten o'clock (by which time she liked them out and she never hesitated to tell her men roomers so before they even moved in), and he spent his weekends, Friday night to Monday morning, with an ailing mother in a nursing home. Mrs McCartney's only worry about David Kelsey was that he would never find a girl good enough to be his wife.

When David answered a knock on his door at five-thirty, he saw that expression of dull surprise and curiosity on the face of Mrs McCartney as she gazed past him into his room. Her lean, gray uprightness and efficiency irritated and repelled David. Behind her quick smile, as false as her teeth, David knew she was reassuring herself once more that his room, *her* property, every thread and splinter of it, was still intact in all its ugliness. It pained David most to think that two sons who lived in St Louis had Mrs McCartney for a mother.

'I'm sorry to disturb you, David,' Mrs McCartney said, 'but Mrs Beecham said she'd like you to go up and see her before you leave.' She leaned forward and whispered, 'I think she's got a little something for your mother, the sweet old thing.'

'All right. Thank you very much, Mrs McCartney.'

'And thank you for the rent,' she said, making a backward retreat. She checked herself. 'You didn't notice that biggest window leaking any, did you? That rain Monday –'

David glanced quickly at the window behind him, a huge window flanked by two small tall windows and set in an oriel bay. 'Not a bit,' he said, 'not a bit.' It probably had leaked, but he did not want Mrs McCartney or her handy man George prowling about his room while he was gone.

'Good. Well, have a nice weekend, David, and give our regards to your mother.'

'I will, thanks.' David waited behind his closed door until her steps faded to silence on the stairs, then went out and locked his door behind him.

Mrs Beecham lived on the third floor at the back. The third floor of the house was much smaller than the others, and had only Mrs Beecham's room, a bath at the center rear, and a room the size of Mrs Beecham's at the left which Mrs McCartney slept in. David knocked gently on Mrs Beecham's door, and her sweet, high voice immediately called, 'Come in, David.' She knew his step.

She was in her wheel chair with some knitting and a book on her lap. On the book stood her rectangular magnifying lens which she moved downward on the page as she knitted and read simultaneously. She was eighty-seven, and she had been paralyzed in her left leg and partially paralyzed in her left arm

16

for twenty years from a stroke. Her daughter in California sent her a little money regularly, but David had heard that she never came to visit her.

'Sit down, David,' Mrs Beecham said, gesturing to a broken straw-bottomed straight chair. 'I was hoping I'd catch you before you took off. Didn't you say your mother was about my size?' She had thrust her chair expertly over to her bureau and parked it sidewise.

'Just about,' David said, as he had many times before. 'Don't tell me you've made something else.' He had sat down, smiling, to be polite, but he leaped up nervously as she drew a pink garment out of her bureau drawer.

'It's just another bedjacket. You know it doesn't take me any time to make 'em, David, and who else've I got to give 'em to?'

David examined it appreciatively, and tried to think what he could give Mrs Beecham in return. He had given her several presents. But presents for Mrs Beecham were difficult for him to think of. 'It's really beautiful, Mrs Beecham. You know, though, she's still wearing that other one you made her – last year.'

'Won't hurt to have two. Two pairs of socks aren't hardly enough for you neither, David. Be sure you bring 'em to me when they got holey. I'm making my new little great-grandchild a coat and bonnet now, but socks for you come next.' She was fiddling with her knitting needles, too old and gray to blush with her pleasure at David's liking the bedjacket.

David stood looking at the pink thing in his hands, abandoning the idea of asking her anything about her great-grandchild, whose sex he had forgotten, because he was not sure her family had been decent enough to send her a picture of it.

'I asked that nice girl downstairs to bring me home a box for it, and I know she will, but she's not back yet. I know her walk already, I do.' Mrs Beecham looked at him brightly through glasses that enlarged and made quite visible to David the cataracts in both pupils.

'What girl?' David asked.

'Effie Brennan. You don't mean to say you haven't met her?'

'Oh, yes, of course, I have,' David said with a smile. 'Well,

Mrs Beecham, what can I bring back for you this trip? Some more of that cheese you like? A plant you'd like?' Her east windows were banked with potted, blossoming plants of all kinds.

'There's not hardly any more room, is there, David?' she said with a laugh. Then she held up a finger warningly. 'There's Effie now.'

'I'd better go.' David unzipped his duffel bag, shielding it slightly with his body, though Mrs Beecham probably could not have seen what was in it at this distance, and put the folded bedjacket carefully into it. 'I know she'll be crazy about that,' he said, standing up. 'Well, until Monday morning. You take care of yourself, Mrs Beecham.'

The old lady seemed in a trance of expectation at the sound of the girl's approaching footsteps, and did not reply to David who awkwardly awaited one word from her as dismissal. Then the knock came, and Mrs Beecham sang out for her to come in.

She fairly burst into the room, her arm full of gold-colored flowers, and David might have retreated out the door without being seen, if he had been ruder or quicker.

'Now here's your box,' Mrs Beecham said excitedly, taking the silver-and-white striped box from the girl's arm. 'Put it in, it looks nicer.'

'Hi, there,' said Effie, smiling broadly. 'So the box was for you.'

'My mother,' said David. 'Thanks very much for troubling about it.' He unzipped the bag and whisked the bedjacket out.

Effie helped him, unnecessarily, to wrap the bedjacket in the piece of tissue that was in the box. Their hands brushed and David drew his back quickly. The girl looked at him.

He tucked the box under his arm. 'I'll be going, Mrs Beecham. Thanks again.' He nodded to the girl. 'Good-by.' Then he closed the door on Mrs Beecham's 'Drive carefully, David,' and on the girl's alert and staring eyes. He heard their rather whining, female voices as he went down the stairs. He supposed Mrs Beecham would be telling her what a fine young man he was. He knew that several of the roomers, behind his back, called him 'The Saint'. It was annoying, and David tried to forget it.

David took a highway northward. Dusk was falling with a

swiftness that meant the beginning of winter, and David was glad. He loved the night better than the day, despite his occasional melancholic moments at night, and he loved winter better than summer. Now in the car, heading fór home, he allowed himself to daydream about the evenings to come, sitting by his fireside with books, or working on furniture down in the cellar, or lying on the floor in front of the fireplace listening to music in the dark. To hell with the flowers of summer, cut roses that perished in less than a week. When he looked out his living-room windows, he could see green ivy, strong and dark, clinging to the rough stone of the house's foundation. He had seen ivy embalmed in ice, still green and alive. It asked for no care, though he gave it some care, and it endured through summer and winter.

At a crossroads of a town called Ballard, about a mile from his house, David stopped at a butcher's shop and bought a steak and some hamburger meat. At another store he bought fresh rolls, salad greens, a couple of pears, and some imported mustard of a kind he had never tried. And at a liquor shop next door, he bought two bottles of Pouilly-Fuissé and a case of Frascati. Then he drove on, turned onto a narrow tar road and then onto a dirt road. Woods of pine trees grew on either side. The car rattled the boards of a little bridge over a stream, and then at the next slight curve, his headlights made the white jambs of his windows flash briefly, like a welcoming hail.

There were no other houses around. David's house was of stone and brick, and had a disproportionately tall chimney at one end, as if the chimney had been built for a house one story higher than this. The color was a dull brown with here and there a shade of gray — the color of natural stone. Someone had once seeded the lawn, so there was some growth of grass now, but this went quickly into woods on three sides. Even on the fourth side, where his headlights had picked out the window jambs, a couple of pine trees grew, taller than the chimney.

David, with one bag of his groceries in his arm, unlocked his front door and automatically wiped his shoes on a rough brown doormat before he went in. He clicked on the light to the right of the door, and with a deep intake of breath surveyed the attractive living room, its smooth couch, its brown and white

cowhide rugs, the mantel with its two photographs of Annabelle, his shelves of books and records, before he went into the
kitchen with the groceries. Within half an hour he had taken a
shower, changed to clean blue jeans and shirt in the bedroom
upstairs, turned up the furnace, stored his case of wine in the
cellar, put his groceries away, and laid a fire. He lit the fire, and
for the second time that evening took down a photograph of a
faintly smiling girl with brown, waving hair that hung to her
shoulders, and gently kissed its lips. Then he made a small
pitcher of martinis, poured two in generous, stemmed glasses
beside a plate of anchovies and black olives, sipped a little from
one glass, then went to work installing a wall lamp he had
brought in his duffel bag. It was a special kind of lamp that he
had ordered from a New York department store by mail and had
had sent to Mrs McCartney's. He fixed it to the wall above the
couch, between some bookshelves. By that time, he had drunk
the first martini, and he carried the second into the kitchen with
him to sip while he prepared dinner. He remembered that he
had used to lift his first martini to an imaginary Annabelle and
say, 'To you,' before he drank, and say it again when he lifted
the second, but he was glad to realize he had not done that in
several months. No use being that absurd. A man could start
losing his mind if he kept that kind of thing up.

While his potato was baking, he put a Brahms symphony on
his stereophonic machine, and set the gleaming mahogany table
with silver, wine glass, and linen napkin for one. Then he laid
a book on geology within reach in case he should want to read
while he ate. He hummed softly to the beautiful first movement
of the symphony, not loud enough to have annoyed anyone, if
anyone else had been present, for having no neighbors, he
played the machine loudly, and now it drowned out his hum-
ming. He moved very smoothly and happily, more smoothly and
far more happily than he did at Mrs McCartney's or at the factory. Now and then he paused, lifted the second martini, which
was still not empty, and looked into the living room with expectantly raised brows as if Annabelle, sitting there, had said
something to him or asked a question. Sometimes, too, he imagined her in the kitchen with him.

And sometimes, after the two martinis and a half bottle of

wine at dinner, he imagined that he heard Annabelle call him Bill, and that made him smile, because when that happened, he'd gotten tangled up himself. In this house, his house, he liked to imagine himself William Neumeister – a man who had everything he wanted, a man who knew how to live, to laugh, and to be happy. David had bought the house in the name of William Neumeister, and the few local tradespeople, the garbage collector, and his real estate agent knew him as William Neumeister. David had picked the name out of the blue one day, had at once realized that it meant 'new master' in German and that it was therefore rather silly and obvious why it had occurred to him, but the name sounded good to him, a comfortable mouthful, and so he kept it.

At first, nearly two years ago, when he heard that Annabelle had married Gerald Delaney, David had merely wanted to escape, at any cost, the pressure and the pain of his depression. He was not the sort to throw up his job, stay drunk for weeks, or any of that. On the contrary, he had tried to work harder to shut it all out until he could recover enough to think what had to be done. He had wanted privacy and a change of scene, and because of his job the change of scene had been impossible. But he dreamed about a change of scene, and as he dreamed he enriched his fantasy. Why not, for a time, imagine it had not happened, Annabelle's horrible mistake of a marriage? Why not, just for a while, the blessed relief of imagining that Annabelle had married him? And what would he and she be doing? He would certainly have moved out of his small apartment in Froudsburg and into a pretty house somewhere. Without hesitation he had made the split as it remained to this day: the ugly boardinghouse in Froudsburg where he worked, and the house in the country into which he put ninety per cent of his earnings and as much time as he could. He had not wanted to make the house traceable to David Kelsey, so he had invented the other name, and with the new name came to some extent a new character – William Neumeister who had never failed at anything, at least nothing important, who therefore had won Annabelle. She lived with him here, he imagined as he browsed through his books, as he shaved on Saturday and Sunday mornings, as he puttered about his grounds.

He had not acquired the house overnight. It had taken him weeks to prepare William Neumeister's references: one from a 'Richard Patterson', who subscribed to a mail and telephone service in New York City, and who replied to the querying letter of Mr Willis, the real estate agent, recommending William Neumeister in the highest terms; another word of commendation from 'John Atherley', in whose name David had maintained a room for a week or so in a Poughkeepsie hotel, where he had picked up Mr Willis's letter. A last small precaution was joining the library in Beck's Brook, a town a little north of Ballard, an action for which no references had been asked. In addition, he had borrowed a few thousand dollars (since paid back) from his Uncle Bert, so that his down payment on the house could be substantial. Real estate agents were not apt to be suspicious of people who could pay in cash a third of the value of a house. He had told his uncle he wanted the money because he was thinking of buying a house, and a few months later said he had changed his mind and would continue living in the boardinghouse. At the First National Bank of Beck's Brook he had opened small checking and savings accounts simultaneously, again using Patterson and Atherley as references for William Neumeister, but evidently these were never investigated, as David received no letters from the bank.

His house had the tremendous virtue of never being lonely. He felt Annabelle's presence in every room. He behaved as if he were with her, even when he meditatively ate his meals. It was not like the boardinghouse, where with all that humanity around him he felt as lonely as an atom in space. In the pretty house Annabelle was with him, holding his hand as they listened to Bach and Brahms and Bartók, making fun of him if he were absent-minded. He walked and breathed in a kind of glory within the house. Sunlight was like heaven, and rainy weekends had their peculiar charm.

At night, he slept with her in the double bed upstairs. Her head lay on his arm, and when he turned to her and held her close, the surge of his desire had more than once reached the summit and gone over with the imagined pressure of her body, though afterward, his hand, flat against the sheet, reported only emptiness and aloneness. On one Sunday morning, he threw away the bottle of Kashmir that he had bought because Anna-belle had often worn it. He did not need such things to recall her. The perfume was even too much.

On Sunday evening, after a dinner of charcoal-broiled steak that he had cooked in the fireplace, David sat down at the beige, Japanese-style desk in the extra room upstairs, opened his fountain pen, and spent perhaps ten minutes in thought. When he had composed his letter in his mind, he took from a cubbyhole that contained nothing else the two letters he had received from Annabelle. Their envelopes were postmarked Hartford, Connecticut, a town David knew slightly and considered nearly as ugly as Froudsburg. He knew the rows of red brick houses with ten feet of space between them and that space cluttered with garbage cans and children's play wagons. He knew the flapping clotheslines and the tangles of television aerials on the roofs. He knew even Annabelle's street, though when he had gone there, he had not wanted to identify her house in the red row. It would have been like pressing his fingers against a painful wound, instead of merely looking at it.

He read her last letter thoughtfully, though he knew it by heart. Her handwriting was a little on the large side, its lines very straight.

July 3, 1958

Dearest Dave,

I was so happy to hear from you – but if Gerald happens to see the envelope, I have to go thru the old explaining and reassuring. I'm glad your job continues to go well. The folks at home often write me what a success you've become. Congratulations!

I too remember the happy days we had together. My life here isn't very exciting or interesting but – that's life, I guess. Gerald's shop is doing fairly well, but we have expenses coming up. I do think of you since you asked and would love to see you, but it would be hard to arrange without a lot of trouble blowing up. I hope you've met some friends where you are and are not spending too much time alone. I know you are superior to most people, but as Mr Soloff (one of my music teachers) used to say, you can get a little something from everybody, even the humblest. No, I do not keep your letters, as Gerald might find them. I tell him you write me now and then to tell me how you are getting along. I know you are getting along very well. After all, Dave, you do have your work to occupy you.

23

This letter is so long already and I've got tons of sandwiches to make for a picnic tomorrow!

With my love and good wishes always,

Annabelle

Those tragic phrases – *I have to go thru the old explaining ... My life here isn't very exciting or interesting* – though they had disturbed him daily since he received the letter, now fell painfully and fresh on his heart. She didn't love Gerald and never had. It was a marriage that should have been undone, and David had tried to persuade her to undo it when he had first heard about it, when it was only a month old. He shook his head and ground his teeth again at the thought that he had ruined everything, made the crashing blunder, by staying on that last month in Froudsburg, just because Cheswick had told him they wanted him to stay, and because the job was new to him, and because he had thought, for the $25,000 they were paying him, he had better know every detail of the factory's operation. He could have learned his work in two weeks, and actually he had. He forced his anger to subside, and pulled a piece of paper in front of him. No use reading her other, earlier letter, which was shorter than this, and which he knew by heart too, unfortunately, because it did not cheer him. He had not replied to her July letter. He had wanted to have something definite to ask her before he risked trouble for her by sending another letter. The idea of trouble from that mushy beast of a husband was more infuriating than any other aspect of the situation. He looked like a eunuch, and David cherished a faint hope that he really was.

He dated the page and wrote 'My darling Annabelle', and then before he went on, took an envelope and addressed it, not putting any return address on it.

Your letters [he wrote] are both my only source of happiness these days and also cause my greatest pain. You told me once that you were not in love with him, and I wonder if you have forgotten or have you – not having anyone there to help you – succumbed to what you consider fate? Darling, it is *not* life that you are experiencing in Hartford. Far from it! You're not in love with him and he hasn't even any money. Not that I'd reproach any man for not having money if he's not interested in it or it's beyond his powers to earn much. It's the drudgery and the ugliness that this implies that galls me – plus the all-important fact that there isn't any love to make it bearable. Can you not be objective for one moment and see how it must seem to me or to anyone else looking on from the outside?

Can it be you're afraid to see me? [He crossed that out. He would have to copy the letter. He usually had to.] I want to see you, darling, and I think I have a better idea than Hartford. It's very far off, which will give you plenty of time to think about it. I would like you to meet me in New York. Any day between Dec. 21 and 24 (I know you'll have to be back Christmas). Do let me know soon, so I can be thinking about the day. Tell Gerald you have to shop for something and make it specific. I'll arrange, if you can make it, to be staying at the Alonquin, so for future reference, meet me there on the day you can come in. Or if you prefer, I'll meet your train if you can tell me what it is. Don't forget, you can write me as often as you wish:

137½ Ash Lane
Froudsburg, N.Y.

If you have half an hour, fine, or three hours – wonderful. We'll have tea, lunch, dinner, whatever you like. Or we'll sit in the lobby and talk and have nothing. I'll be cheerful, funny, serious, or anything you like.

Here he had a vision of Mrs Beecham's pink bedjacket. That was funny, but he could not tell it to Annabelle. He did not want to tell her yet about the house where he spent his weekends, about the records and books he was amassing, always with her in mind. And Christ damn it, he could not even ask her to spend a weekend with him *in* his house, because Annabelle would never do anything like that. Her loyalty had been bought by a pig! And not even bought, just reached out and seized. For a moment, he dreamed of proposing his house, telling her about it in his letter, dreamed of her accepting and spending a weekend of the kind he imagined every weekend here – Annabelle here in flesh and blood, able really to eat and drink with him. But it was unthinkable, and he gave it up. He signed the letter with his love, and added a postscript:

It is all very well for you to say I have my work. But I am incomplete without you.

3

Nearly two weeks passed, and there was no letter from Annabelle. David tried to excuse this, but the fact remained that she
could so easily write to him, even if it was only a postcard dropped in a box while she was out marketing. She simply did not
realize what it meant to him to get no word from her at all, he
thought, not even a word that she was considering his proposal
to meet in New York. David imagined that she was considering
it, and not writing until she knew for sure.

The dreary, busy days went by. His working hours were often
hectic. As the chief engineer, he was supposed to know what
was going on and to supervise the work in ten or a dozen quite
different departments. The electronics engineer was incapable
of making the smallest decision for himself and called for David
at least four times a day. Something had gone wrong with a
dancer bar. Was $375 really the right price for a tube? Would
he consider this plate worn out or not? The new kid had done
something to a roller and it was measuring out fifteen-pound
rolls instead of the required thirteen. The factory made plastic
material that was used for car seats, covering for cheap sofas and
chairs, baby blankets, suitcase linings, and whatever else men
like Dexter Lewissohn could think up to use it for. A score of
machines resembling newspaper printing presses unrolled bolts
of white plastic filler between thin pink or blue or green or any
colored plastic material, and at regular intervals this was stamped
with diamond designs, squares, dots or whatever. The results
were horrid. They went all over the nation and were exported
too. You could spill drinks on Cheswick fabrics, babies
could puke on them, just wipe them clean again with soap and
water. The one aesthetic aspect of the production was perhaps
the snow-white bolts of plastic filler, five feet long and three feet
in diameter that weighed almost nothing. They at least looked
clean. But before the stuff was white and on bolts, it had to be
processed and washed and subjected to various rinses (whose
formulae Lewissohn unnecessarily and rather romantically
guarded from competitors), and from the carding stalls the white

wool-like stuff floated out into the air, got into the nose, and stuck to the clothing and the hair. In the 'experimental department' on the second floor, Wes Carmichael and a half dozen other young chemists worked, played, and 'experimented', drawing quite handsome salaries for doing very little. They played at making plastic covering for wire, of the sort dish drying racks are made of, they came up with liquids that could remove stove grease, emollients that were good for the skin, rat poison, and silver polish. They outdid one another in creating cartoons and slogans detrimental to factory morale and effort. On the second floor the men's room was labeled 'Bulls' and the women's room 'Heifers'. The day David had accepted the job, Mr Lewissohn had told him with a happy slap of his palms, 'All our products are turned into dollars and cents in a matter of days.' This was not exactly true of the products of the 'experimental department', Mr Lewissohn's one extravagance for the sake of his vanity. Or David himself might have been one other extravagance. It flattered Mr Lewissohn to be able to say, 'I've got a real chemist working for me. A young fellow who's won three scholarships.'

David disliked his job and, ironically, had taken it only because of Annabelle, and then lost her because of staying on that crucial month to learn the work. David would have preferred a research job. But he had thought that if he wanted to marry soon, he would do well to have some cash in hand and cash coming in. The research job he had had in Oakley the preceding year had not paid enough for him to have put much away in the bank. David had started out very promisingly in the capacity of chemist, and seeing his quickness, Mr Lewissohn had conceived the idea of putting him in charge of the whole downstairs, and so dismissing two or three foremen who were not particularly efficient. This had been just at the time he had intended to go back to La Jolla to ask Annabelle to marry him. He had been writing to her daily, and now he wrote that he would be delayed a month. He hadn't said 'wait for me' and hadn't told her in his letter that he wanted to marry her, because he preferred to say that in person. After all, she had said to him only two months before, 'I love you too, David'. The fact she had called him David at that moment instead of Dave somehow made it all the more serious and true. He hadn't believed it when his Aunt Edie wrote him that Annabelle had married somebody else. David had never heard of Gerald Delaney. He was from Tucson, Aunt Edie wrote him. Annabelle had known him less than a month when she married him, Aunt Edie said, and maybe it was too sudden, but she blamed it on the 'bad time' Annabelle had been having at home. David knew: her mother ailing and complaining, her father ill-tempered, and her two good-for-nothing brothers making her wait on them hand and foot as if she were the Cinderella of the household. But to have married somebody she'd known less than a month! 'Well, it's always the stranger out of the blue who carries the day in love,' his cousin Louise had written him. Louise was sixteen and she had aspirations of becoming a writer. And there had been no use in his dashing out to La Jolla at that point, because Louise said that Annabelle and her new husband had gone off on a month's honeymoon to Canada, she didn't know just where. 'But her mother said she'd be back by La Jolla to pick up her things after the honeymoon. I'll keep you posted, Dave. But don't be too sad, because to tell you the truth she's not good enough for you in my opinion. Water seeks its own level, mom says.'

David had managed to be back in La Jolla when the month was up. He had flown across the continent for one weekend, and he had seen Annabelle at her house. She had come back to pack up a few of her things, because she was going east to live, she said. Gerald was an electrical engineer – by which lofty title David gathered that he could fix a toaster or put new plates in an electric iron. That, in fact, was what Gerald was going to do in the east, set up a little repair shop somewhere. David had been absolutely appalled.

'You didn't know,' he had asked naïvely, 'that I wanted to marry you, Annabelle?'

She had looked inwardly embarrassed, like a small girl with a conscience caught out in a very minor offense. 'Well, Dave – I wasn't sure. Why should I have been?' She was taller than average and had rather large bones, though she was extremely graceful and fond of dancing. At twenty-two, an adolescent roundness still showed in her cheeks. Her lips were young, somewhat thin and soft and as honest as her gray-blue eyes. And she was very serious, seldom made a joke, not having the necessary detachment for joking. 'I'm sorry, Dave.'

'But it's not too late, Annabelle! Do you – You're not in love with him, are you?'

'I don't know. He's nice to me.'

'But you're not in love with him, are you?' David had asked desperately.

'I don't think I am – yet.'

And then had followed the argument that had finally raised their voices, until some brother, awakened from a nap, had shouted down a complaint from upstairs. He had caught her in his arms – and that had been the last time – and begged her to annul the marriage with Gerald. He had told her his life was not worth living if she were not with him, and he'd never spoken a truer word. Somehow he had lost his balance and they had both fallen over a trunk on the floor, and one of his tenderest memories of Annabelle was that she had laughed at that, laughed as she let him pull her up to her feet. Then she had said he must go, because Gerald was due any minute.

'I'm not afraid of him,' David had said. And at that moment he had seen a car stop in front of the house, and one of Annabelle's brothers and a shorter man got out of it. 'But I don't particularly care to meet him either,' David had added quite calmly. 'I love you, Annabelle. I'll love you all my life.' And on those words, which are monumental or absolutely worthless, depending on how you take them, he went out the door, without even kissing her, which he certainly could have done. He still remembered the surprised, puzzled expression on her face, and sometimes he wondered, if he had stayed a minute longer, if she would have said, 'All right, Dave. I'll get a divorce from Gerald.'

On the sidewalk he did not step aside enough for Gerald, whose shoulder brushed his – or rather brushed his upper arm. David had glanced at his face, and what stood out in his memory was the large, fat underlip, suggestive not so much of sensuality as laziness, the small, dark, simian eyes, the smooth, plump jaw that appeared beardless. In later months, the fat underlip had grown to grotesque proportions in David's memory, like part of a monkey's behind. David had thought, *why* on earth? And it had shaken him so, he had not regained the fortitude that day to go back to his aunt's house until it was time to go to bed.

When he had telephoned Annabelle the next day at noon, her mother said that she and Gerald had left. David caught an afternoon plane back east. His family – which was his aunt and uncle and his cousin, David's father having died when he was ten and his mother four years later – knew by then that he was in love with Annabelle. David was sorry that they knew, because while their knowing might have pleased him if he had had Annabelle with him, it now did him not a bit of good. And his Uncle Bert, in his shy but matter-of-fact way, not looking at David as he spoke, had told him he thought this was another case of his 'picking the wrong girl – like that Joan Wagoner.' David had said nothing, but it infuriated him that Bert had put Annabelle on a par with Joan Wagoner, a girl he found it hard even to remember, a girl he had known at seventeen or eighteen! Joan had married some ass too. That was the only similarity. When his uncle and aunt and his cousin had seen him off on the plane, they had looked at him with sad, wondering expressions, as if they had just learned that he had some terrible disease that they could do nothing about.

At that time he had known Annabelle for five months, but what did time matter in love? A second, a year, a month – what they measured didn't apply. When Annabelle had smiled and said 'Hello' to him that spring day at the church bazaar grounds, he might as well have answered, 'I want to spend the rest of my life with you. My name is David. What is your name?' He had been helping his aunt build her booth that day, and he remembered straightening up, dropping the saw, and walking toward the piano music that was coming from behind a big sheet of cardboard. The cardboard leaned against a piano. She was half in sunlight, half in shade, but the sunlight was on the keys and on her wonderful hands. There were little ribbons of black velvet at the bottoms of her short sleeves. Her light brown hair was parted in the middle and fell full and soft behind her head, like a brown cloud. He stood for what was perhaps five seconds – that was something he would never know – and then she saw him, looked once and then again and stopped her playing and said, 'Hello', with a smile, as if she already knew him.

He walked to her house with her that day (eighteen blissful blocks) and he proposed a soda or a Coke and she declined, but she promised to take a walk with him the following evening, after dinner. She couldn't have dinner with him, she said, because she had to cook her family's dinner. She had two brothers. Her mother knew David's aunt, Annabelle said, and David wondered why he and she had never met before, because even though he had been away at school so much of the time, he was home on vacations. 'Bad luck, I guess,' Annabelle said in a drawling way through a shy smile that made her seem younger than she was. She told him the piece she had been playing was a Chopin étude. Walking home that day, David had tried to remember it and failed, but its spirit filled him to the brim.

The third time he had seen her, when they were walking under some trees not far from her house, he had taken her hand, their arms had touched as they slowly walked, touched and separated until it was no longer bearable, and they stopped and turned to each other.

His aunt had liked Annabelle well enough when David had brought her to the house, but her attitude had been, it seemed to David, one of incomprehensible indifference. He hadn't blurted out to his aunt that he was in love with Annabelle Stanton, perhaps because he hadn't thought it necessary, and also because of his desire to keep it secret for a while. But Annabelle – one didn't see a girl like her every day or every year or every lifetime. David could see, when he walked down the street with her, that a few people realized this. Everybody who knew her liked her, and pitied her because she was unappreciated at home. Her brothers had always ruled the roost. Annabelle was the cleaning girl, the cook, their shirt washer and ironer, and if she could play the piano, that was nice, they'd let her, but it shouldn't take her away from her chores. Annabelle had had two years of college, had had to stop for lack of money, and then she had won a scholarship to study the piano, and that had had to stop because her father had a stroke and her mother needed help. David had been so certain, so arrogant, so indignant at her wretched life, he had not even spoken of it much to Annabelle, except to say once or twice, with more violent words that he did not utter choking his throat, 'I'll take you out of all this and soon, very soon.' He was twenty-six then. He had been working at a research laboratory in Oakley for very little pay, and he had intended to go back, but Annabelle changed his plans. He decided to look for a job with a commercial firm, and he had answered the advertisement of Cheswick Fabrics in Froudsburg, New York. He had not set a date for his return to La Jolla, but he had said he would be back at least for a weekend in two or three months, and maybe less. They had known each other six weeks when he left for the east, not long, perhaps, to know someone before marriage, but by then David knew Annabelle was going to be his wife. It was inevitable and right, and it seemed to him that she knew it too.

Perhaps he had tried to hint some of this to his uncle and aunt, he couldn't really remember, but he had sensed that both of them looked down on the Stanton family. It might be true, David thought, that the Stantons had less money than the Kelseys, but was the worth of families to be judged by money? If her brothers drank and loafed around the house, was that Annabelle's fault? David's father, Bert's brother, had left enough money for David's upbringing plus his education, and in fact nobody in the Kelsey family had ever had to worry about money, but not everybody had that advantage. Bert had a comfortable job with an insurance firm, and he had had the job for thirty years. Every now and then, Bert would refer to his brother Arthur's recklessness in business with a sad shake of his head, but David's father had not died poor, and his mother, too, had contributed money from her family. When David was ten, his father had died of pneumonia, and four years later his mother had been killed in a car accident. His uncle and aunt had raised him like a son as far as his physical comforts were concerned, had praised him and been proud of his record in schools. Bert had been shy about accepting the role of father in every sense, but David had not minded that. Bert was a good-natured, benevolent guardian uncle. His wife was less intelligent and more superficial, hanging onto her youth quite successfully at forty-two. Only her letters sounded old, full of out-dated snobbism, practical advice and inquiries as to his finances.

David wondered what his mother would have thought of Annabelle, whether her own willfulness would have prompted her to say, 'Go ahead and get her,' or if the financial and social considerations would have made her against a marriage. David was a little afraid of his mother: in the memories he had of her, he was never more than fourteen, shorter than she, more shy than she, and hampered by schools, infinitely less free. His mother would charter a plane to go to Minnesota or to Florida, would telephone long distance to settle a business matter of his father's. And from another room where they talked together, David would hear his father's contented, adoring laughter as she told him what she had done. Only once in a while, certainly not more than once a month, his mother would sit on his bedside and kiss him good night. David could not even imagine what his mother would have thought if she had known he would be a scientist. 'Go in for science,' she would have called it, and though she might have been excited about it at first, she probably would soon have decided it was too quiet a pursuit for a man. David preferred, however, to think that his mother would have approved of Annabelle Stanton.

In that first sweet fire of his love, David had stopped smoking and drinking, though he had never done either to excess. He had not needed those pale little pleasures any longer. Once at Cheswick he had taken a cigarette with his mid-morning coffee, and it had seemed sacrilegious somehow, a breach of a promise, and he had put the cigarette out. Now he had no taste for tobacco and little for alcohol, except on his celebratory weekends when he imagined that, if Annabelle were with him, they might have taken a cocktail or two before dinner. The wine with his meals was for taste. Once he had written to Annabelle, 'Do you like crème de menthe? Brandy? Chartreuse?' She had forgotten to answer. But then, that question had been put after her marriage to Gerald. Annabelle, David supposed, had little time now for pleasures, and certainly Gerald had no money for brandy.

4

The leaves fell, brown and yellow, and others turned red and clung for weeks longer. It was the first of November, and still Annabelle had not answered his letter. Should he send her another letter, or had she gotten into trouble with the one letter and was Gerald now pouncing on all the mail that came in?

He thought of telephoning her, but he did not want to surprise her and perhaps get a negative answer that she wouldn't want to change later. It was essentially for the same reason that he had never tried to telephone her. He could not have borne her saying, 'I always like hearing from you, Dave, but you *really* mustn't telephone again. Promise me you won't.' And of course he would promise, if she asked him to. This way, not telephoning, the telephone was always open, as a last resort.

In Mrs McCartney's house the girl Effie stared at him and frequently smiled, and always spoke an articulate, complete sentence, such as 'Hello! Why, you're as regular as a clock!' if they met coming back to the house at five-thirty. She now sat at his table, a table for four, at breakfast and dinner, and invariably tried to engage him in conversation before he got his book propped up at breakfast (he did not read at dinner, as it seemed to him more rude to read at dinner than at breakfast), and at dinner her efforts brought knowing smiles to the faces of Mr Harris and Mr Muldaven, with whom she shared the table. Her chatter was no worse than Mr Harris's and Mr Muldaven's grunted comments on baseball and the food. There was at least a warmth in Effie's good humor that made David feel it was genuine. It was the amusement he saw in the faces of the two elderly men that irritated and embarrassed David, their imbecilic enjoyment of what they thought was a boy-meets-girl adventure. He imagined that Mrs McCartney had her prurient eye on them too.

Wes Carmichael, who visited David at least twice a week in the evening, asked David about the girl. He had never forgotten seeing David with her the night he had waited on the front steps, because it was the first time he had ever seen David with a girl.

'I don't know anything about her,' David told him.

'Well, didn't she tell you where she worked?'

'Yes, but I've forgotten.'

Wes greeted this with a mocking laugh that made David stare at him. 'She sure knows about you. Every little thing,' Wes said, grinning.

David watched Wes roll the copper-colored beer can between his palms. Fear had crept over his scalp. Had the girl possibly followed him to the house? But she had no car. 'What do you mean?' David asked.

'I mean, she asks me all about you, and boy, she doesn't forget what I tell her!'

'You've talked to her?'

'I've had a cup of coffee with her, that's all,' Wes said in a calm, placating tone, drank some of his beer, and looked down at the yellow carpet. 'Twice, in fact. I ran into her near the diner. Once *in* the diner.'

David did not quite believe that was all. He could see Wes's guilt.

'It was funny, I'd try to ask her about herself, and she'd steer the conversation right back to you. I told her we worked at the same place, you know, and boy, questions, questions. You've certainly made a conquest.'

'Don't make me laugh.' David closed his eyes and leaned his head back against his locked fingers.

'I'm not joking. She's very sad that you have to be away every weekend. She told me so. Anyway, I certainly couldn't get to first base with her, even if I wanted to.'

'And do you want to?' David asked, opening his eyes.

Wes looked at him with his head on one side. 'No, my friend, I really don't. But there's such a thing as enjoying female company, you know, a beer in the evening, a little gab and a laugh or two and then home again, back to the hellhole. You wouldn't know about that, I guess.'

David was silent.

'While I was talking with her, something funny crossed my mind. I thought, what if old Dave's –' He stopped, his eyes on David's face.

'Go ahead,' David said casually.

'I shouldn't say it, considering your mother.' When David said nothing, Wes went on in a rush, 'I was thinking, wouldn't it be funny if you had a girl somewhere that you went to see on weekends, and all the rest of us thought you didn't care a damn for them – or you couldn't ever look at a girl because of that girl you told me about –' He smiled at David, though he looked a little ashamed. 'It's a bad joke.'

At the word 'joke,' David obediently gave a laugh. 'Yes, it would be funny.'

Wes carried his empty beer can to David's wastebasket, and got a fresh can from the paper bag he had brought. He extended it politely to David, who shook his head. David had drunk one. Wes drank beer more or less on the sly at the factory, but it put no weight on him. Wes was five feet nine, but so slender and small-boned he seemed taller. His fine brown hair was inclined to rise up over his forehead. Most of the time, he looked like a happy, intellectual seventeen-year-old boy, a boy who had had to wear glasses always.

'Speaking of going away places,' Wes said, 'I'd certainly like to have some place to go weekends.' He tipped up his beer can and looked at the light fixture on the ceiling – splayed, tortured metal, two light bulbs and two empty sockets. 'There are times when I envy you this simple dwelling, even if you do have to share the john. At least this *room* is yours. Nobody's going to barge in and demand that you share it with them – unless it's Effie!' Wes finished with a laugh that transformed his face.

'Not with Mrs McCartney on patrol, she won't.'

'Ah-h, all landladies patrol. Things happen anyway.' With an incongruously scholarlike gesture, Wes pushed his glasses back with a forefinger.

Three days later Wes rented a small room on the ground floor of Mrs McCartney's, which had just been vacated by a thin, fiftyish woman who had not been there long and whose name David had never learned. David heard about it through Effie Brennan. He met her on the front sidewalk one night when he was going out for a walk.

'Good evening, Mr Kelsey!' she sang out. 'Did you know your friend Mr Carmichael's going to move in with us?'

David's first thought was that Wes and Laura had really decided to part. Then he remembered Wes's words of the other evening. 'He is? When?'

'Tomorrow evening, he says, if it's okay with Mrs Mac. I just spoke to Mr Carmichael. He was — Well, I ran into him on Main, and you see he'd asked me to tell him when there was a vacancy. He's going to call her first thing tomorrow.'

'I see.' David could smell some scent that she wore, a pleasant scent, more interesting than he would have expected her to use.

She lingered, her smiling face turned up to his. 'He says he won't be bringing much stuff with him. He says it's just going to be an annex to his house. Like a den. He says funny things sometimes.'

David nodded, smiling slightly. 'It'll be nice to have him around.' He waved a hand as he walked away.

He had had no objective when he went out, but now he walked in the direction of Main Street. *It's none of your business*, he told himself, before any of his jumbled thoughts became defined. And maybe he was suspecting things. But he knew he wasn't. He had seen the way Wes looked at women on the street, in Michael's Tavern where he and Wes sometimes went for a beer, even in the factory. Wes bragged of his success with women, any kind of women, he said. 'Act relaxed, as if you're not anxious about anything, but approach them directly,' Wes had said. 'It's a mistake to think women like a subtle approach. Bowl 'em over with a shocking request!' That night David had laughed, amused. Now David realized that what upset him, what depressed him, was that Wes wasn't *better* than he was, that he would fool around with other women, be false to his wife, just like all the other second-rate people who made up the bulk of the human race. David remembered that his respect for Wes had risen when Wes showed him a paper on inert gases he had written just after school. Wes could still do some brilliant work in chemistry, if he didn't waste the next few years at Cheswick. But there would be that blotch, perhaps with Effie Brennan, perhaps with some other woman or women. It seemed inevitable to David that Wes would lose his self-respect, and that this would affect his work, if only because guilt would interfere with his imagination. Or did that make sense? Did anything?

It's none of your business, an inner voice said again, and David stopped a few yards away from the pink-yellow lights of Michael's Tavern. Then he turned around and started back in the direction of his room. He would read a geology book tonight, he thought, and forget about the lot of them.

Wes arrived at six the next evening at Mrs McCartney's, with a suitcase, two strapped bundles of books, and a typewriter. He told David he had left the car with Laura, on the assumption he could ride to and from work with David, and David said of course he could. To avoid disturbing Mr Harris and Mr Muldaven at the dinner hour, David had asked Mrs McCartney if she would mind asking the two men to move to another table, because he knew Mr Carmichael would prefer to eat at his table. Mrs McCartney said she would be glad to. She was already prepared to like Mr Carmichael, simply because he was a friend of David Kelsey, her best roomer.

Effie Brennan was a little nervous at the table that evening, flanked by David and Wes, but she looked happy. She wore a blue and black striped blouse of satiny material that David had heard her say was her best. And she wore her pink coral earrings.

'I don't think this is bad at all,' Wes said cheerfully as he poured ketchup on his meat loaf.

'I don't think you'll get fat here,' Effie said. 'Except maybe at breakfast. There's lots of oatmeal. Bacon Sunday mornings, too, but she's pretty stingy with it.'

David, though he tried, could not think of a thing to say. Neither, he realized, was he curious as to what had happened between Wes and Laura, whether they intended to divorce, whether Laura knew or not where Wes was. And he was not at all interested in the fate of Effie Brennan, even though last night some absurd gallantry had been stirring in his breast, some impulse to protect her innocence. She looked virginal, but who could really tell? David stared at a dingy painting of a north woods landscape on the wall in front of him, looked at the corner cupboard with its hideous display of thick white mugs and a few plates, all from the dime store. The wallpaper was light blue, but not uniformly blue. Its pale sections showed the shapes of pictures and pieces of furniture that had blocked out the light for years.

'What d'you say there, David?' Wes asked in a facetious tone. 'And what're you smiling at? What's funny about my housewarming?'

'Nothing!' David said, knowing he had missed what they had been talking about.

Effie was laughing into her napkin. 'Oh, this one's so absent-minded!' She turned her long-lashed eyes to David.

David ate a few small bites of his sponge cake on which sat a Lilliputian ball of vanilla ice cream. He put the ball of ice cream into his coffee and let it float, and Effie pretended to find this vastly amusing, and did the same with hers.

'Do you have a long drive to your mother's on weekends?' Effie asked him.

'Oh – about an hour,' David replied.

'Do they let you sleep in the building?'

David felt sure Mrs Beecham had told her they did, or Wes had told her, because David had told them that. 'Yes. They're very nice about it. I have a private room and bath. Then they let me take my meals with my mother too, of course.'

'What's the name of the place?'

David crossed his legs carefully under the low table. 'Well, because of a request of my mother's – years ago – I'd rather not say. She's sorry she has to be there and – she has a few friends who see her, of course, besides me, but she made me promise not to mention it to anybody else.'

Effie looked at him. 'I feel very sorry for her,' she said seriously, 'but she ought to be thankful she's got a son as fine as you are.'

Irreverently Wes hummed 'God Save the Queen.' David knew he had had a brace of Scotches, maybe more, before dinner. Now he was all wound up for his evening with Effie.

'I do have a letter I ought to write,' Effie was saying to Wes.

'Write it now. It'll take me a few minutes too.' He winked at her, not slyly but in the straightforward manner that he said always worked. 'I'll see you both about eight?' he asked as he stood up. 'Excuse me.' He bowed. 'I think you both know where I live.' He went out, nodding pleasantly to Mr Harris, to Mrs Starkie the freelance nurse, to Sarah leaning tiredly in the doorway waiting for people to finish so she could clear up, finally to Mrs McCartney, who was just coming in.

Mrs McCartney had an announcement to make, David supposed about the heat or the hot water. She spread her thin arms as though silencing a din of happy banqueters, and said, 'There would've been mashed potatoes tonight, children, but somehow – *somehow* they got burned!' She laughed. 'We could've taken some out of the center, but it wouldn't've been enough,' she added, bringing her head down positively on the last word. 'So I hope you'll forgive me and the cook and I hope you won't starve. Burned potatoes – well, they're just impossible.' With a flurry of her hands, a bowed head, she dismissed herself and continued across the dining room toward the storeroom that led into the kitchen.

'Mrs McCartney,' Effie called out. 'I've been told that if you put a little peanut butter in burned potatoes, you can't taste the burn.'

Mr Harris chuckled appreciatively.

'Oh. Why, thank you, Effie. I'll tell the cook,' said Mrs McCartney, her exit spoiled.

'Just keep some peanut butter on the stove at all times,' Mr Harris said, and laughed loudly again.

David pushed his chair back, ready to get up.

'Can I talk with you for a minute?' Effie asked.

'Why, yes.'

'It's about your friend Mr Carmichael – Wes. He's a married man, isn't he?'

'Yes,' David said.

'Well, it's a little awkward. I mean, I don't like to make dates with married men. I don't think I should go to their room, if they're in a hotel or something, and have a drink with them. I don't want to be rude to him, but I just don't do that,' she said solemnly, shaking her head slowly for emphasis. 'Not that I want to make an issue of it,' she added with a little laugh. 'I thought maybe you could kind of let him know. Only don't tell him I said anything to you. Will you?'

'No,' David said, in a different tone from any he had used to the girl before. He suddenly felt friendly toward her and almost liked her.

'See, I had the idea you didn't intend to come tonight,' she said nervously.

'Come where?'

'To his room. He asked us both, you know.' She smiled her wide, hectic smile. 'Didn't you hear him? He said he was going to get champagne and ice. That's what he's doing now.'

David shook his head. 'I'm sorry I didn't hear anything about the champagne.'

Some of her amused smile lingered. 'But you're going aren't you?' she asked hopefully.

David knew there was no getting out of it, even though Wes would have preferred to see the girl alone, Wes would take it amiss if he declined tonight. 'I'll go tonight, but not the other nights,' David said.

'What other nights?' Effie stiffened in her chair. She blinked her eyes. 'Listen, I hope you're not trying to insult me, Mr Kelsey. I don't have to go at all.'

David bit the inside of his cheek. He had not meant to be insulting, only honest.

'After all, I think he's your friend, not mine.' She got up, and left the dining room.

David was in his room, reading, when Wes knocked on his door a little before eight.

'Effie wants to know if you're coming,' Wes said. 'Come on, old man, you've got every night in the year to read.'

David tossed his book on his bed with a smile. He gave his hair a couple of strokes with a comb, standing before the mirror inside the door of his wardrobe.

On the way out, Wes stopped at Effie's door and knocked. 'Are you ready? I've got David.'

'I'm ready. Just a sec,' she said, and Wes smiled confidently at David. She opened the door a moment later. She carried a tiny pocketbook, and David smelled more strongly the pleasant, not too sweet perfume.

Wes had filled his basin with ice cubes and half immersed two bottles of champagne in it. He told his guests to be seated, then turned the bottles a few times, pulled one out to feel it, and put it back. Effie sat down primly in one armchair, David on Wes's bed. Wes served the champagne deftly – he had borrowed some sturdy stemmed dessert glasses from the kitchen – and they toasted Wes's room and his sojourn under the roof of Mrs McCartney. Wes poured a second round.

Effie's cheeks began to pinken, delicately as the rose. They talked nonsense, and at last David neither joined in nor listened. Wes had opened the second bottle, and mentioned getting a third. The store would deliver it, he said. He opened the window to let the smoke out. Wes sat down on the floor by the girl's chair, and now and then patted her hand or her arm as he talked. Then Effie would take her arm away and look with her pleasant smile at David. 'I wish you'd tell me about your work.'

'Let him tell you,' David said.

'No work. No talk of work tonight,' said Wes.

The girl's eyes grew a little swimmy. 'I won't be here then,' she was saying to Wes. 'I've found an apartment, and I'm moving December first. Ten more days.'

Wes gave a groan. 'But you'll be around. I'll be able to see you now and then, won't I?'

'I certainly hope I'll be able to see you both,' Effie said.

Leaning back against the wall, David watched her casually. He realized for the first time that her hair was almost the same shade of brown as Annabelle's. Her expression had lost its self-consciousness, but her eyes moved from David's face to his brown loafer shoe propped up on his knee, to Wes, to the ceiling, and began the circuit again. Wes's arm was now on her chair arm, and the girl's hand played with the cigarette package in her lap. David was bored, and wished he were upstairs reading. The girl had even commented on his loafers, how good looking they were, and asked him if he always wore chino pants. Who cared? He had said yes. He nearly always wore chino pants, non-white shirts and odd jackets and loafers to the lab, because it had irked him to be told by Mr Lewissohn that he would prefer him to wear business suits, in view of the fact he would often have to talk to 'clients', a sacred word to Lewissohn. Because of all the acid sprays around the place, he wore a long white coat most of the time, and consequently nobody could see much if anything of what he had on underneath. His better clothes he kept at the house in Ballard. People in the boardinghouse, he supposed, thought he had even to economize on his clothing, in order to support his mother.

David was aware that Wes exacted a promise from Effie to take a drive in the country one day soon.

'I'll get the car, all right,' Wes said to David over his shoulder, with determination.

It was all so sordid, David thought. If he wanted a girl, why didn't he go out and buy one? What else did he like about Effie except her body, what else was there of her he could use? She didn't play the piano like Annabelle, had none of the sweetness of Annabelle – only the pseudo-decorousness of the basically coarse young female who reads the women's magazines and the etiquette columns in cheap newspapers that tell a girl how to behave when she is out with men. They focused a girl's mind on sex by harping on 'how far' a nice girl should go. They assumed every man was a lecher. But on the other hand, was there much more to most girls than their biological urges? The only objective of most of them was to get married before twenty-five and begin a cycle of childbearing. Annabelle, at twenty-two, had a brilliant idea for a book on Schubert and Mozart, two composers with the greatest lyric gifts in the history of music, she said. David often wondered what had become of that idea and of the notes she had shown him of it? Had her inspiration gone down the drain with a lot of dirty dishwater? Or was she still thinking about it, still intending to write it, and was it mellowing with time?

They interrupted him, gibing at him for his daydreaming. Effie was standing up, ready to leave, and protesting against Wes's telephoning for another bottle of champagne. Wes begged David to stay on a while, but David with rare firmness toward Wes said he had to do some reading tonight. It was eleven o'clock. David and the girl thanked Wes for his hospitality, and closed the door on his smiling but lonely face.

'I hear if you drink water the next morning, you can feel the champagne all over again,' Effie was saying, giggling. She kept David at his door, saying in a rush of words that an interesting movie was starting Saturday at the Odeon.

'But I'm afraid I won't be here.'

43

'Oh, that's right. But it'll still be playing Monday. Think about it.' And she turned suddenly as if embarrassed and went to her own door. 'Good night, David.'

'Good night.'

In the ten days that followed David's pessimistic predictions seemed to be borne out. Effie went to the movie on Saturday night with Wes, Wes told him. She had let him kiss her – once. Laura called Wes at the factory several times, Wes said, but he refused to speak to her. Once Laura called and asked for David Kelsey. She wanted to know where Wes was staying, but since Wes had asked him not to tell her, David said that he didn't know. Laura persisted, her voice as impersonal as a military officer's. 'Then I wish you would find out for me. It's important.' David asked Wes if there could be some crisis, if he ought to get in touch with her.

'She's got no target for her nagging right now. That's all Laura wants, someone she can yell at.'

It depressed David, and he thought about Wes and Effie as little as he could, though Effie, at breakfast and at dinner, always tried to include him in their conversation, and twice asked him to watch television with them. Wes had gotten his portable set from home. David realized that it was not Wes's morals he objected to, not the morals that depressed him. He was sad that his friend had lost the stature David had given him, sad that Wes had never really possessed that stature.

5

By December twelfth, David could not wait any longer. On Saturday, December thirteenth, at his house in Ballard, he wrote another letter to Annabelle, hiding his painful urgency, he hoped, behind a pretended fear that the letter asking her about Christmas might never have arrived. He was sure it had arrived, it just might have been opened and kept from her by Gerald. Or Gerald might have seen it and forbidden her to answer him. Then for an instant David imagined Gerald reading a certain letter of the other four he had sent Annabelle, one in which he had said he would never be happy without her, that he would move heaven and earth to be with her, and that he had not begun to use – David had forgotten his precise words, but the sense was that he had unlimited power at his command, which he had not yet drawn upon. He had meant, of course, psychical or emotional powers. David believed strongly in the power of letters to sway, to fortify, to convince – and by the same token to destroy, if that was their intention. It had been Annabelle herself who lent him a book of Heloïse's and Abelard's letters. Annabelle knew, too. But if that swine had ever read that letter, he would have done the instinctive thing to protect himself, forbidden Annabelle to answer, perhaps forbidden her to open any more of his letters, if they came. For all his eunuchoid appearance, Gerald laid the law down in the household, according to what his aunt had said, and his aunt had gotten it from Annabelle's family in La Jolla.

David no longer liked to have Wes visit him in his room in the evenings, and noticing this, Wes began to resent it.

'I knew you were chaste,' Wes said with a mitigating laugh, 'but I didn't know you were a prig. All I've done with the girl is take her to two movies.'

'I hope I'm not a prig,' David said quietly. 'I just find it depressing. Nothing can come of it.'

'And what about that girl you said you were in love with? You haven't even seen her for two years. What do you think can come of that? Don't you think she might meet some other fellow who's a little more attentive?'

'I doubt it.' David was driving his car, on the way to the factory on the north side of town.

'Meanwhile, you want to shut out the rest of life.'

David kept silent. A year ago Wes had introduced him to two of his own ex-girl friends, but David had never tried to see either of them again, much to Wes's surprise and disappointment. 'Why, I nearly married so-and-so myself!' Wes had said. That had been just after David had found out Annabelle was married, and it was a wonder he had been able to make himself meet the girls at all. He had declined, he remembered, to go to Wes and Laura's new and happy home, and Wes had arranged that he and David and the girls meet in the Red Schooner Inn for dinner. The girls were friends, and one of them lived in Froudsburg. Wes had harped so on his 'having a little social life' that David had finally told him there was a girl in California he was in love with and intended to marry. David said she was finishing college, and wanted to work a year before she married. This, David recalled, had brought a dubious expression to Wes's face, and he had remarked that she must be an unusual kind of girl, or David must be unusually cold about women. 'It's not that I'm cold to women,' David had told Wes, 'It's the intensity of my feeling for this *one*. Can't you understand something as simple as that?' It was more difficult for Wes to understand that than to understand a complicated chemical equation. Wes even said that the girl – David never told him her name – had made him inhuman, whereas Annabelle had done just the opposite. What was human to Wes, to get drunk and be promiscuous?

But David could not forget and did not want to forget the many hours he had spent with Wes talking of other things than women, the evenings when Wes, mellow on long, slow Scotches, would talk in an entranced, monologic way. Wes was not obtuse in matters of the human heart, but alcohol had to paralyze or at least hold in abeyance his conscious thinking in order for his emotions to show. Wes had invented one night the story of an old woman in rags reverently touching the dead and mutilated body of her prodigal son, who even at the end had not come home, and whom she had had to trudge for miles to see finally in a horrible state. Rhetorically Wes had asked why. And he had rambled on: the prodigal son was childless, had never done anything in life that could be mentioned to his credit, and people had told the mother not to go look at him because it would hurt her, and yet you found her creeping, weeping, on hands and knees to touch his filthy skin with her fingertips. Wes had been talking about the futility and illogic of human relationships. He knew as well as David that they were as unfathomable as the physical universe was understandable and even predictable. That symbol of the mother and the prodigal son had come at the time when Wes had begun having his troubles with Laura, the time of the first dimming of happiness, and

David wondered if in an allegorical way the story could mean that he really would always love Laura, no matter what she did.

The girl Effie had moved on December first to her new apartment, and though Wes said he had been there a couple of times, he still spent half his evenings at Mrs McCartneys, and on the evenings he went out, it was by himself, David knew, because Wes often asked him to go out with him. Laura now knew where Wes was staying, and Wes kept her off, he said, only by a promise to come home on the twentieth of the month. There was a mystery for you, David thought: Laura dying to have him back, according to Wes, only so she could rant and scream at him again, and Wes obeying like a little dog.

'That house is going to be so clean I won't be able to breathe the air,' Wes said. 'An angel would be afraid to walk across the rug. And she'll say, "See, things *can* look nice with you out of the house for a while." That'll be her heartwarming greeting, I'll bet.'

And David thought of Wes's very orderly desk in his office on the second floor of Cheswick.

David turned his car in between the wire gates of the factory's parking ground, and swore automatically, as he had every morning since his letter to Annabelle about their meeting in New York, that if she was unable to come to New York, he would resign from his job and go to Hartford to tackle the Situation more directly. He would demand to see Annabelle, and if necessary talk to Gerald too. What if he presented himself to her jobless? He could make more money in a research laboratory than Gerald was making, sell his house and buy an equally good one somewhere else near his next place of work. And Annabelle would be in it. He'd been entirely too patient up to now, too passive by far.

'He-ey,' Wes said. 'What're you grinding your teeth for?'

David found a space in his usual corner near the east door of the building. A truckload of chemical tanks was being unloaded, and David and Wes had to walk around crates and squeeze past the projecting platform at the end of the truck to get in. Wes said he would see David at lunch, and then took some stairs.

47

David continued on his L-shaped way to his office in the north-west corner of the building. His secretary, a girl named Helen Phimister, had not arrived, and David looked over a small stack of letters in the outgoing box on his desk to see how many he would have to answer personally that day. His dictating period was around eleven. David shared Helen with two other men. He took a mechanics manual from his desktop and left the office.

Mr Lewissohn, chunky in a double-breasted gray suit, pink-faced, smiling, called a hearty 'Morning, Dave!' and waved as he passed. David only nodded, with a smile. He realized that he had forgotten to put on his white smock, that pseudo-scientific uniform of his position. But he went on without it, his well-polished loafers falling lightly and almost silently on the cork floor.

Because he browsed too long in the library, trying to check something for the electronics engineer, David did not realize until one-fifteen that it was time for lunch. He had a bowl of vegetable soup and a cup of coffee, and was back in his office to go over Helen's afternoon's work with her at one-thirty. And then he was not conscious of time until the whistle blew from the top of the building at five. He would have stayed on awhile, perhaps until six, when only Charley Engels the watchman would be down at the main door, but there was Wes to take home now.

And of course there might be a letter from Annabelle at Mrs McCartney's. This possibility, striking his heart faintly but very surely, brought a smile to his lips as he said good night to Helen Phimister.

She smiled broadly in reply. 'Good night, Mr Kelsey. You're looking very chipper today.' She was a pretty, good-natured blonde girl of twenty-two or -three.

'Thanks. So are you,' David said awkwardly as he pulled on his overcoat. A pocket of the coat bulged with a pint bottle of a white emulsion produced by Wes's department, nameless but excellent for the skin, which he was going to give to Mrs Beecham. It was the third such bottle he had given her since he had been at the boardinghouse.

As David and Wes rode homeward, Wes tried to persuade David to come to Effie Brennan's apartment for dinner that evening. 'If you could only have heard her begging me to bring you,' Wes said. 'It's you she wants to see, not me.'

'She's barking up the wrong man,' David said with a smile. By the power of imagination, the power of will, he was putting an envelope, addressed to him in Annabelle's handwriting, on the gray wicker table in Mrs McCartney's downstairs hall.

'She called me in the lab today,' Wes said, 'wanting to make sure. She asked us five days ago, and the least you could do is tell her you're not coming.'

'I asked you to do that for me.'

'Well, I didn't. Okay, hermit. I'm hungry enough to eat for two tonight.'

David grabbed the letter, which he saw was to him, before he realized that it was not in Annabelle's handwriting.

'Ah, the girl,' Wes said with a smile at him, and went on down the hall to his room.

The letter was from Effie Brennan. She had made a painful effort to be light and amusing, and suggested – he was reminded of the excuses he made for Annabelle – that perhaps he had forgotten her invitation, and ended clumsily, '*Please* come, I really have very few guests, and I have missed you very much.'

Perhaps it was the pleading letter, perhaps the desire to avoid an evening brooding over the lateness of Annabelle's letter, perhaps it was the kind things that Mrs Beecham said to him about Effie when he gave her the skin lotion. David took a quick bath, changed his shirt, and went down to speak to Wes, thinking that if Wes had already gone, it was no matter, and if he was still here, well and good. Wes was just about to leave, and delighted to have David's company. David did not join him, however, in his preliminary Scotch before he left his room.

Effie Brennan's apartment was on Main Street, between a women's dress shop and a hardware store, and one entered the red brick building through a door above which hung a dentist's sign: DR NAGEL, PAINLESS DENTIST. David, who had learned some German for his science courses, pointed out to Wes the name, which meant needle, and they both laughed. Effie opened the door for them before they reached her third-floor landing. A very good smell of roasting meat came from the room behind her.

She had Scotch for Wes, and offered David Scotch or martinis, but David smilingly insisted that he would prefer plain soda and ice. He did not even want the ice, as he disliked very cold drinks, but to beg her to leave the ice out seemed too much of an effort, and he felt, too, that it would have deprived her somehow of a little pleasure.

'I planned this menu,' Effie announced from the kitchen, 'to be as *unlike* the things you get at Mrs Mac's as I possibly could.'

They ate in an alcove beside the kitchen, at a white sawbuck table like the picnic tables in public parks. This one was covered with a thin pink cloth, very clean and crisp. Wes soon dropped some of his pot roast gravy on it.

David partook of the wine with pleasure, and wished, after all, that he had contributed the bottle instead of Wes. It was an excellent Médoc, and David wondered where Wes had gotten it in Froudsburg, but he refrained from asking. Nevertheless, Wes noticed that he drank it appreciatively, and said, 'So wine is your weakness. Why didn't you ever tell us, Davy boy? Ah, the connoisseur, the gentleman!' Wes wafted a hand across the table, narrowly missing the wine bottle.

'I think it's lovely to like wine,' Effie said. 'When I was in Canada four years ago . . .'

David resolved to send her flowers the next day. He had a vague memory of having seen chrysanthemums in bunches somewhere recently. Then he became aware of her rather slender hands, gesticulating as she talked, aware of their nail polish, which certainly could be called of a conservative color as nail polish went, but which turned him away from her and even frightened him a little. Annabelle didn't wear nail polish, and she had once told him she liked her nails a little short for the piano.

They were in the living room now, sipping final cups of coffee, and Wes was pointing to a small oil painting that he said Effie had done of a couple of fishing boats tied up at a wharf. It was neither bad nor good, and David made an appropriate comment, and asked her if she did much painting.

'All these,' she said with a wide gesture at the wall on the kitchen side of the room. 'Well, not that one,' she added, indicating a rather competent portrait of a middle-aged man. 'A friend of mine did that. That's of my father.'

Wes went about looking at every picture and finding something to say about each of them. David began to wonder how he could manage to leave before Wes, as he wanted to.

'I'll show you something really mad,' Effie said gaily. 'I wouldn't do it, if I hadn't had two martinis.' From the top drawer of her slant-top desk she pulled out a large sheet of drawing paper. 'Recognize it?' she asked, handing it to David.

To David's surprise and discomfort he saw that it was a portrait of himself.

'It's Davy!' Wes cried, and laughed. 'I didn't know you'd sat for her, Dave.'

'I didn't.'

'I'm enormously flattered that you recognize it. I did it from memory. Memory!' she repeated nervously and rolled her eyes. 'Not that I had much. I mean – well, now I can see what I missed in the eyes.' She went back to her desk.

'But the hair and the whole shape of the face is great,' Wes said.

And that was reasonably true, David thought. There was his thick, dark brown hair – the drawing was in brown charcoal – the straight eyebrows and the mouth. 'I think it's incredibly good, just to be from memory, Effie,' David said, smiling.

She stopped in mid-movement, there was a sudden silence in the room, framing his words in space. It was as if Effie had stopped to drink in his casual words of praise. Then she moved and stood before him with a crayon in her hand. 'I don't suppose you'd really sit for me for one minute and let me get the eyes right.'

David nodded. 'Of course I would.'

Effie worked with a little pointed eraser, and scratched a point on her charcoal from time to time on a sandpaper pad.

'There!' she said finally. 'I've even improved the eyebrows.' She set it up on a bookshelf for all of them to admire, though at everything they said she laughed deprecatingly. 'Portrait of the genius as a young man,' Effie said, interrupting them.

Shortly after that, Wes slipped out of the room, to the bathroom, David supposed, and he found himself with Effie, both of them as tongue-tied as adolescents. She told him he could have the charcoal drawing of himself, if he really wanted it, and he said of course he did.

'I don't know what you think of me. You probably think I'm silly,' Effie said, her eyelids fluttering, unable to look at him. 'But I like you a lot. I wish you wouldn't be so shy with me. *I'm* bad enough.'

In an agony of embarrassment, David stood like a stick.

'I mean, I really don't see why we couldn't see a movie now and then. Or you come here for dinner now and then. I'm not going to cook *you* and eat you.' She laughed painfully.

David braced himself, thinking if he got it over with, everything would be easier. 'To tell you the truth, Effie, I'm engaged and – even though the marriage is a little way off, I'd prefer not to see anybody else.' It was like revealing himself naked for an instant, then clutching his clothes about him again.

But Effie did not look at all surprised. 'Do you see her on weekends? Is that where you go?' she asked almost dreamily.

'I see my mother,' he replied.

'Your mother's dead.'

David's mouth opened and closed. 'And who told you that?'

'Your boss. My boss Mr Depew knows Mr Lewissohn. He had some business with Mr Lewissohn. So we were chatting about you, and I said to Mr Lewissohn, "It's too bad about his mother," or something like that, and he said, "What's the matter?" and I said that she had to be in a nursing home, and he said no, she was dead. It was on their record and he remembered it. I didn't go into it, naturally. I certainly wasn't trying to probe. I just told Mr Lewissohn I must have gotten mixed up.'

David knew his face must be white, because he felt about to faint. 'Mr Lewissohn's mistaken. She's very ill and she may die in a few months, but she's not dead. He's made a mistake about that record.' But David remembered the record now too, the simple '*No*' he had written in a questionnaire's blank two years ago. He hadn't thought of it since the day he filled it out. What if Wes should find out? Or maybe Effie had already told him.

Wes was back.

Effie and Wes had a nightcap of Scotch, and David a cup of

52

coffee – instant coffee, since the pot was empty. Then they got up to leave. Effie looked strange, he thought, and he attributed it to the fact she perhaps did not believe what he had said about his mother. As he was about to thank her for his portrait, which he had picked up, she said, 'On second thought, I'd better spray it with fixative before you take it. Otherwise it'll smear.' Her eyes looked straight into his as she spoke, and he knew he would never see the drawing again.

6

A letter from Annabelle arrived the next day, the eighteenth of December. Seeing it on the wicker table, David did not snatch it but picked it up quietly along with a picture postcard with a California landscape, probably from his cousin Louise. He climbed the stairs to his room.

He took off his coat and nervously hung it, yanking its front straight on the hanger, closed the wardrobe door, then sat down at his writing table, the better to bear whatever the letter might contain. It was two pages, written only on one side, and his eyes swam over the whole thing before they focused.

Dec. 16, 1958

Dear Dave,
Pardon me for taking such a long time to answer you – but I think I have a good excuse! I have just had a baby, an 8½ pound boy. There were some complications – or rather some were expected, so I was afraid to say anything before 'it' was actually here, but now everything is fine. I hope you can understand, Dave, that with a baby to take care of it is impossible for me to think of going anywhere. He was born Dec. 2, at 4:10 A.M., which makes him two weeks old to-day.

Dave, I really can understand that this may come as a surprise to you, but it shouldn't. I am happy – at least right now – and though I might have been equally happy or more happy with you, that is just not the way things worked out. To think of anything else except the way things *are* is just to live in a world of the imagination – fine for some things but not for real life. Don't you agree?

I'll have to take a job as soon as I'm able to arrange about the baby, as Gerald has made a bad mistake about his shop (against everybody's advice) and consequently has had great expenses. Enough of that.

I must end this as I have a million things to do. I'm sorry I can't see you, especially just before Xmas. Are you going to California for Xmas? I do think of you, Dave.

With much love, as ever,
Annabelle

David stood up and faced his triad of windows. A baby. It was unbelievable, just unbelievable. His stunned brain played for a moment with the idea she had only made this up, perhaps to startle, to hurt him so that he would not try to write her again — her objective being to make him stop hurting himself. If she had been going to have a baby, wouldn't she have said so months ago? Wouldn't any woman?

He sat for a long while on his bed, frowning with an attentive, puzzled expression at the carpet, until finally a knock on the door roused him.

It was Sarah, saying something about dinner.

'I'm not feeling well tonight. I won't be coming down,' David said to her.

Her presence reminded him of where he was, and when he had closed the door after her, he listened until her footsteps were out of hearing, then picked up Annabelle's letter, his eyes falling on certain words though he refolded it quickly, put it back into its envelope, and set his ink bottle on it with a thump. He took his coat, left his room without locking the door, and went quietly downstairs just as Wes came into the hall from the dining room.

'There you are. You're not feeling well?' Wes asked with concern.

'I'm all right. Not hungry tonight.'

'You're *green*. What happened?'

'Nothing. I'll just get a little air. See you later,' he added weakly, and went out the front door.

For the first time in months, perhaps ever on his walks, he went to Main Street, where there were lights and people. Many of the stores were closed, but many also stayed open for Christmas shopping, and there were people enough on the sidewalk, the dull-faced peasant types that from David's first days in the town had surprised him by their preponderance and repelled him. Aware suddenly that he walked on Effie's side of the street, he crossed over so as to have less chance of running into her. The windows of cheap shoes, women's dresses, drugstore windows crammed with toys, flickered past in the corner of his left eye. Constantly he stepped aside to avoid the oncoming drifters, gawking at the windows. A huge, dangling Santa Claus, laughing drearily on a too-slow phonograph record, made him dodge sharply, but when he looked he saw that the black oilcloth boots were at least four feet over his head. A record store boomed 'Hark, the Herald Angels Sing'. Through this chaos David carried precariously the small, concentrated chaos of the Situation like a ball held up in the air by jets of water from below it. When the sounds and the light grew dimmer, and a dark, silent vacant lot stretched out on his left, he found a thought in his head: Annabelle was not herself now, wasn't able to see anything in perspective, because of the baby. No, he didn't think she had lied about the baby; Annabelle wouldn't stoop to trickery. But it was no wonder she was immersed, drowned now in what she considered reality. Naturally, a baby was real, pain was real, dirty diapers, hospital bills, and of course the stupid husband. What Annabelle couldn't see now was that there was a way out still.

If Annabelle could not come to him he would go to her. He decided to go this Sunday, when he would most likely find Gerald Delaney at home too. He would go to his house in Ballard Friday evening as usual, and leave around nine Sunday morning for Hartford. He would not call her first, he thought, and give her the opportunity to beg him not to come. He would call her in Hartford and insist upon seeing her and Gerald too. Then he began to plan, as methodically as he could, his argument.

David credited himself with an ability to maintain a self-possessed manner, regardless of his emotions. And though the letter from Annabelle had been shattering, had prevented him sleeping the night of the evening he received it, neither Wes nor Mrs Beecham – who measured him for socks – nor anyone at the factory commented on a change in him Thursday and Friday. He remembered the flowers for Effie and sent them to her with a thank-you note. On Friday, around 5:30 p.m., Wes left Mrs McCartney's in a resigned and cynical mood to go home to Laura.

With a swiftness that made Wes drop a package he was holding, David swung around and caught Wes by the shoulders and shook him. '*Try* it again, for Christ's sake! You've had your vacation!'

'Good God, Dave!' Wes said, readjusting his jacket. 'What on earth's the matter with you?'

'Nothing! But you – If you go back with a bitter attitude, where do you think you're going to get with her?'

'Maybe I don't want to get anywhere with her.'

'You said you loved each other once.' David tried to quiet his hard breathing. 'I'm sorry, Wes.'

'Christ. I thought you were going to beat me up.' Wes's expression was still resentful. 'To tell you the truth, I've been invited to Effie's for a bracing Scotch or two before I face – home.'

'Go ahead, go ahead.' Then David sat down on his bed and put his hands over his face, waiting for Wes to be gone, for him to be quite out of the house, before he started on this most important of journeys.

It was at least a minute before he heard his floor creak under Wes's steps and the door open and close.

7

Sunday morning, it rained, starting a little after 6 A.M., when David got up. On the radio, he heard that the rain was expected to turn to snow. In his pajamas and robe, David had a leisurely breakfast of boiled eggs and an English muffin and bacon – though he had no appetite, the importance of eating had registered on his mind, and the breakfast went down dutifully. Then he played some Haydn on the phonograph and drifted about his house, looking at the backs of his art books, at his framed manuscript page of a Beethoven theme which had cost him a considerable sum, at the gold-leaf-framed Leonardo drawing which had cost more, and at his silver tea set on a table in a corner of the living room, which he realized with a little shame he had never used once.

It rained all the way to Hartford, and grew perceptibly colder and foggier as if he were forcing his car into Hyperborean realms. David still heard the Haydn in his ears, and he hummed with it as he casually rehearsed his lines. Not one line did he compose verbatim, however. In a situation like this, he preferred to rely mostly on inspiration. Having vowed he would enter the city properly this time, he again got shunted onto an overpass that brought him out finally in a factory district, not unlike the neighborhood of Annabelle's house, but miles away from it, he knew. He was forced to ask directions twice at filling stations.

Talbert Street. A name evoking nothing, named perhaps for some ephemeral good citizen, or maybe just slapped on for no reason at all. After sighting the street, David drove two or three blocks to a drugstore to telephone. He knew her number by heart.

A man's voice answered.

'May I speak to Annabelle, please?'

'Who's calling?'

'David Kelsey.'

'David?'

'Yes. David.'

It seemed longer than necessary before she came on.

'Hello?' she said, and at her voice he relaxed like a bow unstrung.

'Hello, darling, it's David. I'm in Hartford and – well, I want to see you.'

'Today?'

'Yes. Now. Can I come up? I'm very nearby.'

'I'm on my way to church, Dave.'

'Church?' he said with surprise.

'Yes, but I suppose I – I was just going with a friend.'

'Well, break it, Annabelle, would you? Annabelle?' But she was already off the telephone, talking perhaps to the friend.

'Hello, Dave. Can I meet you somewhere?'

'I'd rather see you at home. I'd like to speak to Gerald, too,' he said with determination.

And again she went away, and he heard unintelligible hums, the deeper hum of a man's voice, and then the telephone was hung noisily up.

David banged his own telephone back on the hook, and wrenched the booth door open. Immediately he checked his anger, so that even before he was out of the drugstore he felt cool and collected once more. Let Gerald be the only angry one in this scene, the ass. David drove to Talbert Street and parked his car almost in front of the house. He rang the Delaney bell, one of four in the two-story red brick building. He looked at the sprinkling of yellowed grass on the tiny lawn, at the foot-high hedge full of gaps where people had trodden through, despite the wire someone had strung. Thinking he had waited long enough, David rang again. A prim, freckle-faced little girl in Sunday best opened the door and walked by him, staring at him. David heard a woman's high heels on the stairs. The door opened and there she was.

'Dave, why did you?' she asked, smiling. 'Sunday of all days. Ouch! That's my hand.'

'Annabelle –' Her hair was shorter, and she looked a little tired under her eyes, but the color of her eyes, that dusty gray-blue, and her wonderful mouth were still the same. He looked at the swell of her breast under the brown tweed dress, at her still slender waist.

'What're you staring at?' she asked with a shy laugh that made his own heart dissolve in tears. 'How'd you get your hair so wet?'

He said something that came out simply gibberish. Then he was leaning against the doorjamb, tiredly, though he held her tightly in his arms, his lips against her skin just below the ear. He could have spent the rest of his life there.

'Listen, I came down to avoid a scene – with Gerald,' she said, pushing back from him. 'You shouldn't have told him your name.'

'I want to see him. Or do you want to come out and talk to me first? My car's outside.'

She shook her head. 'Gerald'll be down in a minute, if I'm not back. I don't know if I can see you at all today, Dave. Except now.'

58

'What are you, a prisoner?'

'When it comes to you –'

'Annabelle?' from upstairs.

She looked at him, beseechingly, and he was reminded of her eyes in La Jolla, when she had come back from her honeymoon.

'Fine. Let's go up,' David said, taking her arm.

'Annabelle? You coming up?'

'Please, Dave –'

But he pulled her firmly toward the stairs. 'Yes!' David shouted up.

Gerald retreated a step toward the open door as David, still holding Annabelle's arm, arrived at the second floor. He was short, round-shouldered in his shirtsleeves, and baby-faced, and David suddenly realized what was so strange about him: he looked like one of those glandular cases whose name David had forgotten, whose voices never really change, who are practically beardless, wide in the hips, high-waisted – and Gerald was all of that, except that his voice did sound a trifle more like a man's than a woman's. 'Mr Kelsey?' Gerald said.

'Yes,' David replied pleasantly. 'Pardon the intrusion. I was just passing through.'

'Dave wants to come in for a few minutes,' Annabelle said to Gerald, who was standing sideways in the door now as if he would block it.

David made Annabelle precede him into the apartment. He had expected clutter and the dreary appurtenances of an existence such as theirs, but the sight, the tangibleness of it all now made it far more horrible to him. There was the picture of a hideous, gray-haired relative on the television set beside the aerial, a pair of mole-colored house slippers in front of the armchair in whose seat lay the gaudy comic section of the Sunday newspaper. Glancing at Gerald's shoes – small, unshined – he noticed that the laces were not tied and deduced that he had interrupted Gerald in his reading.

'The place is a little untidy,' Annabelle said. 'Sit down, Dave.' She gestured to a green sofa that looked more worn than their year and a half here would seem to have warranted.

'Thank you.' David pulled off his damp raincoat and tossed it over one arm.

'Well, you don't have to stand there scowling at each other,' Annabelle said. 'Would you like some coffee, Dave?'

'No, thanks, Annabelle.' He looked at Gerald, who was standing with folded arms, regarding David with a frank impatience for him to be gone. 'To come to the point quickly, Mr Delaney, I love Annabelle, and I intend to make her my wife.'

'What?' Gerald said with a slow smile of amusement, dropping his arms now and resting his hands on his hips that looked more capable of childbirth than Annabelle's.

'Oh, Lord, Dave,' Annabelle moaned.

'Listen, Mr Kelsey,' Gerald said slowly, and as if to back him up, or as if Gerald had meant listen to it a squeaky wail came from another room, and Annabelle made a start toward it and stopped. 'As far as I'm concerned, you've been rude, vulgar –'

'Just a minute,' David interrupted.

'– all the time Annabelle and I've been married. I don't like your letters and I don't want any more of them!'

'I didn't know I'd sent any to you.'

'You've sent them to my wife and –'

'I suppose you read them. You look like the type. It's usually a woman's vice.'

'David!'

Gerald's cheeks were becoming as pink as his rubbery under-lip. 'In a way – in a way, I'm glad you came up here today, because I can see you're just what I thought. You're a nut, a real nut.'

David gave a little laugh. That eunuch! For him to have married Annabelle was a piece of grotesquery – like a hunchback in a fairy tale capturing a princess. 'You're the picture of health, I must say.'

Then there was a burst from Gerald, answered by David, both were shouting at once, close together, and Annabelle, trying to separate them, got struck in the hip by the back of David's hand.

'Get out!' Gerald said, pointing to the door. 'Get out now or I'll call the police!'

'Annabelle will put me out and nobody else,' David said, picking his raincoat up from the floor, wishing he had buried his fist up to his elbow in that inviting pudginess below Gerald's belt. It would have laid him groveling on the floor, might even have killed him. Boldly, David kept his back to Gerald while he straightened his raincoat, turned it inside out, and laid it over his left arm. Then he looked around for Annabelle, remembering from his own smarting hand that he had struck her.

She was coming into the room with a cup of coffee for him, held out like an offering, and for some reason David found it very amusing and grinned broadly at her as he took it. 'It's not very strong,' she said apologetically. 'Gerald doesn't like it very strong.'

'And you?' he asked. It was indeed abominable coffee, so transparent he could see the circle of the cup's base through it. He thought of his espresso machine at his house, and he looked once again at Gerald, who was spraddle-legged, his absurd fists still clenched. 'Mark my word, Gerald. Annabelle and I loved each other before she ever met you, and those things don't change,' David said.

'For Chrissake!' Gerald slapped his bulbous forehead. 'Ask her! Ask her!'

'You can remember, can't you, Annabelle?' When he turned to her, he felt his thirst in body and soul. All his anger subsided, and the coffee cup nearly slipped off its saucer. She was looking at him, wanting to say, 'Yes.'

'I remember, but it was a long time ago, Dave.'

'Less than two years. You told me that you didn't love Gerald.'

'How could I have?'

'In La Jolla,' David said.

'He's insane. If you're not out of here in one minute, Mr Kelsey –'

'I guess there're different kinds of love, Dave. When you're married, it's different.' Her voice shook.

'Different from what? People fall in love and they get married –' He stared at her, at a loss to express himself by only the one word 'love.' He plunged on. 'Doesn't it mean caring, providing, being thoughtful – sacrificing?'

'Yes. Oh, Dave, we can't stand here all day arguing.'

'But I do all that for you,' he stammered. 'More than this –'

Again there was no word for that lump of flesh with the unfortunate ability to reproduce itself. 'I want to speak to you alone, Annabelle.' Setting his cup down, he took her hand to lead her toward the door, but her hand stiffened and drew back, and then Gerald's face was near his, and David drew his fist back.

'Dave, *please*!' Annabelle hung onto his raised arm with both hands.

David relaxed. 'I'm sorry. I'm really sorry.' He would have been ashamed to hit the absurd little man, was ashamed that he had almost hit him 'I mean what I say' he said quietly to Annabelle, looking into her warm eyes that were now full of tears. Then he kissed her suddenly and briefly on the lips, before Gerald could bustle up, and the kiss was over when David's hand flattened against Gerald's chest and shoved.

Gerald recovered his balance before the back of his legs struck the sofa. He uttered a filthy curse, which David ignored.

'Obviously Sunday isn't the day to call,' David said. 'I love you, Annabelle, and I'll write to you.' He pressed her hand, then walked to the door and went out, hearing Gerald's bluster – in a tone of pretended incredulity – as he descended the stairs.

Though he kept walking toward his car, David debated turning back and demanding to talk to Annabelle alone, taking her out by force if he had to. Certainly he could handle Gerald with one hand. He felt he hadn't been definite or strong enough. But he reflected that his exit had not been bad, and that a return might spoil it. He would write to her, and persuade her – really persuade her – to meet him somewhere, even if it was only in Hartford. He thought of Gerald's physical appearance – unredeemed evidently by any brains, grace, or sensitivity – and David felt quite secure again. He had not driven half a mile, when he pulled against the curb in a quiet street, turned off his motor, and sank with fatigue over the steering wheel, his mind reverting to Annabelle as it always did before he fell asleep, not tackling now the problems, the Situation – only Annabelle's clear and innocent face, her body that he had so recently half embraced. He knew, like a quiet, still fact that she would one day be his.

8

He wrote her that evening, before the horror of what he had seen that morning had a chance to dim.

Dec. 21, 1958

My darling Annabelle,

I'm tempted only for your sake to apologize for my behavior this morning, but being bitterly sorry I wasn't more forceful, I can't apologize. I am depressed – and yet this whole day is different and enchanted because I have seen you at all. I had a glimpse of your piano in the next room, just the end of an upright that I can't believe does your playing justice. I wanted to ask about your book on Mozart and Schubert and wanted to ask and say so many things and couldn't. All I achieved, I suppose and I truly hope, is convincing Gerald that I mean what I say. I hope he is thoroughly upset, because he should be.

If at all possible, would you wire me at home (collect so it won't appear on your phone bill) what morning or afternoon you can meet me in Hartford next Monday, Tuesday or Wednesday? I'll manage somehow to get off from the factory. Seeing you is more important than my job – which I took only because of the money, which was because of you. I do not mean to reproach you. I've enjoyed the money and put it to good use, and I'd like to tell you how, but I'd rather tell you when I see you.

I can't end this letter without saying frankly how depressed and surprised I was to find Gerald the person he is. I had gone along with the letters from the folks back home that he was 'okay' and that sort of thing. I find him [here he crossed out the phrase 'a little monster'] so far unworthy of you, I cannot put my reaction and opinion into words. If he has any endearing qualities, tell me – when I see you – as I'm quite willing to listen, just so I can think about them for the remaining time you'll have to spend with him.

Yours forever and ever,
Dave

P.S. Forgive me, but I could not take any interest in the child, even though it is half yours.

The postscript set him off on a disturbing line of thought: would he have to take the demi-monster when he and Annabelle married? Without pondering it for long, he thought that he could persuade her to present Gerald with the child –

wouldn't she realize that it would inherit its father's physique? – because he and Annabelle would have a child or children of their own. He went out to mail the letter, drove the mile or so to the little town of Ballard, where there was a big green mailbox on the main highway. Then he realized the letter would have a Ballard postmark, if he mailed it here, and he did not yet want Annabelle, or Gerald, to know that he ever went near Ballard. There was nothing else to do but drive to Froudsburg. He wanted it in the mail as soon as possible.

9

David's sleep grew worse. It was not that it took him long to fall asleep, as a rule, but that after an hour he awakened, and with that bit of refreshment could not get back to sleep until dawn. The noises in Mrs McCartney's house were like repeated sound effects in a repeated unpleasant dream. There was the faint but no less annoying, weatherstrip-muffled *thump – thump – thump* of some window upstairs as the wind stirred it in its jambs. Mrs Starkie, second floor back, in Effie's old room, snored. Mr Harris not only went to the bathroom every night around 3 a.m., but was now and then awakened with a Charley horse and stomped insanely on the floor with his bare heel until it went away. Once a month he presented an apology about this to the dining room. Most of the sounds were just mysterious creaks, as if someone else who could not sleep were walking his room and treading on squeaky spots in the floor. David was often cold, and had to add his overcoat to the thin blankets that covered him. Forcing himself to lie still in order to get as much rest as possible, it was easy to imagine that he lay in a waking coma or state of paralysis.

There was still no telegram by Tuesday evening, and David made himself late to work Wednesday morning, waiting for the ten o'clock mail. He stood anxiously in the front hall, watching for the mailman through the glass of the front door. Mrs McCartney, having been told in answer to her question that he was waiting for the mail, asked if it was about his mother, was she worse, and David said it wasn't his mother, she was about the same.

'You'll be spending Christmas with her, I suppose,' she said with a small Christmas smile.

'That's right. I certainly will.' Then he saw the mailman coming through the light rain, and opened the door to meet him.

'Merry Christmas!' said the mailman, and handed David all the mail for the house, two dozen square envelopes that were mostly Christmas cards, some gaudy with wreaths in their corners, a few with the scrawly, uneven writing of the aged. And one was Annabelle's. David dropped the other letters on the wicker table and tore open hers.

She said she could not see him. He only glanced over the letter, breathing hard with anger, like a nervous child about to burst into tears, his lips open over his set teeth. She thanked him for the diamond clip – bought by mail, sight unseen, from an Olga Tritt advertisement he had seen in a New York newspaper two weeks ago – but said she could not think of accepting it, as it was much too expensive a present.

David rushed out the door and turned his face up to the rain as he strode to his car in the alley.

At Cheswick there was only a pretense of work that day. The pockets of white coats bulged with pint bottles. Everyone seemed to be laughing – David thought once or twice at him. Mechanically, with very little effort, he kept a pleasant look on his face, returned 'Merry Christmas' merrily, and he had not forgotten the present of perfume for Helen, his secretary. David patiently double-checked every matter that he had to attend to that day, aware that he was completely unable to concentrate. Though it was Annabelle and her letter that kept him from concentrating, he was unable to think clearly even about that. In the quiet of the lunch hour, standing by the window in his office, he reread it. What pained him was her attempt to be gentle, to be kind, perhaps because she had known he would get it on Christmas Eve. *You must realize it's Xmas and I have so much to do, but not so much that I don't think of you. Don't let this spoil your Xmas in any way.* As if he could even have any kind of Christmas without her! The letter was a combination of haste and tortured thought: *Your visit — though I naturally enjoyed seeing you — did not help matters with Gerald, as you can probably imagine.* Naturally enjoyed? Why naturally under those circumstances?

He stood in Wes's department that afternoon, hoisting beakers filled to the 500 cc. level with seventeen-year-old Scotch contributed by Mr Lewissohn. The bonuses had been generous this year, David's had been $1,000, and everyone felt pleased with himself, with Christmas, with his work, with his boss. David looked at Mr Lewissohn's ruddy solid, merry-with-success face, and realized he had no energy and no passion even to dislike him today. After a sip or two, David poured the rest of his Scotch into Wes's willing beaker.

'You wouldn't like to come by after work?' Wes asked David for at least the third time. 'There'll be other people there, not just Laura. She's making eggnog, but you can have coffee.' Wes's eyes pleaded with him.

'Thanks, not now,' David said, unable to manufacture an excuse.

'Off to your mother, eh?'

Wes's inflection on 'mother' made David look at him. 'Oh, I may not go till tomorrow. They have some party planned for tonight,' David replied, carrying it off with the boldness of despair.

'She lives in a nursing home?'

'Yes,' David said. There were two nursing homes within an hour's drive of Froudsburg. He had ascertained that before he gave out his story.

'Not in a house?' Wes asked.

'No,' David said firmly. And why do you ask, he started to say, but couldn't.

Finally Wes nodded, and David wondered if Effie had dropped any hints to him, or told him that his mother was dead. 'Effie asked about you,' Wes said. 'I hope you sent her a Christmas card, anyway.'

'Do you see her?' David asked, more hotly than he intended.

'Now and then. Whenever I please.'

On this rough-edged exchange they parted, David turning away as Wes did.

Even Mrs McCartney was dispensing hospitality in her 'parlor' whose threadbareness somehow relieved its gloom and its air of never being used: *someone* had worn out the carpet, had let his cigarettes burn out on the top of the mahogany music cabinet, and had gathered the half dozen cattails that appeared to have been chewed by mice.

'David, would you take this up to Mrs Beecham?' Mrs McCartney said in a tone of seasonal sweetness, extending a sloppy cup on a small plate on which sat a half slice of store-bought fruit-cake. 'Sarah's busy making more nog.'

David did not answer at once, and Mrs McCartney with a puzzled expression started to speak to him again. Then he said, 'Maybe I can help her get down,' and went out and climbed the stairs three at a time.

Mrs Beecham protested and laughed, and said she couldn't get down *in* the chair, even if two men carried her.

David picked her up chair and all, kicked the door open with his foot, and with Mrs Beecham laughing and holding firmly to the banister with her right hand, they very slowly got down. A cheer went up as he carried her into the room and set her gently down on the sofa. He had left the chair in the hall.

When David extricated himself from the parlor group and went up to his room, he found a small package wrapped in tissue paper on his bed. A card in the shape of a Santa Claus dangled from it and written in the white of the beard was 'To dear David from Mollie Beecham.' The straggly writing, the clumsily tucked corners of the tissue wrapping, the thin, yellow, foil-threaded ribbon sent a torrent of pity through him, and as he stood there with the little package that he knew contained socks knitted by her hands, he thought that this might be as near as he would get to the spirit of Christmas this year. He pulled out a drawer in the bottom of his bureau, and opened a round stud box of worn dark brown leather. Among buttons and a couple of odd cuff links – all his good cuff links were at his house – he found a ruby pin set with seed pearls. Having nothing to wrap it in, he took one of his white handkerchiefs, folded it as neatly as he could around the pin, cut a square from a sheet of typewriter paper, and wrote: 'To Mrs Beecham with a Merry

Christmas from David.' He took it to her room, tiptoeing as if she were lying in the room asleep, and put it on the table where she kept her sewing articles. The pin had belonged to his mother, and though David had never been close to his mother, he ground his teeth and jerked his head away as he turned to go to the door.

That evening at his house, during his ritual two martinis, he laid fir branches along his mantel, brightened them with holly, and on the cocktail table where the two glasses stood, he set up a little angels' merry-go-round, lit its three candles, and turned off the Mozart Divertimento to listen to its simple, ever-changing tune of some nine notes. He had banked his few presents, most of them from a box from California that had come several days ago, at one side of his fireplace. In the total absence of Annabelle, not a present or even a card from her this year though last year there had been a present of an alligator key case, it was easier to feel that she was with him, that some of the presents were for her from other people, but that their presents to each other had been kept separate, to be opened together in some other room.

After a simple but properly served dinner, he lay on the cowhide rug in front of the dying fire, his arms crossed on his chest. Their weight was Annabelle's head resting there, and through the aroma of mingled firewood and fir, he could still detect the perfume that he knew. The concrete reality of the diamond clip he had sent her, that she had held in her hands at least and perhaps was holding at that moment, was a foundation on which to build the tallest of fantasies throughout the four days to come. With Annabelle he would plan voyages around the world, debate in advance about schools for their children (he liked to imagine they had a little girl already four and a boy two), consider a job offer in Brazil or Mexico, talk over the placement of a barbecue pit in the back patio, and whether they could afford to buy a small sailboat for next summer. He always saw Annabelle as more practical but also more impulsive than he, and almost never saying no to anything. He dressed her in silks, in fine wools, in mink and ermine. They sat in a box at the Met and heard *Die Zauberflöte, Elektra,* and *Wozzeck,* and when they went to a party together, they were always liked though a little envied by the married and the unmarried. When he bought a suit on his own, which he insisted upon doing, Annabelle sometimes made him take it back. There were certain ties of his that she liked, others that she didn't like that he seldom or never wore. He made up her favorite foods, and pretended that she did not like shrimps or eggplant.

The house was for dreaming, not plotting or fretting, and not a single worry about anything, any suspicion, any failure, any delay – because not even time existed here – clouded his visions as he lay before the fireplace, while his music, like incense, influenced his moods, the noble mathematics of Bach, the heroic tenderness of Brahms.

10

Mrs Beecham was extremely touched by David's gift. ('Why, it's too beautiful for an ugly old woman like me.') She went on so about it, words of praise that David could not reply anything to, and when for the third time she asked at what shop he had found such a pretty thing (she was aware that Froudsburg offered little), he blurted out that it had been his mother's.

'But she didn't like it very much,' he hastened to add, when Mrs Beecham's mouth fell open. 'I don't even know how I came to have it.'

'Why, shouldn't you give it back to her?' Mrs Beecham asked, and David suddenly realized the error in tenses he had made.

'That's why I have it, I suppose. She doesn't like it.'

Then Mrs Beecham looked at him tenderly, and grotesque as her enlarged eyes were behind the thick round lenses, something within David's heart stirred, awkwardly, unused to such a look. It's just that the lenses magnify the look, David thought suddenly, and smiled.

'Well, it'll still be yours, David,' she said, holding the little pin in her boney sapless fingers. 'You know it'll never go out of this house, and when I die, I'll see that you get it back.'

David so recoiled, for safety's sake, from the blunt truth of this statement, that it missed him, emotionally speaking. He left her room as soon as he could.

At his writing table in his room, David wrote Annabelle two letters in the week between Christmas and New Year's, the second more violent, more derogatory of Gerald than the first. He demanded, in all fairness, that Annabelle write him a real letter, one that she really meant, one over which Gerald didn't seem to be hanging, reading and passing on every word as she wrote it. David loathed the holiday coming up, New Year's, even though he would be at his house and perhaps not hear a single car horn or drunken hoot. He received a letter from Annabelle, very short and not at all in answer to his, the same day that the little package containing the diamond clip arrived at Mrs McCartney's by special delivery. The note was intended to be very kind, very grateful, but she was sending it back. Gerald himself might have written it. David missed in it that one word, or two, that he had always found in Annabelle's letters, words in which her own feelings showed through. My God, he thought, it's as if she's become a puppet of that freak!

Surely she'd write him another letter. He had asked her some specific questions in his last letter, how many hours a day was she able to practice her piano, did she have many friends in Hartford, did she ever go to the theater, did she like espresso coffee, and again what did she intend to do about her Mozart-Schubert idea whose outline David had once seen? He felt reasonably sure she would answer those questions, perhaps after New Year's when she would have more time, and he thought also that she would apologize for the coolness of her note concerning the return of his Christmas present, and explain that Gerald had wanted to see the note to make sure she was really returning it. She would tell him how much she wanted to keep it, because it was from him.

On New Year's Day, David awakened in his house from an unrefreshing sleep with a dream of Annabelle's letter still damnably in his head. He had seen every word in his dream, and she had said that she loved him, she had put herself in his hands, asked him to make plans for her freedom from Gerald and promised to do anything that he proposed. And David awakened to this gigantic trickery of his own dreaming processes, to the empty house, to the first hours of a new year, stunned and shaken. It seemed a bad omen. Never before had he had a 'bad dream' in his house. But later that morning as he was polishing brass and silver, it occurred to him that he could as well take the dream as a good omen as a bad. Perhaps such a letter was on its way to him. It had been stupid to feel downcast, simply because he hadn't the letter in his hands. This more cheerful attitude stayed with him, even for several days after he went back to Mrs McCartney's and the factory.

Twice David saw Effie Brennan at the boardinghouse, both times as he was returning from work around five-thirty. She came to visit Mrs Beecham. The first time, Effie had a blossoming geranium in a pot, sheltered from the cold by a green paper wrapping that was open at the top. She had asked David to come upstairs to say hello to Mrs Beecham with her, and David had politely declined, politely asked Effie how she had been, and she asked him the same thing, and that had been that. The second time Effie had been standing in the front hall, looking down at the mail on the wicker table as if she expected to find a letter there for herself, and as he closed the front door, she whirled around and smiled at him.

'Why, hello, David. We meet again. There's a package for you.'

He picked up the little package, a book he had ordered from New York. They chatted, saying nothing. The weather was cold, and it would get worse. David felt as guilty in her presence as if he had committed a grave and shameful offense against her. It was that she knew — at any rate, she believed — that his mother was dead, though this fact and the fact that she had told him so to his face did not plainly come to David's mind as he confronted her. He looked at her hair, short but fixed in wide curls that rose crisply around her dark blue beret, hair that was almost the same color as Annabelle's with its touch of red, and he remembered that Annabelle's hair, too, was short now, though he always thought of it as long, the way it had been in La Jolla. David could not face Effie's clear, direct eyes.

'By the way, your portrait's got the fixative on it now,' she said. 'If you'd like to have it, it's yours. If you don't want it, no offense taken.'

'I'd like very much to have it.' He ground his palm on the newel post.

'Why don't you stop by some evening?'

'Thanks very much, I will.' He smiled, then began to climb the stairs.

She followed him. He opened his door, went in, and was about to close it when she said his name.

'There's something else I wanted to say to you,' she said quietly. 'Can I come in a minute?'

With a small, nervous sigh of exasperation, he stepped aside for her, closed the door which put them in darkness until he crossed the room with two long steps and pushed the button of the lamp on his writing table.

'Oh!' she said, looking about. 'I didn't realize you had such a big room. And don't they keep it nicely for you!'

He nodded, slowly unbuttoning his overcoat. 'Would you like to sit down?'

'No, I won't stay.' Her eyes had fixed on his face again. 'David, it's about that night at my apartment. I'm sorry I was so probing about your mother.'

'You weren't probing,' he said quickly.

'I meant about whether she's dead or not. I'm sure you have your reasons − I mean you said it was a mistake on the record. Anyway, since it isn't my business, I'm sorry I said anything. The other thing I wanted to say is that I haven't said anything to Wes about it.'

'What does it matter? It's perfectly all right,' David replied, his back to her as he hung up his overcoat.

'I saw you were upset by it that night, that's all.'

Silence.

'If you think Wes is acting a little different lately, it's not because of that,' the girl added. 'He's annoyed because you never come by his house.' She smiled her wide smile.

David shrugged. 'All he tells me about is quarrels. I don't like to go into a house − where a man and wife are quarreling all the time. I'm not a psychiatrist. I don't know how to help him.'

'You could help him just by going to see him. Honestly David. They don't quarrel when people are there, at least not when I was there. Wes thinks his wife's temper has driven a lot of their friends away. Well, maybe it has, but if you like Wes –'

David shifted on his feet.

'Wes is so fond of you, *really*,' the hortatory voice went on. 'It seems to me that you could do him a small favor. Even if you hate women, a visit of half an hour isn't like living with one.'

'I just can't face it,' David said with the bluntness of impatience.

Effie looked at him, disappointed. 'I know. I understand. You can hardly bear for me to be in your room, I can see that,' she said, walking toward the door.

Words of apology, of insane protest, stuck in his throat.

She turned at the door. 'What girl hurt you so much?'

'No one.'

'I'm sure there was someone. I'm not asking her name, just – how long ago was it?'

'There's no one,' he said quickly. Still frowning at the floor as he had been for the past minutes, he moved toward the door to open it for her. She spoke as his hand touched the knob.

'You're so young, there's so much ahead of you, I hate to see you unhappy.'

'But I'm not unhappy.' He had an impulse to open the door and push her out. Women! Their prattling little minds and tongues, their so-far-and-no-furtherness, but please come so-far, and their tedious obsession with the idea that human bliss is based on getting a man and woman in the same house together!

'Good-by, David.'

'Good-by.' He was trembling as he closed the door, his anger almost at the exploding point.

He yanked off his tie and whipped it in the air, making a loud crack, and hung it up on the rack in the wardrobe. Tonight, he thought, he would read about ocean bottom cores and get the mess of his own life out of his head. He unwrapped the package, looked with the pleasure of anticipation at the brand new jacket of the book, and tossed it on his bed. Maybe tomorrow, David thought, he would ask Wes to come by and talk. There was still half a bottle of Scotch in his wardrobe. He kept Scotch always, as a courtesy to Wes, though Wes usually brought his own.

His new book restored him. He read until after 2 a.m. and finished it. The book had just been published, and it mentioned a second voyage that the same group of scientists of the Dickson-Rand Laboratories were going to make four months from now for the purpose of taking sample cores from the bottom of the Indian Ocean and the China Sea. The place names called to him romantically, pregnant with adventure. Dickson-Rand was where he had wanted to work when he met Annabelle. It was a wild thing, but perhaps he could –. His thoughts were checked as he struggled vainly to fit them to the circumstances with Annabelle. He had thought, *after everything is settled*. But after all, why should it take longer than four months to settle everything? Then, suppose it did take longer? He returned to his first idea, that he might at least write to Dickson-Rand, which was in Troy, give them his résumé, and ask if there was a place for him. It cheered him a little to think of his résumé with its impressive number of scholarships and prizes, plus the statement of highest commendation from Professor Henkert of Oakley, California.

David woke up early, and wrote the letter to Dickson-Rand before he went down to breakfast. He felt unusually well all that day, despite having had only three hours' sleep. He talked with Wes at lunch about the book on ocean cores, especially the climatological aspects of the core findings, which he knew would interest Wes. A light of interest came in Wes's face, but it faded when Wes said that he envied anyone who could go on such a trip, but that he certainly couldn't, because Laura wouldn't hear of it. He made David see Laura as a female spider, every leg gripping a few web strands, keeping an eternal vigil for untoward vibrations and the threatening quiver of a breath of air. When Wes went to work, he went off with one of those strands attached to him, and he followed it back at night to the web and the spider.

'Maybe you'd like to come by tonight,' David said. 'I've still got some Scotch in my wardrobe.'

Wes smiled gratefully. 'Around nine? A little earlier?'

'Okay. Earlier. I'll lend you that book, if you want to read it.'

David had two letters that evening, one from his aunt, whose handwriting he recognized, and the other typewritten. He turned it over and read:

G. J. Delaney
48 Talbert St.
Hartford, Conn.

He opened it in his room, panic-stricken at the thought that something had happened to Annabelle, that she was in a hospital dying, or had already died.

Dear Mr Kelsey:

I have two words for you: get out. I want no more of your letters and neither does my wife. I could sue you for libel on what you have written already. They have laws for people like you who deliberately attempt to destroy somebody else's marriage. Your insults against me make me sick and are no better than a delinquent might produce, not a man who thinks he is a big shot scientist.

I have seen both your insulting letters to my wife in which you suggest she is going to meet you at such and such a place. Nothing is more off the beam, Mr Kelsey. If my wife even wanted to meet you, don't you think she could have done it by now? She shares my opinions that you are about one step away from a mental institution and that you had better cut your connections here – or else. We do not want to hear from you again. If you do choose to keep it up I'll take steps myself and I mean that.

Yours,
Gerald J. Delaney

David started to put the letter on his table, and instead dropped it on the floor. By the time he had hung up his overcoat and removed his rubbers, which he had stomped as dry as he could on the doormat downstairs, he had made up his mind not to answer the little pig. Lumping Annabelle in with his 'opinions' indeed! 'Libel.' David wondered if Annabelle had read the letter and had been unable to keep him from sending it? He would write to Annabelle tonight, he thought, right after dinner and before Wes arrived. And again he was tempted to tell her that he owned a house, a good-sized comfortable one, where she could go at any time and never be found by Gerald. Then he decided once more to wait.

But he began the letter before he went down to dinner, and

in the course of it, he told Annabelle that he had a house that he had furnished for two, specifically for himself and her, and that she was not only welcome to come there at any time, but that her being there would give him the greatest happiness. He was not telling her its location, as he did not want Gerald to know it. He was calm but eloquent, and said he had done with letters, with insults on paper, with questions that could never be answered because of the meddling bore, the eunuchoid moron (he could not completely control his choice of words) she lived with. '... If I come to Hartford, it will be to take you away with me. I should have done so the last time ...'

Wes Carmichael came that evening bearing beer and a bottle of Hennessy brandy. He sat on the edge of David's maroon armchair with a beer can in one hand and a glass with two inches or so of Scotch in the other, and he told David that he no longer had a cocktail with Laura before dinner, so these were the first drinks he had had. The words gushed out of him like so much dross he had to get rid of before they could talk of anything else. Last Sunday he had had to shave himself at the kitchen sink, because the bathroom basin was full of combs and brushes soaking in ammonia, and the toilet was soaking in something else, and the tub was full of clothes. And the cleaning mops and scouring powders, the spot removers, the variously colored sponges, each for a specific purpose, the disposable toilet mops, the steel wool, the stove cleaners, the glass wax and the floor wax and the furniture wax, the Clorox and the ammonia and the silver polish that came tumbling out of the cabinet below the sink or the one in the bathroom every time he opened them. 'I swear if I ever get away from her and start living in the ordinary world, I'll succumb to the first germ that hits me.'

David did not listen attentively, heard only phrases here and there, and a few times he laughed, because Wes liked him to laugh. Then Wes himself joined in with loud claps of laughter, like a purge.

'Stay a bachelor,' Wes said, pouring himself more Scotch. 'Are you really going on this expedition if they take you at that lab?'

'That depends on something else. Another job I'm considering.'

'Where? I'll go with you!'

'I can't talk about it yet. As soon as I can —' David rubbed his palms on the edge of his chair seat. He had suddenly thought that Annabelle might not get his letter tomorrow, since he had dropped it in a box only at eight-fifteen tonight. She probably would not get it until Saturday morning. That meant, if she telephoned him or sent him a telegram, he would not be here on the weekend to receive it. He decided that he would call Mrs McCartney Saturday evening at eight or nine to see if any messages had come for him.

Then Wes began to talk of the topography of the ocean bottom as he looked at the pictures in the book, and David with relief passed into an objective and logical world. They talked until after midnight, and David walked down with Wes to his car to say good-by. He felt well again, lucky, and blessed: he was only twenty-eight, Annabelle twenty-four, and the best years of their life lay before them.

The next morning there were three inches of snow on the ground, fluffy and soft as a fallen cloud. David loved the snow, better the light snows than the heavy. They transformed the scenes that he knew, hiding their dirt, blurring the angles that evoked old thoughts, disappointments, and the drearinesses of his daily routine. The snow freshened his own hopes, and it was one of those Friday afternoons when he felt sure a letter from Annabelle would be lying on the wicker table when he went back to the boardinghouse at five-thirty. But there were only three letters on the table, and none was for him. And there couldn't have been an answer, anyway, to his letter of last evening.

In his room he packed some books in his duffel bag and a bottle of ink, which he had remembered the house needed. He whistled softly to himself, anticipating the weekend which would be quieter than usual with the new fall of snow expected tonight, quiet except for his music and the sounds that he made himself. He would think over everything this weekend, and it just might be that this was the weekend on which he would go, on Sunday, to Hartford, for the all-important next meeting with Annabelle. By Sunday night, he thought, all might be arranged, Annabelle might be in the house, hanging up her clothes, getting acquainted with the house, flinging her arms around his neck and kissing him. And perhaps she wouldn't want to share the bedroom with him until they were married, he thought, whistling more loudly until a smile made whistling impossible.

On an impulse he ran up and knocked on Mrs Beecham's door. She was knitting something brown – David didn't ask what this time – and let the knitting lie in her lap while she talked to him. Now David was fluent and at ease when she inquired about his mother, and they talked about the snow, and Mr Harris who had sprained his ankle somehow and wouldn't be able to stomp out his Charley horses for a while, and David felt happy and blessed in the warmth of her voice and her smile and her good wishes for his weekend.

Hardly had he started downstairs when Mrs McCartney called to him. He was wanted on the telephone.

David picked it up quickly, thinking it was Wes. 'Hello?'

'Hello, Dave? This is Annabelle.'

'Darling! Are you all right?'

'I'm all right. But Gerald saw your letter. He happened to come home for something at four o'clock and the mail arrived and I couldn't help it, Dave. He took it from the mailman himself and opened it.'

'Well – a scurvy thing to do, but I couldn't care less.'

'Maybe *you* couldn't. Dave, don't you understand the situation? He's my husband.'

'The situation – of course I understand it, better than you, I think, Annabelle. Did you see my letter at all?'

'Yes. I read it.'

'Well?' he blurted, hopefully, cupping his hand around the mouthpiece so that his voice would not carry through the hall.

'Dave, this business about your house – that's why I'm calling. You don't seem to understand when I write to you. I can't ever come to your house, Dave, not the way you want me to come.'

'Naturally, I was thinking – you'd finally get a divorce.'

'Dave, I don't want a divorce. Can't you understand that?'

He wet his lips. 'Is he there with you? Now?'

'No.'

'No? Listen, Annabelle, would you like me to come to Hartford? Right now?'

'No, Dave, that's why I'm calling. How can I say it? You've got to stop writing me, Dave. It's just causing more and more trouble. Gerald's fit to be tied and I do mean that.'

'I don't give a damn about Gerald!'

'But I do. I've got to. Just because you can't understand —'

He stood open-eyed, open-mouthed, his mind at a loss for a single word, as if he confronted a problem too big and cumbersome even to be taken in.

'Dave, forgive me for saying it like this.'

'It'll be all right,' he mumbled. 'Don't worry.'

'What?'

He had mumbled, and he couldn't repeat it. 'Good-by, Annabelle.'

'Good-by, Dave.'

Walking away, he tripped over his duffel bag, picked it up, and went on. He got into his car and automatically started for the town of Ballard and his house, took the same abbreviated route he always took, but he did not stop at the delicatessen in Ballard as he usually did, because he could not bear to provide for himself for tomorrow. Once in the house, he frowned even harder as he went about the simple business of unpacking the duffel bag and changing his clothes, because it seemed that here, in this happier half of his existence, there would surely be the answer, the explanation, the direction he must take. Finally he played music, and sat on his sofa, staring into space across his folded arms, no closer to coming to grips with the matter than he had been just after her telephone call.

Only after his second absent-minded shower that night, after midnight, did something that might be called a thought form in his mind: Annabelle might *think* she meant what she said. Otherwise how account for the sincerity and the seriousness in her voice? Annabelle didn't lie. In which case, the situation called for more persuasion on his part, a power to convince her, and he had not lost an iota of his faith that letters could.

But that night he felt as spent as if he had walked to Hartford and back, or as if he had been pummeled until he hadn't the strength to stand up, and his desire to write her another letter at once was also feeble, like the thought that had occurred to him, which after all might *not* be correct. Tomorrow, perhaps, he could think more clearly.

In the dead of night, more snow began to fall, like billions of white, silent tears.

II

Saturday he did not write another letter to Annabelle, because he was still considering going up to Hartford on Sunday and bringing her back with him. Letters had their time and place, they influenced, but they were not action, after all.

He was up early Sunday, shoveled the snow from his steps, and then set himself to finish the sanding and shellacking of a piece of wood that he chose to call a figurehead, actually a section of hand-carved molding that must have graced half of some late nineteenth-century doorway. It was something over three feet long, and had two floral designs among its sweeping scrolls, no human face, and it was strangely incomplete looking, but he still called it his figurehead, and when he had bought it from the puzzled junk dealer for fifty cents, he had imagined it beige or brown or whatever color the real wood was. He had thought at once that Annabelle would like it, perhaps as a lamp base, perhaps simply lying on the long table in the living room, purposeless and beautiful. He worked briskly but without haste, and he was putting on the first coat of shellac when he heard the shift of a car's gears. A shift to a lower gear. He climbed the stairs to the living room. He had jumped at the first sound from the silent, snowy outdoors, and now his heart pounded crazily. A maroon car, an old one, was coming up his driveway, taking the curve so that it faced him now. David made out the color of a Connecticut license plate. He tried to see through the windshield. The car was only fifteen feet away, on the straight stretch to his door, when he saw that it was a man driving and that no one was with him. David's disappointment barely registered as such. He was as tense as if he were prepared for a physical fight, and his reaction might have been just as hostile if a stranger had driven up to ask him a direction. But in this case he could see the driver was Gerald.

Gerald got out of the car, scowling suspiciously at the house, and leaving the car door open, he came to the door and so moved out of David's line of vision. Gerald knocked. David stepped near the front door, so that he could not be seen through the windows. He was not going to answer. Let Gerald think he had come to the wrong house. David clenched his fists until they burned with unreleased strength, furious that Gerald had found his house, invaded his doorstep. Gerald's knock came again, more angrily.

'Kelsey? Open up!' Gerald said threateningly in his rather high voice. Then immediately the steps crunched away in the snow in the direction of the garage.

David moved to a side window. Snow had obliterated the tracks of his car wheels, but Gerald stood on tiptoe and looked through the glass in the top of the door. As if this didn't satisfy him, he yanked at the door, piling up snow as he opened it wide enough to go in. And there sat his car with the keys in the ignition, his initials on the alligator key case that Annabelle had given him. David imagined Gerald's filthy, prying hands on it.

David flung his front door open and yelled, 'Get out of there!'

Gerald came out of the garage. 'Oh, there you are. What's the matter? Scared to open the door?' His voice was high and hoarse.

'Just get out,' David said, his feet planted in the snow, his fists clenched again.

'Not before I have a talk with you. Let's go inside.' He fairly snorted with petulant anger, his stocky figure advancing so confidently that David thought he might have had a few drinks. 'Come on, you're going to get cold,' Gerald said in a superior tone, reaching out for David's arm.

David recoiled, but also slashed at the arm with his fist, and Gerald staggered and nearly fell.

'Good God,' Gerald said, doubled over with pain, clutching his elbow. 'Listen, Kelsey, I've got a gun on me. I don't want to use it, it's just for my own protection, but –'

David's laugh drowned him out.

With a scared expression, Gerald looked at the open door of the house, as if he were afraid to go in now. 'You're nuts, Kelsey. You're out of your head.' He still held his elbow.

'I said get out. Leave.' David walked to his door to close it, not wanting Gerald even to see the inside of his house. He tripped the latch so he could get back in again and closed the door.

Gerald looked up at him, his fat mouth turned down at the corners. 'I said I wanted to talk to you. I know where you live now – on your weekends. I suppose this is where you intended to bring my wife. Well, I'm here to tell you I've had enough of you and Annabelle's had more than enough.'

'Why don't you use your gun, Gerald?' David said recklessly, his thumbs hooked in the pockets of his blue jeans, his whole body exposed to Gerald's silly gun. He was rigid and shaking with cold.

Gerald put his right hand in the pocket of his overcoat and started toward David, who at the proper moment came down a step, lifted a foot and pushed Gerald in the chest.

The gun went off as Gerald struck the ground, as if it were a sound of his own impact. And it was the noise and the disorder more than anything else that inspired David to yank Gerald to his feet and shove him toward his car, but Gerald fell again, yelling with panic or pain.

'*Don't touch me!*' Gerald said shrilly, and an instant later David saw his round cheeks shake like blubber when the underside of David's fist struck him in the side of the head. Now Gerald held his ear like a small boy about to cry, and like a small, angry boy he scowled at David, pulled the gun from his pocket, and said through his teeth, 'Get back, David.'

But David could not stop his pleasure, and he launched what seemed to him a very slow blow at Gerald's soft chin, saw Gerald's face with its hypnotically fixed expression rise a little in the air and turn backward, and now there was a crack as he landed, but not the crack of a gunshot. Gerald's head had hit the steps in front of the house, and there he lay.

David picked up the gun that had slid away in the snow, stuffed it back in a pocket of Gerald's overcoat, and pulled Gerald to a sitting position. Gerald was out cold. With one hand, still strong with his wrath, David dragged Gerald to his car, stuck him behind the wheel, shoved one leg in, then the other, and slammed the car door. He started toward his house, then got a thought that struck him as absurdly considerate an instant later, that Gerald might well freeze there before he came to, thought of turning on his car motor to warm him — but there might be a danger of carbon monoxide poisoning. With a bitter smile and a curse in his head, David opened the door again, grabbed a handful of snow, and smeared it all over Gerald's repulsive face.

'Wake up, you slob,' David said. 'Wake up and get out of here.'

He was bleeding from the left ear, David saw. Then he realized the blood was coming from the back of his head. David thought of feeling the wound to see how bad it was, but couldn't bring himself to touch that round, idiotlike skull. Gerald's hairless hands lolled foolishly in his lap. Gingerly David took one wrist and felt for a pulse. There was not only no pulse, but the wrist felt doughy and unnatural. Suddenly David thought he might be dead. David straightened up and folded his arms, staring at the gross annoyance that refused to revive.

'Gerald!'

Then David stuck his hand under the fat jaw to feel for the more reliable pulse in the throat. There really was none, and he thought the skin felt even a little cool, not so cool as his own hands but not nearly so warm as a throat should feel. David looked off at the road, invisible except for its levelness and a short, snow-covered length of rail fence. Not a soul in sight, not a car. Turning, he stared for a moment at the edge of the quiet woods, a hundred yards away. David thought of taking Gerald to a hospital, which might be twenty miles from here, he didn't know. Or the police. What should he do?

Then as he shivered violently with cold, he realized that he would be blamed. He gave another bitter smile and shook his head, with a purely rhetorical exasperation.

He went into his house and sat down, chafed his hands and stared at a radiator cover across the room. Of course, he could drive to some deserted spot miles from here, he was sure he could find one, and either leave Gerald parked in his car or send the car with Gerald in it over a cliff. He could say he never saw

83

Gerald, at least not today. A terrible, terribly obvious question came to him: how had Gerald found the house? Who told him? Who knew?

Wes?

That meant Wes would have had to follow him here at some time. And how would Gerald have found Wes?

Mrs McCartney? Could she be indulging him in his fairy tale about visiting his mother every weekend? It seemed unbelievable.

David got up restlessly, and another idea came to him: he was William Neumeister in this house. What was Gerald doing here talking to William Neumeister? He went to the front door, though he had been on his way to get a sweater, opened it, and saw that Gerald had not moved, but he went out anyway and this time only looked at his white face, the fat chin sunk down on the shirt collar, the heavy head pulling the body a little way from the seat back, as if in another few minutes the chest might fall against the steering wheel and keep the horn blowing forever. David pushed his shoulder. The whole body moved stiffly and remained in a precarious balance on the right haunch.

He closed the car door and more hurriedly now went back into the house. He was debating going somewhere to call the police – he had no telephone – versus driving Gerald's car, with him in it, to a police station. And he decided to do the latter, because he did not want any police in or around his house. Or he wanted at least to postpone that as long as possible. There would no doubt be an examination of the spot where it had happened, to see if his story held water. The story William Neumeister was going to tell would certainly hold water.

David changed to an Oxford gray flannel suit, black shoes over which he pulled galoshes, and a dark blue overcoat. He also put on a hat. Then he reluctantly took a plaid steamer rug from the foot of the couch in his study upstairs, and carried it down to cover Gerald Delaney. He went back into the house: he had forgotten Annabelle's photographs on the mantel. First he turned them down, but on second thought stuck them between books in a bookshelf. He drove Gerald's car, with Gerald a hump in the front seat, to the next town, rather redundantly called Beck's Brook, on the highway north, where there was a drugstore from which he could make a telephone call. David asked the operator the location of the nearest police station, and was told there was one in Beck's Brook at Broadway and Horton Street.

'Shall I connect you?' the operator asked. 'Is this an emergency?'

'No, I'll just go there,' David said.

He had taken the precaution of stuffing into his pocket some unimportant letters and an electric bill that had arrived at the house for William Neumeister, and of leaving his billfold at home.

12

David told his story in a simple, straightforward manner, and any nervousness, and he certainly had some, he thought could be attributed to the shock of the incident. He said that the man — whose name he pretended not to know, letting the police find it in Gerald's wallet — had arrived at his house in a belligerent mood, addressed him as Parker or something like that, and eventually pulled a gun.

'My fingerprints may be on the gun,' David added. 'I put it back in his pocket.'

The single shot had made a hole through Gerald's overcoat, but Gerald had not been hit. David had frankly admitted that it was the push he gave him against his front step that had killed him.

They asked for David's name and some identification, and the letters seemed to do, for the nonce. David gave as his occupation 'free-lance journalist'. Quite by accident, David had put on cuff links with the initial N on them, which he had whimsically bought one day, and perhaps the police officer noticed it when he signed, in a stubborn backhand, the name Wm. Neumeister, and perhaps not. At any rate, the police seemed much more interested in the corpse, in finding what his motive had been, than in David. The police were two, an older man of some higher rank, and a younger, heavy-set man with a simple yet alert face.

And of course they wanted to go to the house to look around the scene.

Riding back with them, pointing out the turns, David thought that his only mistake so far had been a trivial one; he had not known, and it had been obvious, whether today was Saturday or Sunday. It was Sunday. Now it was Sunday afternoon at four-ten.

The tracks of Gerald's car were quite clear in the snow, and the snow on the ground between where the car had stood and the house was torn up and scarred, the dark earth showing through, as if they had wrestled with each other violently. The blood was fresh and bright red in the snow below the first step.

'You're absolutely sure you never saw that man before?' asked the older man.

'As sure as I can be of anything.'

'And he never went in the house?'

'No.'

'Can we have a look inside, anyway?' asked the older man.

David nodded solemnly, and pulled out a key ring on which only two keys were fastened, one for the front and one for the back door. He let the police precede him. The living room was in order.

'Nice house,' said the older officer. 'No phone, you say.'

'No.'

'Like to get away from it all when you write, eh?'

'I suppose so.'

The younger officer opened the front door. From the threshold they had a better view of the tracks to the garage, Gerald's going all the way, David's halfway, and the two sets merging in confusion near the house. David said that the man, when he arrived, had looked into his garage, and that David had then gone out to ask what he wanted.

'Oh. Then you didn't just open the door to him,' said the older man.

'No. He knocked, and by the time I got to the door – because I was in the cellar – he was by the garage looking in the window. I went out to see what he wanted.' It wasn't, somehow, the way he had told it at first, and the young policeman stared at him.

'I thought you said the argument started on the front steps.'

'We walked back toward the house. I wanted to get rid of him. He looked drunk. He wanted to come in the house to find Parker, he kept saying. We were on the front walk when he started threatening me with a gun.'

The two officers seemed to ponder this, then the young one shook his head in a puzzled way.

'Maybe he was looking in the garage to try to check on the kind of car you have. Maybe he was hired to kill you – or this Parker.'

The older officer smiled a little at the younger. 'Got any enemies, Mr Neumeister?' he asked, pronouncing it 'Newmester.'

'Not enemies who'd kill me.'

'Well – I guess this'll have to be explained from the other side. We'll see who Delaney knows in Connecticut. Mr Newmester, we'll put a guard on the house, have a man out there on the road in a car tonight and the next few days.'

David nodded. 'I'll feel more comfortable with one there tonight. But I'll be leaving early tomorrow and I'll be gone for a few days.'

'Where?'

'New York. I'm going there on business.'

'Can you tell us where we can reach you?' asked the young officer, pulling a small notebook from his pocket.

'I'll be at a hotel, I can't say which one. If you want me to keep in touch with you, it's probably easier if I call you.'

'What hotel do you think you'll be at?'

'I usually try for the Barclay,' David said very calmly, the vision of the Lexington Avenue corner gliding into his head as if the Barclay were an old haunt, though he had never paid any attention to the Barclay.

'Can you call us around six p.m. Monday? Tomorrow?' asked the older man. 'Here's our number.' He handed David a small card printed like a business card. Beck's Brook Police Headquarters, Broadway and Horton Street, Beck's Brook, New York.

Then the door closed with a solid, double impact, and David, instead of being relieved at his aloneness, felt confused and dangling. Suddenly he was shaking, every nerve jumping and twitching. He grabbed his head and sat down on the sofa, holding his head in his arms in an effort to steady himself. What if they should come back, he thought, and see him like this?

He made himself sit up straight, and slowly the seizure abated. He'd go to work tomorrow as usual. He'd call the police around six from some place in Froudsburg, and by then he'd know if they wanted to see him again, he thought. He would tell them he was at the Barclay, and if they tried to reach him there later, it would be awkward, they'd have caught him out in a lie, but it wouldn't be a crime, after all.

David got up and turned on another light. They would tell Annabelle tonight, in a matter of minutes, perhaps this very minute. David imagined the young policeman with Gerald's driver's license in his hand, asking the Hartford operator to give him the telephone number of the house in Talbert Street, and Annabelle answering. 'You're Gerald Delaney's *wife*? Your husband has been killed, ma'am...' And Annabelle breaking down in tears, because whether she loved him or not, the news would be a shock. Would she immediately think he did it, because Gerald had been on his way to find him? Only for a second or two anyway, because the police would tell her the Neumeister story. *Gerald dead.* It didn't register on him as yet. He could not take in what it meant to himself. One thing, however, he did see clearly: Annabelle must never know that David Kelsey had given Gerald that fatal push. Annabelle would never believe it had been an accident.

13

When David left the house the next morning at a quarter to eight, the police car – turned a different way from last night, and perhaps a different car – stood on the road that went to Ballard. David forced himself to stop and speak to the man in the car, and once he had begun telling him he was going to New York for a few days, he felt quite calm and at ease.

'Yeah, the sarge told me,' the man said with a friendly smile.

David drove on to Froudsburg. It was his habit to go by Mrs McCartney's Monday mornings to change from the clothes he had worn Friday to clean clothes for the factory. As he entered the house, Sarah was coming down the stairs with Mrs Beecham's breakfast tray.

'Morning, Sarah,' David said.

'Good morning, Mr Kelsey. Oh!' She looked up at him, lipstickless, a pimple on her right cheek. 'Did the man find you? The one who was here Sunday?' The mild interest on her inanimate face indicated an unusual excitement.

'No. What man?'

'I dunno who he was. He was asking everybody where you were.' She pushed the dining room door open expertly with her right elbow, tipping the tray not quite enough to make the dishes slide off, and she disappeared.

David went up to his room. Perhaps the information hadn't come from here, he thought. With his door closed behind him, he stood for a moment, hardly breathing, looking all around his room, finding no change in it. In spite of the cold day, he put on chino pants and a blue shirt, and took from his wardrobe a brown tweed jacket that in its four years had never been cleaned or pressed. He felt quite certain that Mrs McCartney would be waiting for him in the front hall, and sure enough she was there, hovering by the wicker table.

'Your friend didn't find you Sunday, David?' she asked.

'No. Who was he?'

'Didn't say his name, at least I didn't hear it. Effie Brennan was here, and she told him where he could find you. We didn't know, you see, and my goodness but he was persistent! It was very important, he said.'

David stared at her. 'Did he say what it was about?'

'No, just that he had to find you. He wanted to know where your house was, and I kept telling him you visited your mother in a nursing home on weekends,' Mrs McCartney said with a smile, but David thought he saw suspicion in her eyes.

He frowned. 'I never saw the man —'

Here Mrs McCartney broke out in a shrill laugh that seemed to David maniacal. 'Between you and me, I think Effie told him a story. He'd been drinking. I could smell his breath. Smelled like whisky, it did indeed.'

David also gave a laugh. 'I suppose she did give him a story,' he said, and walked on. At the door, he turned and asked defiantly, 'What did he look like, by the way?'

'Oh – not very tall. About thirty, I'd say. Kind of ugly. Kind of fat lips.'

David squeezed the oval doorknob, not yet opening the door. 'And where did Effie say I was?'

'Some town not far away, she said. I didn't hear her, because she went out to the curb to talk to him. She's a dear girl, isn't she, David?'

David nodded. 'She is,' he said weakly.

That afternoon, there was a local newspaper on the counter in the factory's cafeteria. David was alone, having avoided Wes and a couple of other men with whom he sometimes lunched, by going down late. He found it on page four:

MYSTERIOUS CALL RESULTS IN DEATH
FOR HARTFORD MAN

Ballard, N.Y., Jan. 19. – Gerald J. Delaney, 31, an electrician of Hartford, Conn., was fatally injured yesterday when his head struck the brick steps of a house during a fistfight with William Neumeister, 30, of this town.

Neumeister, a free-lance journalist who claims never to have seen Delaney before, stated that Delaney called at his house on County Road at approximately 2:30 P.M. Sunday, and shouting a name resembling 'Parker', made threatening remarks to Neumeister and finally pulled a gun.

In the course of a struggle on the front walk, Delaney was knocked down and his skull fractured on one of the front steps of the house. Neumeister drove the dead man in the latter's car to the police station at Beck's Brook and reported the incident.

According to a medical report issued by Dr Serge Oskin of Beck's Brook, Delaney had been drinking, though not enough to have incapacitated an average man, unless Delaney was a type particularly susceptible to alcohol.

Delaney is survived by a wife, Annabelle, 24, and a son, Gerald J. Delaney, Jr., seven weeks old. Police are still trying to clear up the mystery of his actions.

David refolded the paper and put it back where it had been on the counter. Was it reassuring or not? It was not reassuring that the police were still trying to clear up the mystery of his actions. Wouldn't the police ask to see David Kelsey? Annabelle would certainly tell them Gerald had left Hartford to talk to David Kelsey, and the reason that wasn't in this paper, David thought, was that they hadn't had time to get that information before the paper went to press.

He went out of the cafeteria, down some stairs to a hall lined with green lockers, to a telephone booth. A vision of Annabelle in tears had suddenly forced him to move. He thought he knew her number, but he was not sure enough of it, and he asked the operator for information in Hartford. He had been wrong in two digits.

A woman's voice answered, but it was not Annabelle's voice. While he waited, he heard an unintelligible conversation in the distance, women's voices, whether in the apartment or over the switchboard, he could not tell.

'Hello?' Annabelle said.

'Annabelle, it's Dave. How are you, darling?'

'Oh, Dave!' she gasped. 'I'm alive, I guess. I don't know.'

'I just saw a paper –'

'Dave, he was going to see you. I tried to stop him – but he went out Sunday morning, just to see Ed Purdy, he said, but I knew. That's where he got the gun – at Ed's – and the liquor.'

'Ed gave him the gun?' David asked.

'He knew where Ed kept it and he took it. Ed said he asked for four drinks and drank them right down, and he's not used to drinking.'

'Well – he was going to shoot me?'

'I just can't believe that,' she said, breaking into tears. 'He wanted to give you a warning, that's all. He saw your letter. I *told* you, Dave – that's what caused it all.'

Her accusing tone froze him. 'I'm sorry, Annabelle,' he said contritely. 'I'm very, very sorry.'

'It's too late now. Gerald loved me. That's what you never understood.'

'I do understand.'

'But you didn't. I called you to try to make you understand. All you could say was "I have a right to write you" or something like that. Now you see what it's brought on, don't you? Are you still there, Dave?' she asked in a child's voice, full of tears.

'Oh, Annabelle, I'm here and I love you!'

'I've got to go now, Dave.'

And before he could say anything else, she had hung up.

That evening, David made a call to Joseph Willis, his real estate agent, and told him he wanted to sell his house.

'I heard about the trouble Sunday,' Mr Willis said. 'That's not what –' He stopped.

David remembered Mr Willis's habit of leaving sentences unfinished. And of calling him 'Newmaster.' 'No. I've been thinking of it for quite a while. I'm going to be traveling – abroad – and the house would just be an expense.'

'You can always sublet. Hate to lose you as a tenant.'

'No, I'll sell even if I take a loss. I should have my things out in about a week.'

'Well, you won't have to take a loss, Mr Newmaster,' Mr Willis said with a laugh. 'I've got two people who want a house around that area and in that price range.'

'Good. The sooner the better, Mr Willis, because I'd like the money before I go abroad.'

'I think we can manage it. Can I show the house any time I want to?'

'Any time at all.'

They set a time to meet at Mr Willis's office in Beck's Brook next Saturday morning to make the mortgage arrangements, and it was Mr Willis's opinion he could have the house sold by then, in which case the bank would give David back all the money he had put into it.

David hoped so, because he thought William Neumeister might have to disappear without trace, in which case he would not be able to receive the money the house would bring. He recalled William Neumeister's signature on his mortgage, the same signature with which he had registered with the electric company and the propane gas company and with which he had paid his bills for the Ballard house from Neumeister's checking account (if he wanted the money from the checking and savings accounts, he'd have to go in person to Beck's Brook and close them), and for the first time, he felt a doubt of William Neumeister's luck. Annabelle's words had made him afraid, had made him ashamed of the William Neumeister game. He would have to be careful in Beck's Brook. It scared him to think of facing the Beck's Brook police again as William Neumeister. It was as if since his house was shattered, its privacy gone, so was the character William Neumeister. He felt he wouldn't be able to bring it off again.

Putting the house up for sale at this time might look suspicious, but he had been unable to postpone it a day longer. He was afraid Annabelle might ask to see the spot where Gerald had died, that the police might want him to tell her, first hand, how it had happened. It was unthinkable to keep the house. In fact, it was not even safe to go back there. And yet the thought of hiring someone to pack up his things was distasteful to him.

But Mr Willis would probably telephone someone on his list of prospective clients, someone who would never have heard of the Delaney-Neumeister story. Mr Willis would be the only person who knew he had put up his house for sale the day after Gerald's death, and Mr Willis, like Mrs McCartney, thought highly of him as a tenant.

In the Froudsburg *Herald* on Monday evening, there was a picture of his house, showing the front steps against which Gerald had fallen and also a small, fuzzy picture of Gerald, ugly and grinning. And Effie had directed Gerald to the house. That enigma panicked David. If she knew that much about him, she would start trying to find out why he kept the house in the name of Neumeister, and very likely, out of spite because he had rejected her or out of a sense of justice, she would tell the police that Neumeister and Kelsey were one and the same. David was unable even to face that possibility.

Should he call up Effie – which was what an innocent man would do – and ask her if the man she had talked to on Sunday had told her his name or what he wanted? Could he dare deny flatly, if Effie asked him, that the house in the newspaper photograph was his? What was he going to say when Effie told him that the man whose picture was in the paper tonight was the man she had talked to?

There was no way out except to deny everything.

It was after 8 p.m. David dreaded the strain of another telephone call, having gotten successfully through the call to the Beck's Brook police at 6 p.m. and to Mr Willis immediately afterward. David put the newspaper back on the sideboard. He was the last one in the dining room.

Sarah, nearly finished with her clearing, said a dull 'How are you tonight, Mr Kelsey?' and passed him with a tray.

David went upstairs for his overcoat, got Effie's number from the little book by Mrs McCartney's telephone in the hall, then went out and walked almost to Main Street to reach a certain shabby pharmacy that had a telephone booth. He called Mr Willis again and asked him please not to put a FOR SALE sign on or around the house until after next weekend. Then, though he had intended to call Effie Brennan, he found he was not up to it.

He walked back through the slush to Mrs McCartney's, wondering how he would get through the evening, how he had gotten through the four or five hundred other evenings he had spent in his room. It was as if his wretched room itself had suffered an invasion. The Neumeister part of his life had entered the Kelsey Monday-to-Friday part, and like certain chemicals on mixing had set off an explosion. David was not used even to thinking about his weekend life during his working days and evenings. Now his weekend existence had, in fact, been destroyed. *Slush-slush-slush* went his shoes on the filthy sidewalks.

And there was Annabelle angry, loathing him, angry and mistaken, and he himself too distraught to think how to set things right again. That should be his number-one project – Annabelle. He decided to attempt a letter tonight, a calm, sympathetic letter that would make Annabelle feel less hostile toward him and help him also to clarify his own thoughts. He immediately felt better with that plan in mind for the evening.

As soon as he turned on the light in his room, he saw the little rectangle of paper on his bed that meant a telephone message:

Miss Brennan called at 8:30. Wants you to call back. FR 6-7739.

He would not call her, he thought. He could conceivably be out all evening, returning too late to call her back. But she'd call again tonight, or call tomorrow at the factory, he knew. At some point he would have to face it. He took a deep breath and walked to his door again. He walked back to the same pharmacy and called her number.

'Oh, hello, David,' Effie said in a friendly, excited voice. 'Did you see the paper tonight?'

'The paper?'

'Yes. The man who was killed, you know – He's the man who was at Mrs McCartney's yesterday asking about you. His picture's in the paper tonight. Look at it, Dave. Gerald Delaney. You know him, don't you?'

David's heart had taken only the mildest dip. 'No, I don't.'

'You don't? He knew you. Well, I thought you'd be terribly interested.'

'No. I mean, I'm only interested because he seemed to know me.' David looked out of the telephone booth at a middle-aged man just a yard away from him, inspecting a row of pocketbooks. He had the feeling the man was listening, knew that he lied, that the man was a police detective ready to arrest him as soon as he came out of the booth. 'They told me at the house he was drunk,' David added, dry in the mouth.

'Oh, not drunk. But he'd had a few all right.'

David sensed her caution. She was waiting for him to say more. 'And where did you tell him I was? Mrs McCartney said you made up a place.'

'Well, I said – Oh, David, can I see you tonight? Can't you come over?'

He hesitated. 'Not very well, Effie. I've got some work to do tonight.'

'Look at the paper, David. They've got a picture of the house. It belongs to William Neumeister.' She pronounced it 'Newmester,' the way the Beck's Brook police had. 'You know him, don't you?'

'No,' David said.

'You don't? In Ballard?'

'No,' David said with very genuine impatience.

'But I saw you going there once, David. You put your car in the garage.'

'*I* did?'

'Look at the picture in the paper. William Newmester. Maybe I'm pronouncing it wrong. I know it's the house. First on the right on County Road with the big chimney.'

'It must have been somebody else you saw there.'

'I guess I know your car, don't I?'

'I don't think I've ever been in Ballard,' David said stubbornly.

Now she was silent.

'But I'll take a look at the story, Effie.'

'Listen! If you recognize the man, would you let me know? Call me back. I'm kind of curious.'

'Sure, Effie.' He dropped the telephone on the hook. The last moments had exhausted him.

It was probably with Wes that she had seen him at the house, David thought. He had never seen Effie with anyone else who had a car. Even if she hadn't been with Wes, she would tell him all about this, because people always spilled out an exciting story, one with a mystery in it and the death of a man she had spoken to just before he was killed. David remembered Wes asking suspiciously, 'She lives in a nursing home? Not in a house?'

David dreaded tomorrow and seeing Wes. And maybe, like Effie, he would telephone tonight.

He went back to the boardinghouse. He could not even start in his mind the letter to Annabelle.

14

Wes, however, was his usual self the next day. David met him at ten in the morning in a corridor, and Wes kept him a minute or two telling a long joke about an old maid and a burglar which David managed to laugh at, and then Wes slapped him on the back and walked on.

David began to feel easier. Maybe he could lie his way out with Effie. Maybe she had not been with Wes when she saw him at the Ballard house. If he kept insisting it hadn't been him she saw, what could she do about it? And by this weekend, he would be out of the house.

The vertical hands of his wristwatch that evening reminded him to report to the Beck's Brook police — but that had been last night at six, he realized. 'Okay, we'll check again,' the police voice had said, but they hadn't said when they would check at the Barclay, and they hadn't told him when they wanted him to check with them again. Perhaps they didn't want him to call again. Perhaps he was overanxious. David remembered that quite by accident, when he spoke to the police, he had not said where he was calling from, but suppose they were calling the Barclay in New York at this moment and learning that William Neumeister was not there and never had been?

For a moment, David debated going to New York and staying overnight at the Barclay as William Neumeister. It would at least be on record. Or should he simply call the Beck's Brook police again, voluntarily? Appear to be co-operative? He put his overcoat on and left the house.

He called from the pharmacy near Main. A young voice answered.

'Hello,' David said. 'This is William Neumeister again.'

'Oh-h, Mr Newmester. Well – nothing to report from here, I guess. You're still in New York?'

'Yes. I may be here for – anyway, over next weekend, I think,' David said, and as he had last night, he lowered his voice somewhat, because he thought he had talked to the police officers on Sunday in a hypercautious growl in an effort to seem calm.

'I see,' said the young voice. 'Well, thanks for calling us.' And there was even a smile in the words.

David walked back to the boardinghouse, had his supper, started to read a book that he had brought from the factory's library, and then decided to take a walk. Gerald was probably buried today, he thought, and it had been on his mind all day to write a letter to Annabelle. He wanted to write the letter before he settled down with his book, and he began to think about the letter as he left the house. Platitudes of sympathy came to his mind first, and he discarded them with disgust. *I want you with me now*. After all, that was all he wanted to say.

It took him until eleven to produce a ten-line letter that satisfied him. He did not say anything about wanting her. He was sympathetic.

The next day, Wednesday, just after the lunch hour, the intercom announced all over the building that David Kelsey was wanted on the telephone. David went back to his office to take it, knowing that his secretary was with Lewissohn that afternoon. David had a ghastly premonition that it was the Beck's Brook police wanting to see him. Annabelle had told them that Gerald had been trying to find him on Sunday. Or they had called Effie and asked her why she had sent Gerald to the house in Ballard and she blurted out that she had seen him there. '*You're* David Kelsey?' the plump, alert-faced young policeman would say. 'Sunday you said your name was William Neumeister.'

A deeper older voice said, 'Mr Kelsey? Sergeant Terry of Beck's Brook speaking. Do you mind if we ask you a few questions?'

'No.'

'Uh – you know a Mrs Annabelle Delaney of Hartford, don't you?'

'Yes.'

'You know that her husband left Hartford to go to see you last Sunday?'

'I was told that.'

'Where were you Sunday, Mr Kelsey?'

'I was visiting my mother – at a nursing home.'

'A nursing home where?'

'Hazelwood, it's called. Five miles north of Newburgh.' It was one of the two nursing homes that were approximately an hour's distance by car from Froudsburg.

'Newburgh,' the man repeated, as if he were taking notes.

The voice continued in an easy tone: 'I take it you read about Delaney's death in the papers.'

'Yes – and I called Mrs Delaney when I heard about it.'

'Do you know William Newmester?' he asked with a note of hope.

'No, sir, I don't.'

'But you know a Miss Elfrida Brennan.'

'Yes. I know her slightly.'

'You have any idea why she sent Delaney to his house in Ballard?'

'Well, I spoke to her on the phone. She said she didn't really know of a house there – that she just made up a place to tell Gerald to go to that day. He'd had a few drinks, I heard.'

'Yes. Do you have any doubts, Mr Kelsey, that Miss Brennan's telling the truth? This is strictly confidential between us, so you can be honest with me.'

'No, sir. I have no reason to have any doubts. Why?'

'Well, we're trying to find Newmester. Mrs Delaney wants to see him. Talk to him y'know, and ask him what happened. Newmester's in New York and he won't be back till next week.' The voice sounded unbelievably casual.

'Oh,' David said.

'We don't think Newmester's got any reason to hide, and yet we don't know. He's not at the hotel he said he'd be at in New York, and we thought Miss Brennan might know him and might be trying to protect him.'

'Well, I don't know anything about that.'

'Uh-hm. When did you see Delaney last, Mr Kelsey?' the lazy voice continued.

'I saw him three or four weeks ago when I went up to Hartford.'

'Did he seem hostile when you saw him then?'

David took a deep breath. 'Frankly, I've never paid much attention to Delaney. I'm a friend of his wife's.'

'Just a friend, Mr Kelsey?'

'Yes,' David replied, thinking the truth included friendship, after all. 'Isn't that what she told you?'

'Ye-es, she did,' the man drawled, and he sounded as if he believed it. 'Delaney wasn't by any chance jealous?'

'I don't know what his motivations were. Maybe his wife knows. You might ask her.'

'Hm-m. She said her husband had a bad temper.'

'Sergeant, I've seen Delaney only once in my life, and that was in Hartford three or four weeks ago.'

'I see. Well, thank you, Mr Kelsey. One thing more. Can you give us the telephone number of your landlady?'

David gave it. A moment later, walking away from the telephone, he felt a sink of defeat: the Beck's Brook police would very likely remark to Annabelle that he had been visiting his mother over the weekend. Annabelle knew his mother was dead.

And there was the other little matter that Annabelle wanted to see William Neumeister.

Mrs McCartney was waiting in the hall that evening, and she began to talk as soon as she saw him. The Beck's Brook police had called and asked her a lot of questions, and she was at great pains to tell David that she had given him the highest kind of 'references'. Mrs Starkie had been standing by, too, to corroborate everything that Mrs McCartney had said to the police. Mrs Starkie joined them in the hall. So did Mr Muldaven. Mr Muldaven had also been in the house when the police call came.

'I told them you were the finest young man who'd ever set foot in this house,' Mrs McCartney averred to David.

David listened for Annabelle's name, but he did not hear it. The police had been interested only in his personal habits, and in where he had been that weekend, and Mrs McCartney had told them he spent *every* weekend with his mother, and had for the two years she had known him.

'Who is this Newmester?' Mrs McCartney asked.

'I don't know,' David said.

'Don't you worry about anything, David,' Mrs Starkie put in.

'Thank you.' David had not known he had such a champion in Mrs Starkie, whom he hardly so much as greeted when they encountered each other in the house. 'Would you excuse me now?' David asked, ignoring a babble of questions. 'I'd like to go upstairs.'

'Of course, you would, dear boy,' said Mrs McCartney, patting his sleeve. 'You go ahead. Everything's going to be all right.'

It was a pleasure to climb the stairs and leave their voices behind him, a pleasure to close his door and snap the lock under the knob and breathe again! Why hadn't they mentioned Gerald, David wondered. Why hadn't the police told Mrs McCartney that he knew him? Were they saving that for something? If so, what? Had Annabelle really not told them he was in love with her? Maybe he was going to be saved by the very gun Gerald had carried. A drunken mistake with a flourish of a gun was disgrace enough, but if a story of jealousy of his wife's lover came out, that would make Gerald a premeditating killer.

David was once more at a table with Mr Harris and Mr Muldaven, and they asked him for the fifth or sixth time at least if he was sure he had not known Gerald Delaney somehow, from somewhere. But when David, summoning all his patience, gave them a quiet 'No, absolutely not,' the two men began to mull over the incident with an objectivity that David found quite comforting. What interested them and the rest of the people in the house was that Gerald Delaney had been in such a temper that Sunday morning, and that he had been carrying a gun pretty clearly intended to be used on David Kelsey. What amazed them all was David's calmness about it. If Mrs McCartney and her boarders ever found out, David thought, through the Beck's Brook police or any other way, that he *had* known Gerald Delaney, he would say he had been told by the police not to discuss the situation with anyone. The Situation. It was all part of the one Situation, after all. He could not eat Mrs McCartney's slimy boiled chicken with its soggy rice. He ate tasteless white bread with his pat of butter, and the two aging men at his table, though they relished their morsel of butter, always scraping the last bit of it from the little squares of cardboard it was served on, pressed their portions on him as if he deserved special treatment because of what he had been through.

He had a fear that someone in the house, perhaps Mrs McCartney herself, might invade his room tonight to ask him more questions, so he went directly from the dining room to get his overcoat. It crossed his mind to kill two hours of the evening at a movie, but this seemed analogous to drinking alcohol, and he made an effort to collect himself. He decided to walk for precisely an hour, then go back to his room and read until he became sleepy, read all the night, if he couldn't sleep.

'Dave!'

Wes's voice had come from a car in the street. David walked toward it.

'I want to talk to you, Dave. Can we go to your place or what?'

David hesitated, but he thought of no way to get out of it. 'Let's go to Michael's.'

'Fine.'

David got in. Wes said nothing more. The unpleasant silence lasted until Michael's Tavern was in sight. Then Wes said with his usual cheer, 'I guess they're asking you all kinds of questions at the house. I mean about this Delaney thing.'

The bar was dimly lighted, and at this hour rather quiet. Wes motioned David to follow him to a back booth, greeted Adolf the barman, and gave an order for two Scotches with water as he walked past.

'If you don't want it, I'll drink it,' Wes said to David.

There was another silence, until Adolf brought the two drinks on a tray, served them, and left.

'Effie called me tonight,' Wes began, looking down at the table. 'Seems the police called *her* and —' Wes held another match to his half-lighted cigarette. 'They called her because she told that Delaney fellow to go to the house in Ballard, you know.'

'Yes,' David said.

'But you weren't at the house.'

It was half a question, half a statement. 'No,' David said, frowning a little.

'But you know that house, don't you?'

'No, I don't.'

Now Wes frowned and smiled at the same time, as if he didn't believe him. 'Do you know this fellow Newmester who lives there?'

'No, I don't.'

Wes rubbed his freckled forehead with his fingertips. 'Well, Effie and I happened to see you go there once, Dave. That's why I asked. No other reason.'

'See me go there when?'

'Remember the Friday I went back home from Mrs Mac's and I said I was going to stop by Effie's for a drink? I don't know why I did it, but I said, "Let's follow old Dave tonight and see where he really goes weekends." I wasn't intending to snoop, Dave, I was just in the mood to do something a little nuts, I guess. So Effie got in the car and we spotted you crossing Main going north, and we followed you, that's all. It's none of my business, Dave, and I haven't thought of it since. I just thought, well, his mother stays in a house not a nursing home, or something like that. Or maybe the place was a nursing home, I didn't know.'

David looked at him. He could see that what was troubling Wes was not Delaney's death, or that the house didn't look like a nursing home, but that the whole story of his invalid mother might be a myth.

'I mean, I didn't think any more about it, Dave, until this business came up – with Effie. She thinks the house where the man was killed is the same one we saw you go to. She called me up to see if I didn't think so, too, and I do. I could see part of that big chimney in the photograph. And she gave the guy directions to it, after all.'

The bald-faced lie, David thought. There wasn't any other way, 'I told Effie I didn't know that house,' David said. 'If she thinks she saw my car going there, she's just mistaken.'

'Oh, no, Dave. Maybe you just dropped something by there that day, but we saw you get out of the car and open the garage door. *You*,' Wes said with a grin, pointing at him. 'We were on that road before you turn into the driveway, but it was still close enough to see you.'

'I can't even think of anyone I know around there,' David said, feeling a little nauseated from Wes's cigarette smoke.

Wes only stared at him disbelievingly, still smiling. Then he shrugged and puffed again on his cigarette. 'I don't want to pry, Dave, I really don't. I'm sorry. Don't take it – Don't take any offense, will you?' His brown, gold-speckled eyes almost pleaded.

'Of course not!' David said generously. 'I just think there's some mistake.' He looked with insane bravery and calm into Wes's eyes again and asked, 'Effie told the police she saw me at that house too?'

'Oh, no, she didn't.' Wes chuckled, about to drink the last of his first Scotch. 'Sweet little kid, she told them she made up some directions and didn't even know if there was a house there. She just wanted to get a drunk out of Mrs Mac's place, she said. You see, she thinks you might be seeing a girl there, and she's so crazy about you she's making the supreme sacrifice.'

David's deliberate smile became a smile of relief. What a piece of luck! He couldn't have told Effie better what to say. 'The most mixed-up story I've ever heard.'

Wes looked at David slyly, as if reassessing him in the light that he might be spending his weekends with a girl, might have been all the time Wes knew him. 'A mixup,' Wes repeated sarcastically, and pulled his other drink in front of him. 'There are some pieces I don't get either.'

David was silent.

'Why don't you go by Effie's and pick up your portrait sometime?'

'I don't know why,' David said quietly.

Wes laughed. Then a moment later, leaning across the table, 'Tell me how you knew Delaney.'

David looked at him, for the first time sure that Wes and therefore Effie did not know about Annabelle. 'I don't,' he said.

Wes frowned. 'Dave, you can't expect me to swallow that one!'

'I don't care what you swallow, Wes, or what you don't.'

'All right, Dave, don't get sore at me. If anybody ought to respect privacy, it's me, and I do. Whatever I know, and it sure isn't much, won't go any further Dave.' But he was still waiting to hear about Delaney.

'I can't understand why people're so curious,' David said with irritation. 'Good God, I wouldn't be.'

'Human nature,' Wes said cheerfully. 'And don't forget, that guy was looking for you to do you some damage. He had a gun. Maybe you forgot that detail.'

'I didn't forget,' David said with boredom.

'You wouldn't've had some girl in common, would you, Dave? That's my last question.'

'Don't be silly.'

Wes had a third drink, after asking David if he minded sitting there another couple of minutes, and Wes courteously brought up a different subject – the latest satellite firing in Florida. As he was driving David home, Wes remarked that David's name had been in the paper that evening and asked David if he had seen it. David had not. It had been a small item, Wes said, saying that Delaney's wife had told the police that Delaney had been looking for David Kelsey – something that anybody at Mrs McCartney's could have told them, too, David thought. Apparently, Annabelle had not yet told the police Gerald had been jealous because David Kelsey was in love with her. David hoped she had not, and not merely for his own sake, but because if Annabelle wanted to keep it a secret, it seemed she attached importance to it and respected it. David had not even thought to look at the evening paper, and he admitted to himself it was because he had been afraid to look.

'Got to rush home to the little wife,' Wes said as he let David out. 'We haven't eaten yet. I told her I had urgent business and walked out, she thinks to see Effie. It's going to be great.' Bolstered by the Scotches, Wes smiled broadly and waved good-by.

In his room David took off his overcoat and flung himself face down on the bed, one arm under his head, the other out at his side, around an imaginary Annabelle. He pressed his mouth against her cheeks, and then her lips, and floated away to that sanctum of calm, that swiftly rising awareness of her presence that brought a pang at its peak, and that he made linger by his concentration. It struck him that it was the first time he had been with Annabelle in this ugly room. Yet even the sourish, dusty smell of the counterpane seemed funny and pleasant now, because he shared it with her.

15

David worked late in his house on Friday night, packing a trunk and suitcases, wrapping his dishes in newspaper in readiness for the barrels that a storage company was going to bring Saturday afternoon. And he was up early Saturday to continue the dismantling of lamps, the tying up of mattresses, until eleven when he had an appointment with Mr Willis. He was sorry he had agreed to go to Beck's Brook, because he did not want even to be greeted by one or the other of the two police officers there, and he was on the brink of going somewhere to telephone and ask Mr Willis to come to his house instead, when he heard a car outside. He looked through his front window. The car had stopped thirty feet away on the drive, and due to the sunlight on the windshield, he could not see who was driving it. Then the door opened and Effie Brennan got out.

'Jesus!' David said, turned around and rubbed his palm across his forehead. He walked to the stairs and ran up. In the half-empty bedroom he paced slowly, trying to ignore the urgent, metallic rap-rap-rap of the front door knocker.

It went on and on and on, until David wanted to scream from where he was for her to go away.

'David?' Her voice came feebly into the closed house. 'It's Effie. Can I come in?'

Rap-rap-rap.

Then a blessed silence.

But she had only gone to the back door, and the knocking and rattling started again. 'David? Are you in the basement? It's Effie.'

And suddenly he dashed down the stairs as if he were racing to put out a fire that had started on his back doorstep, yanked the door open, and said, 'What the hell do you want?'

She was in flat shoes, and his words seemed literally to knock her over backward. She staggered, regained her balance, and quickly her eyes filled with tears. 'Oh, David, I just wanted to talk to you for a minute. *Please.* I'm your friend, David. Or is there somebody else here?'

'No.'

'A friend of mine lent me her car. I thought I'd just drive up and say hello. I won't stay long, David,' she said as she moved past him, leaving a trail of scent behind her.

David scowled.

She turned and looked at him, still frightened, still wide-eyed with shock, as if she might run suddenly out the open door, which David hoped she would. 'This *is* your house, isn't it?'

A tangle of shame and wrath kept him from answering anything. He moved toward another door, his hands in the back pockets of his blue jeans.

She followed him. 'David, don't be angry with me. I think I said what you'd have wanted me to say. To the police. I said I made it up about this house, you know. I didn't tell them you — that it was your house.'

He said nothing.

'If that's what you're angry about. Is it?'

'Why don't you leave, Effie?' he asked, turning to face her. 'I'm not in any state to talk.' His voice cracked foolishly and he could see his own trembling.

Prying, snooping, she had crossed the kitchen and was looking into the disordered living room. He wanted to hurl her through a window, anything, to get her out. 'You're moving,' she said, and David burst out in an insane laugh, rocking on his sneakered feet, his head back. And she looked at him as if he were a ghost.

'Yes, moving today,' he said loudly and cheerily.

Her eyes looked at him steadily, but again as if she were trying to choose the right instant to dart away from him, out of the house, and David wondered what could be so frightening about himself, standing there with a genial, inane smile on his face. 'Who is William Newmester?' she asked.

'A friend of mine, a very, very good friend,' David said promptly.

'He lives here?'

'He certainly does.' With those words, a sour anger began to grow in him.

'You told Wes you didn't know him.'

'I didn't want to go into it with Wes.'

'And you spend all your weekends with Newmester?'

'Yes. Dear old Bill.' He smiled a little.

'Were you here Sunday – last Sunday when the man arrived?'

'I happened to be out.'

Effie nodded and looked uneasily about her. She was holding a large brown pocketbook with her two hands, fumbling along its top. 'Is there a girl here, too, David?' she asked shyly.

He only stared at her.

'Please don't be angry. I don't know why you're angry, since I only want to do the right thing. I even lied to the police to help you.' She was getting her courage back, and now she smiled suddenly, though her eyes were still wary of him. 'I know you want to keep it a secret, whatever you do here. You don't owe me anything, I know, but I asked about a girl – because *I* care, you see? If there's a girl –' She stopped.

'I think I told you I was engaged.'

'You know, I just don't believe that story. Wes told me too. But that just isn't the way things are.'

Something in her words reminded him of Annabelle's letters, and made him still angrier.

'If you're with a girl now, that's one thing.' She bit her under-lip. Then quite flatly she said, 'I love you, David.'

'*Get out!*'

Effie jumped. She took a step back and stood again. 'You've no reason to be angry,' she said, starting to cry. She opened her arms sadly. 'If you're packing up today, I'll even help you.'

Somehow it was the last straw. David moved toward her, and she retreated, protesting, across the living room. They were both yelling at once now, and she kept raising her arms as if to ward off a blow, like a jerking little doll. It was the last straw, this common little stenographer crashing into his house, telling him she loved him, and offering to pack up his possessions that had been meant for only Annabelle to see, offering to destroy what had been created for Annabelle, the rooms and the pictures and the music Annabelle had never heard here, every damned item of which had pained him to touch last night and this morning, because he had put it where it was for Annabelle, and she had never even seen it.

'I think you're insane!' Effie gasped, and now her eyes looked as if they were about to pop out of her head. She bumped against the front door, though he had not even touched her.

'And you're not the first to say it!' he shouted back.

Her breath came with shuddering. She groped for the doorknob, still staring at him with her terrified eyes, as if he had just beaten her within an inch of her life, or had just made an attempt to kill her. He seized the doorknob, opened the door for her, and she darted past him around the door and out, running to her car. David stood watching her, feeling his heart shake his body with every slow and heavy stroke. The car's engine whirred and stopped twice before it caught, and then as it jerked backward in reverse, the engine stalled, and he saw her frantic hurry to start it. Then he shut the door.

David stood looking at a rolled-up carpet for a minute, feeling suddenly very tired, much too tired to think about what had just happened. He felt absolutely justified; that was all he had the energy to realize. He went back to the task he had been at when she arrived, and immediately remembered that he had been going to call Mr Willis. Now it was a bit late, but he was about to try it anyway when he decided he did not want Mr

Willis to come into his house either. David undressed, stood under the shower for a minute to wash off his nervous sweat, then dressed and drove to Beck's Brook.

He did not see either of the two police officers. Mr Willis greeted him triumphantly with the news that a Mr Gregory Peabody had looked at his house and wanted to buy it, and that his down payment would arrive on Monday. Mr Willis asked him if he would be interested in another house in the neighborhood for a future date, and David, dazed with his good luck in selling so soon, said that he would be, and that he was storing his things for only a year or so. But when Mr Willis began to show him maps and photographs of other houses, David realized that he would never want to be anywhere near Ballard or Froudsburg or Beck's Brook again.

'I really can't think about it at the moment,' David said. 'I've got too much else on my mind.'

The men from the storage house came in the afternoon, bringing a dozen large barrels for his books and dishes. They were due to come back on Monday morning, when David would not be there, and load the barrels and the furniture, everything that was in the house, onto their truck, to be stored in the name of David Kelsey. It was dangerous, he well knew, but he saw no other alternative – at least no honorable one. He could have stored his things in Mrs McCartney's name or Mrs Beecham's, he supposed, and if it all crashed down on his head, he wouldn't be at all interested in having his clothes and furniture back, anyway, but to have hidden behind their names would have been disgraceful. And a concocted name would have presented the difficulty of identification when the time came for him to get the stuff out of storage. So if the police or even the people at the storage house noticed that Neumeister had deposited his things in the name of Kelsey, that was just his bad luck. None of his suitcases bore any initials. He kept out one good suit and a white shirt. But the only things he was taking from the house were the two pictures of Annabelle and the few letters she had written him, and some papers from his desk, including his insurance policy that named Mrs Annabelle Stanton Kelsey as beneficiary.

He sat for a while on the sofa, which was already tied up

with newspaper. The house was filled with a shocked silence, like the silence after the explosion of a bomb. The words he had said to Effie came back to him now, repeating themselves like maddening echoes in his head. Had he really said, 'I despise you! Get out or I'll throw you out!'? He had certainly said Neumeister was a good friend of his, and he had told Wes that he had never heard of Neumeister. What was Wes going to make of that? What was Effie going to make of it? David stood up with a thought of talking to Effie again, asking her – But he remembered her terrified face, and he knew now he had made her his enemy. She'd talk to Wes all right, probably immediately.

To hell with it, David thought. He was again worried about the wrong things. Annabelle was the only thing worth worrying about.

As for knowing or not knowing Neumeister, he'd tell Wes, in case Wes brought it up, that he'd told a slight lie to him in denying knowing Neumeister – who really did own the house in Ballard, and who was a friend of his – but that the police had asked him not to discuss the thing with anyone, because of Neumeister's accidental and unfortunate connection with Delaney's death. David smiled a little bitterly, and from a silver box, still unpacked among some other small things on the floor, he took a cigarette and lighted it. William Neumeister smoked a few cigarettes on his weekends, and this one was a last salute to him. It was dry and crackly. David inhaled it, even though it gave him no pleasure.

The doorknocker sounded, and he walked to the door quite calmly. There stood the young officer from Beck's Brook.

'Afternoon, Mr Newmester. Well! You're moving?'

'Yep. I'm going to be traveling for a bit. Do you want to come in?'

'Thanks,' he said, coming in. 'I saw a little activity around the place, so I thought I'd drop in and see how you are.'

'I'm fine,' David said.

The young officer pushed his cap to the back of his head. 'You weren't ever at the Barclay, were you?'

'No. I had to stay somewhere else the first night and the second I was told I could get in, but —' David made a gesture as if it were too unimportant to go into.

'We tried to reach you at the Barclay Thursday, because Mrs Delaney was here.'

'Here?'

'She came to see us. She wanted to see the spot where her husband died. She wanted to talk to you, see, so we put in a call for you at the Barclay. We thought, if you were willing, you could've come up and talked to her, because she'd've waited a couple of hours, but we just took her around outside here and she went back. She was with another woman. Very pretty girl, she is.' He looked with a dreamy smile at David, as if her image were still in his eyes.

David looked out a front window. That ground, and Annabelle's feet. It was almost incredible, having hoped for so long to bring her here, and then that she had actually come when he was not here, and gone away again.

'You moving out?' the young officer asked.

'Yes. I'm going to be traveling for a while. I'm selling the place.'

'What're you asking?'

'What I paid. Twenty thousand. Seven and a half acres go with it.' David frowned. 'Did Mrs Delaney stay very long?' he asked, prodded by a tremendous curiosity.

'Oh, just about ten minutes. You shouldn't be so surprised, people're always like that. They want to see where it happened and they want every detail you can give 'em. Unless they're old people. Old people don't want to hear details, y'know, about car wrecks and things like that.'

David nodded, wondering if Annabelle still wanted to see William Neumeister, and if she were going to persist until she did. 'Do you think I should telephone her?' he asked.

'Up to you. I guess I would. You could probably tell her what she wants to know on the phone.' He drifted toward the door. 'Got her phone number at the station if you want to drop by for it. Otherwise it's Hartford, Mrs Gerald Delaney. Information'll give it to you.'

'Was she very upset?'

'Kinda teary, but she held up okay. Nice girl, you can tell. And with a two-months-old baby. Jesus! I think her name's Anna. Something like Anna.'

16

On Monday evening, David drove to Hartford. He had set out at a quarter to six, and he arrived at eight-thirty, in a nasty little rain. He had wanted to ring her bell without telephoning first, but now he felt it would be rude not to call, so he stopped at the drugstore he had called from before, dialed her number without checking on it, and Annabelle answered. He told her he was in Hartford.

'Can I see you, darling? Are you free?'

'Yes – I'm free. Did you want to come here?'

He left his car where it was, dashed obliquely across the street, nearly got hit, and strode on down a dark sidewalk with his face turned up to the fine rain which had suddenly become beautiful and refreshing. Someone was coming out of the house as he arrived, and he lunged and caught the door before it had time to close, ran up the steps and knocked.

'Dave?' Annabelle called.

'Yes.'

A latch turned, the door opened. Annabelle looked at him in surprise. 'You got here so fast.'

He held her close and pressed his lips against her cheek. She stirred in his arms, and it was not until her hand pushed his shoulder that he realized she wanted free and he immediately released her. His eyes devoured her as his arms had. She was pale, even her lips colorless. Only her eyes seemed the same, looking up at his face sadly, and as if they spoke to him in words she couldn't utter. He searched them for words of love, and instantly found them, found also regret, apology, hope, and tenderness. It was as if she said to him that she had been longing for him to come, that she needed him, that she had been afraid he might not come. He put his hands on her shoulders and bent to kiss her again.

'You hung up soon,' she said, drawing back, 'I didn't tell you that somebody's coming over.'

'Who?'

'A friend. Mrs Barber. She'll be here in a few minutes.'

'Oh. But at least we have a few minutes. I have so much to say, Annabelle. Isn't there ever any *time*?' He passed his hand across his damp hair.

'Take off your coat, Dave,' she said more kindly, and David's face spread in a smile.

She sat down tensely on the edge of the sofa, her hands in her lap.

He sat down on the sofa also, not too close to her. 'I'm sorry you've been unhappy,' he said, and watched her eyes fill slowly with tears.

'It's all such a mistake. I can't believe it sometimes. I think – Gerald's going to walk in the house, but no. Gerald was here – and now he's not here.' She wiped a tear away impatiently.

Her words, which meant little to him emotionally, seemed classically trite – as if Annabelle felt she had to put on a traditional show. David looked from her to the television set with the gray-haired nonentity on it. 'I want you to come with me, Annabelle,' he said suddenly, turning back to her, seizing her hand, though it grew stiff at his touch. 'I'm selling my house, but I want to buy another house, one you'll like and help me choose. It can be anywhere, depending on where I work, and I'll work anywhere, almost anywhere. I'd like to be with Dickson-Rand in Troy. I want to start a completely new life. Let's both start over. Do you –'

'No,' she interrupted more loudly. 'Honestly, Dave, did you come here to talk sense to me or not?'

He looked at her closed hand, which had just come to rest, with tired slowness, on her thigh. It had a plain gold wedding ring on it. 'I didn't mean to say it all at once. There's always so little time – or none. I'm sorry, darling.' And he ground his teeth, because he could see from her tense expression that she was nearly out of her mind from fatigue and worry, the worries he so wanted to relieve her from.

'I just have nothing to answer to an outburst like that. You talk as if I have no child, no responsibility to Gerald –'

David was suddenly aware that she wore a man's white shirt with her patterned cotton skirt, realized with discomfort and revulsion that the shirt was probably one of Gerald's. 'I know all that takes time.'

'Time? A long time. My life's torn apart now and you come with your crazy plans. My first duty is to my child.'

'We'll take her with us,' David said quickly. 'That's understood, darling. I was talking about the future. You've got to think of that too, haven't you?'

'It's a boy, in case you've forgotten,' Annabelle said, wiping her nose with a Kleenex she had taken from the shirt pocket.

A boy, of course. David had been picturing a miniature Gerald, when he thought of the child at all. He asked her if she were going to stay on in the apartment, and she said there was the lease to think of, and that she had friends in the neighborhood who could help her take care of the baby, because sooner or later she would have to take a job.

'That's not necessary, darling, I've got plenty of money.'

'I can't take your money.'

'What's it for, if it isn't for you?'

She took her hand from his again, and for a moment, he thought she was going to get up from the sofa. 'Where was your house, Dave?'

'Oh – nearly an hour's drive from Froudsburg.'

'In Ballard?'

'No. Practically in an opposite direction from Ballard. The girl at the boardinghouse just made up Ballard, Annabelle. She didn't know where my house was.'

'Why? Isn't she a friend of yours.'

'I didn't want anybody to know about the house, Annabelle. I wanted to keep it just for us – and I did.'

'Near what town was it?'

He sighed. 'The nearest town was – Ruarksville. The house was a mile or so the other side of it. A good ninety miles from Ballard!'

'You told everybody you went to see your mother. Why did you lie, Dave?'

'Because it was the simplest way. I wanted privacy. I didn't want any house guests. I didn't even have a –' He checked himself from saying he hadn't a telephone. 'It was a pretty house. I so much wanted you to see it. I used to imagine you were there with me, and I did everything the way I thought you'd like it done. The bedroom, the living room, the pictures on the walls — even the way I fixed my meals.' He smiled. 'I wish I had some pictures of it, so you could see what it looked like.' And he really did wish that, until he remembered that she would have recognized it from the outside.

She nodded, frowning slightly, her eyes far away, not looking at him. 'Do you know William Neumeister?' she asked, pronouncing it the German way.

'No.'

'Does anybody at your boardinghouse know him?'

'No. Nobody as far as I know.'

'I very much wanted to talk to him. He was away. I went to the house last Thursday. I knew he wasn't home, but I thought somebody there might know where he was. One of the police. I wanted to ask him what really happened.'

David shrugged, and his eyes were drawn again to the smug face in the photograph on the television set. 'He told the police what happened, didn't he?'

'What I can't understand is that Gerald stood there arguing with him — long enough to draw a gun. It doesn't make sense. I know he'd had something to drink, but —'

No, it didn't make sense, and David had thought of it before, but it had to make sense now. 'Maybe he thought I was hiding in the house. Maybe he'd had a little more to drink than you thought.'

'But the doctor didn't think he'd had much. He'd had four at Ed Purdy's and I doubt if he stopped for more on the way.'

'Well, there you are — four, and you don't know how big they were.' David said, and felt his desperation was beginning to show through. 'It was an accident, Annabelle, any way you look at it. He fell and hit a step. It could've happened to anyone going down the steps in the snow that day.'

'But the other man pushed him,' she said. 'I wanted to talk to Neumeister —' Her face, her voice, had twisted again with the oozing tears, the futile tears that David hated to see and could not stop.

'You can't blame Neumeister for resisting a man with a gun.'

She lifted her head. 'But it wasn't an accident that he went to find you. Any man would have, if some other man was writing his wife letters like those. And I asked you to stop, Dave, it wasn't as if I encouraged you.'

'I know.'

'But no, along you come with the worst of all. Threats – saying you were going to come here and take me away. Why, Dave, if anybody saw those letters, they'd say you practically belonged in an institution.'

He sprang up. 'Oh? Any one of those letters – They're perfectly logical letters and you know it. I love you, and why shouldn't I write you letters?'

'Because I'm married!' she interjected.

'I never laid a hand on you or Gerald, and you talk as if I were an idiot or a maniac. If a man can't plead his case in a letter, what's the world coming to?'

'You don't write letters like those to a married woman! I couldn't even go into it with the police, it's so embarrassing!'

The doorbell rang.

'Embarrassing,' David repeated, stunned.

'And all you can say is "I have a right." You have a right then to kill my husband?' She stood up, white-faced with an anger David could see she thought was righteous.

'Kill him, my foot!' he said, and turned away.

'That's what it amounts to.' She walked out of the room.

David heard the release button downstairs. Then a woman's rather slow steps ascended.

'There's no use in your staying any longer, Dave,' Annabelle said.

'What do you mean?' He was walking toward her, stopped because he knew she would not let him touch her, then in desperation caught her shoulders. 'With all my heart I love you and want to make you happy. I might as well be dead myself without you, Annabelle. Just give me a chance.'

There was a rapping at the door.

Annabelle looked at him angrily, as if too angry even to say anything to him, and David scowled, baffled.

'I'll wait downstairs, however long it takes,' David said.

'Do you think I'm going to put you up for the night here?' She opened the door.

There came into the room one of the gray-haired, plumpish, fiftyish women that epitomized to David the word 'neighbor,' possibly 'good neighbor,' plain and dull. 'How do you do?' David said with a little bow, in response to Annabelle's introduction, and saw the woman's smile deflate, leaving pucker lines around her mouth.

'It's – the same one?' the woman asked Annabelle.

Annabelle nodded. 'Yes. We had to have a talk. But Dave's leaving now.'

'I was not leaving,' Dave said softly but firmly, 'unless I'm in the way, of course.'

The woman stared at him as if he were a curiosity, a phenomenon, her mouth a little ajar – like someone in a crowd photograph snapped watching a parade.

'I don't think we finished our talk, Annabelle,' David added.

'Thanks, David, for all your offers. I don't know what else we have to talk about tonight.'

He stared stupidly at Annabelle's brown loafers, her bare slim ankles that without the woman standing there he might have gotten down on the floor and kissed. The taste of blood was in his mouth. He had been biting the inside of his cheek. Annabelle looked at him haughtily, almost as if she were putting on an act for this clod of a neighbor. 'When may I see you again?'

'Dave, please –'

'Annabelle, what's the matter with you?' he shouted, in this last minute seizing her hands, and as she drew back there was a sudden crackling fury from the woman, hands fumbling with his arm that he jerked away from her. Then he stood apart from Annabelle, blinking as the woman shouted and gesticulated.

'Haven't you caused enough trouble, you – you filthy character! Filthy character, you are!' she said righteously, nodding.

'I love this girl and I don't care who knows it!' David yelled back.

Now the woman stomped, tossed her head, and yelled something else that David scorned to listen to as he turned back to

Annabelle. Annabelle stepped away, at the same time opening the door.

'Good night, Dave, please, please,' Annabelle said tiredly.

He only took a long last look, smiling with relief at the kindness in her voice. 'I'll think of you — constantly,' he said, and left.

And for all the time it took for him to walk to his car, his brain was in a vise of self-reproach for having lost his temper. Even in the face of the asinine neighbor, there was no excuse for it. He should have been calm for Annabelle's sake, a pillar of strength, sympathetic, patient, all the things he had not been.

Oh, Christ, how much there was to be done over!

17

Jan. 27, 1959

My darling Annabelle,

A new day is coming up as I write this. I have been walking around the town for hours. How I wish I were a poet to be able to tell you what this day symbolizes to me. It is a new beginning. If you could only see our life together like that, if you could simply believe how much I love you. To speak of myself now, I realize, is selfish. I love you for your devotion to Gerald, I respect your grief, but only because it is yours. I pray to whatever powers there are that your devotion and your love may one day be transferred to me. How can I measure my love for you? It fills me to overflowing. It is strangely tangible and yet intangible. It is like a weight inside me. I could not love you more than I do. It is unbelievable to me that a human being could feel as I do and be utterly without hope of his love being returned. Annabelle, I am quite sure one day you will understand, you will smile again at me as you once did.

As for the present — to return to last night, I reproach myself bitterly for having lost my temper, for having shouted. It is unforgivable. I wanted only to brush away your own tears, comfort you. I want only to make you happy. If you understood that completely, I would be the happiest man alive.

My job here is no pleasure and never was. My plans are, within a few weeks or months, however long it takes, to find a place in a research laboratory. I want you with me. I want to buy a house of *your* choosing. Have you thought of going back to La Jolla for a while? It might be very good for you to get your bearings and all that. If you go, believe me that you are in my thoughts day and night and always. I will love you as long as I live.

Dave

He went out quietly and dropped the letter into a box two streets away. It was 7 a.m. and though when he had walked to the mailbox the town had been colorless as a photograph, on his way back the bricks of a wall across the street had become dark red, and he could see the green in the scraggly hedges. He felt unusually alert, and strangely happy. His letter might erase all the negative atmosphere of last night, might lift her spirits, might suddenly show her everything in a new light. *Some* letter would do it, he knew. It might take a hundred, two hundred letters, but it would not be their weight or their cumulative power, it would be a certain phrase, perhaps one that he did not consider even very important, that would make Annabelle see.

He was whistling as he came up the front walk. On Thursday, he thought, the day after Annabelle received his letter, he would call her from the factory and propose lunch on Saturday. He would take her to some restaurant in the country. Annabelle should see trees, grass, space! The countryside wouldn't be as beautiful, perhaps, as in spring or summer, but compared to that sordid street she lived in, any glimpse of country would be beautiful.

Mrs McCartney was in the front hall when he walked in. 'I just knocked on your door David. Effie Brennan called you a minute ago. Wants you to call her back. She says it's important.'

'All right. Thank you,' David said.

'You have her number, haven't you?'

'No.'

'It's in the little blue book hanging by the telephone,' Mrs McCartney told him, again with the smile and the avidly curious eyes.

David did not want to call her from the house. He waited until Mrs McCartney had gone into the dining room, then went out of the house again. If Effie had told the Beck's Brook police that she had seen David Kelsey in the Neumeister house, then so be it, he thought. It was awkward and embarrassing, but

119

nothing more. If he had to admit that it was David Kelsey who had talked with Gerald Delaney and finally knocked him down, in a fall that happened to be fatal, what then? Did that make him a murderer? If he had tried up to now to conceal his identity because of the Situation, wasn't that understandable?

Wasn't it even possible, David thought as he dialed Effie's number, to make a clean breast of the whole thing and come out in a better position than he was now with Annabelle? Up to this moment, he had been afraid to contemplate making a clean breast of it. This morning anything seemed possible.

'Hello, Effie. This is David Kelsey.'

'Dave – hello,' she said breathlessly. 'I'm sorry I called you so early. Are you all right?'

'I'm all right. Why?'

'I was worried,' she said quickly.

'About what?'

'Everything. Where were you just now?'

'Out mailing a letter.' He had an impulse to tell her he owed her an apology, to apologize for his outburst last Saturday. But now both the incident and whether Effie Brennan was an enemy or not seemed unimportant.

'Dave, I shouldn't have come by Saturday. Once again, I'm sorry.'

'It's all right,' he said, puzzled by her shaky voice.

'I want you to know, Dave, whatever happens, I'm with you. I'm on your side. At least –'

'At least what?'

'I'm confused about so many things. I wish I'd never told Gerald Delaney anything. I want you to know, Dave, that the things you've told me are the things I'll tell too. And even believe. Is that what you want me to do?'

'Tell who? Listen, Effie, I don't care who or what you tell. I'm not trying to hide anything.'

'You're not? I think you'd better, Dave.'

'Why?'

'It's just that I have funny feelings. Anticipating. You know?'

At that moment he had no patience for funny feelings.

'I still have your portrait, but I've put it away, out of sight. Dave, are you still there?'

'Yes.'

'Can I call you this evening? Please. I want to, Dave.'

'Why?'

'Just tell me I can. Can I call you at six?'

'All right, Effie,' he said to get it over with.

'Thanks. Good-by, Dave.'

He hung up, and after a moment thought no more about Effie Brennan, or of what might be worrying her. But in the factory that day, he found himself wondering a few times if Effie had told Wes that she had gone to the house in Ballard Saturday and seen him there. David did not see Wes that day until after four, and then only for a few seconds, when Wes was coming out of a men's room, and David could tell from Wes's smile and the lift of his hand as he greeted him that nothing had changed.

Punctually at six the telephone rang in Mrs McCartney's hall. Effie wanted to see him. She did not want to talk to him on the telephone. David tried to postpone it until tomorrow evening, postpone it forever, not that he was afraid of her, but that anybody breathless, any woman on the brink of tears, made him want to run in another direction.

'It's important, Dave. Please. This once.'

So he gave in and told her he would come over at eight o'clock. But she did not want him to come to her apartment. She proposed a drugstore on Main Street.

'It has booths,' Effie said.

David was a little late. Effie sat in a back booth behind a pink plastic table, a cup of black coffee in front of her. She smiled nervously when she saw him. After he had sat down, she still looked rigid and shy, as if she had to guard against his striking her, or against his resentment.

'Effie, I'm sorry I shouted at you Saturday.'

She nodded, as if in a trance, as if she were unaware of nodding. 'That's all right. I'll forget it. I'll forget I ever went there, Dave. That's what you want me to do, isn't it?'

'I suppose.'

A waitress came, and he ordered coffee.

'I saw Annabelle today,' Effie said.

'You *what*?' He looked at her, nodding again, and he could not believe it. 'She came here? To Froudsburg?'

'No. I went up to Beck's Brook. The police there called me at seven this morning, and they drove me up during my lunch hour. They asked me again if I knew Newmester or knew where he was, and I think they were even wondering if I knew Annabelle, but they saw I didn't. Annabelle wanted to talk to Newmester. It was the second time she'd come to see him. But he couldn't be found.' She paused, looking at him with the wary, troubled eyes. 'They described him.'

David folded his arms over his guilty heart. 'Very well. They described him.'

'They said he was about five ten, medium build, thirty years old, with black hair. Your hair's brown, but – he's you, isn't he?'

'Yes,' David said quietly. 'And so what?'

Her frilly pink blouse rose and fell as she breathed. 'So what is that Annabelle would like to talk to him. The police want to find him too, or the man who used that alias, because they can't find anything – anything about a Newmester who's a freelance journalist. I stuck to my story, Dave, that I'd just made up the house in Ballard and it happened to belong to a man named Newmester. So your name wasn't even mentioned by the police. Or by Annabelle to them. I wanted you to know that, Dave,' she said earnestly, and David frowned down at the table. Effie lit another cigarette. 'Annabelle talked about you later. I asked her to have a sandwich with me.'

David squirmed. Annabelle having a sandwich with Effie. 'And what did you tell her?' David asked.

'Nothing. I swear nothing, Dave. She knows I know you, of course – and I told her I was in love with you. Which I am, Dave. And she told me she's the girl you've been in love with all this time. I think I suspected it when I first saw her. So I asked her and she admitted it.' Effie's voice had dropped so David had to strain to hear, but he had heard.

'That's no business of anybody's but mine.'

'Isn't it? I'm glad to know,' she said shakily. 'She looks like a wonderful girl, Dave – and now she's free.'

'I'm not interested in discussing her with you,' he said quickly.

'Why're you so angry? Well, I know why. You're never going to get her, Dave,' she said, shaking her head. 'Never.'

'What did you tell her?'

'Nothing – except that I love you.'

It exasperated him. 'Why did you say that, that I'll never get her?'

She leaned toward him, wide-eyed. 'A woman doesn't suddenly decide to marry a man she thinks killed her husband, does she? A man she never was in love with in the first place?'

There it was, ugly, crude, coming out of that shopgirl-secretary face. 'That's not true.'

'She said if it hadn't been for your letters, her husband never would've died. She said that, Dave. I don't mean she thinks it was you who pushed him. Did you just push him, Dave, or did you really mean to –?'

'I hit him with my fist and I knocked him down,' David said, feeling his strength leave him. He rested his head on his hand.

'What're you going to do, Dave?' she asked tearfully.

He lifted his head. 'Shut up.' He spoke softly, but he leaned toward her and hit the table top gently with his fist. 'Just shut up about Annabelle.'

'You don't want to hear the truth. I understand that. But you can't keep it up, Dave.'

'Oh, can't I,' he replied, taking her words as some kind of challenge to his perseverance, his character in general.

'No. You're going to drive yourself crazy.'

'I've heard enough lately about insanity. I don't want to hear anything about it from you.'

'All right, you've heard enough. There's just no talking to you. But what're you going to do when the police tell Annabelle there really isn't anybody named William Newmester? Don't you think they'll come to that conclusion sooner or later? And by way of clearing it up, they might want to see David Kelsey.'

'Why?' David asked more softly. 'Just how long do you think they can go on over an accident?'

'Was it an accident?'

'Yes.'

'Well, Annabelle wants to see the man who pushed her husband. She's going to find it out sooner or later. Not through me but some other way.' Now her eyes were glassy with tears.

David's fist was still clenched on the table. 'Naturally, you could drop a few hints, and it wouldn't be coming from you at all, would it?'

'Dave, don't be bitter. I'd never, never do that!'

'Go ahead. I can stand it. Annabelle could stand it, too. Annabelle and I could stand it. Try it, if you think we can't. And suppose I beat them to it anyway? Maybe I'll tell them myself. I'll give them a blow-by-blow description of what happened that day. Matter of fact, I already have. They know damned well it was an accident. But I can also tell them it was David Kelsey who hit him.'

'Suppose they don't believe it was an accident? They'll say you had a motive to kill him.'

'Gerald had a gun pointed at me.'

'They'll still say you had a motive.'

He disdained to answer, and stared at her with a blind hate. She was trying to trap him, trying to blackmail him, to get her grip on him by scaring him, and promising to keep his secrets.

She looked at him with wide-open eyes, as if picking and choosing among a thousand words for the strongest. 'You say you love Annabelle. She loved Gerald. It seems to me you – you not only want to forget that, you don't even give her any sympathy now when she needs it. Not that she'd accept any from you, Dave.'

'Just stop talking about it, will you?' David said softly and quickly, sitting on the edge of the booth seat now, ready to leave.

'That's all you can say. It's – just like that house of yours where you lived hidden away under another name. You're trying all the time to shut out reality.'

'That's a lot of pseudo-scientific jargon.' David put a quarter down, bumped his cup as he stood up, and coffee spilled into the saucer.

'Where're you going?'

'I'm going to the Beck's Brook police,' he said. 'If you'll excuse me.'

'David!'

He did not look back. He walked quickly in the direction of Mrs McCartney's, where his car was. But he had not walked a block before he realized that he could never bring himself to tell those police officers that William Neumeister was David Kelsey. Not that he could not have borne their questions, or that Annabelle might not understand finally that it had been an accident, but that he did not want to betray William Neumeister, the better half of himself who had never failed, who had lived with Annabelle in the pretty house in Ballard, that Neumeister whose existence had made the Monday-to-Friday existence of David Kelsey tolerable for nearly two years. A lucky accident that he had been wearing a hat that afternoon, so they couldn't see that his hair was brown. And they were three inches or so off in his height. Had fear made him stoop?

The police wouldn't get Neumeister tonight, and maybe not any other night. It was very difficult to get hold of somebody who didn't exist, and thinking of this, David began to laugh to himself.

Abruptly he turned and walked back to the drugstore. Effie was just coming out the door.

'I'm not going to talk to the police,' David said.

'I didn't think you would. What are you going to do, Dave?'

'I'll just take my chances.'

On Thursday morning he called Annabelle. She was not in. Nobody answered the telephone until four forty-five, and then it was not Annabelle but a strange female voice. David suspected it was the old witch who had plucked so insanely at his sleeve, and he declined to give his name, only asked if Annabelle would be in it at six, at seven, at eight? The woman thought she would be in at six.

David called at six from the squalid pharmacy between Mrs McCartney's and Main Street.

'Yes,' Annabelle's calm voice said. 'I'd like very much to see you Saturday, Dave.'

'I'll be there by noon. Or would you like me to come earlier?'

'Noon is fine.'

Noon is fine. Noon is bliss! Noon is when time starts again! He ran into the inward leaning tree on the way back, though it was not even very dark, the tree he had so often dodged and barely missed on his nocturnal walks. He bruised his forehead quite painfully, but this seemed a good omen, a sign of a great change, simply because he had hit the tree after missing it for two years.

He talked to Mr Harris and Mr Muldaven at the dinner table that evening, and even dug up two jokes to tell them, of recent Wes Carmichael vintage.

18

There was an adolescent girl in the apartment on Saturday, who Annabelle said was going to babysit. The baby was in a large pen affair in the living room, propped up against a pillow, sucking the nipple of a bottle which he constantly dropped, and which Annabelle patiently put back into his mouth. She moved in her smooth, unhurried way, and David stood with his overcoat in his arms in the middle of the floor, following her with his eyes wherever she went.

'Dave,' she said, stopping at the door to the bedroom, 'maybe you'd like a drink before we go? There's some bourbon.'

'No, thanks,' he said, smiling.

She seemed in a good mood, almost the way he remembered her in the best days of La Jolla. She even wore a dress with little ribbons at the bottoms of the short sleeves, like the dress he had first seen her in. He felt optimistic about the afternoon.

'You don't want to sit down, Dave? I've still got one or two things to do,' she said. 'I'm sorry to hold us up, but you were so ear-ly.' She drawled the last word, as she had drawled certain words in La Jolla when she was happy.

She disappeared, reappeared, bent over the pen, tickled the baby's chest, and as she picked her green cloth coat up from the armchair, David sprang to hold it for her, dropping his own coat accidentally on the floor, leaving it there until Annabelle had her coat on.

'What's your favorite restaurant in the country around here?' David asked as they walked toward his car.

'You won't believe it, but I don't know any places in the country.'

David knew four. He had consulted roadmaps for suggestions and even an old Duncan Hines in Mrs McCartney's bookshelf in the dining room, but the most promising was one he had seen advertised in a Hartford paper that he had bought that morning: King George's Inn, Old Mail Road off Route 21A, since 1889, wines and spirits, quiet atmosphere, superb cooking and a view of some river whose name he had forgotten.

'I quit my job,' David said.

'You did? When?'

'I gave notice last week. I'll be there three weeks more, though. February twentieth is my last day.'

'What're you going to do then?'

'Try to get in at Dickson-Rand in Troy. I wrote them. They should be interviewing me in a few days.' He glanced at the houses as they left the city. He wanted to see a certain kind of house, somewhere by itself, snug and preferably made of rock, and say, 'What do you think of a house like that?'

'You're not worried, quitting your job before you've got another?'

'Not a bit. I couldn't have made myself stay on any longer anyway. If I get in at Dickson-Rand, I won't be making as much money, unless I can get some consulting work on the side, but that's not everything. Let's not talk about that. That's a different perfume you're wearing. You don't wear Kashmir any more?'

'Kashmir. You still remember?'

'I could have brought you some,' he said with bitter self-reproach. 'I bought a bottle a year ago. Then I threw it away.' He glanced at her, awkward as a small boy confessing a misdemeanor, yet longing to elaborate in one long burst on that bottle of Kashmir.

And she seemed to be thinking of what he had said, yet she did not say anything. The silence was so painful, somehow so torturous and embarrassing, he gripped the steering wheel with all his might. Then he pulled to the side of the road and stopped the car. There was a fluttering in his chest, behind his eyes, like tears.

'Annabelle, forgive me today if I say something wrong. I

want it to be a beautiful day. I want you to enjoy it. Please? Forgive me.'

But she looked at him almost in alarm. 'You haven't said anything wrong. Let's go on, Dave.'

Confused between a desire to find more words and to seize her hand and kiss it, he could only stare at her, still gripping the wheel. Then he grimly faced front and pressed the accelerator.

The restaurant was not so attractive as he had hoped, but Annabelle said, 'I think this is beautiful. And I didn't even know it existed!'

David gave great attention to the menu, asked the waiter whether he recommended the sole or the *boeuf bourguignon* – the answer was the sole – and then selected a Beaune of 1949 vintage, which David happened to know was excellent. He proposed the consommé, but Annabelle wanted a shrimp cocktail.

'The shrimp?' he said in blank amazement, then realized he had only made it up that she did not like shrimp. 'I meant, since you're having sole –'

Annabelle laughed. 'I didn't know you'd become such a gourmet.'

'Do you like eggplant too?' he asked.

'So so. Did you want eggplant?'

'No,' he said, smiling. 'I just wanted to find out what you like. What don't you like?'

'Very little. Maybe just kidneys. Oh, and sweetbreads.'

'I know a dish with kidneys and beef that I think you'd like,' he said. 'I've made it two or three times for myself.'

'So you can cook too! You cooked in your house?'

'Yes. Certainly I did.' The waiter poured an inch of the white wine into his glass for his approval, and David sipped it, and nodded to the waiter that it would do.

Her gray-blue eyes gazed quietly into his. Now her eyes were gentle as smoke or clouds, as David always imagined them, as they were in the larger photograph that he treasured. David derived a peculiar nourishment from them. 'Do you see Effie very often?' Annabelle asked, and the spell was broken.

'Almost never.' David's eyes came to rest on her wedding ring.

'She told me she was in love with you.'

'So I heard.' He sipped from his water glass.

'I don't think you treat her very nicely.'

'Why should I? I don't treat her unnicely. I just never see her,' he said, frowning.

'She's a nice girl. It ought to be easy for you to put yourself in her place – someone in love with you and you don't even give her the time of day.'

The slang phrase annoyed him and the whole subject annoyed him. 'She's a very ordinary girl. Let her find somebody of her own kind. Are you possibly thinking I could be interested in her?'

'You don't have to be angry, do you? I just said she was a nice girl.'

David stared at Annabelle in a hopeless silence as the waiter served their first course. Then he said, 'Do you mind if we talk about something else? Anything else?'

'All right. Will you answer a question for me?'

'Certainly.'

'Is it really true that Effie doesn't know William Neumeister?'

'As far as I know. Yes.'

'She told Gerald to go to his house just by accident, you think?'

'I don't know any of her friends,' David said, scowling with impatience. 'If she said it was an accident, I'm sure it's true.'

'I was wondering if she might be trying to protect Neumeister for some reason,' Annabelle said, spearing her first shrimp, dipping it into the red sauce.

'I don't think so. I think she's a very honest girl,' he said with difficulty, as much bothered by Annabelle's casual eating of the shrimp as by anything else.

'Are you telling me the truth, David?'

'Yes,' he said in a protesting tone. 'I told you before that I didn't know Neumeister either.'

There was a silence. David tried to eat his consommé, which was quite uninteresting.

'Don't you think it's odd that they can't find Neumeister? It's as if he's hiding. I keep thinking there's some connection between Effie and him or even Gerald and him.'

'Did you ever hear Gerald mention his name?'

'No, absolutely not. I know I'd have remembered.'

'Did Gerald owe money to anybody?'

'Only a little to a bank,' she replied, and David caught the pride and resentment in her voice.

'Well – you were asking why Neumeister's avoiding the police. First of all, I haven't seen any notices in the paper that he's wanted by the police. Maybe he's traveling and can't be reached. As for his hiding – at least he had the guts to take Gerald's body to the police station. If a man pulls a gun on you, I think a man's got a right to resort to almost anything to defend himself, don't you? An unarmed man?'

'Gerald wasn't a mean man. Why're you defending Neumeister?'

'I'm not defending anybody. I just reminded you that Gerald had a gun and was out of his head besides. What do you expect a man to do?' He realized suddenly how belligerent he sounded, and he was sorry. He thought of the instant his foot had struck Gerald's chest, and the way Gerald, stiff with death and cold, had leaned to the right in the front seat of his car. David's mouth twisted a little, and he reached for a cigarette.

'Since when do you smoke?'

'I smoke occasionally. Usually just on weekends.' The tension left his face. 'I'm sorry I sounded so –'

'You're always sorry afterward.'

Her defenses of Gerald, that worthless eyesore, were still up. Gerald was like a barrier between him and her, a fat, comic barrier that David might have demolished with a derogatory phrase, if Annabelle were not obsessed by her sense of loyalty. She was like the girl in *A Midsummer Night's Dream* who fell in love with the donkey.

'You have funny times for smiling,' Annabelle said.

His smile went away. 'Darling, I'm sorry.'

'What good does that do? I suppose you're sorry your letters drove Gerald to try to look you up and talk to you –'

'Talk to me? With a gun?'

'The fact remains, if you hadn't written those letters, this wouldn't have happened. Nothing of it.' Her voice shook with tears. 'Gerald would be here now!'

What a horrible prospect, David thought. 'I'm sorry the letters did that.'

'You're not sorry. You said you weren't. So don't tell me you are now. You're quite heartless – in a way, Dave. You seem to live entirely in your own head and you don't know anything at all about other people, the people around you.'

The words had a deadly familiarity. Maybe his aunt had said them to him, maybe even Wes. They baffled David, made him angry and ashamed of his anger. 'That's not entirely true,' he said quietly.

'I know it's true from what you said about your house, the way you pretended I was there and all that.' She stopped with a strange gasp that made David look at her. 'I suppose that's normal? To fix up a house to show a woman who's already married to somebody else?'

'Annabelle,' he began, 'if I made up things – about us, it was in order to be able to live at all. It wasn't that I believed it was real, you living in that house with me. Some people take to drink, some to – I don't know what, but I did that.'

She stared at him, and he saw in her face that she still didn't understand. Absurdly enough, she looked a little frightened. Sitting tensely on the edge of his chair, he caught himself, out of habit, trying to memorize every subtle curve in the long line of her face from temple to chin to take away with him.

'I'm not trying to reproach you, Dave,' she said in her slow, serious way. 'I'm thinking of you. I want you to be happy and lead a normal life.'

He gave a groan. 'I love you and that makes me happy.'

'How can it? You imagine it does. And now – you have a perfectly nice girl like Effie Brennan who loves you very much, and you can't even see her. Why don't you try?'

'But I don't want her.'

'Please try it. For me, Dave. I'm asking you to.'

'It's as if you don't understand anything at all about me!' He passed his hand across his forehead, looked at her puzzled, almost angry eyes, and knew in his own eyes now was the same expression. 'Annabelle, this can't go on,' he said, meaning everything. 'I can't bear it. When I'm with you it's like having every pore open, and when you don't understand and you ask me to do the impossible, you don't know what a torture it is to me.' He talked on, unable to stop even when she tried to say something, believing that what he said and the way he said it could not be too awful, too bizarre, because he was keeping his voice low. The waiter might stare at him, but to hell with the waiter. And his sentences might not even be grammatical, but the words were all there, all the words in the English language that could tell her what she meant to him. Then at a repeated phrase from her, he stopped. 'My work? What about my work?'

'I don't know. I just said *maybe*,' she replied, her eyes worried and frowning. 'Maybe you're overstrained –'

'I'm understrained. I'd like a little strain. Why don't you try the wine?'

She took her glass.

Smiling, he lifted his to her. 'I've done this a thousand times with you before.'

She drank, but she did not smile.

He tried to recall what she had said to him, something about adding to his troubles. 'I don't have any troubles,' he said. 'Nothing could trouble me seriously except for you to say you don't care to see me again or something like that. I think it'd kill me.'

'I wouldn't tell you that, Dave,' she said very softly, looking down at the table.

That made him smile again. His left hand felt the square box in his jacket pocket, the diamond clip that Annabelle had sent back to him. At the right moment, he was going to present it to her again. And there would be no Gerald to make her refuse it.

She said she absolutely had to be back by three-fifteen, and it was three-twelve when David turned the car into her street.

'Annabelle,' he said happily, 'will you marry me?'

She laughed, as if surprised.

'You can't exactly say it's sudden.'

'Oh, Dave, I don't know what I'm going to do with my life.'

'Let's work it out together. When can I see you again? I can drive up in time for dinner any night, you know.' He pressed the little box through his overcoat pocket, on the brink of pulling it out.

'I don't know.' And she seemed suddenly anxious, reaching for the door handle.

'Well, think. Monday? Tuesday? Tomorrow? Tomorrow's Sunday.'

'I'm going to La Jolla.'

'When? For how long?'

'I don't know. I was planning to leave Tuesday.' She opened the door and got out.

He got out too, and stood on the sidewalk facing her. 'You'll write, won't you? To let me know how long?' If it was for a couple of months, he thought, he would go out there too.

'Of course I will, Dave.' Then she thanked him for the lunch, words that he hated to hear and to which he made no reply save a smile.

'I'll call you tomorrow,' he said. 'You didn't tell me when I can see you again.'

'There isn't much time, Dave, if I leave Tuesday. I might even be leaving Monday.'

'Say we can have dinner tomorrow.'

'I really can't Dave. There're too many odds and ends to do here. By by, Dave!'

He watched her run up the short front walk, thought of the package in his pocket – wrapped again and with a new card – but it would take too long, she wouldn't have time even to accept it, even just to poke it in her pocket and run upstairs. But David walked back to his car whistling, feeling rich, not yet beginning to relive and explore the three hours and fifteen minutes he had spent with her. Parting from her always left him stunned, and yet for several minutes it was as if she were not really gone from his side. Then finally he would have to speak to someone, or think about some practical thing, and the sense of her presence would slowly fade.

David telephoned her on Sunday. She was leaving for La Jolla Monday for an indefinite length of time, and a friend of hers was going to see about subletting the apartment. She sounded hurried, and he did not want to add to her distractions at that moment by telling her that he might come out to La Jolla too, as soon as his three-week period at Cheswick was over. David had to show the incoming manager how the factory worked. The man was bright but ordinary, had a wife and three children, and his objective was the salary. The job was made for him, David thought.

On Monday he had an answer from Dickson-Rand. They were interested, and in five days he was to go up for an interview.

19

Nine days later David received a letter from his Aunt Eddie saying that Annabelle was not in La Jolla and that her parents knew nothing about any idea of hers to come. David sank down with the letter on his bed, and for a few seconds his thoughts drew a protective veil of incredulity over the wound: Annabelle's mother or one of her lousy brothers could have said she wasn't there just out of malice. He stood up, still feeling sickish, as if he had been hit in the pit of the stomach. He thought of all the days he could have spoken to her, even seen her, if she had been in Hartford, when he believed she was three thousand miles away. A sudden idea of calling her in Hartford made him feel weak. If she were in Hartford, it meant that she had been trying to avoid him. He thought of the three letters he had written to her and sent to La Jolla, wondered if someone in her family had opened them, or if they had been decent enough to send them on to Hartford?

David put on his coat and went downstairs. Mrs McCartney, crossing the hall toward the dining room, nodded to him with a twitch of a smile. Mr Muldaven, unlocking his room door on the right of the hall, hunched over his key and did not speak. To hell with them all, David thought. Nine more days and he would be gone. Two days ago the Beck's Brook police had dropped a small bombshell in the house: they had telephoned Mrs McCartney to ask if David Kelsey was still living there and, not satisfied with the fact that he was, they had quite a chat with her. They had told her that David Kelsey's mother had been dead for fourteen years, and that they had had this information from an old friend of David's from his home town in California, but the name of the friend was not mentioned. Mrs McCartney, while eating this up, regurgitating and chewing it like a cud, professed to David to believe it a ridiculous lie. She had told them that he did have a mother and had spent every weekend with her for the past two years he had been living under her roof, but they had not believed her. David had listened to her in the downstairs hall, pretended to be as puzzled by what the officer had said as she, and had escaped as soon as he could to his room, where he tried to get a grip on himself. After all, Mrs McCartney hadn't said the police would call back or that they wanted to see him. He would face it out in the house, he thought, and stick to his story that he had an invalid mother. Then just as he had been about to go down to the dining room that evening, he had heard Mrs McCartney's light, rapid knock on his door, and he thought, she's coming to tell me that, by the way, the police want to see me, and his nerve left him.

'They said if you had a mother, where was she, and I couldn't tell them, because I didn't think you'd ever told me,' Mrs McCartney said, her avid eyes fixed on David's eyes. 'Because she wasn't in the nursing home in Newburgh. Or if she was under another name there, nobody at the place knew you.'

At that instant David felt he couldn't have kept the lie up if his life had depended on it. The vision of a nursing home didn't come to him, he couldn't think what she was ill with, and he admitted – he had foreseen it in a split-second as a casual admission, but in two seconds he had begun to perspire and twitch like a criminal – that his mother really was dead, and that he went to New York on weekends just to get away from Froudsburg and to be alone for a couple of days a week. He said he had made up the story about his mother as the simplest way to avoid social obligations on his weekends, and that as time went on he had not known how to get out of it and had had to embroider it. And he had said he was sorry. Mrs McCartney had nodded and smiled understandingly and with her head higher than usual had turned away, a proud ship sailing out of his room with her cargo of possible dirty linen.

Then David gathered his nerve, walked out of the house, and telephoned the Beck's Brook police station from the pharmacy. Soberly and calmly he told them the same story he had just told Mrs McCartney, his words coming in a steady flow, and he apologized for the discrepancy in his story, but said he had not thought it of any importance. He said that in New York he stayed sometimes with friends and sometimes at a hotel, and that sometimes he went just for a day. His only purpose in going to the city was to get away from Froudsburg, a town he did not care for. It was Sergeant Terry to whom he spoke, and the sergeant seemed to be even amused by the made-up story of the invalid mother.

'As long as you're not doing this for the purpose of bigamy, Mr Kelsey,' said Sergeant Terry.

'Never been married even once.'

'You were in New York the Sunday Delaney was killed?'

'Yes, sir.'

'Staying where?'

'I didn't spend the night. I went to a museum and a movie and then drove back to Froudsburg.'

'Were you with anybody? See anybody you knew in New York?'

'No, I didn't. I was alone.'

'Um-m. See, we told Mrs Delaney you said you were with your mother, and she told us your mother was dead.'

'Yes.' David knew how it had been. He frowned, gripping the telephone, waiting for the sergeant to add that Mrs Delaney told them he spent his weekends in his own house.

'Ever see Mrs Delaney in New York on any of those weekends?'

'No, I did not.'

'Ever try to? Ever ask her to meet you in New York?'

'No,' David replied so calmly, it sounded false. 'What're you getting at, sergeant?'

'Were you ever in love with Mrs Delaney?'

'What's that got to do with anything?'

'Mr Kelsey,' with a chuckle, 'it's the only thing that makes any sense. Are you in love with her now?'

David hesitated, protecting not himself but the privacy of his love.

'All right, Mr Kelsey, is this the reason why Mr Delaney came to talk to you with a gun?'

'It could be.'

'It must be. Had you ever made any threatening remarks to him, Mr Kelsey?'

'I certainly did not.'

'You're sure?'

'You can verify me by asking his wife. The one time I ever spoke to Delaney, she was with us.'

'I see. Well – a darned good thing he didn't find you that Sunday.'

'That's what I think too.'

'All right, Mr Kelsey. Maybe we will verify a few things with Mrs Delaney.'

'I hope you do, sir,' David said firmly.

When he had stepped from the booth, one of his legs had almost given way under him. That had been Monday. He had thought: Annabelle was in La Jolla, and the police probably wouldn't take the trouble to telephone her out there in order to check his story. He might have a reprieve of weeks before the ax fell.

But now as he walked the darkening streets of Froudsburg with his aunt's letter in his pocket, he felt that his life depended on whether Annabelle were in Hartford or not, and it had nothing to do with his conversation with Sergeant Terry. What he had to find out was whether Annabelle had been lying to him in order to avoid seeing him. And after walking the streets for half an hour, he still couldn't summon the courage to call and find out. The dreary phrases of his aunt's letter depressed and angered him: *Why don't you give the girl up, Davy? ... Her parents say she's just like her grandmother so-and-so who never did marry again though she was only twenty-two when her husband died. The family isn't good enough for you, Davy. ...* He walked the gloomy streets, taking the darkest ones, as if their heavy shadows might steady him and let him go to that grimy pharmacy and telephone.

He saw the face of a clock in a dimly lighted hand laundry. Seven-ten. Four-ten in California. Which was it? Why did she avoid him? Was *she* playing a game, and would one day she rush into his arms and laugh and cry and say she loved him and had always loved him? He blew on his cold hands, turned up his coat collar, and pushed his hands back in his pockets. Every man he saw was carrying a bag of groceries, on his way home to his wife. David wondered if he would be able to find a house he liked within driving distance of Dickson-Rand? This time he would live in it seven days a week, no more split life and schizophrenia, no more hiding from half the world. And maybe in three months or in six Annabelle would want to come and live with him. It was unreasonable of him to expect that she would marry him less than a month after her husband died. David felt suddenly so calm and reasonable himself, the prospect of calling her in Hartford and of her answering the telephone began to lose its horror.

A block away a Bell telephone sign projected from the front of Michael's Tavern. The telephone booth was at the back, directly under a television screen that had not existed the last time David had been here, and which was now crackling with Western gunfire and horses' hoofs. He hesitated a few steps inside the door, replied with a nod to Adolf's greeting, then went on toward the booth with a determination to make more noise, show a little more life than the television screen. What was ever ideal and perfect anyway? Annabelle would not be in a pink or blue nightgown, as he liked to think of her. Most likely she would have a drooling baby on her lap.

'Dave!' a surprised voice said. 'Well, how do you do?' It was Wes, sitting in a booth opposite a woman with brown-streaked blond hair. 'Sit down, Dave. This is Helen.'

David's first thought, not an intelligent one, he immediately realized, was that the woman was Laura, and he had been ready to run. Still flustered, he stammered, 'How do you do, Helen?' and did not know how to extricate himself from Wes's grip on his left wrist.

'Helen, this is my most distinguished colleague, a man who will one day win the Nobel Prize, Mr David Kelsey, chief engineer of Cheswick Fabrics, but leaving us for better things and greater glory. Sit down, Davy boy.'

Helen chuckled, the red-caked lips parting, and her hand slid forward on the table, ready to take Wes's again.

'I'm going to make a telephone call,' David said.

'You make it and I'll order you a drink. Break down, fellow.'
He yanked David's wrist.

Smiling, David twisted his arm, but Wes held on with drunken obduracy. 'Nope. Just that call,' David said.

'Isn't he good looking?' said Helen, as drunk as Wes.

'Calling that girl?' Wes asked with a wink.

David yanked his wrist free and Wes spilled out on the floor. Instantly David had him up again and back on the bench, and Wes's surprise struggled with anger for a moment, then his lips smiled uncertainly.

'Good grief!' Helen said, edging away from David.

'Davy, old boy, your nerves're getting you. I said sit down and have a drink. Well, you *are* calling that girl, aren't you? Is she going to marry you, Dave? I certainly hope so.'

David could neither speak nor leave, nor did he have a clear idea of what he wanted to say to them. Perhaps nothing. He turned away and went on to the telephone booth.

Just as he dialed the operator, the booth door was pulled open.

'Don't do it, Dave. You're making a mistake,' Wes said. 'Seriously, I've been talking with Effie and she says –'

'Let me alone, Wes.' David tugged at the door to close it, but Wes had the door handle and the door barely moved. David sprang up from the seat, got out of the booth, repressed his impulse to lash out with his fists and walked with Wes, who was still talking, back to the booth. Helen smiled at them with unseeing eyes. As soon as Wes had sat down again, David went back to the telephone booth.

The operator was saying, 'Hello ... your call, please ...' and David told her the number.

Buzz. Click. Jingle-jingle-jingle-jingle, and then he sat staring at the remaining quarter and dime on the little shelf, stiff as a piece of iron, awaiting the voice that would stop the ringing in Hartford. It rang eleven times, which he did not want to count but did, then a voice said, 'Hello?'

'Annabelle, this is Dave. You're really there?'

'Yes, Dave. I – well, my plans about La Jolla –'

'Never mind. I'm glad you're so close! How've you been? I wrote you three letters to La Jolla. Did you get them?'

'I got them. I'm a little out of breath. I just ran up the stairs – You won't be much longer in Froudsburg, will you?'

'Nine more days. Annabelle, I'm spending next weekend around Troy. I'm going to look for a house, and I was hoping you could come with me. At least Saturday. I could bring you back Saturday night, if you'd prefer that.'

There was a pause, and he said, 'I want you to see the lab, Annabelle. The grounds are beautiful. I went up for an interview a few days ago. They've accepted me. I told you that in my letters.'

'Dave, I don't see how I can.'

'Then let me drive by and see you on the way up?'

She made excuses. He interrupted her, pleading. Perhaps on the way back, when he could tell her if he'd found a house. Fifteen minutes even, if he could just come by. He had a little present for her, he said, though he didn't tell her what it was, and as soon as he mentioned a present he was sorry, lest Annabelle think he felt he had to lure her. Finally he abandoned hope for the weekend and asked when he might see her at any time, any evening.

'I don't *know*.'

And though it seemed strange she didn't *know* when, he was even more disturbed by the anguish in her voice. 'Is there someone there with you?'

'Yes, there is someone.'

Silence. And he didn't quite believe there was someone with her, because she had said she had run up the steps.

'Dave, I hope you find the kind of house you're looking for. I'll be thinking of you. I really ought to go now, because I hear the baby crying.'

He squeezed the telephone, searching frantically for words. 'Don't just go like this. Can I call you tomorrow?'

'All right, Dave. Only I don't know when I'm going to be in. I have to do some marketing – and I'm out tomorrow evening.'

And what was she doing tomorrow evening? He wanted to know only so he could think of her doing it. 'All right, then. I'll call you Saturday. As soon as I've found a house. Would you mind that?'

She said she wouldn't mind it. They exchanged good-bys, the deadly clichés that put an end to voices. David sat there, trying to breathe slowly before he went out and possibly had another encounter with Wes.

Wes sat with one elbow jutting out, one hand on a thigh, nodding as if he had heard and understood everything. 'Well, is she going to marry you? Is she even going to see you?'

Helen laughed emptily.

Because he had not a positive thing to say back, David's frustration rose like a black cloud before his face. Wes reached out to grab his wrist, and David recoiled. 'Don't touch me!'

He walked to the door and banged it open with the side of his fist.

When he got back to Mrs McCartney's, there was a message that Effie Brennan had called and wanted him to call back. David wadded it up and threw it in his wastebasket.

20

Though it might have been suspected at Mrs McCartney's that he went to New York to see a girl, Effie Brennan within twenty-four hours had assured Mrs McCartney that he was in love with a certain girl who lived way up in New England, in fact she thought the girl was going to school in Maine, 'so much in love he won't look at another girl.' Witness herself, David supposed, attractive and willing and not even honored by a movie invitation from David Kelsey. Effie called David again to tell him what she had told Mrs McCartney, and to ask him if she had not said the right thing. She said that Mrs McCartney had called her to poke about and ask if she knew what he did on his weekends in New York.

'Thank you. You did say the right thing,' David said, for the first time grateful to Effie, grateful to her for not disclosing Annabelle to the people in the house.

What pained David most, even tortured him, was that Mrs Beecham knew now that he had no mother, and that the bed-jackets she had knitted, the potted plants, the crocheted doilies, and the box of stationery Christmas before last had had no recipient. David had gone to her and apologized, tried to explain, and it had been one of the few times since the age of fourteen that tears had come in his eyes, and all in all with his getting down on one knee to her, he supposed he had made a fool of himself, but Mrs Beecham was the only one in the house who counted, and he had tried to tell her that. She hadn't said much, just looked bewildered and disappointed. But on the other hand, David thought with some amusement, his non-existent mother had sent Mrs Beecham quite a few presents, too.

The talk of a girl had caused a startling change in the attitude of the people in the house. David knew what they were thinking: not that he had done anything specifically wrong or evil, but that he was a man with clay feet like all the rest, a man in love with a woman whom for some reason he had not yet been able to marry and evidently didn't even see very often, a man like most others and not a sexless saint. Now their eyes wavered when they looked at his face. They were like children for whom some legend had exploded.

On Saturday morning, David had a letter from Annabelle in the ten o'clock mail. He hoped she had changed her mind about going with him to look for a house, but the letter did not even mention that. Standing in the downstairs hall, he read it quickly, suffered a sense of shame like a slap in the face in public, though no one saw him, stuffed the letter into his pocket, and went out to his car. He had his route planned, and he concentrated on that for a few minutes as he drove. On the dull throughway north, the letter returned to reproach him. Annabelle had said she wished he would not be insistent about seeing her at this time, when she had her hands so full with the child and things to settle up around the house. It was worse than that, and he could not bear to recall the very phrases. Nothing about being questioned by the police. Yet the very coolness of the letter suggested to David that she had been questioned, that she might have told them about his having a house, might have told them about all his letters: Annabelle was not the kind of girl who would write all that out in a letter. Yet wouldn't the police have tried to see him immediately, if she had told them all that? Wasn't it more likely that Annabelle would try to hide or minimize those facts in order to make Gerald appear less a killer?

David simply didn't know. But he made a mighty resolution to change his attitude toward Annabelle, to be less importunate, more thoughtful, more patient. He would mail her the little present, a hand-woven stole he had found in a store on Main Street, and also the diamond clip, and in Troy he would look for some music books for her, Mozart and Schubert and Chopin and whatever else he could find that she might like.

The house he liked best out of five on Saturday was overshadowed by one he found Sunday afternoon, a two-story house of red and white brick, mottled and weathered to a rough texture, with a gray stone chimney at either end. Inside, the floors and several of the walls were made of planks ten inches broad and six inches thick, according to the agent who showed him the house. Two of the rooms upstairs had sloping ceilings and embrasured windows. It was a twenty-minute drive from the Dickson-Rand Laboratories, and the nearest house was a quarter of a mile distant and not visible. The house had been occupied until two months ago, so everything was in working order, and the price asked was $18,000, but the dealer confided that he thought it could be had for $15,000.

'Then get it for fifteen thousand,' David said. 'I want it.'

'Just like that?' the man asked. 'You don't want to sleep on it?'

David shook his head, smiling, happy. Twenty minutes before, he had been discouraged, thinking he would have to settle for something he was not enthusiastic about. If the agent had not had his office in his home, so that he could be reached on Sunday, he might never have found the house. David said he could make the down payment right away, and that the check would be in the mail that night.

Then he started in a general direction southward, undecided whether to telephone Annabelle, drive to Hartford to see her, or to get his things moved into the house before he told her. The image of the house with woods flanking one side and a fairly well-tended lawn on the other side backgrounded his thoughts, a concrete thing, home, an anchor. Why *wouldn't* Annabelle like it? He had not found a single flaw. Wide staircases, generous closets, high ceilings. Thirty years old, and maybe a bastard style, if one wanted to be an architectural snob, but it was unpretentious, it looked more American than English, it was neither formal nor informal.

He decided to tell her on the phone. He would be cheerful but careful not to be too cheerful or too anything. The main thing was not to appear to assume she would live with him there, nor to appear she wouldn't. After he called her, he would stop at the best restaurant he could find on the road and have a good dinner, preceded by a martini or two martinis, one for Annabelle.

It was around 5 p.m. when he stopped at a filling station, ordered gas, and went into the office to call her. There was no answer, though he had the operator ring more than twenty times.

She was still not home by nine, when he reached Froudsburg, and he gave it up. He had decided by then that he might do better writing her a letter.

He wrote to Annabelle, describing the house in some detail, and then in a cheerful mood typed a letter to his aunt.

... I don't know why you are all so gloomy out there. Can't you absorb any California sunshine? I talk to Annabelle quite often and see her too. Naturally, she's a bit low because of Gerald, but grief passes in normal people. The grandmother you mentioned must have been a psychotic if she spent a lifetime grieving ... I am moving to a wonderful house I bought today, a bargain at any price, as they say. This because I'm at last changing my job. From now on I continue my school in a sense, though I'll be paid for it. I am going to be working at Dickson-Rand Laboratories. This is the lab that reports California's earthquakes before California knows it has had them. My immediate superior will be Dr Wilbur Osbourne, of whom you may not have heard, but he is world renowned as a geophysicist and quite an eccentric, I hear. Since I am told I am too, perhaps we'll get along...

Then he wrote a letter to the Red Arrow storage company of Poughkeepsie, asking that the articles deposited in the name of David Kelsey be delivered to the house outside of Troy, and he enclosed a little map that the real estate agent had given him. Reluctantly, he signed the letter William Neumeister, and he hoped it would be the last time he would have to write that name.

He waited until the following Wednesday at noon, two-and-a-half creeping days, before he telephoned Annabelle. She sounded very cheerful, congratulated him on finding a house so soon, but when he tried to set a date when she might drive up with him to see it – and it could have been any one of eight glorious days starting Saturday, because Dickson-Rand was giving him a week's leave to get settled – Annabelle hedged and postponed. She even said she was considering going to La Jolla.

'I really was going three weeks ago, Dave, but the baby had a fever and I didn't dare leave with him. I didn't mention it, because I know you're not interested in babies, but I have to be. Then I wanted to see Mr Neumeister, if I possibly could.'

'Have you seen him?' he asked.

'They still can't reach him. The man who's handling his house said he told him he was going to be traveling, but he hasn't left this country, because one of the police in Beck's Brook has checked with the passport – the passport something or other. Now they're checking the references he gave the real estate agent. That should lead to something.'

David's guilt created a feeling much like anger. 'Have they put anything in the papers about it? Maybe they should do that.'

'Not that I know of. I guess it isn't that important. It's just important to me.'

'Well, what do you think he can tell you, Annabelle, that he didn't tell the police?'

She didn't answer. 'Dave, Sergeant Terry called me last week. He's the one in Beck's Brook.'

'Yes? What about?'

'Mostly you. He asked if there was anything between us. I told him no, Dave. I didn't see it would do a bit of good to – I mean, I told them Gerald was a very jealous type, but he had no reason to be where you were concerned, because whatever there'd been between us was over a long time ago. That's essentially the truth, and I thought it was better for Gerald and you *and* me. Don't you agree?'

'Yes,' David murmured.

'I told them Gerald had been drinking – which they knew. I didn't tell them about your letters. That would only complicate things and make the situation sound more serious than it was.'

The Situation, the Situation. David asked, 'Do you think they believed you?'

'Why shouldn't they?'

'That's right. Why shouldn't they?'

'Dave, don't be angry about *this*. It's absurd.'

'I'm not angry.' And yet he was.

'They said you told them you were in New York that Sunday. Is that true, Dave?'

'Yes. I was.'

'And that you always went to New York on your weekends. That's not true, is it?' she asked. 'Didn't you spend most of them at your house?'

'Yes,' said David. Every question was like a driven nail.

'Why did you lie? Why do you lie, Dave?'

'That house was yours. And it's gone now. I don't want to discuss it. With anybody. I've bought a new house and I – My things're going to arrive Saturday, so the house'll be a mess then, but I wish you could see it, darling, even with the things not arranged. I've got a piano, you know. I don't think I ever told you that, did I? It's a Steinway baby grand.'

'Really, Dave? Do you play now?'

'I play Chopsticks – chords,' he said, 'just so it gets a little exercise. I have it for you, Annabelle.'

Silence.

With a lump in his throat, he went on. 'I want you to see where I'm going to work too. We could drive up there in twenty minutes from the house. You've got to let me bring you out this weekend, Annabelle.' He waited. 'Annabelle, do you ever think of us together? Do you ever think we might –'

'I guess sometimes – I think of it.'

She promised to send him a postcard in regard to the weekend, and David left the telephone booth radiant. He felt optimistic for perhaps five minutes, until the Neumeister business began to prod at his brain. So they were checking Neumeister's references. Would he never be done with Neumeister? David wanted to forget him, like a silly game, like a bad dream, like a self-indulgence that made him ashamed of himself. And now they were checking his references, all because of a whim of Annabelle's to talk to him! They wouldn't be able to find his references either, and what then? John Atherley, or had it been Asherley? And Richard Patterson. David began to whistle loudly. Like a scared boy in a dark cemetery, he thought.

On Friday he said good-by to twenty or thirty people at Cheswick, some of them a little jealous, David thought, because he was doing what they wished they could do or wished they had the courage to do. Some of them, too, had heard that David had been fostering a curious lie about an invalid mother. It was inevitable: Mr Lewissohn's secretary had checked his questionnaire for the police, she had told someone else about the police call, and finally a few who had asked him, as Wes Carmichael had, to their homes on weekends and been refused on the grounds that he had to see his mother — these few heard the story and remembered it. David could see behind Wes's joking remarks and smiles that he was a little worried because the thing had come out in the open.

'Listen, Dave,' Wes whispered to him in David's office, 'you weren't by any chance seeing Delaney's wife — ever. I mean in that house.'

'What house?'

'Newmester's,' Wes said, pronouncing it in that manner that always made David think for an instant that people were talking about someone else.

'I told you I didn't know him,' David said, frowning.

'All right, Dave, it crossed my mind, that's all. We're good enough friends for you to tell me, aren't we? If it were true and I knew it — Well, I haven't any ax to grind about it,' he added, retreating before David's frown. 'I'm sorry I brought it up.'

'I never met Delaney's wife. I never met Delaney,' David said, his voice cracking.

'Well, where did you go weekends, Dave?'

'I just don't care to answer that. I went to New York most of the time. What I do weekends ought to be my own business.'

'Okay, Dave,' Wes said in a placating tone, but he was angry.

David knew he had sounded angry too, but he didn't care.

'Let's go back and join the boys,' Wes said.

There was another gamut at Mrs McCartney's. Mrs McCartney had a special dinner for him, turkey with accessories, shared by the entire dining room, and even preceded by port wine in thick, stemmed glasses. Everyone asked him about his new job. He explained how cores were taken from the earth and the ocean bottom and marveled to himself that there could be a room of twelve or more living, breathing people of whom only one or two had ever heard of taking sample cores. When he went out of the dining room with Mr Muldaven, Effie Brennan was sitting in the straight chair in the hall.

She got up and greeted him with a smile. 'Finally caught you, Dave.'

'Hello, there. Why didn't you come in the dining room?'

'Oh, I knew it was a special dinner for you. I don't belong here any more. I was hoping you might come by my place for a last talk, Dave,' she said, turning her pleading eyes up to him.

David realized he owed her a great deal, but at that moment the prospect of going with her to her apartment was the last thing he wanted to do. 'I was going to see Mrs Beecham for a while,' he said. 'She's expecting me.'

'All right. I can wait,' Effie said with a smile. The tip of her slightly upturned nose was pink and shiny from the cold. 'She'll be going to bed soon, won't she? You'd better hurry.'

'Effie, I've still got some things to do. In the way of packing, you know.'

'But this is important, Dave, honestly.' She came closer to him, suddenly earnest and straining. 'I want to talk to you.'

It would have been easier to get rid of a bulldog with its teeth sunk in his wrist. 'All right. Let me go tell Mrs Beecham.'

He had no appointment with Mrs Beecham, and he was grateful that Effie walked toward the front door, from which she could not see the top of the first flight of stairs. David went into his own room, spent a few minutes puttering around, got his coat, and went down again.

21

Back through the door under the sign of Dr Needle, painless dentist. It was the second time David had been to Effie's apartment, and it seemed smaller and more cluttered. A round, orangey-pink cake stood on the coffee table with a big D on it in black chocolate.

'That's for you,' Effie said, hanging up her coat in the foyer closet. 'I made it – and Wes may come over tonight. In fact it's practically certain. Maybe in half an hour.' She was so tense her voice sounded hysterically shrill.

Her nervousness made him nervous. He opened his arms stupidly and said, 'Well, that's very nice. We'll all have coffee and cake.'

'I'll bet old Wes won't have any coffee *or* cake. I've got Scotch for him. You – I've got a bottle of Sauterne for you.'

Good God, David thought, then reproached himself for his ingratitude. 'I'm honored,' he said, smiling.

'Sit down, Dave.'

He waited until she had sat down in an armchair, then he sat down on the sofa.

'Dave, before Wes comes,' she said, 'I wanted to tell you Annabelle called me today.'

'Why?'

'Well, why not? Just to be friendly.'

'But why did she call you?' It was Annabelle's calling her and not him that galled him.

'Dave, I happen to think it's nice – even remarkable – if a woman can be friendly enough even though I happened to send her husband to the house where he was killed.'

'All right.' David looked away from her face.

'What I wanted to tell you is the police, the Beck's Brook police, aren't going to stop looking for Newmester.'

'Oh? What're they doing about it now?'

'Annabelle said they're looking up everybody by that name, but they can't find any journalist nor anybody by that name who's around thirty and answers that description they've got.'

David had to smile. 'There must be a William Neumeister somewhere who answers that description.'

'You're awfully casual, Dave.'

'All right, Effie. Thank you for telling me. But I wish you'd stop trying to alarm me, because I'm not afraid of anything.' He stood up.

'I think you are. I think you'd lose Annabelle if she knew. She wouldn't care to see you any more. I know that.'

Here was the blackmail again. 'I'm not so sure of that.'

'I think you are. Meanwhile you expect me to protect you. You just take it for granted I will.' Her voice had begun to shake with hysterical, incredible tears. 'And I have – with the police and with Wes, too.'

David glanced at her uneasily. 'I've told you what happened at that house was an accident. And if I wanted to buy a house under another name, what is it to anybody?'

'I'm even trying to persuade Annabelle to drop this business of finding Newmester,' she interrupted him. 'But I can't help it if the police are interested now. Annabelle thinks Newmester tried to kill her husband in that fight. Maybe out of self-defence, but that he tried to and did and that's why he's hiding out now and maybe going under another name.'

David laughed.

'You're lucky, Dave,' she said, her eyes narrowing.

'I think Neumeister's lucky. But Neumeister's finished now. He's disappeared and forever.'

'Annabelle told me they're checking the references you gave when you bought the Ballard house. They won't stand up, will they?'

David shrugged. 'Not if they look hard.'

'Have you thought of getting yourself a real alibi? A real house or a person you could say you were with on those weekends?'

'You?' David asked, smiling.

She got up and stood by the dark window, looking out. It was so silent he could hear a clock ticking in the bedroom. He felt a nervous amusement, something quite uncontrollable, at least for the moment. He thought of a funny remark, and set his teeth together to keep from saying it. 'I'm sorry, Effie,' he said.

'Oh – let's open the Sauterne.'

He got up to help her with it in the kitchen. Great play of hands over the corkscrew. David chose to think it funny. There was no other way to take it.

'You must be looking forward to your new job. I've never seen you in such a good mood.'

'I think I'll be this way from now on,' David said. He noticed some gray in Effie's hair, just two or three gray hairs, in the bright light of the kitchen. They were somehow comforting.

She had a glass of wine, but she insisted the whole bottle was for him. It touched him that the Sauterne was bona fide French and quite good.

'You've found a house, Wes told me,' she said. 'Where is it?'

'I wouldn't know how to say. Near Dickson-Rand, which is near Troy.'

'But what's your address? Where can I write to you?'

'Dickson-Rand, Troy, New York.'

'Oh, Dave, I'll miss you,' she said in a sentimental tone, and started toward the cake as if to cut it, but there wasn't a knife, and she went off to the kitchen came back with one, awkwardly laid it on the cake plate, and sat down again.

'This is one of those silly cake knives you get by sending off four box tops and fifty cents,' she said. 'Someday I'll really have to start collecting silver.'

Her eyes gave him a sensation of being slowly drained, and realizing this, the situation seemed vaguely comical again. She put a record on the phonograph, assuring him she would play it very low, asking him if he minded French records. David happened to have the record himself, though he didn't tell her so. He remembered going into a music shop to buy something else and hearing part of the French record, liking the piano in it and thinking Annabelle might like it. Effie sat down again and took another cigarette.

'Will you be seeing Annabelle very much when you're in Troy? That's not so far away from Hartford as Froudsburg, is it?'

'About the same. Yes, I certainly expect to be seeing her,' David said. 'Anyway, I think she'll be moving from Hartford soon.'

'Oh? To where?'

'Well, I'm not quite sure yet.'

'You're still – very much in love with her?'

'Of course,' David said, and then Effie's wistful, almost tragic smile made his own confident smile leave his face and he looked away from her out of pity. He poured his glass half full again. Effie still had most of her glass.

'When will you know, Dave?'

'Know what?'

'Whether she's going to marry you or not?'

'I know now. She is. I don't say next month, but –'

'That's why I asked you when you'll know.'

'I don't see that it matters much when,' he said quickly, and at the same time the doorbell rang.

Effie pressed the button in the kitchen, then with her old nervousness back – such an unpleasant contrast to Annabelle's calm – she said she'd fix Wes's drink right away and began to clatter the ice tray.

Wes came grinning broadly, chucked Effie under the chin, and accepted the Scotch and soda as soon as he had removed his overcoat.

'I didn't really think you'd make it tonight, Dave,' Wes said for the second time. 'Good for you, Eff.'

'Why, it was easy,' said Effie. 'He came along like a lamb.'

He hadn't, David thought. Effie had tricked him into coming by telling him she had something of the greatest importance to tell him. That Neumeister story – she hadn't told him anything that he had not known or could not have predicted for himself.

David sensed a falseness in Wes's good humor, and he suddenly realized that it had been many weeks since Wes had come to see him in his room at Mrs McCartney's. David also found himself recalling the incident at the factory today, the incident at Michael's Tavern, and he felt self-conscious and ashamed. He was sorry he had sent Wes sprawling on the floor, and sorry he was going to leave before he had attempted to patch things up. Wes and Effie had a second drink, and because they pressed him and David wanted to be agreeable, he accepted a Scotch and water. He had drunk more than half the sauterne. David watched Wes's face as a spate of silly words came out of his mouth, accompanied by Effie's giggles at regular intervals. He fingered the wristwatch under his cuff, and when Wes ended a story with a clap of laughter, David stood up and said, 'Take my watch, Wes.' He handed it to Wes.

Wes looked at him in surprise. 'What do you mean?'

'I'd like you to have it. You like it, don't you?' He knew Wes liked it, because Wes had often told him he thought it was a handsome watch.

Wes took it uncertainly. 'That's an expensive watch, pal.'

'David,' Effie said reproachfully, 'that's a lovely watch.'

'That's why I want him to have it,' David replied, opening his arms and letting them drop at his sides. 'What's so funny about that? I'll get myself a new watch.'

'A Vacheron Constantin? On your new salary?' Wes asked. 'The liquor's gone to his head, Eff.'

'I want you to have it,' David said. 'I'm tired of it, in fact, and you like it and it keeps wonderful time and the big second hand's very useful.'

'No, Dave.'

'Take it! I can't understand what all the fuss is about!' David shouted, and then smiled at Effie's startled expression.

There was silence then, and finally Wes said very seriously, 'Well, thank you, David. If you ever went it back –'

'I don't ever want to see that watch again. I'm going to buy a new watch.' David was amused by their startled faces, by the puzzled glances they exchanged. 'Put it on, put it on,' he said to Wes.

'Two wristwatches,' Wes said, fastening the alligator strap. 'I've always wanted to be rich enough to wear two wristwatches.'

David gave a sad, disappointed laugh, and sat down.

Wes cleared his throat and drank, deeply. 'If this is an evening for farewell presents, why don't you take the sketch Effie made of you, Dave? She got it framed for you.'

Effie looked suddenly panicky. David watched her with curiosity. 'I destroyed that sketch – I'm sorry to say.'

'Really?' Wes frowned. 'Destroyed it, Eff?'

'Yes, I did.'

'Why?' Wes asked.

And Effie got up and went into the kitchen without answering.

Rather grateful that she had destroyed the sketch, so that he would not feel obliged to hang it, David followed her into the kitchen. He had meant to ask if he could help her, but she wasn't doing anything. 'Would you mind if I had another drink?' he asked, expecting the pleased surprise he usually saw on people's faces when he accepted or asked for a drink, but Effie's face grew more troubled.

'Maybe you shouldn't have any more, Dave,' she said.

'What? I bet I could drink that whole bottle and never show it. Never feel it and never show it.'

Wes had come in and heard him. 'Famous last words.'

'Do you want to bet?' David asked.

'No, no, I don't want to bet,' Wes said, glancing at Effie as if they had a secret of some kind.

'In that case, I'll have just one, if nobody minds,' David said, looking at Effie. He reached for the bottle and poured a generous amount, but not foolishly much, he thought. Three fingers or so. He set the bottle down and gave it a push toward Wes, whose glass was empty, dropped two ice cubes into his glass and added a little water from the sink tap. Wes and Effie stared at him as if they had never seen anybody fix a drink before.

Then Wes solemnly half filled his own glass, plopping his ice in, adding the token inch or so of soda. David smiled at him, but Wes did not return it. Wes went into the living room.

'Dave,' Effie whispered, coming toward him, 'I'm sorry I said that – about the sketch. It's not destroyed and you can have it if you want it. I thought of destroying it, that's all.'

Her muddled sentiments were of no interest to him at all. 'I see,' he said politely.

'I thought if those police from Beck's Brook ever came here and saw it – That's why I haven't got it hanging. It's in the bottom of a drawer. They'd recognize it as Newmester – wouldn't they, Dave?'

'As him?' David said with an incredulous smile. 'Yes. But so what? That's all in the past. Why be so dramatic about it?'

But she still looked dramatic, and shocked. 'All right, Dave,

I hope it's in the past.' And after a couple of her famous nods, she went out of the kitchen into the living room.

David lifted his glass, shut his eyes, and took three big swallows. Neumeister. He hadn't thought of him in days until tonight, and there was little Effie, keeping his precious secret. Neumeister had served his purpose, sailing serenely, victoriously, over tumultuous waters, up and down riding the waves, a strong ship in full sail. Neumeister had never lost. It was too bad Annabelle had never known Neumeister – even though Neumeister had in a way lived with her. Well, he had been over all that, he remembered. He had come to the cold and terrifying conclusion that if he ever told Annabelle that he was William Neumeister, she'd never get over it, never believe that Gerald's death had been an accident. Very well, Neumeister was gone now, and might as well be dead and buried himself. David swayed a little as he rounded a kitchen cabinet, and he was careful to walk straight as he entered the living room.

Wes and Effie stopped their murmuring when they saw him. Effie put some new records on and she and Wes started to dance, but Wes said it was too slow. Wes was showing his drinks now, and, when he went to get a refill, tried to take David's empty glass with him to the kitchen. David held onto it, saying he didn't want any more.

'Don't if he doesn't want it, Wes,' Effie said.

'He was boasting he could drink the whole bottle!' Wes's good-natured smile was back.

David let him take his glass.

The next hour or so was unclear to David, and he thought it strange that so little alcohol could affect him so much, though the effect seemed to be only in his vision. Wes, on the other hand, was going to pieces, dancing clumsily with Effie, occasionally making a wild gesture or a wild statement: 'I'm *glad* you destroyed that sketch of Dave, I'm really glad, Eff. Shows progress. No more will the little maiden pure sit home and wait while her beloved chases after a – a myth!'

David ignored it and looked up at a corner of the room, put his head back against the sofa, and listened to the piano on the phonograph.

Then Effie said, 'Wes!' in a teary voice, and David saw her press her hands together in a ludicrous despair, as if the evening and her two guests had slipped out of her control. And Wes was stumbling toward David, smiling slyly and pointing at him.

'Isn't that true, Davy boy?' Wes asked.

'Be careful, Wes. Leave Dave alone,' Effie said.

'I didn't even hear what he said,' David told her calmly.

'I said you don't want a girl you can have, you want a girl who doesn't want you. It's a neurotic symptom,' Wes said cheerfully, rocking on his heels with his hands in his pockets. 'I'm thinking of your welfare. I'm trying to give you some good advice. I don't care *who* she is.'

'Dave, I haven't been talking to him about this. Honestly. Don't let it —' Effie made a jump to protect a glass on the coffee table, but Wes knocked it over, anyway — his own, and empty.

David looked at him placidly. 'Since you don't know what you're talking about, I'd appreciate it if —'

But Wes didn't stop. The boring, half-jocular advice went on and on. *That girl*. No name mentioned. That girl who was finishing college or something. And did it drive him so crazy he had to spend his weekends drunk maybe? Or maybe with another girl? David took a cigarette, then threw it down on the coffee table unlighted. He kept his composure, but the words fell on his shoulders, the top of his lowered head, and seemed to cling to him. Even Effie was begging Wes to stop.

'You don't understand,' David said into his hands, and heard Wes laugh.

'Effie's been telling me,' Wes said explanatorily, 'that she feels sorry for you. She thinks it's hopeless.'

'I didn't say exactly *hopeless*,' Effie bleated.

David had stood up. 'Sorry for me?' he asked with a smile.

'You did say it,' Wes said to Effie, 'so why deny it?'

David lit the cigarette now. Easy to see why Effie called it hopeless. Hopelessly in love perhaps he was, and that was why he'd never been able to look twice at Effie. 'I'm going to marry the girl and that's that,' David said, interrupting Wes. 'It's embarrassing to have one's private life discussed, but since you brought it up —'

'I didn't mean to embarrass you, Dave. I'm interested. Eff

and I are both interested, because we like you. And Effie more than likes you.' He gave David a light, friendly pat on the shoulder.

'I don't want the girl I intend to marry to be discussed by anyone. I hope someday you'll meet her, but it'll be under my roof, our roof. We're going to be married in a very few months, maybe less than that, and anybody who says anything different just doesn't know what he's talking about.' David crushed the cigarette out quickly in an ashtray. His heartbeats shook his chest and even jarred his vision. 'There never has been any doubt in my mind that I'd marry her,' he went on, though he did not even want to go on. He took a step toward Wes, who retreated a little. And now it was David who went on and on, talking over Wes's attempts to put an end to it, Wes's apologies, as if Wes's slight figure in the brown suit were an obstacle between himself and Annabelle that had to be crushed and swept away by words. Then he saw his own arm go out in a swing at Wes, and Wes ducked and stepped back, though David's fist had been at least a foot short of hitting him, and it hadn't been David's intention to hit him. His words suddenly stopped.

Wes's baffled, angry face weaved a little and turned away. Effie clung to David's arm, saying something to him, and David wanted to tell her that her concern wasn't at all necessary, but he felt in the grip of something, unable to move or speak, and his body was rigid and trembling.

'Just don't say anything else about her to me, ever,' David said, his voice shaking with fury. He reached for his glass, finished it, and looked back at Wes's scowling face.

'Boys, boys,' Effie murmured with a try at a smile. 'I think I'll put on some coffee.' She went into the kitchen.

David kept looking at Wes, somehow expecting retaliation from him, either in words or in action.

'Well, how's anybody supposed to feel who's just been swung at?' Wes said resentfully.

David gave a little smile. 'Let's have some coffee.'

But the resentment did not leave Wes's face. 'I'll tell you one thing,' he said in a lower tone, 'if you ever got that girl, you wouldn't be able to do anything with her. You're in such a state – You don't know it, pal, but you're all in knots.'

David couldn't believe his ears for a moment, then when it dawned on him what Wes meant, it was like an electric charge hitting him. 'You dirty liar!' David said between his teeth. He walked past Wes to the front closet, not even hearing Effie's words behind him, only their high-pitched whine that was like a razor scoring the surface of his brain. 'Good night and thanks, Effie,' he said quickly, plunging his arms into his overcoat, opening the door for himself.

The bang of its closing behind him was a sound of delicious finality. The unjustness, the stupidity of it! The vulgarity! The falseness!

'Take your watch, Dave!' Wes's voice called down the stairs.

David made the front door boom, too.

22

David's anger stayed with him for days. It generated heat and energy, spoiled his sleep, and as he tossed in his bed, he tried to reason his anger away, went over Wes's words until they were drained of their emotional effect and became even meaningless, yet the core of his anger remained. He put his energy into arranging his things in his new house, and worked all night the second night. Yet the conversation of that evening kept going through his mind. Effie had said he was lucky. David could not see anything lucky about David Kelsey. Maybe William Neumeister was lucky. Effie was worried because they were still looking for William Neumeister, but William Neumeister's luck was not going to run out in a hurry. Effie's words acted on him as a challenge. He felt like calling up the Beck's Brook police and giving them a full account of Neumeister's doings since he had apparently disappeared. Oregon, the state of Washington, Texas, California – there was no telling where Neumeister's far-flung journalistic activities had taken him. David began to smile, and impulsively he reached for the telephone. But he had hardly picked it up, when he realized that the Beck's Brook police would most likely want to see him.

Very calmly, David changed into the Oxford gray suit he had

worn as William Neumeister that memorable Sunday afternoon. He had not the cuff links with the N on them, because he had thrown them away when he was packing at the other house, but he had the same hat, and he even remembered the tie he had worn, but he chose another. He removed his driver's license from his billfold, just in case they would ask for that for identification, and he racked his brain for a way of identifying himself as Neumeister. He had destroyed every Neumeister bill and receipt. He'd have to bluster his way through it, he thought. This interview would either allay all suspicion or it would be the finish, and he was in the mood now, and the mood might not come again. No use waiting until tomorrow or the next day to get hold of some card or other to sign with Neumeister's name.

He would bluster through. And he would not forget to slump a little.

Beck's Brook was approximately ninety miles south, and he arrived at four-fifteen on Sunday afternoon. There was only one man, whom David had never seen before, in the station, and David had to introduce himself with considerable explanation. A good sign. The man picked up a telephone and called Sergeant Terry. David hoped the sergeant was unavailable, but he was at home.

'He'll be over. He wants to see you,' said the officer.

David thanked him and sat down. A certain arrogance that he had felt since he had decided on this expedition rose in him more strongly now, and he struggled to put it down. He must appear somewhat solemn, even slightly depressed, and above all co-operative.

The sergeant arrived after David had been waiting perhaps fifteen minutes. 'Well, Mr Newmester. I'm glad to see *you* again,' he said as he approached David with slow, heavy strides.

David stood up. 'How do you do, sergeant?' he said pleasantly. 'I was in the neighborhood and I remembered I'd never called Mrs – the woman in Hartford. I don't have her address. Delaney, isn't it? But I've forgotten the first name.'

'Gerald,' said the sergeant. 'Where've you been?'

'I've just made a trip to California and back,' David replied. 'Why?'

'Well, Mrs Delaney wanted to talk to you. We were doing our best to find you.'

'Oh. I didn't realize that. What's the trouble?'

'No trouble. Just that Mrs Delaney wanted to talk to you. She wanted to see you and ask you just what happened that day,' the sergeant said somewhat reproachfully. 'I don't know what papers you work for, but they're not in the state of New York.'

'Well, a couple are,' David said with a slight smile. 'I supply science editors with material for their articles. Not very often I have anything under my own name in the papers.'

'I see,' said the sergeant, his doubt, or annoyance, still apparent. 'Well, Mrs Delaney would like to see you.' He moved behind the desk, at which the other man sat watching them both over his newspaper and pulled out a drawer. From a folder he took a sheet of paper and copied something from it on a slip of paper. He handed the slip to David.

'Thank you,' David said. It was Annabelle's address and telephone number.

'Where you living now, Mr Newmester?'

'I'm not settled anywhere just now. I'll be in New York for a while, and I expect to go abroad in a month or so,' David replied, remembering what he had said to Mr Willis about traveling.

'Yes, so your rental agent said. You know, we couldn't even find the two people you gave Willis as references. Patterson and – What was the other?'

'John Atherley,' David said promptly, confident suddenly that the name was Atherley and not Asherley. 'Have you tried South America?' he asked with a reckless inspiration.

'No,' the sergeant replied, straightfaced.

'I had a letter from John a couple of months ago. They're both in Cali, Colombia, doing organizational work for a mining concern. They're industrial consultants.'

'Oh.'

'But what's the trouble? Why did you want to reach them?'

'Thought they could help us find *you*.'

'Gosh – if I'd known you were going to all that trouble – There wasn't anything in the newspapers, was there? I'm a pretty thorough reader of the papers.'

'Oh, no, we didn't put anything in the papers,' the sergeant said, shaking his gray head slowly, still looking dubiously at David. 'We thought your references might know where you were, and when we couldn't find them, we began to think something was fishy.'

David smiled, and looked surprised. 'Sergeant, I'm sorry you had such difficulties. It's my fault, I suppose, for not contacting Mrs Delaney as soon as that other officer mentioned it – that day I was packing. To be honest with you, I wasn't looking forward to it, and I put it off and then it went out of my head. I thought she'd be hysterical or even blame me for it. Does she?' he asked anxiously.

'I don't think so,' the sergeant said. 'She's a pretty level-headed woman. She just wants a firsthand account of what happened.'

'She'll get it,' David said with resignation. He watched the sergeant move toward the telephone on the desk. If the man was going to ask him to talk to her now, David thought, he would claim an urgent engagement elsewhere.

But the sergeant turned and said, 'Is this why you moved out of your house so soon? This Delaney story?'

'No,' David said. 'I admit it upset me a little. Maybe it did make me move sooner than I'd intended, but I'd been planning a couple of years' work that would keep me traveling, and that's the reason I got rid of the house.'

The sergeant nodded, and stared at him. 'Would you like to talk to Mrs Delaney now?'

David gave a little shrug and was about to say he might as well talk to her in person, but the sergeant had already picked up the telephone. The folder with Annabelle's telephone number was still open on the desk, and the sergeant read it to the operator. In the interim of waiting for the telephone to be answered, David said as casually as he could, 'Or you might set a time when I could come to see her. I'm pretty free tomorrow and Tuesday.'

The sergeant did not answer. He frowned attentively as if he were listening to something. The moments passed. Was she not at home? Or had the Hartford operator even begun to ring? Sergeant Terry was patient. David slumped, his tense shoulders aching, and turned a little, just as Sergeant Terry said, 'I see. Thank you, operator.' He hung up. 'She's not in,' he said.

'I'll call her tomorrow,' David said with a sigh. 'I'm sure I can manage to see her.'

'Do that. And by the way, Mr Newmester, give us one place – one specific place you can be reached or where there's somebody who knows where you can be reached. Just in case this slips your mind again.'

David smiled a little. 'I'm really not as invisible as you think, sergeant. Tonight I expect to be at the Hotel Wellington in New York, Fifty-fifth Street and Seventh Avenue. And – at the *Times* office in New York, there's a Mr Jason McLain who knows where I am ninety per cent of the time. Want to write that down?'

Sergeant Terry wrote it down. 'Mr Newmester, we have nothing against you and we don't *want* to have anything against you, but we're going to find out if you contact Mrs Delaney, and if you don't – Well, that's all we want from you and all *she* wants from you.'

'I understand,' David said, making an effort to hide a surge of resentment. After all, it was almost over. The sergeant was walking with him to the door. David waited for the sergeant to say good-by first.

'I'll call Mrs Delaney early tomorrow and tell her you came in,' said Sergeant Terry. 'Good-by, Mr Newmester.'

'Good-by, sergeant,' David replied with a wave of his hand.

And when he drove away, he turned in the direction of New York, even though the sergeant might not have been watching. It occurred to him now that it would be wise to trade in his car for one of a different make and color, in case Sergeant Terry had noticed it when he came in, and in case David Kelsey had any more dealings with the Beck's Brook police. But having to trade in his car was a small nuisance compared to the achievements of the day, he thought. Sergeant Terry had seemed a little suspicious, no doubt of that, but it was nothing serious, or he would have been questioned a lot more thoroughly and perhaps held at the station. He would write to Annabelle in lieu of seeing her, and he felt sure that the letter he would write would satisfy her. Annabelle, alas, wanted to hear about *Gerald*, not necessarily see Neumeister in the flesh. He had imagined going home to write the letter, but that made no sense, if he would have to go to New York to mail it. He continued in the direction of New York. He could borrow a typewriter at a hotel, he thought, the Wellington Hotel, where he would register as William Neumeister, and he hoped the Beck's Brook police would call him there to check on his whereabouts. If they didn't, perhaps he would call them. David began to whistle. Annabelle might get his letter Monday, if her mail came in the afternoon, but most likely she would get it Tuesday. If the police got upset because he didn't speak to her Monday, he would say he hadn't been able to fit Hartford into his schedule on Monday, and that he had written her an explicit letter.

He arrived in New York at midnight, put his car in a garage off Eighth Avenue, and walked to the Hotel Wellington. No luggage, he told them, he would be here just overnight. He asked if he could rent or borrow a typewriter for an hour or so. When they brought one up to his room, he sat down at once, while still as much in the mood as he would ever be, to write the letter to Annabelle, which would be only half deceitful after all, he thought. Without pausing, he wrote two full pages on the hotel's stationery, leaving in fact little room for Neumeister's backhanded signature. Then he took some stamps from his billfold, marked the letter airmail, and dropped it down the chute in the hall.

Then he was suddenly tired. He blotted his perspiring forehead with a handkerchief. Lies, he thought. He had been lying steadily since four o'clock that afternoon, and he had done it with surprising ease. Standing in the middle of his room, he felt a little faint. It was as if he beheld for the first time a criminal side of himself that he had not known existed. Nonsense, he thought, and began to undress. It had all been necessary; if he hadn't lied, Annabelle or the police would have lied in accusing him of murdering Gerald, and wasn't his the lesser of the evils? He felt faint only because he had forgotten to eat any dinner. But now he had no desire to play any more with the Beck's Brook police. Annabelle would probably tell them the letter had been written on Hotel Wellington stationery, and that was good enough. He fell into bed.

The next morning, Monday, he breakfasted in the hotel, paid his bill, and checked out. He bought a few phonograph records, and in the early afternoon saw an Italian movie. He considered looking at cars in Manhattan, but the thought bored him, and he decided he could risk getting one in Troy. He started for home. Tuesday morning in Troy, he chose a light blue Dodge convertible, two years old and a year younger than his black two-door Chrysler. The car would be delivered next Monday. Annabelle, he thought, might like light blue, though he really didn't know. The rest of Tuesday he spent on the house, and that evening, when he thought the house seventy-five per cent presentable, he telephoned Annabelle.

A man answered, and David asked to speak to her.

'Who's calling?'

'David Kelsey.'

A moment passed, and then Annabelle's voice said, 'Hello, Dave,' warmly and happily, as if she were glad he had called.

'Hello, darling. I called to – to give you my new phone number.' The presence of the man in her apartment threw him off. 'Got a pencil?'

'Yes, in just a minute. Dave, I heard from Mr Neumeister today.'

'You did?' For an instant, it had actually taken him by surprise. 'You saw him?' he asked more carefully.

'I had a letter. A very nice letter. I'll let you see it. He sounds like a very nice person and – well, I feel so much better, I can't tell you.'

'What did he say?'

'He just told me what really happened. In detail. That's all I wanted to know. Mr Neumeister's in New York now. He's just back from a trip to California.'

'Oh. Did you learn anything new?'

'Of course. Well, maybe I didn't, but I was glad to hear it from him. He was at the Beck's Brook police station Sunday. He hadn't even known we were trying to find him.'

'I told you you should've had something put in the newspapers and you might've heard from him sooner.' David stopped, his easy flow of words shut off. 'Can you get a pencil?' he asked. When she got one, he gave her his number and address and the address of Dickson-Rand. The man with her was murmuring something, rudely, while she was trying to write, but David could not hear what he said. 'I was wondering when you might be free to visit me. I've got the rest of this week free and next weekend, too. I could drive over tomorrow and pick you up.'

'You talk as if I'm a couple of blocks away.'

'You're not far.'

But she couldn't make it this week, and she wasn't sure about the weekend. She absolutely had to get some sewing done on Saturday, and she had guests for dinner Sunday. David had a premonition of defeat about the weekend.

'It's my only time off, Annabelle –' He broke off, knowing it was useless. 'Okay. Next week then. Shall I call you or would you call me? Reverse the charges. Any time day or night.'

'I'll remember that,' she said with a smile in her voice. 'And I wish you much luck and success and all that in your new job.'

He laughed at her formality, then froze at the prospect of the 'good-by' that was coming in a matter of seconds.

'Thank you for calling, Dave. Good-by.'

'Good-by,' he said, and sat for a few minutes looking at a big, shiny avocado that crowned a basket of fruit, an avocado that would be perfect in a day or so, that he had thought of using in the luncheon with Annabelle.

That evening he had two martinis before his dinner, and for company at the table propped open a pamphlet on nuclear radiation that had been written by a scientist of Dickson-Rand. It crossed his mind, like a subtle temptation, to use the name William Neumeister in this house too. Neumeister was so much more cheerful than David Kelsey. Neumeister had reason to be. Annabelle had said he sounded like a very nice person. David felt that it was going to be hard to imagine Annabelle in this house with him, if he were only David Kelsey. He need not have bought the house in Neumeister's name, he thought, and he hadn't, but merely to pretend, only to himself, that here he was William Neumeister who had never failed in anything – David checked himself. He had made a decision to abandon that silly game, and he would stick to it. It was nothing but a crutch, and it had been weak of him ever to use it. It was no better than Wes's drinking to avoid the painful decision to do something about his wretched life with Laura.

David went to work on Monday. His job in the rock analysis laboratory, the caliber of the people, the atmosphere, all matched his expectations. The grounds, spacious and well-kept, put him in a good mood every morning as he walked the flagstone paths from his car to the geophysical laboratory. Tall blue spruces grew near the administration building. There was a sundial that was also a bird bath and frozen tight now, a tennis court, a loggia with a grapevine growing on it, and stone benches here and there where in good weather one could sit and talk with a colleague. David's superior, Dr Wilbur Osbourne, was a small, stooped man with humor in his eye and an easygoing manner that did not suggest an eccentric character. And then before David had worked five days, Dr Osbourne closeted himself in his office, locked the door, and refused to be disturbed by anyone and refused to take any telephone calls. He even spent the weekend in his office, sleeping there by night on his leather couch. He was thinking out a problem. There were other odd ones. A young engineer in David's department was enamored of rain, and would stand out in it bareheaded and with his face turned up, David was told. Another man brought his gray Persian cat to his office every day. Another, Dr Gregory Kipp, walked the two and one half miles from and to his house morning and evening, regardless of the weather.

Most of the men, like David, had no private office, but worked on their feet in big rectangular rooms that held vacuum tubes, rock separators, mass spectographs, and other machines for the analysis of physical matter. There were five or six students from Utica working toward degrees in physics. David's routine job was to tend the rock-separating machines and spectographs, and to remove the dust they produced, record its weight and affix a label. He was also to work with Dr Osbourne on two or three projects that were outgrowths of that last voyage of the *Darwin*, Dickson-Rand's own ship. He could not have wished a more altruistic job: the Dickson-Rand Laboratory received hundreds of rock and soil samples per year, and gave its analyses free of charge to private citizens and to commercial firms. It was a far cry from the practices of Cheswick Fabrics, Inc.

Effie Brennan sent David a present of a gray linen tablecloth, darker gray napkins and four bamboo place mats. 'Be happy in your new home,' said her card. It was quite a fine linen set, one that met David's standards, which were the standards he set for Annabelle.

Annabelle was unable to make a date with him during the second week he was in his new house. David felt restless and unhappy. He had called twice, both times in the evening. The first time there had been no answer, and the second time he had gotten Annabelle just as she was going out somewhere and had no time to talk, but she had said that every night that week was impossible, and so was the following weekend.

It was now March seventh, a Saturday. The day before, David had accepted Dr Osbourne's invitation to dinner at his house on Saturday evening. Dr Osbourne had invited him the preceding Saturday, but David had declined, thinking he might be able to see Annabelle. When Dr Osbourne repeated the invitation, David had awkwardly said he would not know if he were able to come until Thursday evening, a time he arbitrarily set to call Annabelle with a last hope for the weekend.

'Well! I didn't know you were so popular,' Dr Osbourne had said cheerfully.

David, after a moment's hesitation, decided to wear chino pants, loafers, and a tweed jacket to the Osbournes'. Informality went unnoticed among the Dickson-Rand personnel. He followed the little map that Dr Osbourne had drawn on a scrap of graph paper, and arrived at a massive two-story house set back on a dark lawn. A light came on in the hall, and Dr Osbourne greeted him with a handshake. A colored maid took his overcoat. Then they went into a solid, old-fashioned-looking living room where a fire was burning in the fireplace. Mrs Osbourne, a plump woman with fuzzy gray hair, was sitting on a sofa, cracking nuts in a silver bowl.

'Hello-o, David,' she said, as if she had known him all her life. 'Pardon me for not getting up, but once I'm ensconced here – My, you are tall, aren't you? Wilbur said you were tall. What will you have to drink?' And a walnut cracked in the silver nutcracker.

David liked her at once and at once felt at ease. They did not think it odd that he declined a drink and they did not press him. At their insistence, David sat on a hassock near the fire while

Dr Osbourne drank his bourbon and his wife her sherry. Mrs Osbourne said she couldn't understand how anyone could go around in cotton clothes in such weather.

'This boy runs on intellectual heat,' said Dr Osbourne.

'Tuh!' from his wife.

The dinner was substantial and the dishes arrived in heavy silver tureens. There was a joke, that David paid little attention to, about the tureen's bearing the initial of Mrs Osbourne's maiden name. For the benefit of his wife, Dr Osbourne went over David's achievements at his school in California and his credits with the laboratory in Oakley, and though David usually squirmed at such times, he was flattered by Mrs Osbourne's knowledge of what her husband was talking about, and gratified that Dr Osbourne rated him highly and considered the laboratory fortunate in having him.

'I hope I am here the rest of my life,' David said.

'Why, Wilbur was telling me you've already bought a house,' said Mrs Osbourne. 'Tell me where it is.'

David told her and said it had formerly been owned by some people called Twilling.

'Twilling? The Twilling house? Wilbur, why didn't you tell me it was the Twilling house?'

'Because I didn't know, my dear,' said the doctor.

'Why, I know that house well. I'm a friend of Mrs Twilling, you see, and I used to visit her. Wilbur doesn't happen to like Mr Twilling but that's neither here nor there,' she said with a smile.

'Twilling's an ass,' said Dr Osbourne, pouring more wine for David and himself. 'Never associate with asses or their wives. Life's too short.'

'To return to the house,' said his wife, 'it has a lot of charm, hasn't it? And you can't say there isn't enough room there. You're not going to be lonely, all by yourself?'

'Why should he be lonely?' asked Dr Osbourne. 'Besides, he may be doomed to matrimony. I daresay that's what you're feeling around for.' Dr Osbourne's eyes kept moving over the things on the table as if he were looking for something that was missing. David had passed him the salt earlier in the dinner.

'Well, I hope that's in David's picture – *some* time,' said the doctor's wife.

David sat up a little. 'Matter of fact, it is. I don't know when it'll be – the date – but certainly before this year is out. Before the summer is out,' he said with more conviction.

'Why, congratulations, David! Where is she and what's her name?' Mrs Osbourne asked.

He hesitated, wondering if he had already gone too far, until both of them looked at him expectantly. 'She's in Connecticut,' David said. 'Her name's Annabelle.' And he felt immediately better, happier, more sure of everything. The Osbournes were his friends. He suddenly even wanted Mrs Osbourne to meet Annabelle. Yes, he wanted that especially. 'You'll like her,' David added with a smile.

'Hmph,' said Dr Osbourne. 'Just when you're about to get married, you leave a highly paid job for a much less well-paying one.'

'Yes, but I explained why in my letters, sir. I never liked the job in the plastics factory.'

'Why'd you take it in the first place?'

'I thought I wanted the money then – in order to get married,' David said, feeling himself grow warm in the face, with embarrassment or anger.

'To the same girl?'

'Yes, sir.'

'But you had that job nearly two years. What's holding her up? Can't she make up her mind?'

'Wilbur!' his wife admonished. 'Maybe David doesn't want to answer all those questions.'

The ice cream had arrived, garnished with the walnut halves that Mrs Osbourne had been preparing in the living room.

'No, it's perfectly all right. I don't mind answering them,' David said in a frank manner.

'Is she interested in your work?' asked Dr Osbourne.

'Well –'

'Good.'

Mrs Osbourne began to talk of something else with David, and the burning left his cheeks, but he felt in Dr Osbourne's silence that he was still mulling over the unanswered question – the Situation. Dr Osbourne's first-class brain, so used to the abstract, was trying to put together the two or three pieces of concrete fact he had picked up, and from them infer the truth about David Kelsey. David felt suddenly panicked. It was as if Dr Osbourne were going to spring up suddenly with a great 'Good God, man! You mean to say you've been obtuse enough to fret away more than two years on a Situation as utterly hopeless as this?' From Dr Osbourne, David could not have borne that. He would have gone to pieces. But the word 'hopeless,' David thought angrily, was merely an echo of Effie Brennan's idiotic remarks, or of Wes Carmichael's.

'You're too warm, David?' Mrs Osbourne interrupted herself. 'Would you like to go in the other room?'

'No, I'm perfectly all right. Thank you. But I realized I didn't answer one of your husband's questions and I didn't want him to think I was avoiding anything. The question was what's holding us up — Annabelle and me. She's had some trouble in her family, you see. A death — or two. And I suppose that's what's delayed us. Nothing more than that, sir.'

There was a terrible silence, and Dr Osbourne stared at him with his terrifying air of wisdom, and of disbelief.

Again Mrs Osbourne tried to dispel the horror with a polite statement of understanding, and again the horror stubbornly remained. It was worse. Did Dr Osbourne think he was merely eccentric or really off his head, David wondered.

They had coffee and brandy in the living room. David nearly sat on their Sealyham before he saw him. He managed to get through the next forty-five minutes with no more strange outbursts, but he felt visibly rigid and unnatural. The brandy, of which he drank two small snifters, did not help at all. They said good-by in the front hall, and Mrs Osbourne told David that he must come again. David felt that she deliberately left the hall sooner than she might have, in order for her husband to say something to him alone.

Dr Osbourne jerked his head back as he often did before a statement of importance, then said, 'Sorry I pressed you on a personal matter, David. It's only that I'm interested in how you work, you know. Personal problems can be damnably upsetting and can interfere with the imagination. I don't have to tell you that, do I?'

'No, sir. But I don't consider I have a problem. I mean, even if I do, I can keep it separate from my work. Believe me, I know. They're two separate worlds to me. I've been this way all my life.'

Dr Osbourne nodded, but there was something dubious about it.

David drove home slowly, following Dr Osbourne's map backward in his mind until he was on his familiar road. He decided that the evening hadn't been as awkward as he had thought. Certain phrases that he had said and that Dr Osbourne had said flitted across his mind. Well, what was so bad about it ? The pain and the awkwardness had all been inside his own head. He felt that he always exaggerated his own disturbance, thinking that it stuck out all over him, while it was really inside him and invisible to another person. Believing this, he began to feel much better. He put his car in his garage and went into the warm, comfortable house. He had left a standing lamp on in the living room, and its light fell directly onto the telephone on the table at the end of the couch. Had Annabelle called earlier and had he missed it?

The light focusing on the telephone seemed to tell him so. Quickly he looked at his watch. Ten minutes of eleven. She would not likely call again. But suppose he had missed a call from her? So tenuous was her impulse to call him, he knew, that if she missed him once she would probably not gather the inspiration to call him again. Why should he feel so strongly that she had called him tonight? It didn't make sense, in view of the fact she hadn't once called him here. Twenty times he had thought he heard the telephone ringing and had nearly broken his neck running downstairs from the bedroom or running in from outdoors, only to realize just before he lifted the telephone that it was not ringing.

He went to bed, but the brandies and the coffee kept him from sleeping. He felt wide awake and hopeless of sleeping for hours. A disturbing feeling that something was the matter with Annabelle – she was sick or had had an accident – made him want to telephone her, but suppose nothing was wrong and he simply woke her up and annoyed her ? Suppose she thought he was a little off his head for getting premonitions? He vowed not to telephone tonight, no matter how he felt.

He put on a robe, went into the sitting room, and addressed an envelope to Mrs Beecham at Mrs McCartney's. He wrote her a letter telling her about his new job and his new house, about the eastern windows of his kitchen and living room and bedroom that were so good for plants, and he promised to bring her a praying begonia that he had just bought, because he did not remember that she had any. At that moment, David felt a great desire and need to pay her a visit and to have a long talk, though he knew the impulse might not last. It even occurred to him, though he did not put it in his letter, to invite her to spend a day with him here, to fetch her and take her home again in the evening. After all, he had turned over a new leaf. David Kelsey. Nothing to hide. He sealed the letter, stamped it, and put it on the table by the front door.

Suddenly he felt infinitely better and almost cheerful. He got a beer from the refrigerator, thinking it would help him to get to sleep. As he got into bed with the beer and a book, a thought came to him: he ought not to call Annabelle for ten days. He had been importuning her — just because he wanted her to see his house, just because she was free now — and Annabelle had never liked that. Let her miss his calls a little, and be glad when she heard his voice again.

He thought of her just before he slept, saw her standing in the living room in Hartford, saw her figure turn as she went about some ordinary action, and it was like a little knife in his heart.

Exactly ten days later, on a Tuesday, he called at seven in the evening. A childlike voice answered and said, 'Hello?'

'Hello. Is Annabelle there, please?'

'Uh–uh. She's out with Grant.'

'With what?'

'*Grant*. Barber,' she added. 'They went to the movies and she won't be back till late.'

'What's late? What time?'

But the child had hung up.

David sat, frustrated, on the sofa for a minute. Grant. He thought of Ulysses S. Grant's bearded face with cap and cigar, thought of an army tank moving on crude tractors. He stood up. Was Barber his last name or was he a barber? David shrugged. Had Annabelle ever mentioned the name Barber? He thought she had, but he couldn't remember when or how. He'd try tomorrow night then. It was only one more day to wait.

23

Annabelle was in the next evening. David had rehearsed himself well, and his tone was cheerful and light. He proposed a Saturday lunch at his house, and he would come and get her and bring her back.

'I just don't think I can get away that long, Dave,' she said with a sigh.

'Well, a shorter time – without lunch?' he asked, dismal already. There was such a long silence, he said frantically, 'Hello? Operator, are we cut off?'

'No, I'm still here.'

'Please, Annabelle,' he begged, all his composure and resolution gone. 'It's been so many weeks now. I'm just asking for a couple of hours.' The whine in his voice mortified him. 'Well if you can't –'

'All right, Dave, maybe around three?'

'You mean, can I pick you up at three? We'll drive back to my place?'

But she didn't mean that. She hadn't time for the drive. She suggested going somewhere in Hartford, begged off going to his house on the grounds of taking care of the baby, and David, half defeated, said: 'We'll go anywhere you like, Annabelle. I'll pick you up at three.'

'Maybe earlier. Can you make it at two?'

After they had hung up, he thought it was not impossible that he could persuade her to drive on to his house with him. Not impossible they could have dinner here Saturday night. If she had to get a baby sitter, that could be arranged by telephone. Or should he call back and suggest she bring the baby with her? He gave that up.

He walked around his house for a while, hands in his pockets, went upstairs twice, strolling about and judging everything with Annabelle in mind. He had started to mention the piano again on the telephone and had checked himself. She knew about the piano. He couldn't tempt her with material things (or was a piano really a material thing?) and it was shameful to think he could. He hadn't written her any letters lately. Would that have helped?

'To hell with it all!' David muttered suddenly, and went downstairs to get a beer. He thought that beer had a sedative effect, and beers were also nourishing. His appetite was bad lately, and he was losing weight.

The telephone rang and David flew to it.

He heard the operator saying, 'Seventy-five cents, please,' and David said quickly, 'Tell her she can reverse the charges,' but he was drowned out by the clanging of coins.

'Annabelle?' David said.

'Dave? This is Wes.'

'Oh! Hello Wes.'

'I just called up to see how you are. I'm with Eff and a couple of other people. Well, how are you?'

'I'm fine, thanks. And you?'

'Very fine. Greetings from Michael's Tavern! Why didn't you phone or something in all this time?'

'I don't know.'

'You sound gloomy tonight. Want to talk to Eff?'

He almost said no, and said nothing.

'Hello, Dave. How are you?' Effie asked.

'Very well, thanks. Thank you for your housewarming gifts, Effie. I should have written you a note. They're very pretty. I use the place mats every day.'

'You did write me a note,' she said with a laugh. 'A very nice note. Have you forgotten?'

'Must have. Sorry.' He wet his lips.

'Has Annabelle been to see you?'

'Why, yes,' he said so loudly, it roared in his own ears. 'She was over a couple of times. She likes the house. Haven't you spoken to her?' he asked politely, loathing the idea they might have spoken to each other.

'No, I haven't. Well, you're on better terms then. I'm glad.'

'Oh, fine terms.'

'Would you like to speak to Wes again?' shakily. 'Here he is.'

'Hey, who's Annabelle or Plurabelle or whatever?'

'Oh – my car,' David said.

'Ha ha ha. Is she the girl? The famous girl?'

'No, she is not,' David said.

'Come on now.'

'Can I speak to Effie again?'

But Wes paid no attention to that request. He asked David about his job, and then said that Effie wanted to come up and see him. 'With me, if –' Wes hesitated, and David heard his breath against the telephone. 'Dave, I'm sorry about that night. I guess we were both a little loaded. I certainly was.'

'That's okay, Wes. We can let it go, can't we?' At that moment, he had only a vague memory of the evening. More important was that he wanted Wes as a friend. 'I'd like you to come up some time, Wes. I'd have to make you a map to get here. I can mail you one.'

'Will you do that, Dave? Right away, so you don't forget?'

'I will, Wes.'

'Can I bring Effie up when I come? You can say yes or no,' Wes said in a lower tone. 'She can't hear us now.'

'It makes a different atmosphere,' David said, 'having her. Maybe some time but –'

Wes said he understood. He said he would come up some time by himself, and David said if he made it on a Saturday, he could put Wes up for the night. Wes sounded delighted.

'You needn't tell Effie – about the first time you come up,' David told him.

David had a funny feeling after he had hung up, that the conversation really hadn't happened. It seemed incredible, unspeakably shameful that he had uttered Annabelle's name to Wes, even though he had done it accidentally. And Wes had repeated it. David shuddered at the thought Effie might break down and admit to Wes that Annabelle Delaney was the girl he loved, and tell Wes all the rest of it too. Or could he trust her? Wouldn't Wes, anyway, remember that Mrs Gerald Delaney's name was Annabelle? It scared him. He tried to imagine Wes sitting with him in his living room, and this was frightening too.

But why, David Kelsey? What was the harm or the danger there? Why should he have set up a law for himself that

Annabelle had to be his first visitor, the first person beside himself to set foot in the house? And after all, Annabelle might still get there before Wes did. He had a date with her Saturday.

Remembering Saturday, he felt better, and almost jubilant.

He sat down and drew a map for Wes to get to his house from Troy. He wanted to add a little note to it, but he found he had nothing to say, or was not in the mood.

David made such good time Saturday on his way to Hartford he had to kill an hour in the town. He parked the car at a meter, and walked along one of the business streets, looking into the windows of jewelry stores. It occurred to him that he had never before thought about what kind of wedding ring he would give Annabelle. The one she wore was one of those plain bands of gold, solid and convex, that had become too common in the world for David's taste. He preferred the very thin silver rings, set with tiny blue or white diamonds.

When he drove up to the red brick apartment house promptly at two, Annabelle was standing on the steps waiting for him. She waved to him, came toward the car, and David jumped out to meet her.

'Hello, darling! Both of us on the dot!' He touched her arm and kissed her quickly on the cheek – not a rehearsed move, and he felt somewhat awkward, having to press her arm to keep his own balance, and he noticed with dismay, too, that she drew back from him a little. She wore a black cloth coat that was new to him and a black hat like a thick beret.

'I know what your eyes are like now,' David said. 'Star sapphires.'

She smiled and looked away from his face. 'Is that your car?' she asked with surprise.

'Yep, a new one. I mean, a different one. I decided to trade mine in for a convertible.' He opened the car door for her.

'I don't think – I want to drive anywhere, Dave. I haven't that much time. There's a new restaurant just around the corner. A Chinese place.'

'Let's drive, anyway,' he said, smiling. 'I want you to try the car.'

She shook her head. There was a funny tenseness about her.

Reluctantly he closed the door, had to slam it twice to make it catch. 'All right. We'll walk.' He knew now it was hopeless that she would drive with him to his house.

The Chinese place was called the Golden Dragon, small and gaudy, but at least it looked quiet. They took one of the semi-circular booths. David asked if she had had lunch, hoping she hadn't, but she had.

'You haven't,' she said. 'Please have something.'

He was hungry, but he ordered only tea, for both of them. It would have been depressing to eat when she did not. He noticed she did not have her wedding ring on, and he wondered what that might mean. 'If you'd like a drink along with the tea – now or later?'

'No, thanks, Dave. I love this Chinese tea.' And patiently she waited for it, not looking at him.

They had been here before, he thought, the lunches that he rushed to so confidently, and then – It was like a crazy chess game in which he advanced one position and then had to retreat to the position he had been in before. He pulled an envelope out of the inside pocket of his jacket. 'I wanted to show you some pictures of the house.' He had brought the pictures along, reluctantly, in case she wouldn't be able to drive to the house with him, and he had thought it defeatist to anticipate that, and yet here it was – a lot better than nothing, after all. Among the pictures were two interior shots, one of which showed the piano with its top up.

'It's just – spectacular!' Annabelle said in a tone of awe, and David laughed.

'It's for you. It has to be pretty,' he said. 'Now *when* are you going to come and see it, at least?' Her hand, the ringless hand, was only inches from his, which rested on the red upholstered bench. He took her hand gently, hungrily, and a sigh came from his chest and for an instant seemed to drain his strength.

'David, I think I ought never to see it.' She rushed on before he could speak. 'I don't know how else to say it. However I say it, it's bad, I know – and not nice.'

'Well –' he stammered, and released her hand because she wanted him to.

'It's harder for you, if I see it, that's what I mean to say. I know it's beautiful. You've spent a lot of money –'

He groaned. 'I hoped you would like it. I hoped you would like me – *love* me. And I think you would, if you gave me a chance. You don't give me much of a chance, Annabelle. You don't give me much of your time. With no time together, it's hard to tell – I mean, look at both of us, sitting here stiff as pokers,' he said with a laugh. 'Is there any need of it? Couldn't you have visited me weekends, lots of weekends, and brought the baby with you, if you had to?'

'Women don't usually visit single men on weekends,' she said, smiling.

'Oh, *rot*!' Then, seeing she was shocked at his tone, he said, 'Well, we could've had the baby as chaperon. We still could. How about it?'

She shook her head and with a forefinger drew back into place a strand of hair that had been disarranged since she took her hat off. She waggled the half-empty teacup in its saucer, staring at it. 'Would you like to see Mr Neumeister's letter?'

'Of course I would.'

She took it from her pocket and handed it to him.

David unfolded it and read it quickly but with interest, almost as if he had never seen it before. His eyes paused momentarily at the two typing errors he had deliberately made and corrected with a pencil, his own typing being rather good. 'It is a nice letter,' he said when he had finished.

'I was darned glad to get it. I'm going to keep it.'

And David saw the start of tears as she replaced it in her pocketbook. 'I'm glad you have it,' he said gently. 'I still want to know – when you might come to the house.'

'Oh, Dave – you make it so hard for me to talk to you.'

'Good God, I don't mean to. What're you trying to say? I'll help you.'

'I think you'd better turn loose of me – emotionally and every-other way. You know you said – or maybe you didn't exactly say it, that after Gerald died, there'd be a chance for me to see.' Her eyes still staring at the teacup, were suddenly brimming with tears. One zipped down her cheek, and David pulled out his pocket handkerchief.

'Darling, here.'

She got her own Kleenex from her pocketbook. 'Well, it's no different now, Dave.'

'You're still in love with Gerald?' It was easy for him to ask it, because he had never believed it. 'But you're not going to stay a widow all your life, are you?'

'No,' she said matter-of-factly, and put the wet Kleenex back in her bag.

'Well, how long do I have to wait?'

'That's what I mean. I'm afraid it can't ever be – with us. That's what's so hard to tell you – because you won't understand. Even I don't understand.'

Tears in her pretty eyes. She seemed to be going through more torture than he was. He slid closer and put his arm around her, pulled out his handkerchief again. 'Darling, I can't stand to see you –'

'Please, Dave.' She pressed him away.

And he had only wanted to wipe her eyes, as one wipes a crying child's eyes. 'I don't think you understand *me,* Annabelle. You don't understand the kind of feelings I have for you. They're deep. They won't go away.'

She said nothing. And the tears still oozed. Now she was using his handkerchief.

'Had you rather I took you home now? Would you like to rest for a while and maybe I can see you this evening?' he asked, desperate as to what to propose.

'I'm busy this evening – Dave, do you know what I've been trying to say?'

He nodded, mute.

'That it's useless for you to call me any more? That I can't see you as a friend, because that's not the way it is with you, on your part,' she said in a rush, 'and that I do know what all this has been for you. It must be like a nightmare. I'm not heartless, Dave.'

'Heartless! I never thought –' He stopped. It was as if he had bumped suddenly against a stone wall. He blinked, frightened.

'You do understand, I think,' she said, so gently and yet the words were terrible.

David tried to smile. He poured more tea for her and himself.

'I had a letter from your aunt in La Jolla. She's quite worried about you, Dave.'

'Aunt Edie? What in hell is she writing you about?'

'About you – in regard to me. I answered her letter.'

David frowned. 'What did you say?'

'What I've said to you. That I understood and felt very sorry. But that it couldn't be helped – by me, I mean. Dave, I may marry some day, but it won't be you. Maybe something's the matter with me, I don't know, but that's the way it is.'

'You're talking about – somebody in particular?'

'Yes. I think so.'

'Grant?'

'How'd you know?'

'Who is he?' David asked, frowning harder.

'He lives in Hartford. He's an accountant. The son of one of my neighbors. I've known him quite a while,' she said rather apologetically.

'Barber. You mean the son of that old woman who tried to start a fight in your apartment?' David asked incredulously.

'She didn't –'

'An accountant!' David smiled a little.

'I only said I was going out with him,' Annabelle said, flushing.

'You didn't. You said you were thinking you might marry him.'

'Well, what if I am?' Her hands were on the edge of the table, as if she intended to jump up and leave.

David's amusement struggled with a sense of imminent danger. He spoke calmly. 'Annabelle, what is it? That you've had a chance to spend a lot of time with him? Give me a chance. Are you trying to crawl back into some dreary life? Can't you – can't you treat yourself a little better?'

'He likes the baby and he's very kind,' Annabelle said quickly. 'I'm sorry I brought it up, Dave.'

'So am I.' He sat back against the bench. 'I know you so well,' he said with a little laugh. 'Why don't you know me as well?'

She didn't answer. She looked around as if she were trying to find the waiter.

'Annabelle, how would you like to live in Troy for a while? Bring the baby. I can find an apartment there for you –'

'Stop it, Dave.'

He still felt more amused than angry. He could imagine what

Mrs Barber's son was like, and he couldn't believe that Annabelle would make the same mistake twice.

'There's one more thing, Dave,' she said, opening her pocketbook. 'This – I simply can't take it.' She pulled out the little beige box that held the diamond clip he had mailed to her a couple of weeks before.

'It'll keep,' he said.

'Take it. Please.'

He took it slowly from her hands. For some reason, he thought of the Steinway and saw its black form in miniature, the size of the little beige box. 'They'll keep,' he said. 'Everything'll keep.'

'Except me.'

'Including you.'

'Dave, would you mind if we took off now?'

'I don't mind anything you want,' he said. 'Waiter!'

Outside, David felt a leap of nausea in his stomach. The air was cold on his forehead. He took a couple of deep breaths, and the nausea passed in a few seconds. Annabelle was silent and she walked quickly. David wanted to appear relaxed, untroubled by what she had said to him, and he really felt unperturbed, but the fact remained, he was taking her back to her apartment that would lock her up from him. And he realized he was afraid to ask when he might call her or see her again.

'Has Effie been to your new house?' Annabelle asked.

'No.'

'Aren't you going to have her up?'

'I really hadn't thought about it.' His hands were perspiring. He ought to get a hamburger somewhere before he started the drive home, he thought, because he felt a little faint.

After he left Annabelle, he drove to a bar and had a double martini, two in one, and then went to the men's room and was sick. He asked the barman for a drink of water before he left, and he smiled at his pale face in the mirror. Grant Barber. David felt himself rising to the challenge. And what an absurd challenge it was, what a silly rival!

24

Wed., March 25, 1959

Dear Annabelle,

I have let a good deal of time go by on purpose. Or maybe four days isn't a lot of time to everybody. It depends on what you do with it. Every time I see you, I grow more confident about us, and if I felt or showed any resentment of Mr Barber, it was only momentary. But please don't use him, darling, as a wedge between us. If you want more time to consider, I'll give you more, all you want. I'm not one to be discouraged by the presence of some dummy male figure. I won't call you, if that bothers you. I'll wait for you to call me. (Tyler 5–0934) Call collect, of course, or drop me a note.

The weather's getting better. The baby's getting bigger. Aren't there some cheerful aspects to all this?

The house will still be here, even prettier in summer. The sailing of the *Darwin* (Dickson-Rand's ship) has been put off until mid-July, due to a delay in getting some instruments we need. I expect to go with them, a two-month cruise and maybe longer. So don't think I am pressing you, darling. Though the greatest thing I can think of is that we might be married before July. Things being what they are at the lab (everybody's treated like a privileged character) I bet they would let you come with us on the voyage. The China Sea and the Indian Ocean. Would you like that? One man has already gotten permission to take his wife, a young fellow too.

Please do call me, darling. One call would brighten my whole weekend. Wes is coming up Saturday morning. I think I've mentioned Wes Carmichael to you a few times. A friend from Cheswick. I thought you'd like to know I'm not leading the life of a hermit. I had the Osbournes here once for dinner. They were impressed by my cooking. Isn't it time you sampled some too?

All my love, darling, and forever,
Dave

She would get the letter by Saturday, if not Friday, if he mailed it tomorrow morning, and he thought it more likely, somehow, that she would call him this weekend, knowing that Wes was in the house.

The telephone rang the next evening when David was under the shower, and he jumped out, grabbed a towel and ran downstairs. He had been listening for the telephone. It had become a habit with him to leave the bedroom and bathroom doors open always, so he could hear the telephone, if it rang.

It was Wes, calling to say he couldn't make it on Saturday. His voice sounded grim.

'What's happened?' David asked.

'It's Laura. She's stirring up all kinds of hell about Effie.'

'At this late date?'

'It's not funny. I might get fired, Dave. Effie could lose her job, too. I passed out in Effie's apartment and spent the night there. Effie's super's wife told my wife. I don't even know how she found out who I was. Isn't it great living in a small town?'

'Well, does she finally want a divorce?' David asked, thinking that when the chips were down, it would be Wes who wouldn't want a divorce.

'Nothing so nice. She just wants to embarrass both of us all over town. Effie and me. But Effie's behaving very well.'

'Good old Effie!'

'I wish I could see you. You've got the right attitude. This town's full of prigs.'

'Come on up, Wes.'

'I can't. I've got to stick around and try to calm Laura down. Effie at least had the guts to call her and tell her what happened. I fell asleep on the sofa, period. But I'm worried about my job, Dave.'

'Who told Lewissohn?'

'Laura,' Wes said loudly. 'If that isn't something for a wife to do! Jeopardize her means of –' Then he laughed.

'Come up, Wes. You can't do anything about it over the weekend.'

'No, I have to see Lewissohn tomorrow. We're having a little talk. Gad, you'd think we were living in the Victorian age. And I never even necked with her on a couch! I might as well have spent the night with my sister!'

David said he could still come up, if he changed his mind, that the refrigerator was full of food, and if he couldn't make it this weekend, then maybe he could next weekend.

'If you lose your job, maybe you could get on at Dickson-

Rand,' David said with sudden exuberance. 'Want me to find out?'

The operator interrupted, and Wes dropped some more coins.

'Let me see what happens here. With Laura, you know, I have to make more money.'

'No, you don't. That's nothing but habit.'

'You're in a good humor. What's happening with Annabelle?' It brought only a throb, like a delayed reaction.

'Dave? That's Delaney's wife, isn't it?'

David couldn't speak.

'What's the matter, Dave? I was just wondering – You know her, don't you?'

'No,' David said, knowing it didn't make sense and that Wes wouldn't believe him.

There was a long silence.

'Dave, I'm not your enemy. But I could tell that night. You do know her. Is she the girl, Dave? You do know this fellow Newmester too, don't you?'

'No, I don't.'

Another silence, and though David thought there must be a phrase, a statement he could make, that would sweep away Wes's suspicions, he didn't have it in his head, and if it had been in his head, he thought he might not have said it.

'All right, Dave,' Wes said softly, and in it David heard disappointment, resentment, and disbelief. 'Effie –'

'Effie doesn't know anything about this,' David said.

'All right, Dave. Well – I'll call you – about the weekend after this.' Now he sounded as if he didn't want to come.

And David, when he put the telephone down, had lost his desire to see Wes. Effie must have told him a lot, he thought. And even if she hadn't, Wes had seen him go into Neumeister's house. A few more questions that Effie answered yes to, and Wes would know the whole story. And Wes couldn't be trusted, David thought. He would have a few drinks – or maybe he wouldn't even need them – and call up Annabelle and tell her that David Kelsey and Neumeister were the same person.

His thoughts swung the other way: Wes wouldn't and couldn't do a thing like that. What did Wes have against him that would make him do a thing like that?

On the other hand, mightn't Wes and Effie put their heads together and decide the only way to end an apparently 'hopeless' courtship was to tell Annabelle the truth?

'Damn them both, damn them both, damn them both,' David chanted.

He finished drying himself and dressed.

That evening he could scarcely eat his dinner. Maybe they would call Annabelle tonight. Annabelle would telephone him immediately, or more likely telephone the police. The Beck's Brook police would be very interested.

But then, since Wes was in such hot water because of Effie, he probably wouldn't be spending this evening with her. It was rather contemptible of Wes, David thought, that at the first real counter-attack from his wife, he cringed and tried to go crawling back to her. He had mentioned needing to make a big salary only because presumably he was going to stay married to her.

David drank no coffee that evening, knowing already that he was going to sleep badly. Around nine, when he was trying to read, he had an impulse to call Effie and find out how much she had told Wes, but his pride kept him from it. The safest was to assume she had told him everything now.

The telephone did not ring the rest of the evening, though once, at a quarter to eleven, David ran down from the bathroom to see if it was ringing. The toilet made an odd ringing sound as the tank refilled, and it was not the first time David had been fooled by it.

That night he felt he did not sleep at all, though he had something that passed for a dream, or a nightmare. It was about turtles, little turtles that crawled across the tile floor of a darkish room. They came in a flow, diagonally, and David, crossing the room, took great pains not to step on them. In a corner of the room, he saw his bed at Mrs McCartney's, and under the thin blankets the contour of a small figure. He drew the covers back and found a beautiful young girl, naked, whom he recognized as Joan, a girl he had been in love with at seventeen or eighteen. 'I'm still in love with you, Dave. I guess I always will be,' she said. And David replied with quiet assurance, 'Love is like that' (though Joan had never cared for him, and the curious thing about the dream was that during it he felt he had dreamed of seeing Joan before, so that the dream now seemed reality and not a dream). Then came a series of pretty images: a large white blossom which, when he held it by its base, opened like a spider's web or like a cage. David exclaimed about its beauty, but he could not get the three or four other people (two women and another man) in the room with him to take any interest in it. He peered into the white cage and saw some small, dark, moving things like insects. Then he realized they were the turtles. One, larger than the rest, was injured, as if someone had stepped on its back. Its shell had been crushed and blood oozed out. In a sudden agony of compassion, David tried to think how best to put the turtle out of its pain, called frantically to the other people in the room, then began to push the blood back into the shell and to try to reshape it. 'You know well enough what to do about that,' the other man in the room said to him rudely. Then the turtle began to retch, silently and horribly, and vomited what seemed to be its stomach. The shell was suddenly empty. David, exhausted by witnessing all this, asked the man to take the shell away and bury it. Then, with an interest more scientific than merely curious, David took the vomited part to a water tap and washed it off in order to see it better. It had three sections: the first the shape of a turtle's head, the next fat and pinkish like lung tissue, then a waist and a fatter part again. It began to writhe, as if to get out of his hands, and David realized to his horror that instead of a dead organ he held the whole turtle, all that was within the shell – the turtle's soul, it seemed – in his two hands. He woke up sweating and panting, and his heart beat faster and faster as he reviewed the dream and its horror. He got up and dressed.

The weekend dragged, and by mid-afternoon on Sunday, David was depressed and a little frightened by a feeling that something was supposed to be happening and wasn't happening. It was as if his house were a stage set without actors or action. And all he could do was wait. Annabelle had surely gotten his letter on Saturday, his cheerful letter asking her to call him. Here it was Sunday. Was she spending the whole day with Grant Barber? And how had Wes made out Friday, trying to hold onto his job? The realization that Wes knew about Annabelle was like a small explosion in David's mind every time it occurred to him. It was a far more important matter than the presence of Grant Barber, who was nothing but a potential mistake, a cipher.

For the first time in this house, David realized that he was too disturbed to concentrate on a book. Dr Osbourne wanted him to read the book over the weekend. It consisted mostly of tables and graphs of radiocarbon analyses. David made four or five plunges at it, but after a few moments, his thoughts would drift to Annabelle and fasten: Annabelle was hearing, at that moment, about William Neumeister. Wes was telling her. Wes was drunk. Or Effie was telling her in her sweet, earnest way. 'I thought you *ought* to know, Annabelle.' David cursed Effie Brennan again.

At eight-thirty that evening, David called Effie. Anger had swallowed up his pride. If Effie had stood in front of him and said she had told Annabelle who William Neumeister was, David thought he would have struck her. The telephone rang more than ten times, and David was about to give it up, when Effie answered, breathless.

'Hello. It's Dave Kelsey.'

'Dave! Oh, how nice! Oof! I just ran up the stairs. I thought it was my phone ringing. How are you, Dave?'

'Okay, thanks. And you?'

'I'm all right. Wes told you about that mess we got into, didn't he?' she asked with a silly, easy laugh.

'Yes, he did. Some of it. Has he still got his job?'

'Uh-huh, and so have I. My boss wasn't so bad about it. He's got a sense of humor. I don't see what's so earth-shaking about a man passing out and spending the night on somebody's living room sofa. It was only Laura that made it so awful for poor Wes.'

'I quite agree,' David said tensely. 'I didn't really call up about that. I'd like to know what you've told him about Annabelle.'

'Nothing, Dave!' she said with a gasp. 'Absolutely nothing. I promised you. Remember?'

'Yes, I remember. Well, Wes knows her name, knows who she is.'

'He knows her name because you said it that night on the

phone. He told me you did. I was shocked too, Dave. You were expecting a call from her?'

'And you said, "Yes, that's the girl"? What else did you tell him?'

'Honestly, Dave, I didn't. Wes guessed it. He said, "Isn't Annabelle the name of Delaney's wife?" and I said, "I don't know," but Wes jumped on it. He remembered it from the papers. Honestly, Dave, I never even told Wes I'd seen Annabelle, but Wes remembered I did say I'd met the girl you – you were in love with and I'd said I didn't think – Well, I didn't think she'd ever marry you. But I guess he knows now the girl is Annabelle. But it was your voice that night, Dave –'

'All right, all right.'

'Dave, don't be angry.'

'Oh, no. Of course not.'

'But I didn't tell him anything! Wes just said, "So that's why Delaney had it in for Dave." And he said Newmester must have been a good friend of yours, because – Wes's idea is that Newmester was trying to protect you that day by fighting with Gerald Delaney. Wes thinks you were in the house that day and that Newmester – Wes doesn't suspect anything about you using the name Newmester, and I'm certainly not going to tell him anything, Dave.'

'Thanks, thanks,' David said, weakly relieved, yet still loathing Effie merely because she knew as much as she did, and that she had learned it all by prying.

After he had hung up, he tackled the radiocarbon book again, and now it was interesting. He skimmed through it, concentrating only on the chapters beside which Dr Osbourne had put a small, neat check in the table of contents. He read steadily for nearly two hours, until he began to feel sleepy. When he thought of Effie and Wes again, they seemed miles away and quite removed from him. If Wes didn't know the Neumeister story, then he obviously couldn't tell it to Annabelle. And Effie wouldn't. Apparently he could depend on her. William Neumeister – good old Bill – had come through again. A pity David Kelsey couldn't be such an all-round success.

When he went upstairs and glanced into the bedroom, he had a funny illusion: he thought he saw Annabelle lying on the bed, face down, with her arms around the pillow. He had left one lamp on in the bedroom. But the bed was made, its surface smooth, he saw as he blinked and stared at it. Had the illusion been due to eyestrain, he wondered, or to a quirk of his brain? Matter or mind? That was a question for a metaphysician.

A whole week passed with no call from Annabelle. David went to dinner one evening at the home of Kenneth Laing, a thirty-five-year-old physicist in his department, and the other evenings he spent at home. He was tempted every evening to call Annabelle, especially the evening he came home from the Laings': couldn't he tell Annabelle the telephone had been ringing as he came in and that he had called to see if it had been she? But he knew Annabelle would find the story only pitiful. She called him so seldom. She never *had* called him in this house, David realized. And maybe she never would. That thought drove him from his armchair, and he hurled the book he had been reading against the pillows of his bed. No use thinking things like that, playing little games with himself, holding his breath as long as he could and betting – against whom? – that the telephone was going to ring before he had to breathe again. No use running down the stairs *every* time he flushed the toilet. But if he ran down the stairs half the time, what was to tell him which half of the time he should run down?

What would somebody else do? What would William Neumeister do? William Neumeister would go up to Hartford, pack her things and drag her out of that apartment, David thought. And another man, any other man, what would he do? David broke his pacing of the floor and ran downstairs to the telephone and called her.

A strange female voice answered, a middle-aged voice.

'May I speak to Annabelle?'

'She's not here. Who's calling?'

David, suddenly realizing who it was, felt a wave of anger break over him. 'A friend,' he said nastily. 'Can you tell me when she'll be back? I'll call again.'

'Oh, well, they went to the movies, y'know. Then they'll probably have a cup of coffee and something at the Sweet Shop –' She chuckled with vicious satisfaction.

'How very charming. She and Grant, you mean.'

'Yep,' said the crude, smug voice. 'Listen here –'

'Mrs Barber, you listen to me. I advise you to tell your son to keep his distance from Annabelle, understand? There's some people I don't like her associating with and he's one of them.'

'Are you that David? I thought you were that David. You've got a fine nerve calling that nice girl up and making trouble after all the trouble you've made already. I'm going to tell the police! I'm going –'

'Shut your stupid mouth! I'd like you to leave a message for Annabelle to –'

But Mrs Barber had hung up.

David slammed the telephone down. 'Bastards!' he muttered. Then he put his head back and laughed at the idea of Mrs Barber calling the police about him. He laughed long and richly with the relief and the satisfaction his burst of temper had given him. It was a great pleasure, a great satisfaction to yell 'Shut your stupid mouth!' to an old hag like Mrs Barber. She deserved it so. David wondered how many people had had the courage to call her that to her face? Not many, he supposed, not enough, anyway. Otherwise Mrs Barber couldn't walk the earth with such unbelievable and revolting complacence. She was the kind of mother who, on producing a clod of a son like herself, would congratulate and preen herself every damned Mother's Day. Her vulgar figure would bustle up to the head of the table at every holiday feast, and no one would praise her greasy cooking more than she herself. It must be great, David thought, really great to have such a high, unchallengeable opinion of oneself, to think that everything one did or possessed or thought or maybe even felt was the best and the finest in the world!

'Good *God*!' David said in total exasperation, almost as furious again as he had been on the telephone.

He thought of driving to Hartford. He could get there by midnight with any luck. But by midnight, Annabelle would probably be in bed, and she'd be annoyed if he called her. Nonsense, David thought. Where had his passivity, his lack of action ever gotten him or anybody else?

Less than ten minutes later, David was on the road.

Just across the Connecticut line, he was stopped for speeding by a traffic cop who, however, let him off with a warning, despite the fact David did not trouble to appear contrite. After that the roads were clear, and he reached Annabelle's street at ten to twelve. A dim light showed at a third-story window, which he thought was hers, though he realized he had never been in that bedroom and he only assumed it had a window on the street. David pressed the bell confidently.

There was a rather long wait, he rang again, and then the release button sputtered the door open for him.

'Who is it, please?' Annabelle's voice called down.

'David,' he replied, climbing the stairs two at a time. 'Are you alone?'

'No. No, I'm not alone.'

'Good.' He smiled at her and would have taken her hand, but she avoided him. 'Grant's here?'

'Yes. Dave, must you? Can't we talk out here? What is it?'

'What it is is that I want you. And I intend to tell this guy Grant off,' David said, moving toward the door that was slightly ajar.

Grant Barber stood there, a fellow nearly as tall as David and heavier, a blank expression on his rather stupid face. His black hair was crew cut.

'Yes, I'm David. How do you do?' David said, walking past him into the room.

'If you're here to make more trouble, Mr Kelsey,' said Mrs Barber, wild-eyed, 'I'm going to call the police!' And she moved toward the telephone, keeping her eyes on David.

David put his fists on his hips. 'I'm not armed, Mrs Barber. What do you think I am?' His voice cracked. He turned suddenly to Grant. 'Mr Barber, you've had your last date with Annabelle, so I hope you enjoyed it.'

'What're you getting at? I think you'd better get out of here, Mr Kelsey. This is Annabelle's house and she doesn't want you here.'

'I don't like you either. But I didn't come here to call you a lot of unpleasant names. I came here to tell you Annabelle's going to be my wife and that I am not pleased about her making dates with men like you, understand?'

'Oh! Listen to that! Did you ever!' The old hag was flapping about again, like a chicken in a barnyard. 'I'll give you just one minute to get out of this house, Mr Kelsey, and if you don't, I'm going to call the law!'

'Just shut up,' David told her.

'Dave, please,' Annabelle said. 'You can't come here and make scenes like this.'

'Darling, I'm sorry, but this is something that's got to be done. I want you to pack your things.'

'Oh, Dave!' Annabelle threw her head back in a gesture of despair that David had never seen before.

He caught her shoulders. 'Annabelle –'

'Get your hands off her!' said the blustering Mr Barber, and David quickly took his hands from Annabelle and hit Grant in the jaw.

The blow staggered him but didn't fell him. Grant backed against a coffee table, upsetting a couple of cups, and David patiently righted the dishes, while Mrs Barber cackled and screamed, and Annabelle held Grant back from coming after him with his fists, though David doubted that Grant would have really tried to take him on. Grant looked scared.

'I think you should, I think you should,' Grant was saying to his mother, and his mother picked up the telephone.

'Don't be a bore,' David said, pulling the telephone gently but firmly from her hands.

'Dave, I ask you to leave – if you care anything about me,' Annabelle said.

'I'm not afraid of him,' Grant was muttering nervously, more to himself than to Annabelle.

'Grant, take the phone!' his mother commanded, but David held the telephone in both his hands, swinging it out of her reach. 'Go downstairs and call somebody, Grant! Or *I* will!'

'Pack your bag and let's leave these people!' David yelled over Mrs Barber to Annabelle.

Now the baby was crying in the bedroom. The sound was another little encumbrance to David. But having gone this far – For an instant, with all three of them shouting at him and somebody in the next apartment thumping on the wall, David lost his momentum and felt a presentiment of defeat. Then he grabbed Annabelle's wrist and propelled her toward the bedroom, and told her again to get the things that she wanted to take with her. Mrs Barber's wrinkled, hideous mouth so close to his eyes filled him with intolerable disgust, and he would happily have pushed her in the face and sent her across the room if he could have brought himself to touch her. Her son was pulling at his shoulder. Then David swung around suddenly and this time the crack of his fist against Grant's jaw was very satisfactory, seemed enough to have knocked his head off, and Grant's shoulders boomed against an opposite wall.

Mrs Barber screamed, and the crazy babble of voices came to a sudden halt.

'*David!*' Annabelle shouted, covering her face with both hands.

'I'm asking you to do a simple thing!' David yelled at her. 'You're coming with me tonight!'

'You're out of your mind!' Annabelle said as if she were in terror of him.

David looked around and saw Mrs Barber crouched on the floor beside her son, who was moving but was too groggy to get up. Slowly David picked up a standing lamp that had been knocked over. An ugly lamp. 'We're leaving,' he said quietly to Annabelle.

There was a knocking at the door. 'Mrs Delaney? What's going on in there?'

Then Annabelle rushed to the door, calling to Mr Somebody, and David closed his eyes and ears to Mrs Barber's yapping and her fist-shaking and her fat, quivering forearm motioning him to the door. A scowling man with black and gray hair came into the room, and David noticed he hadn't quite the courage to clench his fists.

'Mrs Delaney would – would like you to leave or we'll get the police,' the man said to David.

'*Get* the police,' David replied. 'I want these two people removed.' He gestured to the Barbers.

'Is he drunk?' asked the man.

'No,' Annabelle said. 'David, this has gone on long enough. I may as well tell you I'm going to marry Grant and there's nothing you can do about it. Nothing.'

He looked at her, unbelieving, not even feeling angry now, only bewildered by what seemed a small, stupid delay. He glanced at the scowling man who stood rigidly braced for an attack, and at Grant who was getting to his feet. His mother clung to his arm. It would be possible, of course, to knock Mr Barber's head off and thus keep him from marrying Annabelle or anybody else, but that was troublesome, messy, and uncivilized. David laughed. 'I don't believe you. Not for a minute. You're just trying to get me to go quietly.'

'We certainly are,' said the older man.

'Please do go, Dave. It's late and the whole house is upset,' Annabelle said.

'Well, that's a hell of a thing to tell me!' David said, exploding suddenly. 'What do I care if the house is upset? My whole life is upset and now you tell me you're going to make another mess of yours!'

'I know what I want to do, Dave,' she said. 'And I swear, Dave, I'm tired of you meddling in my life. I don't care what I say now or how I say it, I've had enough. I've been patient, understanding – I've taken your insults –'

'Insults?' he said, coming toward her, confused by her beauty, her face that he loved and the words she was saying. Then the older man made a lunge for him, and David veered toward Grant Barber. David hurled a fist at him again, but his arm was caught, and the blow fell short. David's arm felt on fire where the man had caught it.

'Look here, you're going to leave!' the man shouted at him.

Grant, too, had entered the fight, David had one on either arm now, and he couldn't throw them off. He braced his feet against the approach of the door, which Mrs Barber was opening. Another man, two men, appeared in the hall. David bent and hurled himself against Grant, but it was David's own head that cracked against the wall. After that, he might as well have been unconscious, though he was aware that he struggled on with all the strength he could muster, fighting them every inch of the way down the stairs. There might have been five of them grappling with him, pulling at ankles, wrists, hair, anything they could get their hands on, and David fought back with a bitterness he had never known before, as if all five or ten of them were Mrs Barbers that he now had a perfect right to hit and kick at. At the bottom, he and a couple of them fell to the floor, and David felt himself pulled up on his legs again as if he weighed nothing. Then he was aware that his feet dragged the ground, aware of a babble of voices, and of Annabelle's voice among them, and he was unable to reply, might as well have been paralyzed.

They hit his head on the door frame of his car. The car door slammed shut. David knew his eyes were shut, knew he was half reclined on the front seat, and that he was motionless, though his rage still boiled and stormed in him.

When he stirred again, dragging himself up by the steering wheel and accidentally tooting the horn, he saw that there was no light in Annabelle's apartment or anywhere in her building. He cupped his hand around his watch to see the radium dial. It was ten minutes to three. He started the car immediately and drove off. A front tooth throbbed. Feeling with his tongue, he found it was still there and not even chipped. And so what, he thought, so what?

At the moment, he hated the whole lot of them behind him.

25

The next day was a Monday, and David did not go to the lab. He telephoned at nine o'clock and told Rosalie, one of the secretaries, that he had an intestinal virus and had orders to stay in bed one more day. Actually, his trouble was a cut face and very puffy underlip, not to mention a purple eye and various aches, and he hoped to improve his appearance by Tuesday. He was ashamed of having fought physically, and also ashamed of having lost. There was no doubt he *had* lost. But Annabelle, telling him she was going to marry Grant Barber, telling him to his face! Had she thought she had to resort to *that* to get him out of the house? And that nightmarish hog of a woman, pulling at him with those horrible hands!

David paced his house, holding towels with ice cubes in them against his eye, his lips, his cheeks. There was a rip in the shoulder seam of his jacket, and in the afternoon he took it to a tailor in Troy to be mended. It was obvious by nightfall that he was not going to make a great improvement in his face. He debated telling a story of a prowler to the people at the lab. He didn't want them to think he'd been drunk and gotten into a fistfight. On the other hand, why tell them anything? Didn't he have a right to some privacy? Gerald Delaney had gone through life with a lower lip fatter than this, and probably no one had ever questioned him about it. He'd even married Annabelle. David smiled and his lip split. He went to bed very early.

And he woke up feeling like a different person. He could think clearly again. Let her marry Grant Barber, he thought, let her make another obvious mistake. It wouldn't last long. But then he realized the inevitable, idiotic delay that another marriage would mean. And the thought of that swine crawling into bed with her put him into a sweat. Something certainly had to be done. Another letter? He'd given up letters. He could throttle Mr Barber with pleasure, but then he'd be jailed. Hate was a slight relief, hate and contempt for the lot of them. But he couldn't completely hate Annabelle. She was simply duped, right and left. She condemned herself to ugliness and mediocrity, and why?

David drove off to the lab in a quiet, almost repentant mood, conscious that his violence had gotten him and would get him nowhere, and secure with the faith that something, some idea, some solution would occur to him today or tomorrow or the next day. Any problem in nature could be solved. All it took was perseverance. Ponder it, and then relax and let the imagination work. He resolved to concentrate hard on his own work today, be alert and bright with Dr Osbourne at their conference this afternoon, and he felt that, before six, a brilliant move would have occurred to him in regard to Annabelle.

Kenneth Laing gave David a second look and asked him what had happened.

'Oh, I just settled an old grudge this weekend,' David replied with a smile.

Laing whistled. 'Who won?'

'I did.'

No further remarks. Laing was not the familiar type. He kept a certain distance.

That afternoon David got into an argument with Dr Osbourne. David had briefed himself on what they were going to discuss that day, and everything went well until Dr Osbourne said something about the radiocarbon activity of a tufa mass he had examined somewhere, at some time. Perhaps the doctor had even made a joke about it. Less than a minute later, via some exchanges about the significance of radiocarbon activity to living organisms, David found himself in a tangle of illogic, unable to get out of it and blustering in every direction. He sounded off about his attitudes and duties as a scientist. Dr Osbourne protested that those things hadn't any bearing on what he had been talking about. David heard Dr Osbourne and heard his own words too, and it was as if he couldn't correlate them and couldn't shut up either and couldn't change the subject. He harangued against the gabbling scientists who would stop every project that might lead to a homicidal weapon, and at the same time he was decrying – he heard himself – the further investigation of radioactivity anywhere on the globe. And why? Because the discovery that the rate of radioactivity was low and harmless at present would only lead to more tests and more radioactivity on the earth's surface and in the atmosphere.

'I'm confused and amused,' said Dr Osbourne, smiling, but David hardly paused to hear him.

'I don't say I have it all worked out clearly,' David went on quickly, grasping for the hostility and resentment he had felt against Dr Osbourne minutes before and which now seemed to have fled from him. 'I'm not one to make up systems. But in fact I have worked out a system that could make the world a better place. The keypoint of it is the relationship between acceptance and rejection. It would permeate everywhere, from the humblest individual to the men who make foreign policies.' But David had not worked it out, they were only fleeting ideas he had had while standing under the shower or trying to fall asleep at night (and the small hours of the morning were never a good time for him to do any real thinking, despite the apparent racing of his brain), but he babbled on while Dr Osbourne listened with his chin sunk in his hand. 'You have to know what to accept and what to reject,' David said.

'Which nobody can deny. Well, once you get that a little better formulated –'

'But surely you can understand some of it right now,' David interrupted, his confidence rising again.

'My dear David, are you sure that fight you were in didn't jar your brain a little? Or have you had a couple of bracers this morning? Not that I mind in the least, just tell me, because I want to get on with this or not.'

David stood up, feeling vaguely insulted. 'I was trying to say something pertinent to what we were talking about.'

'I'm afraid you didn't. I can't even call what you were talking about a tangent. Now David, I'm not angry!' Dr Osbourne chuckled, but David could see that he was looking at him sharply.

If Dr Osbourne made any comments, David swore to himself, *any* comments on his personal life now, he would storm out of this office and never come back, never say a word to anybody in the lab, just leave.

But Dr Osbourne did not speak. He only nodded a little to himself, as if he had said something inside himself that he agreed with. And his smile was unattractively superior. He made a gesture toward David's chair. 'I'm sorry, David. Now would you like to sit down and we'll go on again – or not?'

David felt baffled. He did not know what he wanted to do.

'Suppose we take it up again tomorrow, eh, David?' Dr Osbourne stood up, smiling. 'We all have our bad days. This wind doesn't make things any better.' He stuck his thumbs in his vest pockets and twisted himself slightly to look out the window behind him.

'Thank you, sir,' David said. Suddenly his underlip felt as if it weighed several ounces. 'If you will excuse me –'

'Certainly, David. There's no hurry with the work around here, you know. I don't want you to feel any pressure.'

During the next hour he experienced something quite new to him. He was unable to work. He was supposed to make an average of graph recordings for one month, something a secretary might have done if she had known where to look, but he could not force himself more than halfway through the task. He tried something more difficult, but this did not go either. Embarrassed by what seemed to him a visible idleness, he went to Laing, told him he wasn't feeling well, and to tell Dr Osbourne that, in case he came down to speak to him. David knew it was most unlikely that Dr Osbourne would come down, and he saw from Laing's face that he thought it was an odd remark.

The unpleasant ambivalence stayed with him on the drive home. Should he turn around and go back to the lab? Should he telephone Annabelle and say something to her that she couldn't ignore, pass off, or forget? Or should he not telephone but go to Hartford again?

When he got home, he cleaned the house, vacuumed every room, and since the house was not really in need of cleaning, it went very quickly. It gave him a feeling of not having totally wasted the day. Then it occurred to him to look for the mail, which he usually did on his way back from work. He put on a raincoat and walked in the mud to the box at the end of his lane. The world looked mysteriously black, not so dark he could not see anything, but as if a solution of India ink had been poured into the atmosphere. He saw some birds fleeing. Then just as his hand touched the mailbox, there was a shocking crack of thunder. Was that an omen? He yanked the box open.

There was nothing personal except a letter from his Uncle Bert, which he had no desire to open.

Back in the house, he cleaned his shoes under the sink tap, wiped them dry with a paper towel and then polished them before he opened his uncle's letter. There was a lot of family news of no great import, Louise had a boy friend they thought was too old for her, and then Bert launched into his well-meant, avuncular advice with the phrase David had heard him say in his mild voice since he was fifteen, 'I know you're old enough to lead your own life now and I don't mean to butt in but . . .' He was worried, of all things, about the field trip in July on the *Darwin*. He thought David's happiness sounded a little false. Was he really happy? What was happening with Annabelle?

. . . In your last letter, you said you two were going to be married by June. Is this really so, Dave? That's not what Annabelle's mother thought when I ran into her on the street the other day. Not that I brought this up, but I mentioned you. To tell you the truth, she avoided talking about you. Please tell me what's been happening, Dave. You know my opinion well enough on this whole thing. It's high time you developed some eyes for another girl. . . .

Had he said he and Annabelle would be married by June? Maybe he had. David put the letter down on the kitchen table before he had quite finished it.

An hour or so later, he was sitting on the living-room sofa, a little high on his third martini. He had started the martinis as a prelude to dinner, and then had decided he had no appetite for dinner. He set the third martini down unfinished, and briskly went upstairs to take a shower and change his clothes. Under the shower, he began to feel more cheerful. He whistled defiantly and began to think of William Neumeister. Lucky old Bill! Somehow that shower reminded him of many happy showers in his other house in Ballard, much, much happier showers. Looking back on it, he felt the house in Ballard was bliss. Gerald had come to an end there, too, at the hands of William Neumeister.

That evening he was William Neumeister again. It helped a great deal. He ate a small dinner and played some records, listening to them on a cowhide rug with an ice pack against his lip and the cold, cut-off tail of a Porterhouse steak against his dark eye.

At the end of 'Verklärte Nacht' he went to the telephone and called Annabelle. He had no resolution about using or not using rough language, in case one of the Barbers answered. He simply felt very confident.

'May I speak to Annabelle, please,' he said calmly. He had gotten the old hag, all right.

'Is this David? David Kelsey?' she asked in a terrified voice.

'No, this is Bill.'

'Who?'

'I want to speak to Annabelle!'

'Listen here, Mr Kelsey, I got news for you. Annabelle's married.'

'Hm-hm,' David said insolently. 'I still want to speak to her.'

'Well, she's not here, I tell you. She's away with Grant.'

'Married?' David asked, with an embarrassing gasp. 'You mean they're married?'

'That's right, and they've got you to thank for it, Mr Kelsey. Annabelle was so upset after Sunday night, the doctor told her she shouldn't wait a minute longer. Grant married her and took her away yesterday, so there. They left town, and they're going to have po-lice pro-tec-tion in case you even *try* to make any more trouble. You'd best remember that.'

'Where is she?'

'Not gonna tell you. Not for all the money in the world.' Bang went the phone down.

They'd gone to Niagara Falls, David thought, if Grant had any say about it. He walked from the telephone into the kitchen and back again. Was it a lie? But that moron Mrs Barber wouldn't be able to lie that well. Involuntarily David shrugged and smiled a little, put his hands in his pockets, and whistled a made-up tune. Then he began to feel odd, opened a window and leaned on the sill, breathing deeply. It did not help. He lost his dinner in the bathroom, and though he listened automatically for the ringing of the telephone downstairs, even the ringing of the toilet tank was lost in the jangle of his own blood in his ears. He brushed his teeth, and avoided looking into the mirror over the basin.

The staircase was partly dark as he walked down, and he realized he was afraid. Afraid of something coming out of the shadows, something coming in the door. The standing lamp, again focusing on the telephone, made the brown-and-beige living room look extremely silent. David had another martini, sipping it slowly as he walked about the house. On the surface, his thoughts drifted between a policy of waiting until Grant Barber showed his true grossness, if he hadn't done this already, and of finding out where they were and paying them a visit. There was no doubt, however, that the old hag's threat about the police was deterring him somewhat. There might be a grain of truth in it. Once the police got hold of you, no use trying to explain. Besides, it would be embarrassing.

Keep cool, William Neumeister. Keep the home fires down. He opened windows, but he felt warm in his chest and in his hands, as if he had a high fever. Annabelle had made a mistake, that was all. Not the first. The second. The last.

What would Mrs Beecham advise him to do, he wondered. He remembered that Mrs Beecham had been sympathetic when she learned that there was a girl he was in love with. Her eyes had lighted up, and they had also grown sad and warm. He had felt as if he had a friend. And she was still there at the top floor back, nearest to heaven at the back door of life. He was on his way to the telephone, when he bethought himself that the telephone was on the ground floor and that Mrs Beecham couldn't get there. Besides, it was nearly midnight.

He woke up at six on the living room sofa, a sordid experience that was rendered less sordid by the fact that his face in the mirror looked much better. He whistled under the shower, shaved, dressed, and went down for a leisurely breakfast, which turned out to be a big glass of milk merely flavoured with coffee, and two shots of gin neat. William Neumeister was going to pull through today, all right. He could tell already that he would do a good day's work, quite good enough to make up for yesterday's mess.

26

'Hello, Dave. Wes. We're in Troy. Are we too early?'

'No,' David said blankly.

'If we are, we'll kill a little time here. So now we take Peterborough Road out of town and I follow your map, right?'

'Yes, that's right.'

'What's the matter? Did I wake you up?'

'No, I was up,' David said. 'Come on out. I'll be seeing you, Wes.'

'Ciao.' Wes hung up.

David looked at his watch. Eleven-five. Saturday morning. It was rather annoying. And the 'we.' Probably Effie. If it was Laura, he thought, he simply wouldn't let them in the house. No quarrels. He would pretend he had some engagement that he had to go out for. David walked restlessly about the house, frowning, glancing here and there to see if anything needed straightening. Nothing did. Then he went to the kitchen, looked into the refrigerator and the freezing unit, where a three-inch-thick steak in waxed paper took up most of the space. It was big enough for six people, which was fortunate.

He put some music on the phonograph, stopped the record

after a minute or two and put on a French woman singer, not the one Effie had played at her apartment. He put a few more French and Italian popular records on the spindle.

David jumped at the sound of a car door slamming. A second door slammed. He went to the front door and opened it. It was Effie with Wes. She carried a basket with a white towel over it.

'Hi, Dave!' she called. 'My, what a handsome house!'

'Hello, there, Dave!' Wes said. 'Good to see you!' He wrung David's hand, stamping his feet on the doormat.

'I brought a few goodies,' Effie said. 'Some fried chicken and a pie. Gosh, a piano! Do you play, Dave?'

They looked over the living room, complimenting everything, and David had to show them the upstairs too.

Now they were in the kitchen, he and Wes, and David was getting some ice out for Wes's drink. Effie had disappeared into the bathroom.

'You lost some weight,' Wes said. 'Are they working you hard?'

'Not a bit. They treat us well.'

In silence they strolled back to the living room.

David made an effort and said, 'I suppose you're going to stay the night, aren't you? Both of you?'

'That was the idea, wasn't it?' Wes said, rubbing his hands together. 'I'm looking forward to that steak you told us about. You know, Dave, I was pretty worried about you after you called Thursday. I'm glad you look as well as you do.'

David nodded, ashamed. *When* Thursday had he called? Had he called the factory or Wes's house? 'So you've still got your job, Wes?'

Wes smiled. 'It blew over, all right. They just like to scare you, and Laura's the same as the rest of them. Things are back just where they were. With her. She's not really worried about Effie, just pretending to be, so I thought, what the hell? I'll spend the weekend with her. At your place, of course. If anybody doesn't think it's respectable, they know what they can do with their dirty minds.' He laughed.

But David saw an anxious, scared expression on Wes's face as he turned to look at Effie coming into the room.

'Dave, I can't get over how attractive your house is!' Effie sat down primly in the center of the sofa.

Wes went to the kitchen to fix her a drink. David declined a drink, but said he would have one that evening with them. The long afternoon ahead took on mountainous proportions for David.

David laid the table for lunch, thinking this might inspire him to make a decision between a ham omelet and a Chinese meal that he could prepare very quickly from packages and cans, but Effie came in and saw him and immediately got out the fried chicken.

'All we have to do is make a big salad,' she said cheerfully.

David fixed Wes a fresh drink and brought it to him. Wes was looking at books in the living room.

'I tried to call Annabelle this week, Dave,' Effie said softly, when David came back into the kitchen. 'I heard about the marriage. I'm sorry, Dave.'

He nodded. 'News travels fast, doesn't it?'

'Well, I'm glad you're not as gloomy about it as I thought you'd be.' She smiled, and angular creases came into her flat cheeks. She wore a slim black skirt and a white blouse full of lacy ornaments. Effie, too, was thinner, her waist quite flat, and looking at her, David could understand why Wes had stopped his campaign for her. There was nothing attractive about her, David thought, except possibly her fluffy brown hair.

'It won't last,' David said calmly. He wished Effie would stop staring at him.

Effie tasted his salad dressing and praised it. She admired also the espresso machine. He braced himself for the next personal assault from her.

'I didn't speak to Annabelle herself. She wasn't there. This was Thursday night – after you called Wes. Do you think she's happy, Dave? I mean, is she in love with this man?'

'No.' He turned from the espresso machine, finished washing the lettuce that the water was running through, then stepped out the door and swung the wire basket until there were no more drops. 'Have you heard from the Beck's Brook police lately?' he asked as he came back in.

'No. Why?'

'William Neumeister went to them and explained why he hadn't been available. He was out of town.'

'You *did* go to them, Dave?' she asked, breathless with surprise.

'And wrote – and wrote a letter to Annabelle explaining the whole damned thing again.' David bent over the salad bowl, dumping the lettuce into it.

'Were they nice to you or –'

'Very nice.' He looked at her.

She might have turned into a pillar of salt.

'Annabelle was very pleased with the letter,' he added.

'She doesn't suspect anything?'

'What's there to suspect?'

Effie looked almost angrily. 'I don't know *how* you can be so cool about it. I don't understand you.'

And just then Wes came in. Otherwise David would have said he didn't know *how* she could get so damned excited about it.

Effie fixed another drink and took it with her to the table. Since Wes preferred beer to wine, David served beer and had one himself. The chicken was very good, the first half of the lunch very pleasant, and then both of them turned the conversation to him. It became personal. It was like an onslaught of little needles that became more and more painful, that he tried to ward off with shakes of his head, silences, with negations, frowns, but still they came at him and made their little punctures.

'So you saw this Grant? ... How did you happen to go up there? ... You really think he's a nice fellow, Dave?'

'He's all right. He's got two eyes and a nose.'

'You said on the phone he was second rate and a moron ... Are you going to stay on in this house, Dave?'

'Yes. Why not? I don't understand the reason for all these questions.'

'I could've predicted this. A girl either makes up her mind right away or you're out ... you're out ... you're out ...'

David got up from the table feeling sweaty and half sick.

After that, it really didn't stop, even when Wes tried to tell a joke, and when Effie tinkled on the piano for a while and Wes pretended to listen and to be amused. If Effie wasn't murmuring to him, Wes was.

'If you'd just tell us what's behind this, Dave – Effie and I are your friends. If you know Neumeister – Is he deliberately hiding?'

When Wes began his pre-dinner drinking at five, David joined him. David had told Wes he could have his room, as there was only one guest room and he thought Effie should have that. David intended to sleep in the room he called his sitting room, where most of his books were. Effie went upstairs around six to change her clothes, and David made a fire in the fireplace, more out of nervous energy than because he or anybody else wanted one.

'Dave,' Wes said, 'I'm sorry we asked so many questions, but you don't know how you sounded Thursday night. You're a lot different now.' Wes spoke quietly and earnestly, though his face had started to get the fuzzy look that came when he was on the way to being drunk.

'Well – how did I sound?'

'You sounded desperate. You said you had to see me. Maybe you'd had a few martinis, but I thought there was some truth in it. I got myself up here, all right. I even offered to come that night. Remember?'

David didn't remember. But what he did remember was that he wasn't drunk. He had had a good day Thursday and a good day Friday at the lab. 'What time did I call?'

'It was about nine. Laura answered. You said hello and you were – very polite to her. Laura was kind of pleased.'

'And what else did I say?'

'You said you were at the end, old boy,' Wes said as pleasantly as if he were narrating a joke. 'And you sounded pretty shaky. You said you were at the end with Annabelle.'

'"The end with Annabelle"?' David repeated, and gave a laugh. 'I must've been out of my head.'

'I said "why?" and you said because she'd gotten married again. You said she'd married another nobody. No, another second rater. A moron and second rate and a lot of other things.' Wes laughed. 'I don't think you think he's a nice guy. But maybe this is the only kind Annabelle likes.'

'That's not true. She fell in a trap just as she did before she married Gerald,' David said.

206

'What kind of a trap? A financial trap?'

'Maybe partly.'

'But there was you.'

'Maybe a trap with me then. I was too intense – or I didn't behave just the right way. But there's still time. This marriage isn't going to last. It's a joke.' David got up and walked to the fire.

'Well, I – I thought you'd given her up, Dave.'

The phrases! *Given her up.* As if one could do it merely by a decision! 'I'd rather not talk any more about it, Wes.' He stared at the flames. In those evenings, Wednesday, Thursday, and Friday evenings, he had played the game again, the William Neumeister game. He had drunk two martinis before dinner. It had been like the weekends in the Ballard house, almost like them. And what had slipped Thursday at 9 p.m., what had happened inside his head that he couldn't even remember now? He'd had a blackout. Wes was watching him.

Effie came down in fitted black slacks, and Wes made her a Scotch and soda and brought in the martini pitcher from the refrigerator to refill David's glass. Then David said he would go out and start the charcoal fire for the steak.

'I'll come out and help you,' Effie said.

'Honestly, I'd rather do it myself.' David shoved his fingers through his hair and felt at the end of his tether. He finished the martini quickly in the kitchen, and went out with matches and the charcoal sack and an old newspaper. No lighter fluid tonight. He wanted to make an honest little fire of paper and twigs and add the charcoal gradually. It was slow going, because even the driest twigs were dampish, but the fire made progress and he enjoyed it – until the kitchen door opened and Wes came out, catching his heel on the step, staggering a little.

'Not going to disturb you, old man, just bringing you some refreshment.' He had a new pitcher of martinis and a glass.

'Thanks, Wes, I've had about enough.'

'Come on.' Wes poured it.

David took it in his smutty right hand, and felt that he was in hell. When Wes had gone back into the house, David picked up the glass, which he had set on the rim of the barbecue pit, and hurled its contents toward the woods.

In the next hour or so, however, David drank at least two more martinis. They were almost a necessary anesthetic. He had taken a shower and put on a clean shirt and trousers. The baked potatoes were done, and Effie had made the salad, putting in an avocado that she had produced from the bottom of her basket. For a short while, David felt gay and happy, not at all annoyed because Wes kept insisting that they postpone the steak. He put out more cheese and crackers and black olives, and then they ran out of ice.

'You know what's the matter around here is Dave wasn't expecting us,' Wes said. 'He doesn't remember calling me, d'you know that?'

Effie looked stupid and astounded. It seemed to David that her face acquired a dozen creases as she tried to digest this terrible information.

'Maybe that was somebody else calling. Who knows?' David said, and his shame suddenly vanished. Wes had certainly blacked out enough in his time. David drained the nearly empty martini pitcher into his glass. It was mostly ice water and little glassy fragments of ice cubes.

Wes had turned the music up and he and Effie were dancing, Wes staggering and stepping on her feet. David laughed, and Effie looked at him in a hurt way, as if he had insulted her. Perhaps she wanted him to cut in, and out of politeness perhaps he should have, but the thought of circling her waist with his arm was distasteful. David had just sat down in the armchair when he heard Effie say, 'Newmester went to the police himself. The Beck's Brook police. They told me so last week.'

'He did?' Wes asked with a laugh. 'You might've *mentioned* it. Hey – am I supposed to believe you?'

Over Wes's shoulder, Effie gave David a slow wink, as if to say she was still in there plugging for him. David squirmed in his chair and looked at the floor.

'I don't think I *do* believe you,' Wes mumbled, amused. 'What's all this about protecting Newmester? Who the hell *is* he, anyway?'

A short, charged silence.

'Did you know that, Dave? That Newmester turned up at the police station?'

'Not until Effie told me today,' David said.

'Well – why'd he go to them, anyway? Did he say he'd killed Delaney or something?' Wes asked with more interest.

'Of course not,' Effie said quickly. 'The police wanted to ask him some more questions. I think Mrs Delaney wanted to talk to him too.' She hiccoughed.

'Annabelle,' Wes said, and David felt Wes's eyes on him. 'She wanted to talk to him?'

'Yes. They said Newmester went to see her in Hartford.'

'Hartford, that's the town,' Wes mumbled. 'Well, what happened?'

'Nothing. I guess he just told her how it was. An accident.'

'An accident,' Wes repeated. 'Hm-m. Well, I don't get it, I don't get it.' He began to dance more vigorously, squeezing Effie in his arm.

'Stop it, Wes! Let me go!'

'I didn't mean it!' Wes tried to hold her, but Effie pushed him violently away.

Effie staggered back herself, toward the fireplace. 'It's you I love,' she said to David. 'You! – Well, why shouldn't I say it?' she yelled to Wes. 'You know it anyway, and what do you do about it? Nothing!'

'What do you expect me to do about it?' Wes asked.

'David! David Kelsey!' Effie cried, bending her knees slightly, extending her arms to him.

David got up from the chair, afraid she would fling herself on top of him. 'I'd better start the steak.'

'Davy!' Effie caught his arm. 'Can't you listen to me for one minute?'

David took her wrist and, as gently as he could, forced her fingers to break their hold on his arm. 'Time I started the steak,' he said.

'Maybe I have had too much to drink, but *in vino veritas*, isn't that it, Dave? Listen, this may be the last time I'll ever – I'll ever see you –'

'Dave hopes so!' Wes said, laughing.

David wanted to laugh, and at the same time the staggering disorder of the two disturbed him.

'I don't see why,' Effie said, addressing herself to Wes, 'my few private words have to be mocked by you, Wes Carmichael.'

'I'm not mocking. Shall I go in another room?'

David was walking slowly toward the kitchen. Hearing Effie behind him, he turned and sidestepped to avoid her, and she caught herself on the doorjamb.

'I know I'm a disgrace — now,' she said, 'but that doesn't change the way I feel about you and what I *know* — to be true. You're wasting your life on that girl, Dave. Take some other girl. Maybe not me,' she quavered.

David made a move to walk away, but Effie held him. There was an angry disgust on Wes's face now as he lit a cigarette and hurled the match into an ashtray.

'Let Davy lead his own life,' Wes said. 'He's going to anyway, whatever you say.' He started for the kitchen with his empty glass, and bumped past David with no apology.

David flung Effie's arms down from his neck, a movement that brought her face against his chest. He stepped back from her, trying to extricate his wrists from her hold, and jerked one arm frantically, suddenly breathing hard with panic. He heard Wes sounding off again in the kitchen, snarling and bitter. But Effie was worse, mewling and whining, clinging like a snail. David retreated half across the kitchen, on the brink of striking her.

'Do' want anything to eat,' Wes was saying, walking off with his full glass.

'Then why don't you both leave !' David said.

Effie clung to the sink edge, looking down at the sink, weeping.

Wes turned pugnaciously, and David walked toward him. Then Wes thumped his glass down on something. 'Awright, I will leave ! I'll leave my gracious host !'

'And take Effie !' David said.

'Or maybe I won't leave,' Wes said. 'I don't know why we should do so much to oblige you, Mr Kelsey.'

'Call me Bill,' David said.

'What ?'

'Dave, watch out,' Effie said, wobbling around from the sink. 'Don't talk, Dave.'

'Who's Bill, Eff?'

'Nobody,' Effie said.

Nobody. David yanked the back door open and went out, slamming the door behind him. The wind blew refreshingly cold on his entire body. He walked past the yellow-red coals of the charcoal fire and went on to the edge of the woods, where he stood with his face turned up to the lopsided three-quarter moon. There was no sound but that of his breathing. He was gasping, his eyes blurred with tears, but he felt quite sober now, absolutely sober. The heavy moon floated through bluish clouds at a steady, easy rate. Once Annabelle had said to him, 'I love you too, David,' and there had been a moon that night, the same moon he was looking at. Where had the words gone to? Weren't they still in the air, somewhere? Couldn't they be found and collected, grabbed with the hands out of the air? Somewhere. Somewhere they were preserved. Things didn't vanish. Truth did not become a lie. Annabelle knew those words still existed. That was what troubled her. There would come a day when she would return to him. There was time yet, much time, only the time was so hard to get through. But one day she would be in this house, or some house with him.

'*Yes,* William Neumeister,' he murmured.

Then he heard a car door slam, a motor start. He listened as it backed, turned, and moved off down the dirt road. Thank God, he thought, and the pressure eased in his chest. He looked up at the moon and felt alone and happy and confident again. He breathed deeply a couple of times, then turned and walked back toward the house, opened the kitchen door and went in, not minding the mess he saw, because there was plenty of time for him to clean it up, alone. Time! Lots of it. He was free to stay up all night, if he chose, to read, to play his music, to write to Annabelle, to lie and dream of her, to dream of her one day in his bed. David seized a gin bottle, in which an inch of gin remained, and poured it into a glass, lifted it with an airy gesture and drank it off. He had a memory of finishing some other bottle once, on a dare, and bringing it off very well. Where had that been? When he set the glass down, he saw his old wristwatch a few inches away on the table. David shrugged.

He whistled as he crossed the living room. There was something like a pleasant, huge cloud in his brain, a weightless blue-gray cloud, the color of Annabelle's eyes. No troubles, no worries could get in. It was William Neumeister's cloud. Deep inside it he was a very clever, lucky fellow, William Neumeister. David climbed the stairs. He wanted to undress, shower the afternoon off himself, and put on his blue jeans again.

He stopped at the threshold of his room. 'Annabelle –'

Her arms were around his pillow, her brown hair on his pillow, and she was sound asleep.

He raced to her and took her shoulders, started to turn her gently, and then with revulsion took his hands away and in the same movement struck out at the face that was lifting itself from the pillow.

'*Davy!*'

He caught her with both hands, tugged her from the bed, and flung her from him. Up she came from the arm of the big chair, wailing at him, and this time David set his teeth and took her by the shoulders.

'Just shut up, shut up!' he muttered, and thrust her from him. He turned to the bed and absently brushed it with the flat of his hand and smoothed its blanket, which had only been lain upon, not under, but he grabbed the pillow from under the bedcover and threw it behind him against the wall.

Effie did not get up. He supposed she was waiting for him to pick her up and comfort her, and he smiled a grim smile and went into the bathroom to wash his hands. He filled his hands with water and washed his face and scrubbed it with a towel. He was through with the house. Effie had ruined it. There was nothing in it that he wanted any longer. Except the pictures of Annabelle in his desk that he had removed from the mantel this morning before Wes and Effie arrived, and perhaps he should also take a few papers from his desk. And he would never come back. Never.

David went into the sitting room, took his checkbook and the cache of extra money he kept in a cubbyhole of his desk, took his billfold and a packet of papers with a rubber band around them that were the only important papers he possessed. He thought of taking some clothes with him, but the task of choosing them and packing them in a suitcase seemed too tedious. He ran downstairs, hesitated for a moment when he realized there were so many lights on, then yanked a trenchcoat out of the front closet.

He propped the garage doors open and backed his car out. Just as he was turning the car to go down the dirt lane, he saw a pair of headlights on the road. David drove quickly down the lane. The car had stopped just before the turn into the lane, and now David saw it was Wes' car.

'Hey! Dave!' Wes called. 'Wait a minute!'

But David drove around him, past him, heading for the highway.

27

He drove just a little faster than the speed limit, and he didn't know or care where the dark highway went to. A sense of futility and of sordidness sat blackly on his brain. He realized that he would have to go back to his house at some time, but he could not bear to think of that now. At least they would be gone when he got back, because he was not going back tonight and maybe not tomorrow. He still seethed with anger and shame at the memory of Wes staggering about the kitchen, Wes telling him he ought to see a psychiatrist! Had Wes ever taken a look at himself, drinking himself to death? The dragging monotony of Wes's marriage depressed David nearly as much as the Situation with Annabelle. Annabelle was married again, true, and that was tragic enough, but at least, David reminded himself, his own attitude was a positive one. He still knew that one day – Could anything that positive be said about Wes Carmichael?

Feeling suddenly tired, he let the car slow down. He drove at thirty miles an hour, his hands relaxed on the bottom of the steering wheel. No, he wouldn't go back to the house tonight, even though he was pretty sure they would be gone. He would stop at some motel and register as William Neumeister, just in case Wes got it into his drunken head to call the police to look for him. He didn't think Wes would call the police. Wes would have another drink, curse some more about David's rudeness, pile Effie in the car with him and drive off. Tomorrow Wes might call and apologize. Effie was a different matter. David was sorry he had struck her. *Had* he struck her? He had thrown her off his bed. The memory of her lying on the floor returned to reproach him. No apology would make up for that. He realized he had gone too far, that he must have had a moment of total aberration to think she was Annabelle lying on his bed, just because Effie's hair was nearly the color of Annabelle's! And he remembered now that he had even told Wes to call him Bill. It was very disturbing. But maybe Wes wouldn't remember, or if he did remember, wouldn't connect Bill with Neumeister. David remembered Effie saying, in an alarmed tone, 'Dave, watch out.' He pressed the accelerator pedal down, and his only comforting thought was that he was putting more and more distance between himself and them.

He saw a signpost with a number of towns and their distances on it, and his eyes immediately found Froudsburg 23. He took the road. It would be late when he got there, and there was nothing he wanted to do there, but he felt drawn to it. Perhaps something would happen, driving those dark and ugly streets again. And perhaps he could see Mrs Beecham.

When he reached Froudsburg, he drove directly toward the house, and at the corner where he turned into Ash Lane he slowed to ease the car over a fat wrinkle of tar that he could not see but knew was there. It was like putting on an old comfortable shoe, going up the driveway, parking his car far to the left against the scraggly hedge where he had always put it. There was a light in the house, but it was in Mr Muldaven's room — unless someone else was there now. David turned the rattly metal door ringer. There was no light in the hall. Mr Muldaven's door did not open, but David heard footsteps, and, to his surprise, Sarah opened the door for him.

'Good evening, Sarah.'

'Mr Kelsey!'

'Is anybody up? Sorry to be calling so late.' He went in.

'Did you want to see Mrs Mac? She's gone to bed,' Sarah told him, her face already fallen back to its habitual apathetic expression.

'Well, I mainly wanted to see Mrs Beecham,' David said

quietly, strangely excited and depressed at once by the familiar smell of the place, a smell of old carpets and of indefinable foods. 'It's pretty important,' David added. 'Could you find her for me, Sarah?'

As Sarah hesitated, Mr Muldaven's door opened. He stood there in a nightshirt, barefoot.

'Why, David Kelsey!' he said, too shy to come into the hall in his nightshirt, but he extended his hand as David approached him.

'How're you, Mr Muldaven?' David asked, touched by the old man's friendliness and by his firm handshake. 'How's everything?'

'Pretty good. Can't complain. We miss you around here, David.'

It was as if all the trouble had never been. Suddenly the house seemed full of old friends instead of cranks and gossips.

'I miss all of you, too,' David said quietly and released the man's hand.

Sarah turned on the stairs. 'You really want me to call her, Mr Kelsey?'

'Yes, please,' David said. 'Tell her it's David Kelsey.' He felt confident that she would be glad to see him.

'Come back and see us some time, Davy,' said Mr Muldaven. 'Come for Sunday dinner.'

'I will,' David said.

'Good night and good luck to you, Davy.'

'Good night, sir. Same to you.'

David thought that Mr Muldaven had never called him Davy before, and he felt sure that he had never called the old fellow sir. David looked up the stairwell, which seemed hallowed by time now, by the better, more serious and dedicated life he had led when he had lived here. He felt that his relationship with Annabelle had been better here, and that thought, that *fact*, was agonizing to realize. And after all, why was he here? He was here because he realized that, and had realized it in the car. He touched the papers in his trenchcoat pocket and, as silently as he could, climbed the stairs.

Sarah was just coming down from the third floor. 'She says you can go in, Mr Kelsey.'

'Thank you. Is anybody else up?' He continued awkwardly, 'Because I'll need a couple of signatures. Maybe yours and Mr Muldaven's.'

'Signatures?' Sarah said as if she had never heard the word before.

'I'll tell you in a couple of minutes,' David said, and stood aside for her to pass him.

Mrs Beecham's door was a little ajar. He knocked.

'Just come on in, David!' said Mrs Beecham in a high, happy, welcoming voice.

David went in, smiling uncontrollably with gratitude and with relief. She was propped up in bed in a white nightcap, a white nightgown with long sleeves and ruffles at the wrists. A small light under a pink half shade burned on her night table. 'I hope you'll pardon the hour,' he said.

'Why, of course I will. What's night or day to an old woman like me? Just hand me my glasses, if you will, David, I want to see you. They're over there by my sewing things. Just to one side, the right side, I think. In the morning when I get up, I don't need them, just to get up and dress, you know, because I know where everything is.'

He handed them to her.

'Now let's see what you're looking like.'

Her right eye, which he saw clearly by the light of the lamp, looked at him through its cloud of cataract, large and curious and kind. David picked up her ruffled wrist and shook it a little, with awkward affection.

'You're looking thinner, that's how,' she remarked. 'What's your trouble, David? Anything?'

'Oh, no, no trouble. I came to –'

'Sit down, David. Pull up the armchair.'

'I came to bring you a little present. In a way, I *hope* it'll be a present.' He felt tortured by his embarrassment, the embarrassment of self-revelation, but he was determined to go through with it. 'Just a little matter about my life insurance,' he said, concentrating on his packet of papers. 'I want you to be my beneficiary. It's just a matter of changing one line. And I'll write the company tomorrow too, of course.'

'What? Beneficiary? Why me, David?'

'Because I want you to have it.'

'Life insurance. Why, you'll outlive me.'

'You never know,' David said quickly, and drew his pen through Annabelle Stanton Kelsey, which was printed, and printed Mrs Molly Beecham above it. He added the address of the boardinghouse. Mrs Beecham protested all the while, but he paid no attention. He handed her the paper and the pen. 'Now I want you to sign this, please. Here where it says beneficiary. Don't argue with me about it,' he pleaded.

She had picked up her mounted reading glass from the bedtable, and she was looking through it at the enlarged fine print. 'Annabelle,' she said, and looked up at him. 'Wasn't that the girl, David?'

Where had she heard? Where had she heard definitely? Or had she, with the wisdom of old age, been able to guess it? Where she had heard didn't matter now. Only that it was the truth and she knew it. 'Yes,' David said with a slight gasp. 'She was the girl. But she wouldn't take it, I know. That's why somebody else's name has to be there, you see.'

'What's happened, David?'

'Nothing's happened! I just decided – I happen to know she wouldn't take the money anyway, so there's no use having her name there.'

'And what about Effie, David?' Mrs Beecham asked sadly, and there was a small note of reproach in it.

David shrugged. 'I haven't seen her – until this weekend. She and my friend Wes came up. They're there now.' David stood up. 'I just had to get away for a while. I'll go back now. I don't know what was the matter with me tonight. I've got to be going now, Mrs Beecham. Please sign that, will you?'

'All right, David. If you want me to.' As if she were indulging a child, she began to write in the large, patient scrawl that David knew well.

He walked restlessly to the door and turned back, came to her and carefully took the paper from her. 'I'll get some signatures downstairs. Witnesses, in case I need them. I don't even know if I need them.' He was suddenly dry in the throat, and the room seemed airless. 'Forgive me, Mrs Beecham.'

'For what, David? Now you get some rest tonight. You

shouldn't drive all that way back to Troy. I think there's a room on the second floor that's free. Not your old room,' she said, smiling. 'A new fellow's got that. Sarah's sleeping in now and she's always up till all hours. She'll show you –'

'No, I'll go, Mrs Beecham. Thank you. Thank you,' he said, opening the door. 'Good night.'

'Bless you, David. And come back to see me.'

Downstairs, David hesitated, then rapped firmly on Mr Muldaven's door, where now no light showed.

David had his pen ready. Mr Muldaven seemed surprised and asked some questions, but David avoided answering them. He only thanked Mr Muldaven and apologized for waking him. And then he approached Sarah, who as it happened was just coming out of the back room left which was the room Wes had had when he stayed here. She was dressed in a ruffly party dress of some kind, and she seemed embarrassed to have run into him.

'I was just going out on a date,' she said. 'Meeting my date at the dance.'

They stood under the ugly hall light and Sarah signed it, resting it on the wicker table where so many letters from Annabelle had lain. How many? Only five or six. David closed his eyes.

He drove Sarah to the place where she wanted to go, a dance hall on the second floor of an office building on Main Street. David had not known the dance hall existed.

Then he was free and alone again, and he felt extremely tired. He drove for half an hour or so, and stopped at a mediocre motel. He wrote *Wm Neumeister, N.Y.C.* on the registration card, and paid his five dollars in advance to a sleepy, gray-haired man behind the desk.

'Want to be waked up any special time?' the man asked.

'No, thanks. I'll wake up,' David replied.

He took a shower and went to bed naked between the clean sheets, dogtired and relaxed, too tired to be disturbed by his hunger, and he fell asleep at once.

When he awakened, it was precisely eight by his watch, and the sun was pouring through the Venetian blinds. He lay for a few moments thinking, wondering if he should call his house before he went back. Apologize. Or make sure they had gone.

Did he owe them an apology, or did they owe him one? He couldn't come to a conclusion about that, and he couldn't have cared less. All he was sure of was that he did not want to come face to face with them. He got up and dressed. He would drive to some quiet place, take a walk in the woods if he could find any woods, and return to his house in mid-afternoon. He needed a shave, but that could wait until he got home.

At the instant David opened the door to go out, there was a knock on it, and the skinny, gray-haired man stepped back, surprised.

'Just going to waken you,' he said. 'There's a –'

'Didn't need it, thanks,' David said.

'I had a call from the police,' the man said with excitement. 'They gave me a license number and it's yours.'

'What?'

'They're looking for somebody called Kelsey. That isn't you, is it?'

'No,' David said. He looked past the man, toward the highway where the office was. There were no police cars.

'Maybe it's a mistake – maybe,' the man said. 'They called me just ten minutes ago, y'see, and I looked over the cards. You didn't write your license number down last night, and I thought, well, there's nobody here named Kelsey. Then as I was walking by – just going to wake up number eight – I seen your license plate. You don't even know a David Kelsey?'

'No, I don't,' David said, walking toward his car. He opened the door.

'You own that car?'

'Yes,' David said.

The old man stood on the low step in front of the door, staring at David's license plate. Then he looked at a card in his hand, checking the number again.

The man might yet call the police and tell them about it, David thought. And the police would make a note of the name Neumeister. David heard his own voice, strangely remote, saying, 'I'd better stop in your office and fill out my license number anyway. I'm sure there's a mistake somewhere.'

'Okay,' the man said, and with an absent gesture toward his office, he walked off.

David stopped his car outside the office, facing the highway, and left the engine running. He waited patiently while the old man looked among a dozen cards, and tremblingly produced one.

'Did they say why they're looking for this fellow?' David asked as he took the card.

'Why, *murder*, they said. *Murder*.'

David's eyes met the old man's for one instant, then he dashed out the door and jumped into his car.

'Hey! Hey, there! Stop!'

David shot up to sixty and seventy, and then with an effort forced himself to slow down. He crushed the motel's card into his jacket pocket. Maybe it wasn't true. They could have told the old man 'murder' to make him be more thorough in looking for the license number. And yet David knew all along that he had been afraid Effie might have been dead. The memory of her falling to the floor, of her lying there motionless, had reminded him of Gerald Delaney's body lying motionless against his steps. For an instant, he thought of returning to his house and facing whatever was there, but the very thought brought panic, and he pressed the accelerator pedal again. No, if she were dead, it was just all up. Everything was all up. David breathed quickly through his dry lips, watching for a deserted road on no matter which side of the highway. He felt that external things – the slowness of his car, the malicious absence of side roads – deliberately held him up. At last there was a one-lane dirt road with a pair of ruts in it, and David took it. He had to bump a couple of hundred yards to reach some trees behind which the car might be hidden from the highway, and when he got to the trees, there was a farmhouse in sight, not far away. He got out anyway, and, with his trenchcoat over his arm, walked back toward the highway.

He hailed the first car, but it didn't stop for him. Nor did the next and the next. Finally, a slow, battered truck stopped, and David climbed to the seat, sweating.

'Thanks a lot,' David said.

The man nodded, shifting the noisy gears. 'How far you going?'

'Oh – the next town.'

Ryder?'

David didn't know if he meant a town or not. He said yes.

'Have to let you off about a mile this side,' the man said.

'That's okay.'

A police car passed them, a highway patrol car. But judging from the truck's speedometer, the police car was going no faster than the prescribed rate of fifty miles per hour.

They discussed apples. The man was an apple farmer. He told David about his orchards and how much better the apples had been two years ago and why. He was a thick-legged, red-faced man of forty or so, and he had a wife and three kids. His life sounded unbelievably uncomplicated and peaceful. David felt a little suspicious of it – as if the fellow were going to turn on him and point to him suddenly and say, 'You're David Kelsey, aren't you?'

He let David out at a turn-off, and David walked on. He loosened his collar and took his tie off. Ryder was a tiny town, everything was closed, and David felt highly conspicuous. In a drugstore, he learned that the next bus arrived in twenty-five minutes and went to Schenectady. It stopped just outside the drugstore. David thanked the man and ordered a cup of coffee. He took a Troy paper from the stack by the door, the same one he had delivered to his house on Sundays, removed the comic section and looked at the first page and the second, the third and fourth. Certainly nothing about a murder. But the paper had probably gone to press early last night, or even yesterday afternoon. David finished his coffee, got off the stool, and walked about the little drugstore, staring at lipsticks under a glass counter, at hideous birthday cards in a rack, wondering what he should do, and knowing very well he was not thinking.

Suppose Wes had just gone into the bedroom, seen Effie unconscious – maybe she'd really been unconscious – and called the police in a panic? Wasn't that most likely what he had done? David cursed his stupidity in abandoning his car. It would be found immediately, and the police would think David Kelsey was either off his rocker or that he knew he was guilty of murder. His picture would be in the papers, somebody on the Beck's Brook police force would see it and say, 'Why, that's William Newmester, the man who had the fight with Delaney!'

David debated going back for his car, hitching a ride back or hiring a taxi. His car was not fifteen miles away.

The Schenectady bus arrived, and because it was standing there and promised movement, he took it. From Schenectady, he thought, there would be frequent buses to Troy.

He reached Schenectady a little after twelve, and immediately asked about a bus to Troy. There was a bus at 2:20 p.m. If he wanted something earlier, he could try the trains, the ticket seller told him. David thought he would try the railroad station.

As he was leaving the bus station, a newsboy approached him with a local extra, and David was about to shake his head when he saw the front page. She lay on the floor, her head awkwardly propped against the leg of a familiar chair. David reached for the paper.

'That's ten cents, sir.'

David's ears had begun to ring.

'Ten cents, sir.'

He pulled some coins out of his pocket and dropped them into the boy's hand. Then he walked to a bench and sat down. He felt he was going to pass out, and he tried to concentrate for a moment on the figure of a man several yards away. Then he looked down at the paper. DRUNKEN WEEKEND LEADS TO MURDER, said the headline. 'The body of Elfrida Brennan, 26, of Froudsburg, N.Y., gave mute testimony ...' David skimmed down the two columns. Her neck had been broken. Wesley Carmichael, 32, a chemist employed by Cheswick Fabrics, Inc. of Froudsburg, and a friend of Kelsey and the murdered woman, said that there had been an argument, Carmichael had driven away in his car to cool off, and had returned to find Kelsey leaving the house in his car and Miss Brennan dead in the upstairs bedroom.

David looked at Effie's picture again, a close-up of her shoulders and her half-averted face, and tried to realize that when the picture was taken she was not alive, and that she had not been alive when he left the house, or that room.

He got up and walked from the station, crossed a street and kept on walking. Dead by his hand. Like Gerald. But Gerald had not been like this. He had been in his senses then, laughing at Gerald one minute, pushing him, and then Gerald had been dead. But this: he couldn't remember having hit Effie, certainly couldn't remember having throttled her or whatever it took to break somebody's neck. And it was unspeakably more horrible to have caused a woman's death than a man's. He dropped down on a bench in a park and passed into a state that was not quite sleeping or fainting, though his thoughts stopped as if some mechanism had been turned off. He sat motionless until his mind filled with an abstract, imageless horror, and he jumped up and walked on. He remembered that the police were looking for him, and now he glanced around the little park and the adjacent sidewalks for a policeman, and if he had seen one, he would have gone up to him and identified himself and collapsed. It was all up, just as he had really known. He had known it from the time the skinny fellow in the motel had asked him if his name was Kelsey. It was another unforgivable blunder of David Kelsey. This time it would be blazoned in every newspaper. This time Annabelle would know all about it.

David began to run, at first fast and then at a trot. He ran for three or four blocks, then walked, and finally stopped a man and timidly asked where the railroad station was. He walked in the direction the man had pointed.

Without any forethought and without any plan, he caught a train for New York. He sat in a corner seat, closed his eyes to the green plastic seat back in front of him, and tried once more to think. But he fell asleep and dreamed that he was being sucked down a deep, blackish chasm that was part of a mine. Nothing pushed him, and his descent had nothing to do with gravity yet he could not stop himself or reach the sides of the chasm to hold onto anything to stop himself, and his drifting, swirling fall produced a nausea that he fought as he had fought against fainting. Then he awakened, not knowing if he had slept two minutes or an hour. His watch said four-ten and meant nothing to him. He saw Annabelle's face when she learned that Effie Brennan was dead and that she had been slain by David Kelsey. David squirmed in his seat and rubbed his moist palms together. William Neumeister would never have made such a stupid mistake. William Neumeister would have been cool and calm in the face of Effie Brennan's maudlin protestations of her love. David saw himself again in Mrs McCartney's second-floor room, saw himself patiently sweeping the floor, quietly lying on the bed with a book, and very quietly standing by the triad of windows, looking out onto a winter view of leafless black trees. That man, too, was William Neumeister.

David sat up and reached for the tie in his jacket pocket. He put it on and tied it, and glanced at his reflection in the window to see if it was straight. He would register in some hotel as William Neumeister tonight, and he thought he would choose the Barclay. A last gamble on William Neumeister's luck. David smiled a bitter smile, and wished he had a cigarette with him. Smoking was permitted in the car he was in. David made a sudden grab for the newspaper, and looked over the double-column story again very carefully, not reading it, but looking for the capital of N of Neumeister. William Neumeister had not been mentioned.

He got a shave in Grand Central Station, then walked up Lexington to the Barclay and registered. When they asked about his luggage, he said it was checked at Grand Central and that he was going to pick it up later. In his billfold he had seventy-nine dollars. His checkbook now, of course, was useless.

His room was pleasant, extraordinarily pleasant to David. The heavy door made a deep, reassuring sound when it closed. The window looked on Lexington Avenue, and he was eight stories up. He ordered two martinis.

He drank the first martini as he strolled about the room. On the second, he toasted Annabelle and William Neumeister. Lucky William Neumeister! It wasn't his fault that all this had happened. It was the fault of David Kelsey, that fool who had never done anything right, never had succeeded in anything – except perhaps passing exams in school – David Kelsey whom no girl looked at twice, except a girl like Effie Brennan! David had an impulse to crash his fist through the windowpane, and he turned suddenly away and set down his empty glass.

'I'll take a shower, Annabelle,' he said, 'and then we'll go out and have dinner. Where would you like to go?'

Under the shower, he sang foolishly, as if he were much drunker than he was.

'William Neumeister,' he said solemnly to himself. Then, 'Mr Neumeister! A letter for you!' He imagined an envelope addressed to William Neumeister in Annabelle's handwriting. 'Mr Neumeister.' It was a pleasant, honest-sounding name, even when he heard it pronounced 'Newmester,' as most people did pronounce it. It was a bit annoying that so many people said, 'Is that 'N-o-y?' if they were starting to write it. Or had so many? David could recall only the police in Beck's Brook doing that. The memory of Neumeister's successful hurdling of the Delaney crisis came back, bolstering and cheering.

David dressed, debated ordering another martini, and decided to get one at the restaurant. 'Tomorrow, Annabelle,' he said into the mirror as he combed his hair, 'I'll buy a couple of shirts and maybe even a suit. I can't go around New York in slacks and an odd jacket, can I? They might not let us in at El Morocco's.'

He thought of signing a large check to the hotel in William Neumeister's name – what else could he do, anyway, if he stayed here very long? – thus getting some extra cash. He could write his bank and tell them to honor checks signed by William Neumeister and to take the money out of Kelsey's account, Kelsey being a dead duck. It rather pleased him to think of exploiting Kelsey and leaving him flat broke. Or perhaps he could risk signing a large check to Neumeister with Kelsey's endorsement and, if the hotel said anything, tell them it was another David Kelsey who had signed it. Kelsey wasn't such a rare name. David lit a cigarette (he had bought some from a machine in the barbershop) and continued strolling about his room. It had occurred to him that the murder story might be forgotten in a few days, a thought that brought delicious relief to his mind. He was beginning to see it objectively: murders, deaths, fatal accidents came by the dozens every week. He had been making entirely too much out of it. Rather, David Kelsey had. William Neumeister knew how to assess such things. David decided it would be quite possible to make out a large check to William Neumeister and sign it David Kelsey. If the hotel wanted to wait a few days before they gave him the money, since it was on a bank in another town, let them take a few days.

'Tomorrow,' he said briskly. 'Tomorrow morning.'

He went to a small but substantial-looking restaurant off Lexington Avenue, the sort of place where he thought his tweed jacket would not be conspicuously inappropriate, and ordered two martinis. The waiter put them in front of him, but David pushed the salt and pepper shakers to one side and set the other glass opposite him.

'William Neumeister salutes you,' he said quickly as he lifted his glass. 'My darling Annabelle, I'm glad you like the room.'

28

The next morning William Neumeister was mentioned in the *Tribune*. David was breakfasting in bed as he read it, and he read it with a profound sadness and regret. It had all come about through Wes Carmichael. He stated that David Kelsey had said 'Call me Bill' the day that Elfrida Brennan was slain, and william Neumeister was the name of the owner of the house on whose steps Gerald Delaney had been killed last January. The police, the paper said, had looked for Neumeister for several weeks following the death of Delaney, but had been unable to find him. Wesley Carmichael – the obtuse ass, even Effie had been brighter – had stated that Kelsey denied knowing Neumeister, yet Carmichael had once seen Kelsey entering his house in Ballard. It was astounding to David that Wes had not yet put one and one together, astounding that nobody else had, and common sense told him that somebody would in a matter of time, perhaps a matter of hours, perhaps now. Annabelle would, David thought. Naturally, the police were now looking for William Neumeister.

David got out of bed. He had known that his days were numbered, but he had not thought the number would be this small. He got some writing paper from the table in the room and wrote to his insurance company, advising them of the change in the beneficiary of his policy. That had been his number-one morning chore, really his only chore for that day. He would have to buy a long envelope to mail the policy back in, and he put the policy and his letter in his jacket pocket so he would not forget to take care of it when he went out.

'Neumeister, chin up,' he said into the mirror. 'After a shave and a haircut, you'll feel better.' He turned to smile at his imaginary Annabelle, knowing she was imaginary, and yet feeling, as he had never felt it before, her presence in that empty space between himself and the corner of the room where a beige armchair stood, seeing her more clearly than he had ever seen her before, in a blue robe whose details he could not see, but she was in it and what else mattered? He kissed her before he went into the bathroom to shower.

It just might be, he thought as he rode down in the elevator, that the police would be entering the hotel lobby now.

But they were not, and David left his key at the desk and went out.

He had certainly enough cash to buy a couple of shirts, but he was reluctant to part with his cash. And Neumeister still seemed a far safer name to sign than David Kelsey. He had a brief fantasy of being accosted by the police and of protesting that he *was* William Neumeister and that David Kelsey was a friend of his. Oh, a sad fellow, Kelsey, always getting himself in messes. But what had Neumeister done to get himself in trouble with the law? Nothing. Sorry, but he could not direct them to David Kelsey, hadn't heard from David in weeks.

David would have gone to Brooks Brothers, but the substantial façade of the store suggested to him that they would ask for some identification, a driver's license, for instance, if he tried to sign a check. Smaller shops were less strict, he thought. At a small shop, he chose two white shirts, one of them the kind that was said to need no ironing, and asked the salesman if he would accept a check. The salesman said he would, if he could show some identification. David pretended to search for his driver's license in his billfold, though William Neumeister had never had a driver's license. And suddenly he came upon the little square card from the Beck's Brook library. He had forgotten to throw it away. A piece of luck – Neumeister luck !

'I seem to have left my license at home. Will this do?'

The salesman looked at the card with its countersignature of the librarian, smiled, and nodded. 'I guess so. Will there be anything else, sir?'

'I could also use a suit.'

The check came to $138.14, and of course was absolutely

useless, as Neumeister's account in Beck's Brook had been closed, and this was a Troy bank anyway. David thought that in due time David Kelsey might reimburse the shop. He would keep the sales bill.

He got a shave at a barbershop in the Fifties. The barber bent to look at him in profile. He smiled. David found him tiresome, though at least he did not try to make conversation. When the shave was finished, the barber picked up a tabloid that he had been reading when David walked in, and pointed to a picture in it. The picture looked very familiar, but it took David a second or two to remember what it was: Effie's sketch of him.

'You look like this fellow,' the barber said, smiling. 'Don't you think so?'

David smiled a little, too. 'I see what you mean,' he said calmly and reached for the money to pay. 'But my name's Neumeister.'

'Oh,' said the barber. And he said nothing more.

David bought an envelope at a stationery store, addressed it with a pen there, and mailed off his insurance policy. Then he walked back toward his hotel. He felt better with his shave, and a clean shirt would pick him up still more. He imagined Annabelle waiting for him in the hotel room, looking at his new shirts, telling him which she preferred him to wear today. Then they would discuss what they would do with the rest of the morning and where they might have lunch. Perhaps at the Museum of Modern Art, David thought, after they had browsed through the exhibition for an hour or so. He would tell her about his new suit – she might not like it, after all – that needed an alteration in the back of the jacket and would be ready that afternoon. Feeling mildly curious about the picture of David Kelsey, he bought both tabloids at a newsstand near the hotel, and took them up to his room.

First, he opened the box with the shirts. He did not really speak to Annabelle now, but he imagined a conversation between them. Annabelle smiled, and pointed to the shirt with the buttoned-down collar, the one that needed no ironing. He put it on, propped his two pillows side by side against the bedstead, and lay down with the tabloids.

228

And here was all the dreary story of Elfrida Brennan's hope-less love for the indifferent young man who was destined to kill her. David glanced over the story, looking for William Neu-meister's name. Again it was not here. But that was just a matter of time too, he thought: the Beck's Brook police would be able to identify the sketch as William Neumeister. Why hadn't he realized that as soon as he saw the sketch in the barbershop? It was just as Effie had predicted, the sketch was going to betray him. Effie was going to get her revenge, all right. He looked at the paper again and made himself read every word. David Kel-sey's car, a light blue Dodge convertible, had been found yester-day on a road off the highway south of Ryder, New York. Darius McCloud, 68, proprietor of the Sunrise Motel on Highway 9, stated that Kelsey had spent Saturday night at his motel, but had registered under another name that he was unable to remember. Kelsey had dashed away, etc., etc., when McCloud had identified his license number as that of David Kelsey. They had inter-viewed his former landlady, Mrs Ethel McCartney of Frouds-burg, who said she was 'shocked and just couldn't believe it.' He had been a 'model lodger.' At midnight Saturday, Kelsey had called at the boardinghouse and transferred his life insur-ance to Mrs Molly Beecham, 88, another boarder who had lived in the house for eleven years. David Kelsey was described as a brilliant but eccentric young scientist, 'a recluse' who had spent his weekends for nearly two years in solitude while giving out a story that he was visiting an ailing mother in a nursing home. The brutal, hit-or-miss harshness of the prose made David feel he was reading about someone else, a case history in a textbook of abnormal psychology. David was more affected by Dr Os-bourne's simple words than by anything else he read: 'I knew David was dangerously strained because of personal problems. He mentioned a girl he intended to marry. In the last weeks, I repeatedly suggested that he take a rest from his work. He did not choose to. It is regrettable that such a talented young man has so damaged his future.'

Damaged. The word held out a sweet hope. He closed his eyes and thought about it. Damaged didn't mean destroyed or killed or finished. If something was damaged, it might be repaired. And then he remembered the sketch, and the Beck's Brook policemen.

He turned to Annabelle on the bed, embraced her, and began to cry. But he cried only a few seconds and jumped up again, washed his face and combed his hair.

'William Neumeister,' he said jauntily into the mirror, 'pick yourself up. You may not be a brilliant scientist, but Annabelle likes you. She likes you a lot better than she ever liked David Kelsey. She's sharing a hotel room with you, and you're not even married.' He spoke quietly, as if Annabelle in the next room might hear him if he spoke any louder. He went back into the bedroom and proposed a tour of the Museum of Modern Art, followed by lunch there, and Annabelle was delighted with the idea.

'Oh, wear the tweed one,' he said. He saw her standing by the closet, one hand touching a hanger. The hand moved, and she took down a very full-cut dress of brown tweed, much like one of his old jackets.

She fastened a broad leather belt around it. Generous folds on her generous figure. Most women, he thought as he watched her making up in the mirror, would have been too vain to wear such a dress unless they were emaciated. She was ready in no time.

They walked to Fifth Avenue and up. It was a beautiful sunny day. They looked at barometers in a shop window, then at women's shoes, then at a travel display with African spears and shields in the window. At the Museum's ticket window, he said, 'Two, please,' and got his tickets and change. He took the tickets to the man in the gray uniform at the entrance.

'Two, sir?' said the ticket taker, looking past David.

'Yes,' David said, and walked in.

There were photographs downstairs. David, that morning, preferred them to paintings. Some photographs had been made through microscopes, showing the paths of atom particles, and these to David seemed the most beautiful, combining art and science. He explained them to Annabelle, the concentric patterns, the magnetic lines. A woman edged back from him to give him room, and David smiled. A tall, gray-haired man smiled at him too. Holding hands, David and Annabelle looked at photographs of people in the dust bowl of Oklahoma and at old masterpieces of Steichen.

The Museum's cafeteria seemed crowded, and after all not good enough for Annabelle on a special day like this. David walked eastward on Fifty-third Street, and chose Michel's, where he also had to wait for a table, but he waited at the bar and had a martini. He had time to order a second, which he did not really want (he pretended Annabelle had declined a cocktail), and he took it with him to his table. Annabelle was really drinking it, he felt, and he was sure not all of its alcohol would have effect on him alone. The lunch was splendid, and, having had no wine, he finished it off with a brandy.

'It's our honeymoon,' he murmured over Annabelle's protestations. 'We may as well pretend it is, don't you think?' He knew it wasn't, of course. They had been married quite a time. With the coffee and brandy, he had a moment of clarity, and saw the curved top of the chair back, empty in front of him. But what was the use of that? With the very slightest effort, he had her back again, smiling, her hair soft and a little long, in her brown tweed dress, and some perfume, more naïve than the kind she used at night, just perceptible to him across the table.

They walked down Madison to pick up his suit. He tried the jacket on in front of a mirror.

'You're feeling fine today,' the clerk said out of the blue.

It rather startled David, but he smiled. 'I'm on my honeymoon,' he said.

'A-ah! Well, I hope she likes it as well as you think she will.'

When David next looked at the clerk, he seemed to have gone sour. Probably envious, David thought.

He bought cigarettes, and at a liquor store a bottle of champagne. As soon as he had the champagne, he realized he could have ordered a bottle in the hotel, but it would have meant an immediate fuss with an ice bucket, and having a bottle on his dresser top would make the room more like home. He also bought an evening paper. It was of slight interest to him to see how things were progressing in regard to David Kelsey, of the same interest, he thought, as a stock market quotation might be if he played, and perhaps not even as much. All relative, because if a man had little money, he valued it, and he did not at all value his life or himself. He had turned loose of himself, he felt, and in that he had found life, perhaps eternal life. He had certainly found happiness. He could certainly look any man in the eye. He had certainly lost his frowns, his sweating, his intolerance of things that were unavoidable, like slow elevators. He was William Neumeister, and even if the police were looking for him, Neumeister's luck hadn't run out. Not by a long shot

In his room, he put the suit box on the bed, opened it, and hung the jacket and trousers on hangers that he hooked over the top of the closet door. 'We'll do something nice tonight,' he said quietly. 'I suppose I should have gotten tickets for a show, though.' The fact that he hadn't depressed him momentarily, but Annabelle did not seem to mind. There were so many good movies in New York, and one didn't need advance tickets for movies. David sat down on the bed, looked at the front page of the folded newspaper which had headlines about a proposed conference in Europe, and then reached for the telephone.

'Information, please,' he said, and waited. 'Would you be good enough to give me the telephone number of Romeo Salta on West Fifty-sixth Street?'

He reserved a table for two at seven-thirty in the name of Neumeister. David had read something about the Romeo Salta restaurant somewhere, at some time, and he had wanted to try it on his next trip to New York. He remembered now that it was one of the restaurants he had hoped to take Annabelle to, when she met him in New York just before last Christmas. But she had not met him.

Then slowly, leaning back against his pillows, he picked up the newspaper. Nothing on the front page. He turned to the second page and saw Effie's sketch of him, and above it, in heavy print:

'DOUBLE LIFE' OF KELSEY THROWS
NEW LIGHT ON MURDER CASE

Sergeant Everett Terry of Beck's Brook, N.Y., today identified David Kelsey, 28-year-old scientist sought as slayer of Elfrida Brennan, as a man who for nearly two years maintained an alias as William Neumeister in Ballard, N.Y.

On January 18th of this year, 'Neumeister' brought the body of Gerald Delaney to the Beck's Brook police station with a story of ...

David could not bear to read it. Farther down the page, his eye fell on Annabelle's name:

Mrs Annabelle Barber, 26, of Hartford, Conn., formerly Mrs Annabelle Delaney, stated that she has known Kelsey for the past two and one half years and that he repeatedly said he was in love with her and intended to marry her, despite her marriage in 1957 to Gerald Delaney.

Mrs Barber, in her Hartford apartment at 48 Talbert Street, gave the following statement today: 'I now understand why my husband was killed. It was Dave he talked to that Sunday in Ballard and not Mr Neumeister. Dave killed him deliberately. I know now that Dave is insane. I was always afraid of him. If he had not bothered us so much with his letters and his visits, my husband would never have tried to see him that day.' She was in tears as she finished.

David dropped the paper and stood up. He walked to the window, pressing his wet palms together, and looked out at the irregular pattern of lighted windows in the building across the street. So he was insane. He laughed a little, nervously. Should he believe them or not? And what did it matter? Annabelle's words were like a hysterical din in his brain. He could hear her voice, angry and shrill with tears, *Dave killed him deliberately*, and something went out of him forever. When he turned from the window, he was another person, not David Kelsey, not William Neumeister, but some other being entirely. It was as strange and inexplicable as a religious experience, he felt, and he realized, too, that this was the nearest he had ever come in his life to having a religious experience.

Fifteen minutes later he was showered and dressed in his new suit and his second new shirt. He had no clear idea of what he was going to do next, and yet everything seemed inevitable and he did not hesitate.

Again there were no police in the lobby, and David could not understand that, could not understand why someone had not rapped on his room door, or picked him up when he had entered the hotel an hour ago. It seemed another piece of the Neumeister luck that he was coasting on. It might not last forever, but it would last hours and perhaps days longer than anybody else's luck. He had left his key in the door, and he did not stop at the desk. He was not coming back.

233

He began walking west. It was a fine spring evening, and perhaps his last, David thought. The eight dollars he had in his billfold was probably not enough for his cocktails and dinner tonight, and he did not know what was going to happen when they presented him with the bill, but somehow it didn't matter.

'Don't be afraid, Annabelle,' he murmured to her, and pressed his right arm, which she held, closer to his side.

But she was afraid. He could feel her shrinking a little, shrinking even from him. She hadn't known that William Neumeister – David Kelsey – was the man who had knocked her husband down against the steps, the man who had shoved his corpse into his car.

'You'll feel better in the restaurant,' David said.

He walked a long way up Fifth Avenue, past Fifty-sixth Street, and it was reassuring that nobody seemed to notice him. David felt determined to bring this evening off well, with no embarrassing snags. With the determination came a great self-confidence. Whatever happened he felt that he would do and say the right thing, and get his way with a mere word or two. He was quite free, he told himself, quite free. A particle in space. Now he held Annabelle by the hand. Her strong fingers straightened, then closed firmly on his. She didn't mind that they had no place as yet to sleep tonight. They'd find some place. Or they'd walk all night, because the weather was fine.

'Neumeister,' he said to the head waiter. 'I reserved a table for two.'

'Yes, sir. Right this way, sir.'

David followed him, beginning to feel euphoric as he walked past the rows of hanging wine bottles, through the pleasant aroma of good food.

'Two martinis, please,' David said to the waiter, and lit a cigarette. 'If you don't want it, I'll drink it,' he said to Annabelle. 'Or would you prefer something else?'

When the waiter returned with the drinks, David ordered a daiquiri.

'A daiquiri, sir?'

'Yes. A daiquiri,' David said.

David took the martini that the waiter had set in the plate next to his and put it near his own plate. When the waiter came back, David indicated that the daiquiri should be put on the other plate. The waiter set it there with a flourish. David drank the first martini, thinking of Wes and of Effie and of David Kelsey's sad sojourn at Dickson-Rand, thinking of all this in a detached, objective way. It seemed a remarkable chain of bad luck, starting way back, starting the day he received the news that Annabelle Stanton had married Gerald Delaney. He saw it all telescoped into five seconds, a whirling, whizzing image of Annabelle spinning in a wild dance, touching him several times and caroming off, out of his reach. He shook his head in discouragement, lifted the second martini and addressed Annabelle, really against his will or at least involuntarily, for he could see that the place beside him was empty:

'You're looking especially pretty tonight. Had you really rather go to a movie than go dancing somewhere?'

She demurred. She would decide after dinner. The full red skirt of her dress, crimson as fresh blood, lay on the bench seat between them and touched the dark blue material of David's trousers.

David signaled for the waiter, looked over the menu and ordered clams, veal *piccante*, a mixed salad, and a Valpolicella.

'Shall I remove the daiquiri, sir?' asked the waiter, reaching for it.

'Oh, no. Leave it.' David frowned, suddenly angry. 'That dinner also is for two.'

'Two, sir?'

'Two orders of everything, please.' He lit another cigarette. The money situation was not important. Had he ever considered money when it was something that concerned Annabelle?

He called for another wine glass. He poured two glasses of wine when the meat dish arrived, ordered two servings of *piselli*, and the more the waiters looked at him, the more nonchalantly he chatted with Annabelle. He had drunk the daiquiri before the clams arrived, and, since he felt the effect, he was careful to eat some bread and butter. The people across the way, a dark, portly man with a mustache and a dark, portly woman, were looking at him and smiling, and finally the mustached man raised his own glass to David. David replied in kind, and they both drank.

'You've got to come aboard the *Darwin* at least,' David was saying quietly to her, 'and see where I'm going to sleep and all that – No, I haven't been on it, but I've seen photographs of it inside and out. It's being overhauled in Brooklyn now.'

He ate well and finished the wine, which had been a whole bottle, not a half. Annabelle remarked that he would gain weight at this rate, and David said maybe that would stop people telling him he was too thin. He had an espresso. Annabelle, rather to his disappointment, did not want any coffee, but he made her taste some from his cup.

There was laughter in the restaurant, the ring of glasses and silver, the aroma of lemon peel in espresso.

'I'll see what I can do around Christmas,' David said to her. They were discussing going to Europe. He proposed a brandy, but she refused it and told him he had probably had enough too. 'I'm inclined to agree,' he replied. He had to make an effort to bring the overlapping images of the waiter together. 'The bill, please,' he said, and with aplomb reached for his billfold, where he knew only eight dollars remained.

The woman next to David smiled at him. David's own pleasant expression did not change.

The bill was $16.37. David laid his eight dollars on it, pocketed his cigarettes, and stood up. The waiter took up the bill and the money, glanced at it a second time, and David gestured to the front of the restaurant.

'I have money in my coat,' he said.

He gave the hat-check girl thirty-five cents. The waiter was standing nearby, smiling pleasantly.

'That's for you,' David said, nodding to the money in his hand.

'Eight dollars more, sir,' said the waiter, and David could tell that the waiter thought he was drunk.

David stood a little taller.

'What's the trouble?' asked the head waiter.

'Perhaps I'd better write a check,' David said, trying to extricate his checkbook from the mass of papers in his trenchcoat pocket. 'You have a pen?'

'Is that a local bank, sir?' asked the head waiter, producing, however, a pen.

'No. It's a Troy bank.'

The head waiter shook his head sadly.

David was embarrassed, and at that moment felt grateful that he was as drunk as he was, because he was able to appear less flustered. He hesitated for what seemed to him five minutes (the head waiter was asking him if he had some identification), but he could not make up his mind between David Kelsey and William Neumeister: he *preferred* to sign David Kelsey, because as low as Kelsey might be his check was good and he did not want to cheat the restaurant. On the other hand, he intended to inform his bank to honor Neumeister's checks, and after all he *was* William Neumeister tonight.

'Annabelle –'

'Are you all right, sir?'

David bent suddenly at the counter of the hat-check girl and wrote *Wm Neumeister* and above it in parentheses *David Kelsey*, tore the check off and handed it to the waiter with a little bow. The check was for twenty dollars. The waiter showed it to the head waiter, who looked at it with interest. David was extending his hand, about to ask the waiter for his eight dollars back, when the head waiter looked at him in astonishment.

'David Kelsey?' he asked, frowning.

The name was a hideous thing.

David turned and fled out the door, tripped on a step and fell on his hands on the sidewalk.

Voices shouted behind him.

He ran, crossing the street. There was a whistle like a police whistle. Ahead of him, a fire engine clanged up Sixth Avenue. David crossed the avenue just behind it and continued westward on Fifty-sixth Street, because it looked darker than the avenue. But he slowed to a fast walk.

'Damn it, Annabelle, damn it,' he muttered. 'I didn't mean to put *you* through this.'

'I don't mind, Dave. The check is good.'

'Sure it is, sure it is.'

He turned south on Broadway, changed his mind and went in the other direction. He saw no sign that he was being pursued. And there was Central Park ahead. He had always wanted to walk in Central Park with Annabelle! To look at the seals and the monkeys, the llamas –

David saw a policeman and bolted, ran three or four steps before he could control himself and realize that the policeman had been paying no attention to him. He looked back. The policeman had stopped on the sidewalk and was looking at him. David turned and walked on. After a few steps, David looked again, and now the policeman was running after him. David clambered over the stone wall that bordered the park and, stooping, ran in a panic through some bushes, ran where it looked darkest, away from the path where a street lamp showed two slowly walking figures. He ran into a tree, hurting his shoulder and the right side of his head. It was vaguely familiar to him, the action of running into a tree. Where? When? He went slowly back to the tree and put his hand on its rough, immovable trunk, confident that the tree would tell him an important piece of wisdom, or a secret. He felt it, but he could not find words for it: it had something to do with identity. The tree knew who he was *really,* and he had been destined to bump into it. The tree had a further message. It told him to be calm and quiet and to stay with Annabelle.

'But you don't know how difficult it is to be quiet,' David said. 'It's very easy for you –'

He saw a policeman on the lighted path, saw him stop a man and speak to him. But David did not know if he was the policeman who had been chasing him. The confusion of it all made David shake his head in perplexity.

'You are much wiser than we,' he said, patting the tree trunk.

Quietly he made his way to the wall again, boosted himself on his hands and climbed over. Annabelle stood there waiting for him.

'Where *were* you?' she asked.

'I'm sorry. I acted like an idiot.' He had to go to the toilet. There were toilets in subways. With a murmured apology to Annabelle, he pushed on toward a subway entrance. But the entrance was closed by a chain across the steps. Grimly, he turned away and sought another entrance. After all, this was Columbus Circle! He saw one far away across a wide intersection of streets, and he plunged toward it. 'Wait here, darling, please,' he said, and went down the steps.

He had to buy a token to reach the toilet, and he avoided

counting what was left of his change, not wanting to know how little it was. The toilet was a block and a half away, underground. Life had never seemed so tedious, and David marveled that so many, many people tried to hang onto it.

With his relief, he had a brilliant idea: he had friends in New York. There was Ed Greenhouse, married now and working at Sperry in Queens, but the last David had heard from him – he distinctly remembered from some Christmas card's return address – Ed lived in Manhattan. There was Reeves Talmadge, Ernest Cioffi, fellows he had known in school. Their names came back clearly, their faces loomed in his memory like the faces of old, dear friends.

'I'm going to call up Ed Greenhouse,' he said when he returned to Annabelle.

They headed for a restaurant's pink neon sign. And there, right beside the telephone booth, was a men's room he might have used free. Closing one eye, David was able to find Greenhouse, Edgar, 410 Riverside Drive. And where, exactly, was that? An orchestra or a juke box was playing 'It was only a paper moon – hanging over a cardboard sky...' A girl was singing, and David closed his eyes and listened for a moment, daydreaming, imagining his encounter with Ed, the handshakes, the greetings, meeting his wife. What was so embarrassing about asking for ten dollars or even fifty or a hundred? Ed would get it back. David opened his eyes and pulled out his change: one dime, two nickels, and three pennies. He had the dime in his fingers when he realized that, if he spent it, he would be two cents short of having the fifteen-cent subway fare.

'You haven't a dime, have you, darling?'

But Annabelle had left her little money purse in the hotel room, and they could not go back there, could never enjoy the champagne that was standing on the dresser.

'We'll just go on up to Ed's,' he said calmly.

He asked the man in the subway change booth where 410 Riverside Drive would be, and the man said to get off at 110th Street. He bought a token, squeezed Annabelle through the turnstile with him, and they caught a train up.

29

It was a huge, gloomy apartment building with the grime of the city in the gray stone curlicues around its double doors. At right and left in the foyer there were long lists of names, and it took him some time to find *Greenhouse, E. 9K.* David pushed the bell, and stood with his hand on the brass doorknob, waiting. He had to ring again, and again he waited, ready to open the door, and still there was no reply. Then a man and woman came in, used their key, and David went in with them. He let them both precede him into the elevator, which was run by a little gray man in a shabby blue uniform. The people got out at the eighth floor, and David said, 'Nine, please.'

At the ninth floor, he looked for the K apartment, bending close to read the markers on the doors, because the hall light was dim. He pushed the bell and heard a pair of chimes.

'Who is it?' a man's voice asked.

'Ed?' David said, smiling. 'An old friend. Dave.'

The door opened a little, and Ed Greenhouse – plumper and shorter than David remembered him – looked at him blankly.

'It's me, Ed!' David said, pushing the door wider. He patted Ed on the shoulder. 'How've you been, old man?'

'Dave Kelsey?' Ed looked completely surprised. His close-set black eyes stared at David on either side of his beak nose, and David remembered that he had used to think Ed looked like a cartoon of an owl.

'Did I change so much in six years? Five, isn't it?'

Ed glanced over his shoulder at a blonde woman who was standing in the middle of the living room.

'Your wife?' David asked. 'How do you do?' He bowed to her. David was in their hall now, but Ed still stood by the half-open door. 'I hope you'll forgive my barging in like this without calling,' David began. 'I would've called, but –' He was suddenly embarrassed, unable to speak of money. And Ed wasn't helping by being so stiff. Ed didn't used to be stuffy, far from it. Frowning, David glanced about quickly for Annabelle, aware that she – somewhere – had shrunk into the background to be less obtrusive.

'That's okay, Dave,' Ed said, moving away from the door at last. 'Honey, this is – this is Dave Kelsey, an old school friend of mine.'

'How do you do?' David said again.

'How do you do?' she said breathlessly, staring at him.

'Am I interrupting something?' David asked.

'Sit down, Dave. Can I get you anything? Coffee? A beer?' Ed preceded him into the living room and turned, his plump, hairy hands that David remembered quite well poised now on his hips. Ed was starting to lose his hair. And he looked rather pale.

David smiled. 'No, thank you. I won't stay long, Ed.' He sat down on the sofa.

Ed did not sit down and neither did his wife. Ed kept looking at her as if he were trying to convey something to her with his glances, and David thought he saw him nod his head a little.

'Am I interrupting something?' David asked again, ready to get up. 'I really shouldn't have burst in –'

'Oh, no, no. Glad to see you, Dave. Liz, I might like a beer and I don't think we've got any, have we? Would you mind going down for some?'

David was on his feet at once. 'Oh, no, I'll go.'

'No, really. Don't even think of it,' Ed said quickly.

'Oh, certainly, I'll go,' said the girl, and started for the door.

'You'll need a coat,' David said. 'It's pretty cool.'

She shook her head with a glance over her shoulder at David, and then she went out, not quite closing the door after her.

'Well –' Ed said pleasantly, and put a shapely pipe in his mouth. He tried to light it, shook the match out and poked at the tobacco with the end of the match, put the match in an ashtray and lit another match. The operation must have taken him over a minute, but David waited patiently for him to speak. 'You're looking fine, Dave.'

'So are you. Married life agrees with you, eh? You've put on weight.'

Ed nodded, but again David saw that cool withdrawal in his expression, as if he resented David's bursting in on him and was even on the verge of telling him so.

David moistened his lips and looked down at the pale green

carpet. It was suddenly impossible for him to ask Ed about his work, as he had certainly meant to do. May as well plunge, David thought. Either that or get up and leave. 'I guess you wonder why I'm here,' David said. 'The fact is – this wasn't a planned trip and I'm out of cash – just out of pocket money, and my banks are out of town and it's hard to get a check cashed. I could write you a check though, Ed, for whatever amount you give me. Fifty would be fine. Less, if it's not convenient.'

'Why, sure, Dave,' Ed said in a surprisingly agreeable tone. 'I don't think I've got fifty, to be perfectly honest, but I can let you have twenty.' He pulled his billfold from a hip pocket.

David stood up, already reaching for his checkbook in his trenchcoat pocket. 'It's a godsend,' David said, suddenly happy and smiling. 'When you're in New York with a girl, you know!'

'Oh? What girl?'

'The girl I'm going to marry. Matter of fact, we are married in every way except the paper way. And who cares about the paper way?' David got a pen from the desk across the room, and wrote the check out on the coffee table. It did not occur to him now to sign William Neumeister's name, but he did want to tell Ed about lucky Bill. 'Remember that weekend we had in Los Angeles? The time we barely got back to your mother's for New Year's Eve?'

Ed nodded, smiling. 'Yes, I remember.'

'This trip has been something like that. I had some wine tonight with dinner. But essentially one doesn't need to – I mean, it's the state of mind that does it – and mine's excellent.'

'Good,' Ed said. Still smiling affably, he tiptoed down a hall off the living room and David saw part of him – an arm and his head – as he very gently closed a door. Then he tiptoed back.

'Somebody in there? Maybe I've been talking too loud?'

'Oh, no, nobody in there. Are you sure you wouldn't like some coffee? We have instant.'

David declined it. He wished Ed would sit down, but it was hardly his place to ask him to. David looked around the room, noticed the dull Impressionist painting reproductions on the walls, the mixture of modern furniture with Victorian, the very messy desk, every cubbyhole jammed and its writing surface chaotic. Then he saw on the floor by the armchair two pink baby rattles. No *one* pink baby rattle. 'Curious,' David said, 'the shape of baby rattles hasn't changed in hundreds of years, has it?'

'No.' Ed chuckled, but David heard a falseness in it, and he felt a little alarmed. 'Where's the girl now?'

'Who?'

'The girl you're with.'

'Oh, why she's –' David gestured airily and stopped. He looked at Ed and again felt embarrassed, wondered if he should say she was waiting downstairs for him. 'She's at the hotel.'

'Oh? What hotel?' Now Ed sat down on a hassock in front of the armchair.

'I seem to have forgotten the name. But I can get there.' David laughed. His legs, jutting out in front of him, did not look like his own. The thighs were thin. He brought his palm down on his knee. 'Well, Ed –'

'Wouldn't be the Barclay, would it?' Ed asked.

'Yes,' David replied, smiling. 'That's it, of course.'

'You're going back there tonight?'

'Yes,' David said. 'But how'd you know?'

'Just a wild guess,' Ed said, puffing his pipe. 'What's the girl's name?'

David had heard the elevator through the partly open door. Ed got up and went to the door and, as soon as he looked out, stepped quickly aside.

'He's in there,' Ed said.

David had jumped up.

Two policemen came in. Three.

'Stay there, Liz,' Ed said out the door.

'Mr Kelsey?' asked the first policeman, an enormous fellow with little gray eyes under his visor.

David whirled away from him, struck a windowpane with his forearm, kicked more glass out and in the same movement climbed out on the sill, grasping a folded awning bar. A hand caught at his ankle, and David kicked it off.

'Kelsey!' the cop was saying in an admonishing tone. 'Kelsey!'

David pressed his fingertips down in a crack between the big cement bricks of the house front and sidled farther from the window. There was a ledge perhaps six inches wide under his shoes. The ledge went on to the corner of the building and disappeared. But there were no more windows between him and the corner.

'Come back, Kelsey! You're going to fall!'

The policeman's hand or his nightstick brushed David's trouser cuff. The cement scraped David's nose as he moved on. Then David paused, out of the man's reach now, and looked back at him. He was a big man and his fear was equally big, David could see that. He was balanced on his hip on the sill, holding to the awning bar that David had caught. Then he pocketed his nightstick and climbed out on the sill and straightened. David edged still farther from him, but there was no need, because the man was not going to turn loose of that awning bar.

Suddenly there were murmurs and shouts of advice from inside the room, as if the people in there had been stunned speechless until that instant. Two other faces leaned out.

'Better come back, Kelsey,' said the big man on the sill, his voice shaking with the fear of death. 'I can shoot you from here.'

David laughed a little. It seemed so silly and unimportant. Still smiling, he imagined the bullet entering his right side, taking his strength in an instant, and he imagined falling backward, over and over to that final kiss of cement below that he could not really imagine. David shut his eyes against the alternately warm and cool flow of his blood into his eyes. Blood made his fingertips a little slippery, too, and he supposed they were cut. But if they dried, he thought, wouldn't they glue his fingers to the cement?

'Dave —' Now it was Ed leaning out the window, and the policeman had disappeared. 'Dave, you've got to come back and face this thing! Come back, Dave!'

But it was Ed who had betrayed him. David could not muster the energy or the interest to spit at him. He felt compelled to look down at the street, at the sidewalk directly below him, half believing that the policeman had fallen, silently, in the course of duty. The view — not emptiness but the presence of lines converging to an imaginary vortex directly below him — was so much what he expected that he lost his fear of it. Down below, a foreshortened figure of a woman pointed at him, and a man joined her and looked up. Two more people, walking from different directions, followed the gaze of the man and woman and were caught too. The four of them formed an ornamental, flowerlike design, their turned-up faces white and mysteriously complex in the glow of a street light.

'Better come back, Kelsey. You're going to fall.'

David's teeth were set and he did not reply. He kept his nose to the cement, and turned his feet a little, so he could stand on the ledge without his heels' overhanging. His heart pounded with an anger he could do nothing about. And now he began to feel tired. If his anger had had an objective, he thought – But he was not angry at the police, or at Ed or his wife, or at anybody. He saw himself objectively, and he felt merely silly, standing on a ledge being stared at, called, asked to come back through the window, and for what? A policeman's flashlight played over his body.

'*Bastard*!' David yelled for no reason at the two gesticulating policemen who were leaning out the window.

'I've got a gun on you, Kelsey. Better come back or I'll shoot.'

'Go to hell!' David said nervously.

'You're a killer. I'm not interested in saving your life.' The big gun waggled at David.

'If you lay a hand on that girl in there –' David muttered.

'What girl? Liz?'

A gust of wind made him cling more tightly. He shut his eyes. Warm blood trickled between his eyebrows and ran cool down the left side of his nose. He wondered if he dared try to make it around the corner of the building and thence to a window? But for what use, after all? It did not matter either whether he fell or remained on the ledge for an indefinite time or forever: the thought gave him a sense of freedom and power, and he bounced a little on his toes. Behind the policeman's thick shoulder, David could see two or three people leaning out of other windows on the same floor. A window went up above him and a woman gave a small scream, but David did not care to look up. Anyway, the weight of his head might have overbalanced him, and he did not want to fall just yet.

'What's going on?' asked a man's voice from above.

'We gotta get this man,' said a policeman, as earnestly as anybody ever pursued the holy grail. Then he turned his head to say something to the people in the room with him, and his voice was an ugly, angry roar.

David closed his eyes, pressed his forehead and nose against the cool stone, and clung harder with his fingertips. Some decision had to be made. Or did it? Why couldn't he stay here the rest of his life? There was something peculiarly fitting about it for David Kelsey – to drop in on an old school friend to borrow some money he could have immediately paid back, and to be betrayed. The memories of Ed Greenhouse came back in a very personal way, a very close way, as if Ed meant something more to David than an acquaintance, which he hadn't: Ed with a terrible nosebleed one day in a classroom, dripping onto an exam paper until he couldn't write any more and had to leave the room, even though two or three fellows, including himself, had given him their handkerchiefs. Ed with a startlingly pretty girl at some dance, surprising everybody by that girl. Had it been this girl, his wife?

He felt his being here at Ed Greenhouse's tonight had been predestined.

'Who is he?'

'Why don't they try to lasso him?'

'What's he trying to do?'

'Is he trying to kill himself?'

'Na-aw,' growled the policeman, still watching him as if he were a laboratory experiment.

David squeezed his eyes shut and tried to shut them all out. He had endured heckling before, and there was nothing at all new about it. This was the way it had been at Mrs McCartney's and a few times at Annabelle's too, on a smaller scale. He shut them out, and Annabelle's face came more clearly to him than he had ever remembered it before, and with it a realization that she existed. It was like those moments on awakening, empty and blank, in the morning, when his first thoughts turned to her and he remembered once more that she lived and breathed, and he was like an empty sail filling and finding its purpose again.

Water, or something wet, splashed on his head, and a woman or a child laughed above him.

'Cut that out!' said a gruff voice. 'We want him alive!'

They won't get me alive, David thought, and like a scream of laughter or defiance that might have come from his own throat, a siren shrieked. David edged closer to the corner of the building, more to change the position of his aching fingertips than to move anywhere, and he concentrated on the image of Annabelle's face with the blind faith that dying men sometimes put in a cross. He realized with indifference that they were fussing around with ladders and nets below, and that they could conceivably reach him, even if he was on the ninth floor. The thought of sending a ladder flying off with a push of his foot gave him some satisfaction. Or would they have the ladder rigidly fixed below? And he would have to turn around to face them. He debated this perilous move very briefly, knowing that the more he imagined it, the more difficult it would be.

He brought his right hand over beside his left, pressed his fingers into the crevice, and turned his body as much as he could before he let go with his left hand and whipped it around his body. His fingers fumbled for a moment to find a crevice, but his right hand held him flat enough against the building, and all in all, he thought, he had done it as gracefully as a ballet dancer making a pirouette.

'Don't jump, Kelsey! We're going to reach you!' a voice said.

It was like looking down on a circus from a swinging trapeze. There was a ring of light around two bright red fire trucks that stood at right angles to each other, and a big spotlight wobbled and found him. Policemen blew whistles and motioned violently for cars to move, but the cars did not move. Cars were chockablock around the corner of the Drive and a side street. David laughed – not because it was all about him, which he did reluctantly admit to himself, but because grown-up people had stopped whatever they had been doing to stare, to get themselves in a traffic jam, to gawk like monkeys with their heads in an unnatural position, just because a human being might fall or jump and kill himself.

'Don't worry, I'm not going to jump,' David said quietly to the heavy policeman who was endangering himself or possibly trying to impress anyone who looked at him by leaning far out the window, balancing himself on one hip on the sill.

A second policeman, of obviously earnest intent, stuck his head out and took the heavy policeman's place, extending something like a yardstick, but on second glance David saw it was a broom and the policeman held the bristle end. 'Take hold, Kelsey! Come on in! We won't let you fall!'

David wanted to laugh and couldn't. A broom! That domestic article, that symbol of home! Now David more courageously looked below him and above. Scared faces stared down at him, a jagged row of them, all upside down and sideways. David felt melancholic.

A whistle screamed for attention. There was a terrible clang of metal as a section of ladder fell, and now David had to laugh as three rubber-clad firemen scrambled to pick the ladder up as if it were a sacred object that should never have touched ground.

'Like some coffee, David?' asked a male voice, and looking at his left, David saw the earnest young policeman extending an arm, a cup of coffee in his hand.

'I'd like my wife,' David said.

'Yeah? What's her name?'

David did not choose to answer. He looked calmly at the black-green line of trees beyond Riverside Drive, and he thought of the boundless woods around his house in Ballard and around the house in Troy that Annabelle had never seen. Or had she? Had she not been there?

'What's her name, David? We'll get her,' said the efficient, obtuse voice.

David cleared his throat and said nothing. He considered once more rounding the corner and fighting his way through another window: but of course they'd be glad to yank him in and he would then have to fight his way out of the apartment. He had a memory of the three or four men attacking him in Annabelle's apartment. There was a limit to human strength, he thought with a sigh, and he felt very tired. He swayed outward, and a wave of surprise, a communal gasp from below made him press harder with his fingers. And here he was again, upright, not fallen at all. David smiled.

David could hear the people giggling nervously too, and the

beginning of a rhythmic handclapping, the kind heard in theaters when the show is late. Firemen shushed it. The ladder was coming up.

'Okay, David, this is it now,' said a calm voice, perhaps Ed's, from the window, but David did not glance that way. 'Okay, David, take it easy.'

He had a feeling William Neumeister was watching him, with an absolute confidence in him. William Neumeister with folded arms and a calm expression.

'We're going to get your girl, David. What's her name? Annabelle?'

David looked up at a star, disdaining to reply.

'She's down there waiting for you, David. Down on the street. You've got to go down that ladder.' The voice was false as false could be.

Nothing was true but the fatigue of life and the eternal disappointment.

The firemen shouted orders and explanations to one another. A little man was crawling up the ladder, even as the ladder was swaying and being raised. David grew alert and felt quite capable of kicking the fellow off the ladder, but he shouldn't, wouldn't do that unless the fellow became violent. After all, what did the man care about him, one way or the other? He was simply doing his duty.

'She's down there, David. See her?' asked the voice from the window. 'She's waving to you.'

David did not believe him, but he looked. He saw no girl waving.

'Hang on, boy,' said the climbing fireman in a scared voice, and it was the closeness of it that shocked David.

There were only a few more seconds left. David blinked and looked around him at his small circle of possibilities: the corner, the window whose half-dozen grasping hands he could not have borne to walk into, above him a dangling blanket that did not quite reach him and might have been meant as a joke or a taunt anyway. Or he could jump. He had been here so often before, he thought, in the center of a meager circle of possibilities, each of which offered essentially nothing. He fidgeted, wondering. Blood had sealed shut the lashes of his left eye.

'Okay, boy. Hold on,' said the fireman.

'*Olé!*' cried a voice from the street.

'They'll get him,' said a deeper voice from above.

There was a girl in a white coat or a light-colored raincoat, hatless, motionless, her face turned up and her hands one over the other tensely in front of her. Her hair was the color of Annabelle's hair, he thought, though in the darkness it was hard to be sure.

'Say hello to her, David,' said the policeman's voice (and he hadn't stopped talking). 'Tell her you'll be down. Just a couple of minutes now –'

The ladder grated on the brick only a few feet below the ledge where David stood.

The girl did not wave to him, which made David think all the more that she could be Annabelle. Annabelle wouldn't have waved, perhaps, even if he had wanted her to. There wasn't any other way, he thought. To be touched by the fireman was a loathsome prospect.

Thinking no more about it, he stepped off into that cool space, that fast descent to her, with nothing in his mind but a memory of a curve of her shoulder, naked, as he had never seen it.

FOR THE BEST IN PAPERBACKS, LOOK FOR THE

In every corner of the world, on every subject under the sun, Penguin represents quality and variety – the very best in publishing today.

For complete information about books available from Penguin – including Pelicans, Puffins, Peregrines and Penguin Classics – and how to order them, write to us at the appropriate address below. Please note that for copyright reasons the selection of books varies from country to country.

In the United Kingdom: For a complete list of books available from Penguin in the U.K., please write to *Dept E.P., Penguin Books Ltd, Harmondsworth, Middlesex, UB7 0DA*

In the United States: For a complete list of books available from Penguin in the U.S., please write to *Dept BA, Penguin, 299 Murray Hill Parkway, East Rutherford, New Jersey 07073*

In Canada: For a complete list of books available from Penguin in Canada, please write to *Penguin Books Canada Ltd, 2801 John Street, Markham, Ontario L3R 1B4*

In Australia: For a complete list of books available from Penguin in Australia, please write to the *Marketing Department, Penguin Books Australia Ltd, P.O. Box 257, Ringwood, Victoria 3134*

In New Zealand: For a complete list of books available from Penguin in New Zealand, please write to the *Marketing Department, Penguin Books (NZ) Ltd, Private Bag, Takapuna, Auckland 9*

In India: For a complete list of books available from Penguin, please write to *Penguin Overseas Ltd, 706 Eros Apartments, 56 Nehru Place, New Delhi, 110019*

In Holland: For a complete list of books available from Penguin in Holland, please write to *Penguin Books Nederland B.V., Postbus 195, NL–1380AD Weesp, Netherlands*

In Germany: For a complete list of books available from Penguin, please write to *Penguin Books Ltd, Friedrichstrasse 10 – 12, D–6000 Frankfurt Main 1, Federal Republic of Germany*

In Spain: For a complete list of books available from Penguin in Spain, please write to *Longman Penguin España, Calle San Nicolas 15, E–28013 Madrid, Spain*

PATRICIA HIGHSMITH IN PENGUINS

'Miss Highsmith is a novelist whose books one can re-read many times. There are very few of whom one can say that' – Graham Greene

'Patricia Highsmith is a mistress of a fine and dangerous art. Let the reader beware' – Isobel Murray in the *Financial Times*

CRIME AND MYSTERY IN PENGUINS

Deep Water Patricia Highsmith

Portrait of a psychopath, from the first faint outline to the full horrors of schizophrenia. 'If you read crime stories at all, or perhaps especially if you don't, you should read *Deep Water*' – Julian Symons in the *Sunday Times*

Farewell My Lovely Raymond Chandler

Moose Malloy was a big man but not more than six feet five inches tall and not wider than a beer truck. He looked about as inconspicuous as a tarantula on a slice of angel food. Marlowe's greatest case. Chandler's greatest book.

God Save the Child Robert B. Parker

When young Kevin Bartlett disappears, everyone assumes he's run away . . . until the comic strip ransom note arrives . . . 'In classic wisecracking and handfighting tradition, Spenser sorts out the case and wins the love of a fine-boned Jewish Lady . . . who even shares his taste for iced red wine' – Francis Goff in the *Sunday Telegraph*

The Daughter of Time Josephine Tey

Josephine Tey again delves into history to reconstruct a crime. This time it is a crime committed in the tumultuous fifteenth century. 'Most people will find *The Daughter of Time* as interesting and enjoyable a book as they will meet in a month of Sundays' – Marghanita Laski in the *Observer*

The Michael Innes Omnibus

Three tensely exhilarating novels. 'A master – he constructs a plot that twists and turns like an electric eel: it gives you shock upon shock and you cannot let go' – *The Times Literary Supplement*

Killer's Choice Ed McBain

Who killed Annie Boone? Employer, lover, ex-husband, girlfriend? This is a tense, terrifying and tautly written novel from the author of *The Mugger*, *The Pusher*, *Lady Killer* and a dozen other first class thrillers.

CRIME AND MYSTERY IN PENGUINS

Call for the Dead   John Le Carré

The classic work of espionage which introduced the world to George Smiley. 'Brilliant . . . highly intelligent, realistic. Constant suspense. Excellent writing' – *Observer*

Swag   Elmore Leonard

From the bestselling author of *Stick* and *LaBrava* comes this wallbanger of a book in which 100,000 dollars' worth of nicely spendable swag sets off a slick, fast-moving chain of events. 'Brilliant' – *The New York Times*

The Soft Talkers   Margaret Millar

The mysterious disappearance of a Toronto businessman is the start point for this spine-chilling, compulsive novel. 'This is not for the squeamish, and again the last chapter conceals a staggering surprise' – *Time and Tide*

The Julian Symons Omnibus

The Man Who Killed Himself, The Man Whose Dreams Came True, The Man Who Lost His Wife: three novels of cynical humour and cliff-hanging suspense from a master of his craft. 'Exciting and compulsively readable' – *Observer*

Love in Amsterdam   Nicolas Freeling

Inspector Van der Valk's first case involves him in an elaborate cat-and-mouse game with a very wily suspect. 'Has the sinister, spell-binding perfection of a cobra uncoiling. It is a masterpiece of the genre' – Stanley Ellis

Maigret's Pipe   Georges Simenon

Eighteen intriguing cases of mystery and murder to which the pipe-smoking Maigret applies his wit and intuition, his genius for detection and a certain *je ne sais quoi* . . .